A STUDY
IN
DARKNESS

HADES' KISS

G.J. BINGHAM

THE CASEBOOKS OF NICOLAUS VAGELLE

For information contact: Drawingfire Publications
https://www.GJBingham.com

Thanks to Kristin McTiernan for editorial support.

Quotes & acknowledgments:

Iliad - Homer (tr: Samuel Butler) (Richard Lattimore)

Odyssey - Homer (tr: George Chapman)

Seneca the Younger (tr. Roger l'Estrange)

Euripides (tr. David Grene and Richard Lattimore)

Female of the Species - Rudyard Kipling (1911)

Strange Case of Dr Jekyll and Mr Hyde - Robert Louis Stevenson (1886)

Library of Congress Control Number

ISBN:

979-8-9891235-0-6 (e-book)

979-8-9891235-1-3 (paperback)

A serial killer works the New Orleans streets.

"The Shrovetide Ripper." Every year more victims join the body count. Enter, **Nicolaus Vagelle,** Criminal Psychologist. Former detective with the NOPD, with that one bad case that compels him to throw off the badge, change his name...until he is lured back into the *dark work, the bloody work,* of justice. These days, he bills himself as a Consultant. And his new obsession becomes the fractured intellect of evil.

Into this gloaming a young, unsuspecting, woman arrives. A Russian immigrant with her own shadowed past. She calls herself **Alya,** "born of the heavens." But she has experienced horror in her life. And now, she will either learn to fight, or be lost to its darkness.

*

"A Study In Darkness: Hades' Kiss." The Casebooks of Investigator Nicolaus Vagelle. *Thriller/Mystery/Suspense.* A Novel-In-Stories—a collection of 6 short stories, 3 novelettes, 2 novellas. These are the chapters chronicling the life of "a knight in dark armor" (to borrow from Philip Marlowe).

*

"Observe, and be mindful of the little things. She can display the most complex of human emotions because she has made a lifelong study of mimicry. But through all of her masks, from sadness to joy, you catch a psychopath when she thinks you are not looking. When she thinks you have not seen her step around the injured child to get to the front of the ice cream line."

*

"He has sharp eyes, hard, dark eyes, that see everything. But not hard when he looks at me. He is comfortable with sharing his space, but after these months, I think maybe he hides his thorns well."

*

"Three a.m. The scream ripped the alley's blackest shadows, only to be swallowed by concrete and steel. But screams here were too common, and this one would go as unanswered as the rest."

Praise for:
The stories of Nicolaus & Alya
*

"An Irretrievable Heart"

"… I enjoy your stories more and more as I read them. The growth of the characters through the stories is realistic and interesting. The twists and turns in the story were placed perfectly, allowing the story to move at a good pace...

"The plot is well thought out, and the tiny breadcrumbs you drop along the way are just the right amount. When a "reveal" is made, there has been just enough information given to make it believable, yet still a surprise. Once again, kudos to you…"

*

"A Hazardous Touch"

"*Wow*! The story moves along well, capturing the terror and sadness of Alya's childhood. Amazing climax with a powerful ending... Great job!"

*

"Hades' Kiss"

"What an amazing way to bring these two complicated people together. The story was riveting and told at just the right pace.

"Alya's angst and Vagelle's reticence stay true to form, yet bend at just the right time, in just the right way...

"...compelling and had a difficult time putting it down. This is a very heavy subject matter and, while difficult at times to read emotionally, this is a sign of your talent in writing. As I read, I felt the emotions of the characters, particularly Posey.

—Kristin McTiernan, "Nonsense-Free Editor"

Author's Caution:

A popular screenwriter recently said of the genre:
Thriller is a cross between Detective and Horror.

Edgar Allen Poe,

in the origins of the classical detective, had encompassed his world in darkness, at times in the extreme. In the following pages, I have chosen to follow the master's traditions.

I dream for those same thrills passed down by all my brilliant predecessors, but not before advising, respectfully:

This book is not for children, nor is it for the overly-sensitive reader. I venture into black waters, and sometimes difficult subject matter, but in the end summation, perhaps you will find a patch of light under the door.

It's called hope.

—GJB

CONTENTS

A Blues Bouquet 1

A Spider Hole Beguiling 17

A Savage Liaison 43

Acheron's Angel 111

A Dangerous Coupling 127

A Sharp-Edged Seduction 145

A Criminal Obsession 179

A Spectral Attraction 247

An Irretrievable Heart 273

A Hazardous Touch 363

Hades' Kiss 379

For Betty, who gifted me with art, music, and literature,

who taught me to understand the true depths of a heart.

HADES' KISS

G.J. BINGHAM

"He knew the things that were and the things that would be and the things that had been before."

"No one can hurry me down to Hades before my time, but if a man's hour is come, be he brave or be he coward, there is no escape for him when he has once been born."

—Homer, The Iliad

*

"There will be killing 'till the score is paid."

—Homer, The Odyssey

ONE

A BLUES

BOUQUET

Alya

I come and go. He makes no demands. He is quiet man. He comes and goes too, and I do not often know where he goes or when he will return. I do not ask.

I think he is man who likes to be alone. Sometimes I ask, does he still know I am here. Once I cut my hair above collar, but he said nothing.

He gave key to apartment—his apartment that is his office too, on third floor of the skinny four-floor building. He gave to me his bedroom "For as long as you need," he said. And he gave no reason to worry. On nights when he is home, he only sleeps in living room.

He has sharp eyes, hard, dark eyes, that see everything. But not hard when he looks at me. He is comfortable with sharing his space, but after these months, I think maybe he hides his thorns well.

He gave to me a job. He pays wages. More than I think I am worth sometimes. Sometimes I do not know what this job is, so I make work myself. I clean, though he never says to clean. I know how to fix small things. Sometimes, when he gives small things to do, odd things, I think maybe he is testing me. It makes me curious about him. Maybe he thinks he is *papa*. He is ten years older than me, but he is not my papa. At fifteen, I ran away from my papa and crossed oceans so he would never find me again. This man is…different, easy with things close to him.

But his job is not so nice. He calls himself Consultant, though I have seen more than that. And I have seen many people who ask the Consultant for help. Many are not such nice people. I wonder what makes a man wish to work for such not-nice people. But I do not ask. Some of my real papa's lessons were useful lessons.

He gives money for groceries, but he often does not tell me what to buy. I know it is time for shopping when I find cash on the black desk. I look in kitchen, and see what is there and what needs replacing. This morning I find cash, and Mr. Vagelle is not home, so I walk to the market. It is not far.

New Orleans is a big city. This market, not so big as others I have seen. The clerk smiles and says, "Good morning, Alya," every time I set groceries on his counter. Today is first time ever he does not say good morning. His head is down, and when I say *Dobroye utro* (Good morning), he does not look up. It makes me nervous, so I look behind me. Maybe police are here looking for Russian immigrant. But no, the store is empty. Except, then I see the young girl.

She is maybe twelve years, but her face is mostly covered with long black hair, so I am not sure. She wears dirty blue dress with small flowers, with hem torn and hanging to her knees. Scabbed knees. Dirty pink socks with no shoes. Maybe she is looking at her socks wondering where her shoes are.

I turn to Mr. Jackson, the clerk, and want to ask if girl is with someone. Is she in trouble? Did anyone ask her? The face of Mr. Jackson worries me. But I cannot stay silent. As Papa said, that has always been my problem.

The girl walks away behind the shelves to the next food aisle, and I start after her. Mr. Jackson says something, and when I turn the corner the girl is not in that aisle. Confused, I hurry to the next aisle then the next. I run to the front of the store. But all I find is Mr. Jackson, where I left him. He lifts his head and his mouth shakes and his fingers shake, and he goes to the rear of the store.

Checking circular mirrors above, I see no one else. I run out to sidewalk and, left to right, I see no little girl. Other people walk here. I stop a young couple and ask did they see a little girl with black hair leave the market. But they did not. I ask another man, but he shakes head like I am crazy, and walks away. I run to the store's corner and see no little girl. I turn and run the other way. I think I am crazy.

Slow walking back to store—but Mr. Jackson is not there. I fill bag with groceries. I count exact money onto the counter and I go home.

I am upset, but put food away.

"If he be Mr. Hyde," he had thought, *"I shall be Mr. Seek."* I set book on the arm of the chair. *"R.L. Stevenson,"* the first book Mr. Vagelle gave to me to read. "To improve your English," he said. *"If he be Mr. Hyde,"* does not sound like good English to me. Anyway, today my head is too busy to read.

I do not know what to do. Sitting at the black desk, I start Mr. Vagelle's old laptop, thinking I will listen to *Angliski* (English) language videos. He wants me to learn better. But I cannot listen with my head full of young girl. She is in trouble. I know about young girls in trouble, and memories make me nervous and sad.

I need air, but I only go outside the apartment door and sit on the landing, and watch light from the first-floor door on the tiles below. Mr. Vagelle might know what to do. It is his job, but Mr. Vagelle is not here and I do not know when he will return. I think what can I do, maybe go back to market store, maybe the little girl returns. But why does Mr. Jackson act so? He acts like he knows the girl…

"Alya?" His voice scares me awake. But it is not Mr. Vagelle. It is Dr. Maiwand, the second floor tenant. "I'm sorry to startle you, dear. I saw you on the stair and hoped nothing was wrong."

"I am okay," I say.

"Clearly, you are upset. Is Mr. Vagelle…?"

"No. He is not here all day. I—I saw something I need to ask him. But when he goes out, and says nothing about going, he may not come home for days."

"He does that sometimes."

"Is everything okay up there?" Mr. Hemmings, the first floor landlord, calls from his door with his usual tone of upset.

"We're fine," Dr. Maiwand says.

"Mr. Vagelle went out early," I say. "I do not know when he is coming back."

"He does that sometimes," Hemmings says, and turns back to his apartment, and closes the door.

"I think Mr. Hemmings does not like me much."

"Oh, he's that way with everyone," Dr. Maiwand says. "Would you like to come downstairs? My mother just sent me a gift bag with her favorite Indian tea, and I was wondering who I should share the first cup with." When he talks about his mother, it reminds me how young he is—and I am younger still—I am twenty. Then I think about the very young girl.

"Not today, *spasiba* (thank you). I should go out."

"I understand." He holds out a hand to help me to my feet, but I do not like being touched. "As I've said before, if you ever need someone to talk to, come down any time. I enjoy the company."

With satchel on my shoulder, I lock Mr. Vagelle's apartment and walk slowly back to market. I am confused still, maybe from sleep, and the sun is too bright and hurts my eyes. When I reach the corner, I see into the alley and a little black hair girl in blue flower dress is walking away. I call to her. She does not look back, but she runs.

Workmen unloading truck, and she runs through them. They yell to her, but when I get there she is gone. They look past my questions and say to go away, they are busy. I continue down the alley. Symbols painted on alley walls, not just usual graffiti but other signs like I had seen in times past. Mr. Vagelle explained to me about voodoo religion. He said some people in this city still believe in this. He does not. But he said it is best not to talk with people about religion.

A man comes from a doorway. He looks down on me. He is very tall, light skin half-caste, with paint spatter on work clothes, and I think to turn back.

"You're in the wrong place, Goldie," he says. "Why you chase that little one? She does not look like a relative of yours. So what do you want with her?"

"My name is not Goldie," I say.

"So, how 'bout I should see some I.D. Let's take a peek in your big purse." Now he shows his shiny silver teeth.

I reach into my satchel and he is curious, and I take out kitchen knife, and his eyes get rounder. He laughs loud enough to echo the alley and feel it in my stomach. He continues laughing and I walk backward, but he does not follow.

I reach corner market and see Mr. Jackson fast-walking away from his store. His door sign says, "Sorry Closed." It is middle of the day and I am too curious, so I follow him. Two blocks later he climbs on trolley car. He does not look back to see me jump on behind woman with a wide sun hat.

The ride takes us all the way to Treme and Congo Square where Mr. Jackson jumps off. He does not look back, so I take my time leaving trolley car with others before following.

I know of this park. I came here a year ago with Mr. Vagelle while he looked for a missing person. Curious, I read the history here. It is known for the slave days. And because of Code Noir, when slaves were made to be Christians. And they were allowed Sundays off to come here, to be together, and to play music and dance. Some claim this is the beginnings of American jazz music. They also say this is where they celebrated their Haiti voodoo.

Mr. Jackson goes to a large black woman in a yellow sundress standing in front of a wide, dark statue. A sculpture of many slaves playing music with a woman dancing. The sundress woman is not happy to see Mr. Jackson.

I stay back in the shade of trees like just another tourist. I am shocked to see the grocer, always so nice to me, but now he is angry and shouting at the woman. It makes me feel…She pushes him away and he slaps her face hard. And I am about to run to stop them, but my feet cannot move when I see Mr. Vagelle hurry forward. Mr. Jackson sees him and runs away through a crowd.

Mr. Vagelle stays to help the woman who sat down hard on the stone of the statue's base. He kneels and takes her hand and his voice is soft and questioning. I am too far to hear. I think to go to him, to ask my own questions, but he gets up and helps her to her feet. They turn away through the park and walk under the arch. As I pass in front of the statue of dancing slaves, I hear tiny sounds from behind.

"Lady?" a girl's voice freezes me. "Lady, why do you follow?"

I am weak and afraid to turn. I do not know why. Maybe I think if I look at her she will run away again. And I will lose her and lose Mr. Vagelle and the large woman in the yellow sundress.

"Do you know them?" I say. "I need to go with them."

"Why?"

"I do not know why. I feel something is wrong, and I need to see."

"What if you do not like what you see?"

"I need to see anyway."

I walk to where I last saw the yellow dress pass through the open market crowd. I hear small feet behind me until I have lost the yellow dress and Mr. Vagelle. Then I turn and the girl is not there. I am chilled on this hot New Orleans day, and gooseflesh tickles my arms.

I move like I am pulled without direction through the open market stalls. I see a vendor's racks with many short blue dresses with tiny flowers matching. I think I am gone blind, but I move on. I see the dress again, far off and moving to the river. I try to hurry and catch, but I cannot gain on the black-haired girl.

Feeling like forever, I keep on, catching a shape or color that could be her. But I am never certain. Something in me cannot stop. I need to know why. And why I am afraid for her. And afraid for my friend, Mr. Vagelle. I might be drunk, but I do not get drunk.

So much time passes, I must stop. Reason says to me, I must go home. I must trust in my Mr. Vagelle to come and tell me his answers for everything. Then I board another trolley for home.

The ride is long and crowds get on and off, and I do not like being so close to people. My nerves stretch like piano wires. If someone touches me, I may scream. Then I see I am not going home. I am going the wrong way from home.

When the trolley stops, I climb down. I am lost. Traffic here is thinner. Houses small and cramped like graveyard stones, one next to another.

"Go on," says the girl in my head, and I cross the broken moonscape of pavement and up a curb and along a tilted sidewalk beneath crosswalk signs. And dogs bark from behind chicken fences, and a child laughs, and another cries. But I do not cry. I have seen too much of life after only twenty years. People could never know how much I have seen. Pain. Hate. Death. And I do not cry. I will not let them win.

"Who must not win?" the girl says.

"Those who wish me to cry."

"Stop."

And I stop at the edge of long grass, in front of a broken-roof house with gray wood and scabbed blue shutters, unpainted for a half century. They call it a shotgun house—long and narrow, front to back—and it stands alone here. Beyond the broken-roof, tall trees begin and the land turns to marsh. Many insects make ugly music that shivers my nerves and upsets my brain.

I continue through the long grass to the front door. The torn screen door lays on its side against the raised base of the house. I do not know why that matters to me. I hear voices inside, and a woman cries then screams words as I climb two steps and look into the sunless shotgun house.

"Why do you come here?" a deep voice behind me says, and I am scared. He grabs my arms and I am blind again with crazy fear. *I cannot be touched.* I try to say it, but nothing comes out. I fight to turn to see him, then I fight to pull free, but my arms feel like wearing lead sleeves. And he drives me into the open doorway where I cannot see, passing sunlight into dark. "So where is your big nasty knife now, Goldie?" Then I know that voice is the tall half-caste with the silver teeth.

"Hands off, Pip!" Mr. Vagelle stands in the hall, his walking stick tight in both hands like he may use it.

"This one's been snooping all over Big Easy," Silver-teeth says. "She's following you."

"She is with me." He does not even look at me, but stares into Silver-teeth's eyes.

"I—" Silver-teeth sets me free and steps back. "I didn't know. Sorry, V."

I hold my arms tight where he grabbed me, and I move to the side, pressing my back against a wall. Now big Pip looks scared.

"I am sorry." Mr. Vagelle moves close to me, but does not touch. "Are you okay?"

"You know this man?" I am still shivering.

"I should've told him about you. He's been helping me."

"How are you here?" I say.

"Come." He leads me to living room doorway where I can see large woman in yellow sundress sitting. Across the room, Mr. Jackson stands twisting his hands and shaking, then I see the plastic zip-ties on his wrists. Mr. Vagelle touches the woman's shoulder. "Matty, this is Alya," he says. "She is my assistant. My friend."

Matty hides her face. Her breathing tells me she cries.

Mr. Vagelle uses cell phone, calls police. He tells them this street and house number.

"We need to wait," he says to me. "I'm afraid I put you in a difficult situation. Would you like to leave before they get here?"

"No," I say. I have moved to the wall again to better see Pip in doorway behind me. My stomach is sick from the touching. "What is *situation?* What does Mr. Jackson do here?"

"I'll explain everything soon."

Mr. Jackson, even with zip ties, tries to run for the door, but Pip moves to block the way. Mr. Jackson spins, dizzy, crossing room to crash through window without screen. He gets up and runs the yard.

Pip is already gone. Mr. Vagelle runs the hallway for the back door and I follow.

I am outside in blinding sunlight. Pip already holds Mr. Jackson's neck in his large fingers and he pushes the face into backyard mud.

"Don't kill him," Mr. Vagelle says.

Pip looks confused. Matty has followed, still holding her face. Her sobs hurt my chest. My world feels like the grip of a tightening blanket.

Then Matty hurries past me, past all of us, into muddier ground and pools of dark water. She sinks to her ankles, and her pushing forward grows more difficult when the wetland sucks at her every step.

I can see past her struggles to the edge of the swamp and clothing scattered across the pools. But it is not just clothing. It is people lying, unmoving, half-hidden by the reeds and tall grasses. Matty drops to her knees screaming at Heaven. She beats her fists in the muck.

Mr. Vagelle stops me from going closer, then he walks at my side because I need to see this and I will not stop.

"Please, Alya," he whispers, but I disobey.

It is a woman and a teen boy lying muddied, but not enough to disguise the blood. A man also lies out there without moving. I see the outine of a rifle in the mound not far off. I have seen enough. I turn away.

"I'm sorry you had to be here for this," Mr. Vagelle says. "I know you have asked me in the past, but it is why I don't always tell you where I go or who I am with. Sometimes…too often, this sort of thing seems to find me."

I still shake and I cannot speak.

"Two days ago, the grocer came to me for help. His arm in a sling, he told me his brother-in-law, Parker, had attacked him. He told a story about his sister, Sam, and her violent husband. And he feared for her safety."

I hug myself and watch moving clouds.

"Do you need to hear this?" He allows for space between us.

"Yes."

"The police could do nothing to help. They are familiar with the family and reports of violence, and Parker had been arrested more than once. Petty crimes. Street brawls. Sam was a regular emergency room visitor with a record of broken bones in her past."

I walk slow, away from the crime, and a soft wind pushes at my back and bends the tall grass, and birds quit the trees and fly as if from a rushing storm. I hear police cars.

"I investigated the husband." Mr. Vagelle stays behind. "Neighbors, workmates, but I could find no one at home here, so I found Sam's sister, Matty. She was also worried about the family. But while her brother-in-law could be a rough man, she said she never knew him to raise a hand to her sister.

"I found Parker last night. Cornered him outside a tavern. I threatened to kill him if he hurt his family again. He was surprised by my words, and swore he had never hurt his wife. Said he loved her more than his own life. When I told him that his brother-in-law had hired me, that I'd seen Jackson's broken arm, that I knew the history of his wife's hospital visits, his look changed from surprise to *something dangerous*. I thought he might attack me, but he ran.

"He was too big to outrun me. I pushed him into a wall, but he was too hurt to resist. He swore again that he'd never hurt his wife. He always took the blame to keep her brother out of jail. The grocery store paid for their house, and Jackson used it as blackmail to keep the family in line. It was Jackson who beat his sister and her children. He was a sadist who resented her marriage and any good that came into her life."

I feel in the grip of Russian winter. I cannot breathe. A fourth, smaller, body in the weeds lay curled as if still in fear. Her black hair stiff with mud and leaves. Her torn blue dress with tiny flowers. Dirty pink socks with no shoes. Because of my life with Papa, I had stopped my tears before I reached this girl's age. No matter the pain, I refused to cry for all these years. Today I am twenty, and I cannot stop them, the tears.

"If you knew all this last night," I force a breath, "why would you send me to his store today?"

"I've seen in the past the way he looks at you. And you are always happy when you walk in his store. But when you turn your back, I see his expression change. I believe he has resented your happiness too. So, I set today in motion. I brought in Pip, who had assisted me in the past, and had him follow you—for your safety. And sending you into that store today, I knew Jackson would see your smile and be reminded of his sister's happiness. When he ran out of his store in the middle of the day, I suspected the worst. But I had miscalculated."

"Mis-calculated."

"I could not have guessed you would return to the store and follow him across town to this place."

Brain fog and rain follow me home in Mr. Vagelle's car. Some hours later I leave the bedroom, and I smell he has made chicken soup. He does not often make dinner.

"I still do not understand," I say. "Why would he hire you to go after brother-in-law, and then this?"

"He came to me two days ago," he says, "asking me to protect his sister from his brother-in-law. But he knew they were beyond any protection. When I found the bodies this afternoon, I examined them. With what water can do, insects and animals, I estimated they have been like this for maybe four days. All except for Parker. He was killed last night while holding his son."

"But not the girl. I saw her this morning. It was her, the blue dress…"

I can feel his eyes on me. He breathes deep. When I turn to him, he is by the fireplace, lowering into his old wingback chair.

"It is a common dress," he says.

In the coming days, I watch him. He goes about his work. Often he disappears, not returning for some time. Or he goes out and I hear him come home in the early hours, then he is gone again before morning. I have seen this before. It is not often, but I have seen him lose, and this is his habit when he does. The black moods, I call it. And I think, why would this man work at a job, a job with so much bad, that gives so much pain?

"If he be Mr. Hyde..."

Two

A Spider Hole

Beguiling

Laine

Spider Hole:

In military terms, a small camouflaged foxhole to deceive the enemy. In naturalist terms, a similarly camouflaged hole, constructed by the trapdoor spider, from which to ambush prey. The spider burrows, takes up residence, decorates the hole with webbing, and constructs a door for camouflage. To lie in wait.

Beguile:

To charm, spellbind, seduce.

The author's pencil scratched its final words, "...the monster."

August limped away after that too-hot summer and the rains turned cool by mid-September. An anomaly here. A chilled damp saturated everything and everyone down to the bones, like a corpse found in the gutter after the floods recede.

It all happened too quickly. I was blindsided. Absolute control spun-off into victimhood by *Moirai*, the Fates who weave all our destinies from birth—or so I would prefer to believe. But no. The Fates, Karma, the Hand of God; it's all bullshit. This began as a killing. Then the net fell from an unseen someone; an adequate enough definition of *blindsided.*

Too many people credit their lives, or blame their lives, to luck, as if buttering their morning toast amounted to a roll of the dice. I tended to fall into the other category, autonomist. I believed that making the odd, rational, choice would be rewarded or punished accordingly.

Four years as a columnist for The Delta Tribune, I felt beholden to read the publication daily, which finally paid off when I answered a classified ad for an apartment in one of the better sections of the city. A one-bedroom, one-bath, with kitchenette, on the fourth-floor of a dark-brick structure devoid of character, and a rent I couldn't pass up. It also happened to be two bus stops away from the Trib.

The landlord, Hemmings, was strategically ensconced on the ground floor, playing his role as the skittish hall monitor. A medical student lived on the second floor. And a recently retired "consultant," whatever the hell that was, had the third. It all felt comfortable enough. Hemmings took my first two months' check upfront with his bon mot:

"Nice to have a broad in the building for once." A term considered bad-taste twenty years before he was born. He grinned in discomfort. Maybe it was my expression. "Um, sorry. I've been binge-watching the Dead End Kids."

Conjuring a smile proved difficult. Now that he had my signature and security deposit, he gave me his list of don'ts.

"It's a small building, Ms. Baker, so please be mindful of the other tenants. No smoke. No dope. I don't expect you to become a recluse like Mr. Vagelle, just below you, but dance in your slippers and try to keep the noise down after ten. If you have a boyfriend, well, try to use his place if you have a loose headboard."

"No worries on all of the above." *He has no filter,* then I immediately wondered if I'd just dropped too much personal information. *Must watch my step with this guy. He may be sharper than he looks.*

My first three weeks in the flat, with the exception of Hemmings popping from his portal whenever I entered the building, I might have been the only inhabitant of a four-story mausoleum. Not a problem for me until, one evening, dodging raindrops and racing up the steps ahead of another squall, the door flew open and a dark, handsome young man nearly bowled me back down.

A smile jumped to his eyes. To his credit, he tried not to leer. After a barrage of apologies and a formal welcome to the building, he dug a business card from his coat pocket. He introduced himself as Dr. Maiwand, who'd recently completed his OBGYN internship, and if I was new to the area and ever in need of—

"I should hurry in before the storm hits," I said, and fled inside. The door to Hemmings's apartment opened behind me, but I sped my momentum up the stairs without looking back. *This place gets creepier by the day.*

At the third-floor landing, I marked Mr. Vagelle's grocery/newspaper delivery outside his door. *Good to know someone still reads the papers.* Then I half-thought to knock, so his groceries wouldn't spoil, but I'd already made my new acquaintance quota for the day. Maybe I imagined a hunchback with one eye, a peg leg and a hook for a hand introducing himself. My adrenalin settled only when the door to my own sanctuary shut me in.

Safety is an illusion until chaos rears its head.

Hoping on a full evening of bliss, shivering in appreciation of the long flannel I had unboxed shortly after move-in, I inhaled the aroma of my first Jack Daniels of the evening. A personal tradition in times of stress, I seldom made it through a second.

Three sips later, I jolted from my easy chair at the sound of a distant *bell* and a commotion from downstairs. But apparently the *jolt* was all in my mind, as it took every bit of sixty seconds to reach my purse and fumble for my petite "self-defense canister." Hard shoes assaulted the stairs with Hemmings bellowing from the ground floor.

"You can't go up! I'm calling the cops! I've got my phone right here! This is me calling the cops!"

"Easy, Mr. Hemmings," said a second voice, closer, probably my neighbor. "I've been expecting him."

Cracking my door, fingers tightening around the small metal cylinder, I got my first view of Mr. Vagelle, the back of his graying crew cut like a dusting of snow. From my angle, he appeared thin, a bit over six-feet and hunched slightly, as he leaned heavily on a cane. He confronted a much larger, skull-shaved, wild-eyed *guest* three stairs away.

"And you've been expecting him for how long?" Hemmings continued. "This is a peaceful house, Mr. Vagelle—"

"My apologies, sir." Without turning he said, "And to you, Ms. Baker. Now, Mr. Durning, you see you have upset the entire house. I will talk with you, but only if you calm yourself. Take an hour. There's a decent coffeehouse across the street, but I recommend a cup of green tea, possibly chamomile."

"Shove your chamomile, Vagelle! I'll not be put off *again.*" Durning eyed me past the older man's shoulder. His clenched fists softened. He pivoted then thundered back down the stairs calling, "One hour!"

Hemmings backed into his apartment. His door lock clicked, and I imagined his eye pressed to the peephole until Durning slammed out. Vagelle hesitated, noticed his groceries against the threshold, ignored them and entered his apartment. He did not close his door. Contemplating the drama, I watched the light of his open doorway. When he did not re-emerge, I took it upon myself to descend to the third level.

"Please come in, Ms. Baker, if you dare so soon after that disturbance."

His apartment was not what I expected. White contemporary furnishings, the exceptions being a single, comfortably traditional, wingback chair to one side, and a modern black, L-shape desk in the corner by the window. A white settee took center stage while Vagelle stood with his back to the door, leaning on his cane, apparently studying the large landscape painting above his artificial fireplace. At the corner of the uncluttered mantle lay a single book, *R. L. Stevenson,* beside a small, unobtrusive, trophy in the shape of a golden bell. Its significance had been turned to face the wall.

"However, I believe you would dare," he said. "Many would have listened from behind a locked door.

He faced me, again not what I expected. His smile tipped to one side, while I thought he should be shaken. Pleasant features, not as aged as I had imagined, possibly mid-thirties; the white of his hair had deceived me.

"I thought perhaps I should have introduced myself before now," I said. "But it seems you already know my name."

"Yes. Mr. Hemmings, always so helpful with the local news. Speaking of which, if you are coming in, would you mind bringing the paper? Just set it anywhere. And you can stow your pepperspray. *I'm* fairly harmless. Fairly." Ah, that disarming smile again.

I pocketed the mini-canister, took up the newspaper and the bag of groceries and set them on the dining table. A table with only two chairs. *A recluse,* Hemmings had said.

"Beautiful." I nodded to the painting. "Looks old. Dark for a landscape."

"It is. Thomas Moran of the Hudson River School, painted during the early months of his Yellowstone trip. An enduring fascination for me, juxtaposing the golden cliffs amid the encroaching shadows."

"I sense a metaphor coming." I refrained from asking where his fortune came from if he could afford an original Moran.

"I would not presume to teach a writer about metaphor. It is my only painting and I believe art should be left to the viewer."

"Writer, huh? Our Hemmings does like to talk, Mr. Vagelle."

"Call me Nicolaus." He gestured to the white settee before the fireplace while he took to the wingback chair. "Come. I'm more comfortable sitting these days. And yes, he tends to chatter, but I knew the name Laine Baker long before you moved in." He aimed his stick at the newspaper.

"You read bylines too."

"Don't be modest. You made a name for yourself early in your career. I've particularly enjoyed your articles on the 'Shrovetide Ripper.'" The stick in his hand incited a sneer and he set it aside, I imagined, with contempt. Not a cheap pharmacy cane. I thought it rather attractive with it's intricately carved silver head, and wondered briefly at the man's vanity. Or perhaps it was simply a gift. The creature crafted onto the head of the stick, worn smooth, possibly from years of abuse, held a familiarity I couldn't quite place.

"You're right, you have known my name for some time," I said. "By the way, that 'Ripper' headline came directly from my editor. At the time, we only had three killings attributed to the madman. He's hardly ol' Leather Apron of Whitechapel."

"Three that first year, then one every Shrovetide since. And he hasn't been caught yet." He glanced at the clock above his desk. If his angry visitor took the full hour, we had plenty of time yet.

"So, Mr.—Nicolaus, what does a *consultant* do? Or should it be, who did you used to consult for? Hemmings did say you were retired."

"Semi-retired. I take the occasional odd-job as an independent contractor."

"I shouldn't pry. Sometimes it's difficult to shut off work. I need to remind myself not everyone is grist for the newspapers." I detected a hint of flavor in the air, something unusual yet familiar, not cologne. Soap? Lilies?

"And I don't mean to be enigmatic." An unexpected smirk came and went. "Consultant, yes. I used to hire out to perform psych-evaluations for a variety of companies. Sometimes with employment applicants or, at times, physicians needing analysis of a patient's mental health. These days that type of client has become rare for an independent."

"I imagine many larger establishments come with their own in-house consultants."

"Blame it on the modern-day, commonplace, standard of insanity."

Had he ever worked as a police profiler? Perhaps in another part of the country, as I'd probably recognize the name had he worked locally. That barely conspicuous sweet flower stink interfered with my thoughts.

"I decided I could afford to limit my practice," he said, "as most who come to me now are looking to find dirt for a divorce settlement, or something equally tiresome."

Was he gauging my responses? Another glance at the clock.

"Would you like me to leave?" I said. "Maybe give you time to prepare before your visitor returns?"

"I've been thinking about that, and wondering. It's an interesting case here. Mr. Durning appears intimidating at first whiff, though after studying him for several weeks, I believe him to be the big barking dog that would never bite. I also saw his reaction to your arrival at the height of his fit."

"I noticed as well."

"It's apparent from your writing that you are one to seek out difficult stories. I wonder if you might like to be a spectator for this interview."

"He's not a client? There would be no sanctity of the therapist couch and all?"

"Just a troubled victim. And I'm not a working therapist. I would be genuinely interested in your opinion once he has left."

A test. "A decent strategy, having a woman's presence as a calming element in the room."

"You also read me well."

And too many compliments. "You won't mind if I keep my hand on the *pepperspray?*"

He then gave a brief rundown on Mr. Durning, who had lost his wife the month before and had come here for help. The police had run through the motions. They wrote a standard report, assigned an officer to make a few calls and ring a few doorbells. Naturally, they'd assumed she either ran off with a boyfriend, or Durning, himself, buried her somewhere and was looking for "police assisted" misdirection.

"I tried to fend him off," he said. "This isn't my line of work. If the P.D. had abandoned their inquiries, he was better off hiring a real private investigator." *He keeps telling me what he is not.* "Unfortunately, a police lieutenant had dropped my name. Said I'd helped find a missing nine-year-old for him last year."

"You worked on the Bunny Arroyo case?" Something—the fragrance maybe—kept pulling my attention to his furnishings. An eclectic assortment of white and black, old and new; like the Moran painting—light and dark—the black-bound Stevenson book against the golden bell, and the overly theatrical walking stick. An apartment composed from the pages of 19th Century literature?

"Unofficially, yes. The detective on the case came to me after they found her body. He was looking for a psych profile on the father. I told him I'd been following the story in *your* paper and, in my opinion, Mr. Arroyo was not her biological father. That's really all I did. No investigating. I didn't even charge the department for an hour's consultation."

"I can't imagine how you came to that conclusion. The relationship. I know a surveillance cam picked up the two at a bus station in Shreveport."

"It was mostly the body language between them." Lifting slowly from his chair, he might have been deciding how much to reveal. He made his way to the window. "I'd been given an early look at the camera footage. It was grainy, but I recognized his neck tattoo, possibly Salvadoran. The girl in the video never stopped crying, and he never spoke to her. That, and she wore a red plastic bracelet similar to others found in south Texas on trafficking victims. Police thought he was just being abusive, slapping her with her own hand. I knew he was slapping her with the bracelet to remind her she was a slave."

"Sharp eyes." *So, he does police profiling as a civilian. And he's letting me know he's read more of my work. He is good, and he wants me to know it. More vanity?*

"My name had been kept out of the papers, as I'd asked, but the lieutenant should never have given my name to Mr. Durning."

"So, now Durning is the dog who can't shake loose of the bone. You."

"I haven't seen him for two weeks." He turned for the door. "But I knew he would be back today."

"Why all of a sudden today?"

We were interrupted by the downstairs buzzer.

"That would be him," Vagelle said. "So you'll stay?"

"I guess you've hooked me."

I moved to his desk chair and out of the line of fire, as he suggested. He placed a notepad and pen at my elbow in the event I was "inspired to jot a few notes." A reporter's habit. The stamped header on the notepad announced, simply, "N. Vagelle, Consultant." I couldn't help noticing his easy gait crossing the room without the walking stick.

Hemmings's voice from downstairs was followed by slow footsteps ascending, and the consultant opened the door before the knock.

The creature who had appeared so menacing just an hour before had transformed. He raised his still smoldering eyes to the consultant. He took in the rest of the room, and me, with a glance. His lips quivered. Knuckles cracked in his heavy fists, but I knew he was finished. A pathetic, beaten man.

Vagelle's body language remained unchanged as he moved Mr. Durning to the settee. He retook the facing wingback chair.

"You know why I came back today," Durning said.

"I do," Vagelle said.

"I wanted to kill..." He deflated. "No. That's wrong. I—I needed answers."

"I know. They found her body two days ago. They interrogated you as suspect number one, held you for twenty-four hours. Your lawyer got you released this morning because they had no evidence to charge you with. You blame me for not taking you as a client last month. You believe I could have found her for you before this happened. You are wrong."

"Do you have any idea," Durning's focus flitted to me then away again, "what it feels like? When you have nowhere to turn...?"

Vagelle scrutinized him like a specimen.

"A man…needs to do something." Another glance to me, then down at his knuckles turning. His pride struggled to rekindle the burning? Pride lost. "I needed to do something."

The consultant rose from his chair, took his grocery bag from the dining table to the kitchen counter, and began emptying its contents. Somewhat discomfited with the interaction, I stared at the blank page of the notepad. *N. Vagelle, Consultant.*

"I was just about to put on a pot of tea for Ms. Baker and myself," Vagelle said. "Would you care to join us? I'm not crazy about chamomile myself, but I do have a nice earl gray. Sugar, Ms. Baker?"

"Um—Yes, that would be fine."

Durning lifted from the settee with effort. He shuffled to the door with his chin to his chest, then stopped to stare at his shoes. He looked back at the settee.

"I'm sorry. I seem to have tracked the rain in with me. I didn't realize…"

"Tea, Mr. Durning?" Vagelle busied himself with minutiae.

"Oh, no thank you." He held the doorknob for several deep breaths. He let himself out and, like a lid tightening on a moth jar, silence engulfed the apartment with the click of the door.

I have always loved the aroma of earl gray, but at that moment I mostly thought of the Jack Daniels forsaken in my apartment. Vagelle's cup rested near the arm of his wingback chair while he contemplated the water stains on his settee.

"So, Ms. Baker, I'm sure you have thoughts on our mini-drama here. What do you think of our widower?"

"The evening has been one surprise after another," I said after a space. "First on the stair. Then you inviting me, a complete stranger, to attend your *drama.* The surprise of Durning's metamorphosis in the space of an hour, then departing after so little explanation of why he returned here at all. It all played out logically enough, yet..."

"Ah, but you came into this finale cold without seeing the rest of the play."

"Yes." After a bit more thought, "The man appears genuine in his grief, as well as his earlier outrage. And his confusion upon leaving—possibly, not knowing why he had come in the first place other than running on emotional steam. He knew there was nothing you could do for his poor wife. Perhaps he needed someone to absorb his own guilt. Perhaps he was the reason for his wife leaving the house that day."

"That word *transference.* "He tipped that cheek again. "You're on the mark. Please, continue the thought."

"Well," I needed a sip of tea to cut what was beginning to feel like an interview, "I don't believe his mannerisms reflected a murderer's guilt. Could be, as you have insinuated, simply a guilt born of his impotence. Impotence in being unable to rescue his wife. The same as his anger directed at you for not assisting him. Why did he come to you initially, if not in search of the *consultant* to tell him what to do or how to find her?"

"Another hint. His wife had disappeared six days before his first visit here." He stirred his teacup absently without drinking.

"Which tells me he didn't wait for the police to end their missing persons investigation. But he saw that they were winding down their efforts and he needed another set of eyes on it. He likely assumed you turned him down because you agreed with the police. He was the most likely suspect.

"Maybe their only suspect."

"I have to admit," momentum prodded me, when I thought to let it drop, "with all the surprises tonight, you surprised me as well."

"How so, Laine?"

"You knew all of this in advance. You knew he would return here after he calmed, and you seemed to know he would have nothing to say. Yet, aside from telling him the few things he already knew, you barely spoke. You asked no questions. Frankly, you barely looked at him beyond that, not even a word of sympathy for his destroyed life. Almost as if you wanted him to turn down your offer of tea and go away."

"There was nothing more he could tell me nor I him. I could say nothing to dispel his future nightmares. And he didn't come to me for sympathy."

"Like I said, just one more puzzle on the evening. Something else I should have anticipated once I'd learned you were a psychologist. That cold reasoning." As if sparked by the thought, I remembered the small Golden Bell Award on his mantle. Its brilliance a curiosity, polished memories of a prestigious dinner presentation for...*a University Honor Society? Psychology Honors.*

"It's what makes me good at what I do." Pushing from his chair with little help from his cane, he returned his teacup to the kitchen then crossed to the dining table where he retrieved the evening newspaper. He seemed to have forgotten his stick. "I suspect you may also have *Psychology major* scribbled somewhere in your schooling."

"I read a lot. Have you ever worked in the theater?" I said. His hesitation was so well-masked, I questioned if I had imagined it. "Just whimsy. Probably that smirk of yours that comes and goes at odd times."

He laid his paper on the desk beside the notepad, "N. Vagelle, Consultant."

"I don't believe you've had time to read the evening edition." His smirk had disappeared. "The police had withheld information on the case, Mrs. Durning's disappearance and murder, until late this afternoon. If you hadn't left work early, they might have asked you to write the column."

"I wondered why I'd heard nothing of Mrs. Durning until tonight, if she disappeared a month ago." I checked the paper's date, today's date, Oct 1st, and scanned page-one. I landed on a column near the bottom: "Shrovetide Ripper Out Of Season?"

Uncertainty, confusion building to outrage—the blood drained from my head, then rushed back in on the boil. The desk chair tipped as I struggled to my feet. I forced a breath and picked up the *news* to continue reading.

"This was my story—should have been my story. How could they run this without calling me?"

The body of Margaret Durning, wife, mother of three, was discovered at 6:30 am on September 27 after the floodwaters of our most recent storm had drained the lower flats of Lafayette Cemetery. Evoking the Ripper's M.O., as described in a brief statement to the press by Lieutenant Murphy, the body was found fully naked with ligature marks on wrists, ankles and

throat. She appeared to have been
disemboweled, but autopsy later confirmed
Mrs. Durning had been forced to ingest
hydrofluoric acid…this is the second such
killing this year. The earlier…

I could no longer see enough to read. Lilies had taken seed in my brain. On autopilot, I righted the desk chair and lowered myself into its grip.

"Not possible. This is not possible," I whispered to an out-of-focus room.

"Of course it is," Vagelle said.

"Of course it is not! Shrovetide Ripper murders during Shrovetide. He's been doing this for at least three years. Three the first year, and…"

"And once every year since. I know."

"This is October first, God-damn it! This is not the same killer. I know him better than anyone. I wrote that… first…detailing the investigation."

"Yes, and you won awards for your coverage. Hey, I'm a fan. I've followed your articles with each installment. Nevertheless, this is our killer. Exact same M.O. down to where the body was dumped."

"It is a copycat!" My head pounded as I concentrated on forming each word. "No serial killer who chooses a specific date…three years in a row, changes…motivation. You're a trained psych—Has that ever been—?"

"Yes, it has, Laine. Seven times this decade. Until we know the killer, we cannot possibly know the level of madness or what might trigger a similar event. Of course psychopathic behavior does not simply manifest at the age of forty, or thirty, or twenty."

"Do not condescend—"

"I can assume, once we get this person behind bars, we will discover more bodies. The M.O. may have evolved. Perhaps the killings have moved to other locales at other times of the year. We need more facts. Never assume the details of a deranged mind."

"Bullshit! I know my killer. This is nothing more than a *copycat.*" The pain pressed like hot wax behind my eyes as my nails bit into my palms. "How could they do this to me! My story! My head...line."

Water ran from the kitchen tap as my thoughts muddied.

"I know the killer too, Laine, and you should know as a general practice, there are details of this crime that were never released to the press. I'm afraid those details are present with Mrs. Durning."

Vagelle set a glass on the desk. I wished he would stop saying my name.

"Just water," he said. "Looks like you could use it."

I wanted to throw the water glass at him, or across the room, anything to hear it break. But my strength had dissolved, so I took his advice. The glass took too long to get to my mouth, but I eventually drank.

"I should go. I—No, I need to clear my head." My knees might have been too unsteady for a climb to the fourth floor.

He materialized in the bedroom doorway with throw pillows and an afghan, which he then spread on the settee.

"Come, rest here a bit." He took my elbow, escorting me to the settee. "I can get you a Tylenol if you like. Or if you prefer, you can stretch out on my bed for an hour. I won't be sleeping much tonight anyway."

"No. No. This is fine. For a bit. Then I really must…"

"Of course."

No sooner had my head pressed into the pillow when consciousness deserted me.

I opened my eyes, having no idea how long I'd slept. I remembered dreaming, but could not recall the dream's contents. All I felt was the residue of a disturbance rooted throughout my faculties.

What the hell time is it? Then I realized for the first time there was no clock above the desk. No clocks in the room. I remembered my cell phone left upstairs in my purse. Everything had happened so fast.

He was still there, Vagelle, his back to me as he hunched at the black desk. He appeared to be writing.

About what? I wondered.

It must be about Durning, getting his thoughts down. Probably an examination of the encounter, or reworking the previous month on paper while its culmination was fresh from last night. Probably still working with his lieutenant friend, fishing for clues to the murderer. Or he might have been writing about me and my part in last night's play. Cataloguing my reactions, my comments—he might even be analyzing me. That's what analysts do. They habitually study the people around them, tracking their behavior, labeling them, placing them into file cabinets for future reference. Looking for cracks in their facade. He had a definite interest in anything related to the Shrovetide Ripper, which meant he had a definite interest in me ever since my first column on the murders. He made a point of saying he *knew* the killer. He also knew me. *How much?*

Such a coincidence, too much of a coincidence that I would move into the apartment directly upstairs from this man.

Could he have been following me all these years from the shadows?

Might he have formed an infatuation with me?

If I didn't know better, I might think he was the Ripper. A case might be made that Durning had come originally because he had suspicions of Nicolaus Vagelle. I knew nothing of the Durning murder beyond what this man told me, or—

Three years since those first murders, I needed to go back and reread every word I had written on them. I needed to find out how much this *consultant-psychologist* might have deduced of my own personality or lifestyle based on my words.

I've never cared much for intrusions into my private affairs, Nicolaus Vagelle.

Paranoid thinking. So unlike me. Thoughts drifted in as wisps of smoke that broke up just as quickly before settling with substance.

My headache lingered. Not as severe, but enough to keep the clouds in front of me. I felt as if I had not only finished the night's tumbler of Jack Daniels, but as if I had finished three more. Had I been drugged? When I spotted my purse on the dining table it occurred to me, for the first time, that Nicolaus Vagelle had spiked my water. I had barely made it to the settee before passing out.

N. Vagelle. *Inveigle—? That son of a bitch!*

"I hope it wasn't too much of an intrusion," he said without turning to see I was awake. "Once you passed out, it occurred to me you might not have locked your door. I assumed your latchkey was in your purse and I didn't want to lock you out. Feel better?"

"Slightly." I struggled upright. I touched my pocket for what he had assumed was pepperspray. His cane tilted against the arm of the wingback where he'd left it, its unique, intricately carved silver head begging for closer inspection. If he needed it as more than just a theater prop, I could certainly beat him to the door. He had not needed it to get to his desk chair, however, and the door might be locked. "What time is it?"

"Four-ten. That's a.m." He turned from his writing with that too-charming smile. "I just put on a pot of porridge for myself if you care to join me. I find it good for settling an upset stomach."

Porridge? What, did you grow up in Whitechapel?

"No thank you." I surveyed the apartment again wondering about more theater props and how much of the decorating looked like it had been bought by the same person, or how much might be stage dressing. *No clocks. What happened to the clock?* The unsettled feeling left by last night's dreams intensified.

"Would you care for another glass of water?"

Again with the water. "I'm surprised you don't work on a computer. Hard to imagine myself getting along without one."

"I'm a bit old school. Of course I know how, but the feel of pen on paper, it's cathartic to watch the movement of letters as I write. It helps the thought process."

I instinctively touched the writer's wart on my middle finger. He caught my move. *He knows me too well. Did he—?*

"But enough about me. I'm sure you're anxious to return to your rooms for a real rest."

"Quite right." I tested my land legs. I started for the table and my purse, but stopped as I reached his walking stick with the *intricate silver head.* "So, Mr. Vagelle—"

"Nicolaus, please."

"Yes, Nicolaus. I'm still curious about a few things." The fingers of my right hand caressed the small, cold cylinder in my flannel's pocket. "I know you are an intelligent man, and it may take some doing for me to catch up."

"Oh, you keep up remarkably well." He leaned heavily on the corner of the desk.

"You've known me for many years, where I'd never heard your name until three weeks ago. You've followed my workings on the Ripper, while having access to police files unavailable to the press, which makes you more of an expert on the killer…possibly. You asked me to sit in on this *interview* with a fake Ripper suspect, then deliberately sent him away without an interview. And you drugged me to get my purse from my apartment, ostensibly to find more information on me. I should think, with your connection to the police, that it would be fairly simple, and not worth all this folderol. My career, my favorite blend of tea?"

He placed himself in front of the painting, no doubt focusing on the center of golden sunlight amid the encroaching shadows.

"I suspect most of what you do is very deliberate," I said. "No wasted movement. The tea, the drugged water, pillows and afghan at the ready. So, now that you've filled in all the blanks about last night, you have nothing more to learn from me, nor I you. There are yet unanswered questions, and you can probably guess what they are."

"I did not lie. The water was not drugged."

"The tea then?"

"You are right, Laine." He turned from the landscape to face me full-on. "As serial killers go, this *Ripper* has proven more artful than many."

A clock ticked from somewhere.

"A significant majority of narcissists live under the delusion of their own genius. No one could possibly be more cunning, and therein lies their greatest miscalculation."

Lilies filled the back of my throat.

"I just needed to clear up a few things before we took this to its obvious conclusion."

As if on cue, the door opened. It had not been locked. Big Mr. Durning stood in the opening, his eyes dagger sharp, no longer the grief-blind widower.

"Mr. Durning. Welcome back." Vagelle seemed to float.

Durning advanced into the room.

"You're here! Thank God!" I worked myself to a pitch as he closed the gap. "You have him. He just admitted it. He killed your wife. I would have been next. He has been preparing for the exact moment to take his revenge for my years of investigating. If you had been thirty seconds late—"

"No!" Vagelle boomed.

Durning glanced at him, confused, and just a moment was all I needed to grab up the cane, touch the trigger beneath its jaw to release the blade, and drive that through Durning's throat. He clutched the stick with both hands. I didn't watch the big man fall, but pivoted on the consultant with the small cylinder already drawing from my pocket.

I learned in a moment that N. Vagelle, *Inveigle,* was precisely as his name implied. Everything about him was deception, including his use of the cane. The cane I had recognized from the designs of a theater marquee—memorable, as I had wondered at the time why anyone would reveal the play's finale before the ticket purchase. And true to his contrived name, Vagelle moved as a berserker, and used the small pillow from the settee like a shield to block the moving cylinder back at me, splashing my face with the acid it contained.

Although the state of Louisiana keeps Capitol Punishment on their law books, I'm told there have been no executions for over ten years. I've been told by others, due to the heinousness of my crimes, the judge has promised to expedite things. It's probably because I am a woman and I've embarrassed law enforcement here for too long. Or it was the killing of a police lieutenant, despite the timely arrival of young Dr. Maiwand, who'd been waiting in the wings.

Autonomy. I insist I am the auteur of my own story. I accept this end. No, I welcome it. The mirror reminds me daily of the destruction of my beauty at the hands of the *consultant,* that duplicitous fraud who followed me after every Shrovetide.

The plotting by him and his friend, Durning, who also turned out to be an alias for Lieutenant Murphy. Their luck and contrivance in finding an available apartment one week after my pay raise from the Trib, in a building so near the newspaper that I had made famous. He had convinced the landlord to place the ad with a reduced monthly rate in The Delta Tribune. He knew I was ready for an upgrade and would see it before the general public. Of course, I couldn't resist.

Who would have thought that oafish police lieutenant could pull off such a performance? The grieving widower. They spiced the act with a fake newspaper printing the details of a copycat killing to coincide with their play.

They couldn't fool me for long, and they knew it. Vagelle couldn't risk letting me return to my apartment for even a night. I was sure to grab an actual evening edition and call the night editor to confirm. Still, I almost had him. I had the "expert psychologist" figured out, him and his deception.

I made one fatal error. Not anticipating the consultant's agility. His handicap pantomime was his most rewarding deception. I could have taken down both of them but for that mistake.

Ultimately, I am resigned to my story's finale. I had designed this life. I am made famous by my coverage of the killings, and I will reach greater fame after my death. I keep the small mirror in my cell to remind me of the face I no longer possess, and the thing that *he* had made of me—the monster.

The Delta Tribune – Sunday Edition

Published at the author's request

(Byline) Laine Baker

THREE

A SAVAGE LIAISON

Nicolaus

"I once knew a man, important in my life, who believed in ownership, who believed he could own a person, and who believed that his ownership justified his violence. Whether or not he believed that to be love, I would never know. He did not live long enough for me to find out. But that was not this life. That was more than nine thousand kilometers ago."

All cruelty springs from weakness—Seneca the Younger

Alya found the note I had dropped into her desk drawer during the night. We were in the habit of calling it "her desk" as, somewhere around her third week in my employ, she settled into that black L-shape beside the window and took control of my books, almost by force. She needed to prove her worth to me, and her skill with numbers, and she had maintained that foxhole for nearly two years. Truth be told, surrendering the mundane chore freed my mind for more urgent problems. Clients seldom sought me out without the spear of urgency at their backs.

"You did not listen to me last night." I turned for the kitchen.

"*Dobroye utro* to you too," she said.

I set a bowl of ice beside the yellow pad as she scribbled furiously to ignore me.

"You like, too much, the dead philosophers, I think," she said. "It is not philosophy to me. More like common sense Russian children learn." She watched the human traffic pass beneath her window while I wrapped a hand towel around a helping of ice. "You will not let this die, will you?"

"The swelling wouldn't be this bad if you had put ice on it when I suggested."

"Now you will hold rag in front of me until I take it, or until ice melts and I need to clean up water. You are stubborn old man." She accepted the towel and accepted the added pain of cold pressure to her cheek. "*Spasiba.*"

She kept her head down, as I returned to the kitchen. She looked up when I set a cup of Earl Grey beside her elbow. I took my own cup to the wingback chair by the fireplace. The fake fireplace. This was New Orleans, after all.

"How long you will sit watching me? I have your ice."

"How long *will you sit…*" I said.

"Please, no lessons today. I have headache. I have *a* headache!"

"You need to take the day off. Go home and rest."

"*Nyet*—No, thank you. I can work."

I returned to my room, allowing her space to settle. It didn't take long. She tapped on my door, brought in the morning paper and the Dostoevsky I'd given her to read. She seated the latter on my bookshelf.

"That was quick," I said.

"I have read too much *Russkiy* (Russian). Do you have Tylenol?" I considered that her way of apologizing.

"By the way, when you reach thirty-one, you won't think it's so old," I said.

She nearly smiled.

These were the early years, the years of bridge building, of finding our place here together. She had shown a unique insight when we first met, even at nineteen. I once heard her explain to a counselor, "Mr. Vagelle, he is always…*odinokiy*. Alone. His landlord calls him recluse, but he is not that, I think. He is used to a privacy, is all."

Another knock brought me from my room. Dr. Maiwand, the second-floor tenant, offered Alya a weak smile from the landing.

"How are you feeling?" he said. "Sorry, a superficial question now that I see the swelling. Is there something I can do for you?"

She flashed unspoken accusations at me.

"Mr. Hemmings mentioned it," Maiwand said.

"His peephole must have telescope if he could see this last night," she said. Hemmings was the first-floor landlord, hall monitor. "Questions can be *superficial* too?"

"You should allow me to look at that. There are fourteen bones in the face, some are delicate and—"

We all turned to the rasp of the street door buzzer. Hemmings's distant voice rose by octaves, competing with others. Heavy shoes drummed the stairs and Dr. Maiwand moved into the room with concern. Instinctively, I grabbed my walking stick from its niche beside the fireplace. I waited until the doorway framed NOPD Lt. Pedersen, backed by a man in uniform. Pedersen signaled for his friend in blue to stay, then crossed the threshold alone.

"Ms. Korikova."

"Pedersen." I moved between them. "You usually wait until someone invites you in."

"Alya, this is an official visit. I'm afraid I have a warrant for your arrest." Handcuffs appeared in his hand, and Alya held a breath.

"If you try to put cuffs on her, you'll need to cuff me too." The cane shifted in my grip as my good judgement wandered off. I had once prided myself on composure.

Dr. Maiwand inched closer to Alya. He knew of her *problem*, and my overprotective instincts. After an indecisive few seconds, with the anxious patrolman advancing behind him, Pedersen returned the cuffs to his pocket.

"Ms. Korikova is under a doctor's care," I said. "If you have a legitimate warrant, I'll call my lawyer and apprise him of the charges. Whatever her offense, if you lay a hand on her, he will be working up other papers within the hour."

"Don't threaten me, Vagelle." Pedersen's shoulders sagged. Regret, maybe. "It's my job. But I think we can trust you to follow us downstairs, Alya. You can ride in my backseat alone, no cuffs, I promise. Your *boss* can bring along any personal items you think you may need."

She touched my arm briefly as she passed.

Three days ago, I get call. A man says his name is Sasha. I do not know him, and I say this. He says he knows my people, though he sounds more American than Russian. He says he knows a friend I left behind. That they were friends in prison. I once knew a friend in prison, in Moscow, but I was just a girl. I do not tell him this.

I have important information, Sasha says. Your momma is very sick. She sends a message to you.

What is message? I say.

I cannot say here, he says. Could we meet for coffee? I am working— Sorry, it is loud in here.

I hear many voices.

I tend bar at Lafitte's, he says. Do you know where that is?

I am confused. He seems to know me. He knows my family, my friend from childhood. I do not want to meet him. But how did he find me? No one back home knows I am here. No one here knows my family name, except Mr. Vagelle. Mr. Vagelle would never tell anyone. But if Mama is very sick…?

I cannot meet tonight.

Tomorrow then? I work late, but I usually take my dinner break at ten. But we need to talk soon. I am worried for you.

Why for me? I do not understand.

I mean for your momma. I know it would hurt you should anything—
I need to get back to work. I will answer everything when we meet. Will you come?

I do not know what to do. I can not think fast enough. His voice is young, and I feel no danger from it, so I say okay.

All night and all the next day I worry on it. I came here at nineteen. I put ocean between me and everyone. And I wished everyone back home to believe me dead. This one phone call brings all the old fears. I will never know peace in life without answers, so I come to the corner twenty minutes early. I stand in gift shop across the street with view of Lafitte's door. This street is always crowded, night and day, and—I hate crowds, but this is a good window to stand behind and make up my mind. At ten o'clock I cross the street.

I walk through crowds of partiers out front, all pushing, all laughing too loud. Two drunk young men, covered in sport labels, bounce against the doorframe on their way out, and I walk wide around them.

He waits outside with his back to parking lot wall, smoking something. I think this is him because he smiles like he knows me, and he drops cigarette. He looks away. I think he is shy. He holds out a hand, but I do not shake hands. Frayed jacket cuffs and collar, his baseball cap stained, jeans dusty, and I suspect he does not belong working inside this place.

But his voice is gentle when he says my name.

I do not know you, I say, keeping my hand in my satchel.

Of course. I am Sasha. I promise I won't keep you long. It is too crowded to talk inside here. His eyes bounce person to person as they pass.

You have message for me?

From Misha, he says, and I fight emotions from my face. About your momma. It is written down. I did not want to lose it. I left it in my car. Come.

He knows the name to say, so I push my doubts away, and follow him through the car lot to the rear Employees Only parking. Fewer people close by. Darker here. I see the broken light on Lafitte's back wall, but he knows the right name, Misha.

He opens the driver door and leans in and comes up with folded white paper. But he stops. Two men whisper, crossing between cars. When I look back at Sasha, he is shaking his head at the men. I grab white paper from his hand and open it. I only remember blank paper and something hits me.

That is all. Then I wake up.

I taste vodka before my eyes open. Childhood memories sour my stomach. The smells of sick and urine and the old mattress beneath my head snap me awake, and the pain of movement makes me dizzy. Voices argue. I can not understand all. I see them like shadows in a room of buzzing, flickering blue light on garbage-stained walls.

He turns. Sasha, looking to see I am awake.

G'wan! Git out! He pushes the two men out to the hall. I will let him know tomorrow, he says. He slams door.

Someone curses far away. Others yell from closed doors.

Talking is difficult. Can I have water, pazhalusta *(please)?*

Sasha comes fast. I try pushing away, across mattress, but my wrists are tied. It surprises me and I fall. He jumps on me. He traps my hands and I scream. I cannot be touched. I try to fight. My head beats mattress and I go blind. I cannot be touched. Mr. Vagelle knows I cannot be touched. But Mr. Vagelle is not here. My throat burns from screaming until more vodka pours on my face and burns my eyes.

Sasha does not expect my crazy. I buck like horse. He falls. Before getting up, I kick him many times. Many times, until I fall back off mattress. I drag my knees across floor, and I finally find my feet. Then I am in the hallway and running, and not seeing, with my hands tied.

I shifted from the monitor to confront Captain Beaudry, who had consented to my supervising the interview. He would have refused, had he believed Alya's guilt, but he was also obliged to go through the motions on the warrant, so here she was. He turned away, knowing my thoughts.

On the monitor, my attorney, Lionel Whitcomb, slid papers across the table to the detectives. The documents had been examined prior to the interview. Sworn affidavits from her therapist regarding his "unspecified" diagnosis of Alya's clinical problem. *Her haphephobia. Fear of being touched.*

"That's enough," Whitcomb said. "I've agreed to Ms. Korikova's statements at her behest, but she is the victim in this. You now know more about the incident than we do. Her condition is non-violent, as the diagnosis clearly points out. She's been traumatized enough, so do not add to her trauma with an aggressive police interrogation."

Detective Calhoun worked her filament eyebrows, searching for an expression. Pedersen remailed silent throughout the questioning, no doubt under caution from superiors aware of his history with Alya and me.

"We've shown nothing but restraint regarding your client, sir." Calhoun leaned into her sincerity. "I've let her tell her story without interruption until—"

"Detective?" Pedersen said. "We should step outside to discuss."

Calhoun opened her folder and brought forward the eight-by-ten color photographs, slapping them onto the table like individual accusations. A close-up portrait of Sasha, eyes wide in death. A full-figure, shirtless, twisted, and lying in a dark pool beside the knife. The grotesque mattress under bright crime scene lights. A close-up on the knife. A close-up on his throat scratches. His bruised abdomen. His broken hand. Extreme close-up on strands of medium length blond hair and dried blood beneath his fingernails. Alya's hair, most likely.

With a smirk to the video camera, Calhoun pushed back from the table to a prolonged squawk of chair legs across tile. I refused to allow her control over my own internal thermostat. Scowling, Pedersen shuffled up the gory glossies and followed her from the room.

Lawyer Whitcomb kept a physical distance while whispering, but Alya's eyes had locked onto the now empty tabletop. Her trembling was noticeable. I imagined the previous night rushing back to her like a fresh assault.

"I am sorry for what you are going through." Rising from his chair, Whitcomb almost touched her hand, but withdrew it after a thought. "This will be over soon. I know, not soon enough for you, but I will get you out of here as quickly as I can."

"I did not do this," she said to the table.

"I know. Do you have enough water there? Let me go out and join the conversation in the hall. Try to stay calm. Say nothing more. They are not allowed to question you without my presence. Do you understand?"

I pushed back from the monitor and followed Beaudry to join his detectives in the corridor. Behind me, the on-screen door clicked, signaling my friend's isolation.

The click followed me into the conversation.

"I shouldn't have to explain the law here," I said. "Doctor-client privilege is not just *his choice*, it's his legal obligation. When she began working with me, I suggested that if she needed someone to talk to, he was an experienced listener. He does not confide in me about Ms. Korikova's visits."

"She couldn't talk to you, her close friend?" Calhoun said.

I regarded her as I would a peevish adolescent.

"All right." Captain Beaudry had the look of a man with a mouthful of something he'd rather not swallow. This was his arena and he typically resented my kicking the dirt here. "Your friend's long-standing psychological *issues* is hardly a defense. That she has been in and out of counseling does nothing for an innocence plea."

Whitcomb shook his head while waiting for my self-control to evaporate. His argument would be better served at another time.

"I see it as further evidence that she could have been pushed over the edge," Calhoun said. "Maybe she attacked and murdered the man she had been drinking with. Does she have a drinking problem?"

"Vagelle…?" Pedersen warned. He needn't have. Calhoun's limitations were obvious to me back before I left the department.

"She left her evidence all over that room," Calhoun said. "And I'll lay five-to-one, when the labs come back, that'll be her blood, sweat and hair in that apartment."

"Why did she go with him to his apartment?" Beaudry pocketed his hands and walked away.

"We have witness statements," Calhoun said. "She went into the alley with the vic of her own free will. We have too much evidence to set her free, and on top of it, she has no citizenship papers or records of any kind."

"No criminal record either," Pedersen said. "Unlike *Sasha Pasternak*, who did serious time up in David Wade Correctional."

"Pedersen!" a sergeant called from the end of the hall and the detective hurried to join him.

"From what I hear, your witness has disappeared," I said. "So unless you can find him, his statement will be filed at the bottom of a can by tomorrow night."

Pedersen returned with a printout.

"What?" Calhoun grabbed the page. "So. Lab results on the knife. I wish you'd have taken my bet. Her prints are on the murder weapon."

"A partial, it says. And smudged, along with others." Pedersen's voice dwindled in its authority.

"She's guilty as sin."

Once Pedersen had Alya and me alone in his office, he relaxed by degrees.

"I don't want you in a holding cell," he said. "The sofa is plenty comfortable and I'll have a blanket and pillow brought up. You'll need to keep the office blinds open, I'm afraid."

"I am okay with cell room. I am strong enough—"

"No arguments, please. I get that from too many around here as is. The officer at that desk out there will stay on, in case you need anything. She'll have to escort you for ladies' room visits."

Alya thanked him. I asked to speak with her alone, and Pedersen exited.

"After all your time working with me, you know what *circumstantial evidence* is. That's all they have, that and their weak assumptions. Whitcomb will have you out of here, like he said, and he'll shred this before it ever goes to court."

"You do not need to say comfort for me. I understand." She searched my eyes for assurance.

"Trust Pedersen to do what's right. He's your friend. I would stay here with you, but I can do more outside with him. The sooner I get on with this, the sooner we get you out."

"The sooner you can have me back at my black desk."

"At least you haven't lost your sense of humor."

She stared at her sneakers. The desk officer had confiscated her shoelaces before the interview.

"I need to ask you one thing," I said. "Do you know how your fingerprints got on the knife? You left it out of your statement, and we need a bit of damage control there. It is something I should know."

"I was stupid. I did not think." She touched her bruised cheek, as if she needed reminding.

"Trust me."

"I did not say. I was shamed—Did not wish you to hear."

I waited.

"He—He had pants off and knife in my face. I grab knife after kicking him. I did not cut him. I dropped knife and ran. I did not cut him."

"I will arrange for an immediate hospital exam—"

"*Nyet!* He did nothing else."

She suppressed the alarm bells, but she would be further hurt if I doubted her. I looked back at her from the door.

"Thank you for telling me."

"I trust you," she said.

"Small-time, no-account, *gangsta'*," Pedersen said. "San Antonio. A typical teen rap sheet. Any number of state-sponsored juvi sleep-overs, 'til he got nabbed at seventeen. Him and his buddies moving drug mules and Mexican girls through Lafayette in a stolen U-Haul. A bunch o' geniuses."

I trust you. Somehow, I needed to refocus.

"His real name was Steven Pasternak. Started calling himself Sasha in prison." Pedersen angled us to the curb in front of Lafitte's Tavern, flicking on the blue light to keep meter maids at bay. Guilt-ridden pedestrians scurried off.

"So, he had no real Russian connections." I watched a walking rag pile attempt a snatch-n-grab with the shoulder bag of a well-dressed tourist. "He lived here all his life?" *Ragpile* apparently failed to see the boyfriend tourist with the Popeye forearms who latched onto his coat collar and flung him into a parking meter.

"I'm getting to that." Pedersen killed the engine. "His mother was Russian. She runs away from her husband with her lover and seven-year-old Steven to the land of opportunity. Loverboy dumps mommy and she becomes a crack-whore. Maybe not in that order. Little Pasternak spends his youth trying to out-gangsta' the other punks he's robbing liquor stores with. Until, like I said, he gets an adult sentence up at David Wade."

"But he's not too stupid. He knows the language, and he needs the protection of a prison *tribe*, so he becomes Sasha from Moscow." My vision stopped at the windshield. I relived Alya's horror story in my head.

"In a nutshell. He got off easier than his pals. An eight-year sentence, because of his age and convincing the heart-o'-gold judge he was trafficked to the U.S. himself as a kid. Just another *victim of circumstance.* Now, he's been on the outside less than a month."

"Okay, so eight years inside and the first thing he does with his freedom is beeline to the Big Easy, phone a Russian woman he'd never met, and tell her stories about her family? Kind of smells like something, don't you think?"

"I remember when you met Alya. I believe you when you say she has no connection to her past life."

We spent minimal time inside Lafitte's. Pedersen asked a number of questions, showing Sasha's photo to the employees who all agreed he'd never worked there. A young woman with green hair met us at the door.

"Could be he was wearing a baseball cap?" she said. "But he walked in sometime after nine like he was looking for someone, then he walked out. Could be."

A manager led us into an office to look at security camera footage. She shrugged, knowing what we would find. Above a 7:55p time stamp, a shadow-faced someone in a hoodie and low-brim baseball cap stepped beneath the camera and killed it with a length of rebar. Pedersen took a copy of the recording with him when we left.

Outside, Ragpile remained on post, hanging off the parking meter and sharing profanities with random pedestrians.

The crime scene.

As we walked in, investigators in white jumpsuits, facemasks, and blue rubber gloves, continued day-two of the evidence sweep, with plenty left to examine. As Alya had described, the first impressions came from a fetid cocktail of mold, old sweat, spilled alcohol, cigarettes, drugs, urine and blood. An attack on the senses for anyone not prepared for it. Pedersen introduced me to the sergeant in the hall, who said he knew my name.

"No one in the building admits to seeing anyone last night, as might be expected," Sgt. Russo said.

"Of course. Do we know what spilled there?" I gestured to the mattress mess.

"Besides the art project of bodily fluids begun sometime during the Civil War? We've got a vodka bottle dropped between the mattress and the wall, still fresh, right next to a family's collection of crumpled beer cans—not so fresh. Plenty of spills here. It's for the lab to determine a date on each. New cigarette burns in the sheet—that's at the lab with the bottle, of course. Vodka fresh, blood stains fresh…"

"The labs already came back with tests on the knife," Pedersen said.

"Six-inch serrated blade matching the wounds on the vic. I read the report. His jeans were found in the corner. They're at the lab as well. By the way, he had a sheath on his belt, most likely corresponding to that knife."

"Something your detective-friend conveniently left out of her analysis," I said.

"I'll be sure to emphasize it in my report and call her by name," Pedersen said. "She's on a short tether with me anyway."

Russo sniggered. Occasionally, I've run into a cop who seemed to be having too much fun with a murder scene. Something in his eyes, or the spread of his teeth. He called to a tech, "Show 'em what you got with the blood." Two steps into the tight room, we checked our footing around the coagulating spill.

"It takes some deciphering," the tech said. "This here is from your vic rolling with his attacker…or attackers. I'm guessing two of them. Those are his palm prints. You can trace the spray there and there along the floor—meaning he was down on his side at some point before his heart stopped. Up the side of the mattress, and the arc up the wall, there, there and there. Mostly, those lines are not arterial spray, but cast-offs from the swinging blade."

"Any signs of sex on the mattress?" Pedersen avoided my look.

"Between man and woman? Recently?"

"Yeah, like last night."

"Not in the last seventy-two hours, but we gotta wait for the lab."

"Your best guess," I said. "Could all this be the attack of one enraged woman? Off the record."

"We got what's probably a woman's fingerprints on the bare floor, several places." The tech stepped carefully between the red and the bed. He pointed to white powder on the tiles. "More prints on the wall, but none of 'em bloody. The actual killing began some five-feet from the bed, not on it. By the spatter, I'd say the vic was already down before the first knife strike, and there's too much blood between the body and the door. A track star couldn't have leaped it getting out of here."

"All the footprints in this, and down the hall, they come from men's boots?"

"We did find a pair of women's sneakers in the corner with his blue jeans. Naturally, if she put on men's boots before running out…"

"Unlikely," I said.

"So, can anyone tell me how her prints got on the damned knife?" Pedersen said.

"The vic's knife." I threw a quick, final survey across the room. "Alya said she got it away from him in the struggle. I'd say she dropped it in the hall as she ran, and one of the killers picked it up on their way in."

"We only got one print from her on the handle," Russo said, "partially smudged. To me, that means someone used the knife after she'd held it."

"That makes as much sense as anything." Pedersen headed for the door and called, "Thanks, guys."

"Nice meeting you, Mr. Vagelle." Russo said to my back.

"Let's finish our rounds," Pedersen said. "But as far as I'm concerned, any case against Alya is already blown by CSI."

What we thought would be a cursory stop at Alya's fourth-floor apartment in the French Quarter slowed us down. The door opened to my touch, but Pedersen held me back, drew his weapon, then led the way.

"CID's been through, but they would have locked up when they finished." Pedersen moved room by room to verify we were alone. "This mess is from them." Open dresser drawers, overturned hamper in the bathroom, laptop missing, handgun missing (what she called her *bedside security*). "They bagged her mini-Mossberg out of caution. It's in their report. Is that registered to you?"

"You need to inform your department, she also carried a Smith and Wesson snubnose in her handbag. With her wallet taken, I assume whoever killed Sasha left with it."

"Which says, if she went into that alley looking to murder him—Does she live with some constant threat? Should I know about it?"

"Let's put it down as related to her other fear." I opened the medicine cabinet. "Your CID wouldn't have confiscated her meds. Early on, the doc had prescribed proxetine for her depressions. It had been here untouched for a year and a half."

"I doubt the average thief would know anti-depressant from XTC. They grab pill bottles out of habit." He holstered his weapon and drew his phone. "Russo. We need your crew back over to the Korikova apartment. Someone's been through here after you. I doubt you'll find much, but we need everything re-printed. We'll wait 'til you get a man here for the door—No. We didn't touch the lock."

From there, we made a stop at my building. Landlord Hemmings yanked open his portal with his patented look of annoyance.

"What happened now! You don't bring Officer Pedersen to my door unless it's something bad. Is Ms. Alya—?"

"She'll be okay," I said. "But she's still in custody. The lieutenant just needs to ask a few questions, part of his official investigation. Can we come in?"

"No. Not unless he has a warrant. I know once you let a cop in, they can snoop and find some reason to—"

"Calm yourself, Mr. Hemmings." Pedersen opened a pocket notepad. "We don't need to come inside. About last night, you said you saw Alya, Ms. Korikova, enter the building. What time was that?"

"Exactly three-forty, a.m. I always turn on the news at three-thirty because my other programs are over by three, and I record the day's events so I can skip the commercials."

"So you were awake and heard her come in."

"I have a buzzer for when somebody keys the front door lock. They don't need to ring if they have a key, but this lets me know that one of my people is coming in."

"You have a buzzer wired to the keyhole. Okay. And you saw her enter."

"No. I saw her on the stairs and it takes some seconds to get to my door. I called to her on the fourth stair."

"The fourth stair?"

"Because she never comes in this time of the morning. So, I see her on the fourth stair and she doesn't look well. Her clothes—well, she always dresses tidy."

"Okay. Tidy."

"But her blouse is torn, and her hair disheveled."

"Disheveled?"

"I wish you'd quit interrupting me."

"Sorry. Go ahead."

"So, when she turns, I see marks on her face and maybe the beginnings of a black eye. Like she's been in a fight. Ms. Alya doesn't get into fights. She is always a well-composed lady. But I see it, and I ask if she's okay. She says she is fine. She continues upstairs. And I say, You do not look fine. And I say, Mr. Vagelle is not in. He went out earlier, eight-forty-seven, and has not returned. And she says that's okay. She says she has forgotten something upstairs that she needs to pick up. And I say, At three-forty in the morning? And she doesn't say anything, but runs up the stairs."

"Okay. Thank you." Pedersen nearly closed the pad.

"Dr. Maiwand, on the second floor, comes out and watches her. He looks at me, and I say, She says she is okay. Then I go back inside. Mr. Vagelle comes in at four-ten and I hear Ms. Alya leave the building five minutes later. She's carrying a laptop. I see it from my window. I believe that is everything."

"Do you ever sleep?" Pedersen said.

"One more question," I said. "What was the state of her shoes?"

"Her shoes? Oh, yes, I forgot. I must be tired. I thought it odd. With all her dishevelment, she was barefoot. No shoes."

"You could see her feet."

"I just said that, didn't I?"

"And the stairway lights were on, and you could see the blood on her feet."

"No, I did not say that! Yes, the lights were on. How else could I have seen her bruised eye? But I never said anything about blood. Her feet were dirty, of course. One does not run around New Orleans streets barefoot without picking up some unsavory something or other."

"But not blood. And none on her clothes."

"I would have noticed that. I would have called the cops."

As we left the building, Pedersen appeared to have remembered the butt-end of a joke. "He's like that every time I come in. Maybe he's the one needs medicating."

"We'll stop at the Medical Examiner to wrap up, though we can figure most of this on our own." Pedersen sped through and around traffic. "I need a serious discussion with Calhoun and our captain, and you can check in on your partner. I guess you can figure what I'm going to ask you next."

"Yes."

"You want to share where you were between eight-forty-seven and four-ten a-m?"

"Frank. If I had been following Ms. Korikova, they'd never have left Lafitte's parking lot."

We found M.E. Gracey in his office, and he led us into the examination room and his work-in-progress, Steven Pasternak. The body lay fully exposed on the dull metal table, flanked by light stands, surrounded by walls the color of dirty snow, and a ceiling blocked with more dispassionate lights.

"I'm still waiting on paperwork, and the go-ahead to begin the cutting," he said. "It's been a busy weekend. Plus, I'm waiting to get the photos back from the lab. Our boy is a complicated canvas."

Prison had made Sasha into a dizzying work of art. Symbolic illustrations, more "storytelling" than most Central and South American cultures with simpler displays of bravado and allegiance.

"Nine deep stab wounds, chest and abdomen," Gracey said. "Not counting the first three defensive wounds to the hands and forearms. Bruising, obvious. Large hands broke his windpipe. Mostly prison-made tattoos here. Russian, of course. Some much older, gang-style, by a young gang—just an assumption considering his age and when he went inside."

"Would it be possible to turn him over?" I circled the body. "Just for a moment. Frank, you say he'd been in San Antonio since childhood. Do you have anything yet on the mother?"

"Little," Pedersen said, as Gracey turned the corpse with his years of expertise. "Not much that can be easily verified."

"It'll take a real expert, but from what I read in these hieroglyphs, he lied a lot on his *mast*—his suit, as they call it. Of course, Russian tattoos are not always literal. But here." I drew a line without touching the corpse. "The first obvious lie. A sun with ten rays, each ray indicates one year in prison."

"Why would he lie?" Gracey said.

"To convince others he wasn't a rookie behind bars," Pedersen said.

"He has a lot of the common Russian markings," I said. "The thieves' cross on his chest with the two church cupolas, indicating two convictions."

"More b-s." Pedersen scratched it into a notepad.

"A spider facing up means he's still an active criminal, something we can believe. Eyes on his stomach says he was gay, or at least the other cons thought so. And here, on his right shoulder—this is why I asked about his mother."

Gracey rounded the table for a closer look. "Yes?"

"The hooded executioner means he'd murdered a relative. Unless he killed his father by the age of seven, before he left Russia, he's taking credit for murdering his mother." I lifted his hand to catch more light. "The tattooed finger ring, a dot inside the circle, is *krugliy sirota*, Roundstone. This tells the world he's an orphan."

"Don't tell me you learned all this from Alya."

"No." I indicated the M.E. could return the body face-up. "But what's even more telling about his character are the tattoos that we can believe. These dots beneath the eyes, and here next to his mouth, and the letters CYKA, *bitch, slut,* the playing cards on his buttocks—hearts and diamonds. These are all forced tattoos. Our Sasha was everybody's *girlfriend* in the cellblock. He'd made a lot of enemies."

"Now you're just showing off." Pedersen continued writing.

"It might be helpful, when you run tests after your autopsy, to determine the age of each tattoo."

"All of them?" Gracey said. "I did say we've had a busy weekend, right?"

"Something else those forced tattoos tell us. They are symbols of demotion. He had status at some point. Then he became a thing worthy of ridicule. Once demoted, his protection disappeared."

"Hell." Pedersen clapped his notepad shut and stuffed it behind a lapel. "You almost make me feel sorry for this douchebag."

"…he stayed alive up in David Wade thanks to him knowing the friggin' language and making the right friggin' friends in there." Pedersen rewound the day in his special vernacular.

Near sundown, we drove into the police parking garage and I let him figure it out for himself.

"The iron bars open and, lickety-split, he heads here for your assistant. Which tells me if, as you said, you never heard of him before all this, when he got out, he was on a mission for someone. Alya said in her statement, he knew things about her family. Probably heard it in the joint, news from inside mother Russia, so—What? Tell me. Her family's connected to Russian gangsters? The friggin' Mafia?"

I disguised a growing anger. Not with him.

He told me nothing I didn't know but, until now, I'd held my uglier side in check. The R-complex, behaviorists called it. So far, I had permitted the details of the investigation to distract my reptilian brain. The details were losing.

These past few years, I had a front-row seat to her struggles. Alya worked diligently to make this new life for herself, this new person. To learn, to grow out of the weaknesses of a traumatic childhood. But now she had become someone's target. She had been abused again. Mentally, as well as physically. And in response to her pain, I felt the chains loosening on my inner animal, readying to obliterate all good judgement. I had jettisoned my psychology studies behind blinding black fantasies.

I opened the car door, reminding myself that action without forethought kills the wrong people.

"…a part of her past you keep to yourself," Pedersen was saying. "Seems like something I should know, don't you think? For Alya? That dead punk back there is not alone in this. Say something to help me out here, pal."

"Get her released tonight."

"I will be safe in my home. Sasha is dead." She continued to argue past the front door and up the stairs to my apartment.

"Pedersen agrees, and I believe you know, Sasha was not on his own. You will stay here until we straighten things out."

"You are employer, not master. This is not part of my job. You are not being fair with me. How is your apartment safer? How long until I get mini-Mosberg back?"

"Make a list. Toiletries, clothes, food, and I will order anything you need delivered tonight." I had gotten rid of my sofa bed two years ago, so I moved her into my bedroom. With her eyebrow raised, and before she could respond, I stripped the mattress and threw a bundle of new sheets across the footboard. "You can busy yourself making the bed and settling in. I'll take to the living room whenever I'm home. Can I trust you to remain in this building while I'm out?"

"I have no say? I am prisoner after all." Arms crossed, she trailed me into the living room.

"You are being obstinate now, but I know you understand. You are under my protection. I'll explain more when I learn more, but Captain Beaudry released you under my supervision."

"*Supervision.* This means you watch me. So you will take me with you when you go out, yes? You take fancy walking stick that you do not lean on. You never explain to me about stick. Why do you not carry gun?"

As I left the building, walking stick in hand, she watched from the third-floor window. She would complain to the glass, but she had known me long enough to figure me out. Her official statement had said others were in the room with Sasha, and someone else had hit her from behind in Lafitte's parking lot. As much as she refused to show it, she was more scared than angry. At least that's what I hoped.

Across the street, a navy blue Chevy Suburban hugged the curb with its engine off and a man slumped behind the wheel. Streetlights glittered with moisture on his windshield and I wondered how long he'd been there. When he noticed my approach, he swallowed a cheek-full of hogie, then checked the other side of his car. He checked the mirrors. He settled the sandwich to his lap and rolled down the window and aimed his open wallet like a weapon.

"Waiting on someone, Sgt. Deacon?" I read the I.D. and badge number. I didn't recognize him.

"Captain Beaudry sent me over to keep an eye on things. He said you'd understand."

"Could be a long wait for you." I leaned on the cane like I needed it.

"It's the job, Mr. Vagelle."

Before I passed his back bumper, I triggered the blade from my walking stick and nonchalantly sliced the air valve on the Suburban's rear tire. I noted the license number then returned to my building. I knocked on Hemmings's door.

"I do not like this. You know I do not like these involvements," he said, the dishtowel scrubbing furiously at the soup stain on his T-shirt.

"Do you still own that shotgun?" I said.

"Unacceptable. This will never come out now."

"Keep it close to you for a few days. No one gets into your building today that you don't know. If they have a badge, tell them to come back with a warrant. If they come equipped with a warrant, call Pedersen to verify."

"I cannot accept—"

"I pay a good price for my little inconveniences, Mr. Hemmings."

His face contorted as he considered more bluster versus my generous contributions to his retirement fund. I headed toward the boiler room and the service door to the alley. I phoned Pedersen on the way.

"Do you have a man on my building?"

"Not yet."

"He says he's from Beaudry. Check on it, please. Got a pen?" I gave him the name, badge, and plate numbers.

"I'll have someone there shortly." He whispered a curse.

"He'll stay parked for awhile."

I next called a close friend at a boutique P.I. firm.

"Patty, do we know anyone up in David Wade Correctional? How's your relationship with your brother these days?"

"I still send him cigarettes to keep other inmates off his back. But he's in Dixon, you know."

"Ask him if he has any friendlies with the Russian side of the yard. Tell him you're calling for a client who will keep him in cigarettes for a little information."

"If I say that client is you, he won't respond well. I'll lie and see what I can get. But I won't get a human on the phone there 'til after nine in the a-m. How's your friend doing?"

"She's fine for now." I thanked her then called one more ally.

"It's me. I need a favor. Do you have any friends who can fly me up to Shreveport Regional tonight? I'm in a hurry."

"Business in Shreveport? Or are you renting a car there and driving to Homer? South Arkansas Regional is a closer drive. How fast can you get to me?"

I checked the time. "If you're drinking, I'm flying your plane."

We touched down without mishap, and he had a rental car waiting. A little less than an hour's drive from the small airport, I entered the town of Homer and found the rendezvous, this town's only Denny's.

At the counter, a thin, middle-aged man in worn overalls and work jacket looked up from his coffee. He tugged on the brim of his ball cap as he blundered wide of me and out the door. At the next stool, sat the only other customer. White shirt, sans tie, sans jacket, spectacles hung on a neck-leash, Warden Moran of nearby David Wade Correctional. I suggested the last booth past the windows. The only morning waitress brought me a cup and filled Moran's with a wink.

"Thanks for the meeting on short notice," I said. "I know it's inconvenient."

"To say the least. But a little birdie says I owe you. A friend of a friend. She knows a lot of people."

"Ms. Gunston."

"And she says you're responsible for sending more than a few of our residents here." He affected the manner of a shrewd interrogator, and slid a business card toward my cup. Unnecessary, as Patty had texted his photo while I was still in the air. He laid his cell phone on the table, red light blinking.

"I have no problem with recording." I showed my ID.

"With your background, I figure you're legit. Ms. Gunston says you're legit. But early morning clandestine meetings give me the hives."

"Understood. So, you know why I should probably avoid being seen interviewing your *residents*."

"She did mention a former inmate, Steven Pasternak. Now deceased?"

"Less than seventy-two hours ago."

"Hence your emergency visit." He measured his response. "I know you understand the political high-wire act. It's always big news whenever a reporter can play the harp for the *penitent* prison inmates."

"If you've talked to Patty, you know whatever you say to me, stays with me."

"Like Las Vegas. If you're looking for names he may have gotten close to in there, it's a long list. And I don't know how much I can say. Maybe if you give me a few clues as to what we're talking about?"

"Sure." Beyond the windows an easy mist descended, casting haloes around parking lot lights. Traffic this time of night was nil. "What I know is, the doors had barely shut behind Pasternak when he beelined for New Orleans, and a particular Russian woman who he never knew on the outside. But he knew her name."

"She may have known another of our inmates?"

"She did not. But he made an appointment to meet with her and gave her a good enough line that she bought it. It almost got her killed. I'm not broken up with the outcome, but I assume she is still in danger."

"And you have little to go on, other than the Russian connection."

"And wondering who was on Pasternak's tail from here to there. He had a spectacular death meant for the headlines. Or to send a message to somebody."

"If you're coming to me, you're probably grasping at straws. And I sense this is personal for you."

"I need to find out what drove Sasha to target her." The mist turned to a hard rain assaulting the windows.

"The guy you saw leaving as you came in, he's another former *resident*. I asked to see him after hearing Pasternak's name. He probably knew him as well as anyone."

"Boyfriend?"

"Or something like it. Pasternak was young when he came to us. Seventeen. So you can imagine he quickly became a target for a number of our old dogs."

"And he knew where to go for protection."

"One in particular, an old lifer named Sergey Breza. Breza was a big dog on the outside, and bigger in the yard. Physically, and with his people. He had been moved here from Angola some years ago because of his moneyed connections. Sasha spoke his language and became a concubine in exchange for Breza's *friendship*. After that, everyone else left the kid alone."

"You said Breza *was* the big dog?"

"Sasha lost his protected status the minute Breza hit the ground. That was three years ago. Whoever had the contract on the old boss worked his magic in here. After that, anyone who may have resented Sasha for his protected status, or his attachment to Breza, well, they took it out on him. They named him everyone's *Prison Pocket*. Pocket is inmate slang for…" He spotted the waitress returning with her coffeepot, shook his head and waved her back.

"I know," I said. "It would be a chore, but what do you think about rounding up the names of Russian inmates released after your kingpin's killing three years ago? Another long-shot. He may still be inside but, if not, it'll give a certain sympathetic police detective something to do."

"You flew all this way to get what I could have told you over the phone?"

"I like to know the man I'm talking to. More importantly, in this case, I hoped to impress upon you the urgency of my inquiry. Whatever this is, it needs to end now."

"Your concerns sound legit enough. If Sasha had a grudge as strong as you're suggesting, I might assume it was connected to the killing of his prison daddy."

"And no one inside would ever give up the inmate on the other end of Breza's shiv."

"Not for a golden limousine ticket to Kingdom Come."

A long drive is always longer in a dark early morning rain, and I was indeed questioning my travel time versus a quick phone call. Driving back to the small Arkansas airport, my pilot growing heavy-lidded, I phoned and got Pedersen out of bed. He didn't complain much.

"Because you need to know," I said, "so our puzzle is now Sergey Breza, Sasha, prison gangs, and Ms. Korikova. Not a small field."

"And Sasha's killers. Who could be linked to any or all of the first three." He drank something, and I heard the rustle of clothes.

"Do you have anyone you can put on gathering background on Breza?"

"Do we assume Breza's killer is still locked up? If not, he may have followed Sasha in his quest. If he was just taking up a contract, it's mafia related. Mafia related gives Sasha motive."

"Let's not assume too much," I said.

"You woke me, remember? Let's not assume all us cops are idiots, eh, Vagelle?"

I let that go.

"The question then becomes," he chewed on his frustration for a moment, "if Breza knew of Alya's history, and who else could've given Sasha her contact info—? I'm thinking somebody in the old country would be hurt if she met with tragedy."

Pedersen called back as I stepped onto the tarmac at New Orleans Lakefront Airport. He hesitated too long before speaking. "Have you spoken to Alya since last night?"

"What!" It caught me by surprise. "No, I haven't. What happened?"

"And you have been out of the city until right now?"

"Say it, Frank!"

"Three hours ago. We found Detective Calhoun's body off Algiers Point."

I waited for the other shoe.

"And your assistant is on early morning walkabout. Are you sure she had her snubnose in her purse when Sasha grabbed her?"

"You're making me troll for answers, Lieutenant. Give me the rest, so I can maybe find you a few answers."

"Okay. River Patrol found Calhoun at the Dry Docks with two .38 holes. One round still lodged in her spine, the second thru-and-thru, close range, to the back of her skull. Your Alya, Calhoun's suspect numero uno, cannot be found and Captain Beaudry is hollering for your arrest, and probably mine, for aiding and abetting. Is that enough for ya?"

"I won't ask how he got an arrest warrant without evidence she committed a crime. But I will ask what happened with the man you had on my building? The one who was supposed to protect my friend, the friend who got beat up by the convict? You know, the innocent one?"

"You know how this works. Warrants are easy given the right motivation, and Beaudry loves you even less at this hour than eight hours ago. He keeps bringing up that whole *under your supervision* thing, and following with a maniacal laugh."

Keeping emotion out of my voice held back my response.

"You know I need Alya's real last name."

"No, you don't."

"We still got at least two killers out there looking for her."

"At least two."

"Damn-it! You want obstruction charges on top of everything, or can I—"

"I said no." I began jogging to my car, ignoring the light rain. It had been too long since I had gotten any sleep, but adrenalin had me wide awake now.

"Have you landed? Boss man has every available unit hunting Louis Armstrong International for you. Are you gonna come in for questioning, or should we expect a big shoot-out if they try to take you in?"

Wrong airport, I didn't say, hoping the troops stayed where they were for a bit. I spun my tires, then slowed to a legal speed and pulled away from the parking lot. Twenty minutes later, I turned into the Long-Term Parking structure across from a Greyhound sign.

I'd realized long ago, how little private life Alya had away from my wing. I had taken her in at nineteen, given her work, and she had become much more than what I made for her. She still had difficulty getting close to others—her haphephobia—which I hoped my *shrink buddy* might help alleviate some, but she was not there yet. Any young man who tried to get close triggered her flight response. So I knew the places where she might turn were extremely limited if she hoped to disappear. Unfortunately, so did Pedersen.

After Calhoun's killing, police would have someone covering my apartment and hers. She would hide her car too, though she had an aversion to tight crowded places like buses and trains.

I walked through the garage and paused as a well-dressed woman, thirty-ish, grabbed her suitcase from the trunk of a steel-gray Tahoe and hurried toward the exit. She smiled as I passed.

"Have a nice trip," I said.

"Oh, I will," she said. "Meeting my fiancé in Dallas, and we'll be skiing in Vermont by Friday."

"Lucky man."

She blew me a kiss. I stole her car.

"I'll never get any sleep!" Hemmings moaned into the receiver. "What is it now?"

"Shut up and listen. Ms. Korikova has not been in since what time yesterday?"

"Um—She went out at ten fifty-five."

"Was she alone?"

"With a woman, young, brown skin, brown business suit. I don't let her in, like you said. I let no one in yesterday. She asks for Alya to come down. Alya does not like the woman, but talks to her on the front step. I can't hear their conversation, but she runs back up to your apartment, then back down with her shoulder bag and a light windbreaker. She has not been back— Is she okay?"

"No. You still have my alternate number? Anything important, use that. This phone will be off." I hung up.

I braked before leaving the garage, as I saw the bus with the Dallas destination display idling outside the terminal. The driver wheeled a heavily loaded flat dolly from the station to the open luggage compartment.

I speed-dialed Gunston Investigations.

"I can get you a car," Patty said before hello. "You don't want to be driving yours around this burg. You're on all frequencies."

"Thanks, but no. I don't want you anywhere close to this. I'm also ditching my phone. I'll give you another number, and if you hear anything about Alya…"

I left the Tahoe idling, and jogged between parked cars to come up behind the Dallas bus. With the bride-to-be nowhere in sight, and the driver turning to check another's tickets, I bid goodbye to my phone, tossing it into the open luggage bay. I grabbed a disposable at the first drug store.

As a matter of covering bases, I drove past Alya's apartment then my own. The stakeouts were all fairly obvious. With no desire to add my presence to the crime scene across the river, I put in another call to Patty. She easily located Officer Calhoun's home address for me.

"For later, I'm assuming," she said. "You know she's a fresh *problem* and her place will be a bug-hill all day."

"Do we have any intel on this Sasha, or Steven Pasternak? Any aliases? I'm mostly looking for known criminal buddies still working hereabouts."

"Our law enforcement pals are engaged there. Someone will leak it to me when they get anything substantive."

"Thanks for that call up north…" Before hanging up, I shared what I had learned from my visit with Warden Moran.

Morning businesses were opening their doors, and I checked in with Alya's *shrink*, not expecting, but hoping, she had turned to him after her ordeal. I caught him before his first appointment of the day and sat for a face-to-face. He couldn't mask his obvious distress as I described Alya's recent horrors. I left his office knowing nothing more than I had arrived with.

"Please ask her to call me when you find her," he said. "Don't put it off."

Likewise, I wasted much of the morning in Alya's favorite Russian grocery store, bakery, coffee shop, and watched the street out front. I absorbed enough caffeine to keep me awake through a bad courtroom summation. I checked in with lawyer Whitcomb who said he would call his friends in NOPD and hospital emergency rooms, and anywhere else he could think of. Then I wasted the rest of the day in my stolen Tahoe.

Rather than driving endless loops round the Big Easy, I parked at the end of her block, watching her building, watching the *undercover* watchdog across the street, and trying to think like a Russian woman. I couldn't even think of a sarcastic metaphor.

Why leave my apartment late at night? Hemmings's description sounded like Lt. Calhoun, but Alya would not consider her an ally. Maybe because the woman was a cop. Maybe she had invented a decent enough lie. But why? And did Alya witness Calhoun's killing?

Cruising Lakeshore Parkway, the eastern sky already darkening Pontchartrain's waters, I turned off at the West End Marina. A place we had in common. The place we had first met. I cruised as slowly as traffic would allow.

Would she simply run to disappear, get as far from the city as possible, just as she had fled Moscow as a teenager? Perhaps she saw that Russian gangster as a simple extension of her lifelong flight. Sometimes I think I know her mind, but is it merely my ego that refuses to believe she would leave without saying goodbye?

I considered spending the night at the *safe house,* but my brain needed immediate shutdown and it decided without me. The Tahoe was comfortable enough to pass out in.

Three a.m. found me parked four doors down from Calhoun's building, drinking gas station coffee, eating granola. Her second-floor apartment was dark. Investigators had finished their work there.

Dumping half the coffee in the gutter, I pocketed a penlight, and waited for headlights to pass before mounting her front steps. I picked the lock on the street door and took my time up the stairs. The yellow police tape on the door of apartment 2E had been cut, and I listened for movement inside before picking that lock as well.

The apartment, typically overturned by investigators, let in enough street light to keep me from banging my shins on the furniture. It also silhouetted the person on the couch.

"I hear they just caught up with your phone outside Natchitoches." *Pedersen's voice.* "How'd you know she had no roommate?"

"I rolled the dice." Relaxing a bit, I checked the corners for a SWAT team. "So, you figured I'd come prowling here. Well done."

"And too many of you Peter Gunn types still believe *all us cops be ign'rant.*"

"Not really. I also gambled that if you were here, you didn't really want to shoot me for breaking and entering."

"Now, that is a gamble." His shadow lifted. He flicked on the table lamp. "So, what now? What were you hoping to find out about Calhoun?"

"I wondered what story she gave Alya to get her to leave my apartment. And that got me thinking about her fixation on a woman who was so obviously the victim in this. Also, who else might be involved. There is no way to convince me my friend murdered a police officer in cold blood."

"I think it's a pretty big stretch to assume a woman in my department would have connections to your Russian pals."

"Just looking for answers, Frank. You come up with a better thought, I'll listen."

"Maybe she hated pretty blondes." He peeked between the window blinds. "Did you buy a new car?"

"It's a loaner."

I squatted and poked the tip of my penlight through a pile of scraps from an overturned wastebasket. He pulled cushions off the furniture then kicked through fallen books that had been yanked, just as discourteously, from their shelves. I ended my trail of paper debris in the second bedroom, Calhoun's office. Again, anything not taken by investigators had been scattered. Three desk drawers had been dumped from a spindly-legged, aluminum desk built more for utility than style. All that remained of her computer was the cables and keyboard, which I lifted looking for Post-Its and secret codes. *Speaking of cliches,* I thought. I upended the desk lamp for the same reason, *no stone unturned, cracked open, ground to dust.*

"You trip over something important in there, you'll let me know, right?" he called from the kitchen. "You will let me know, right?"

Lifting the lamp had shifted the light enough for me to notice scuff marks on the hardwood floor. The desk legs had dragged only a few inches, but it made me wonder why the desk had to be moved at all. Holding the lamp as a spotlight, I kneeled closer. Beneath the desk, I checked the drawer trays. I checked the wall behind the desk. Another small ding where the back corner of the desk had dented the plaster, almost imperceptible, but enough to raise another question mark. Scooting the desk away from the wall, a rear leg wobbled. My thought bubble expanded.

"Yes?" Pedersen leaned a shoulder to the doorframe with an open book in his hand.

"Give me a hand." I set the lamp on the floor, took hold of one side and waited for him to take the other. We turned the desk upside down and I unscrewed the wobbly leg. I removed the footpad and inset screw. A small key fell into my hand. A Post Office box key.

"You're almost too lucky," he said.

"Persistent," I said. "Most people have secrets worth hiding. Cops are just better at it."

He held out a hand. I pushed mine into my pocket.

"If you want to leave this apartment without cuffs, you'll hand it over," he said.

"Only if I have your word you'll call me with the details when you find them."

"And will you give me your word you won't go on a killing spree?"

"Alya is innocent."

"I know."

"Then you know there is not much I wouldn't do for her."

We remained locked, testing each other's sincerity, until I dropped the key into his palm. Aside from a few details, I already knew most of what he would find in Calhoun's mailbox.

Alya would not be found until she was ready. Pedersen would find the evidence, Alya's innocence, and Calhoun's criminal involvement. That left me cruising for something I didn't yet know I needed. Proofs. As the city came to life, I strolled

Lafitte's empty parking lot. The security camera had not been replaced.

The man I had named *Ragpile* watched me from the corner of a dumpster. Before I could confront him, my phone rang.

"Got something for you," Patty Gunston said. "A call this morning from my brother up in Dixon asking more about the reward for talking with his Red yardbird pals."

"I'm guessing he survived asking them questions." My eyes were on Ragpile, wondering about his interest in me. "You wouldn't have called unless he had actual information."

"Naturally. Everyone had heard of the hit on Big Breza at the time. Rumors of it being sanctioned from Moscow. It would have taken a madman to go after a boss on anything less. Then more rumors that someone's family *back home* received a big payout."

"Prisonyard boredom has been the death of many," I said. Ragpile looked to be retracing my steps through the parking lot while pretending to be high. A less than convincing act.

"They didn't mind chatting about more money in the wind either. Breza's personal toyboy, your Sasha, got mentioned. Being on the receiving end of abuse after Breza's fall, as you suggested, in his delirium he started shooting his mouth off about getting even. This pisses off the man in Moscow and more money gets offered up for Sasha's head."

"But our Sasha-clown gets short-time lucky and is released before the contest begins. All this would become more than a rumor, spreading like a gasoline fire through the Russian populations of every prison in the state."

"Bingo."

"But most of this I already knew, or assumed. Tell me what makes this worth paying your brother more than a few cartons of cigarettes."

"Minutes before I called you, I got another call from David Wade. Moran's former trustee pal, the guy who had been close to Sasha, has spread a little more joy. He'd gotten those rants first hand. Over the years, Breza had cozy, late-night discussions with your boy about the boss he knew put the contract on him. And Breza had so many inner-prison connections, he knew how to strike back at Moscow should anyone manage to collect on the contract."

"He had Alya's family name." I left Ragpile to his parking lot search, for now, and re-boarded the Tahoe.

"Seems so. Though how anyone from there found her here is beyond me."

"Only one person can tell us that."

The lay of the land.

I paid my respects to the Calhoun crime scene, Algiers Point. Across the water from the French Quarter, "the Crescent" was where the Mississippi made its sharp eastward turn before heading down to the Gulf. A point of land known to be the second oldest neighborhood in the city. Some families still claimed heritage back to Colonial times. Some called them liars, but not to their faces. Still, it remained a relatively calm section of the city until recently, with hourly ferry rides shuttling tourists wishing to escape the Mardi Gras madness for a breath or two. After dark the Point allowed for the detached safety of a scenic skyline and jittery river reflections of the city lights.

Alya would have been brought here after dark, but not on the ferry, so I drove the Crescent City Connection Bridge following Calhoun's likely route. Then I turned north towards Morgan Street and the Dry Docks. In the daylight hours, not quite as romantic a spot for a shooting or a prisoner exchange but, even late at night, too well-trafficked for either.

If Calhoun's killers were the same wild-boys who'd stabbed Sasha nine times after strangling and beating him, perhaps she anticipated a joyless meeting and this was her location of choice. Across the river, not too isolated, this was a place she might not be recognized. She would have met them with a gun in one hand and Alya in the other. I drew my phone.

"Pedersen. Algiers Point," I said. "Did your crime scene kids determine the lieutenant was shot here? Or was the body dumped?"

"What are you thinking?" he said.

"I'm thinking it's a bit too busy for a prisoner-cash swap, even after dark. You got a Military Academy up the street, and a Marine Corps Support base, to say nothing of all the Coast Guard along here. Had the killers suggested someplace further out, maybe Calhoun made this a safer middle ground—in her mind."

"Not dumped. Many nine-eleven calls. Gunshots heard." He hung up.

With police cruisers yet sweeping the waterfront, I parked my stolen Tahoe in the alley of a leaning, rot-walled tavern that suggested a more local, rather than tourist clientele. I ordered a late lunch of crawdads and beer to blend in. Zydeco remained the jukebox racket of choice in here, though I imagined most of the Marines preferred Led Zeppelin.

The place had a decent afternoon crowd with bar regulars easy to spot. At the nearest table a half dozen Marines in civvies, haircuts high-and-tight, Corps tattoos, proved their patience as a wobbling crone carried an unbreakable stream of one-sided, hard to decipher, conversation with each of them.

"…yep. A sight, fo' sshure. Dem mo'fekers don' care 'bout nuffin', fo' shhure. Dem mean bad times fo' everybody else. Bop-bop, and alls dem oders run for de hills…" She staggered and grabbed the closest Marine to steady on. He finally interrupted her.

"Ma'am."

"Shhorry, boy—I mean shhir." And she continued her stream.

One of the Marines spotted my expression and rolled his eyes.

"Day off?" I said.

"Off day," he said.

That got her attention, and she swerved to the bar at my elbow just as I rose and slid my tip to the bartender.

"—an' yer leavin' already? Fo' shhure you can spot a gal de price of a Maker's? Or at least a beer?"

"Gladys," the bartender said. "If you can't leave the customers some space, you'll need to shove off."

"No worries," I said and slid another ten his way. "Wet her whistle on me." I nodded to the Marines and made for the door.

"I'll thank you for her," the bartender said to my back. "But the rest of us are hoping on that whistle going dry enough to stick her tongue to her teeth."

Outside, I leaned on the Tahoe fender and waited. I heard her coming.

"Blessh you, mister. You a kind gentleman, fo' shhure." She patted my chest then started back for the tavern.

"So, you probably never witnessed so many police on this strip before."

"Oh, no, fo' shhure." She was thrilled to continue her conversation, as I suspected. "I runned off, bangety-bang. But yep, en'nertainments all night n' day. Crazy, dem. Sho'nuff crazy, mister."

"All night too? You said, bop-bop. You heard the shooting? You must've been scared."

"Scared as I'd like to tell. Not just heard, I seen 'em. Bop-bop."

"No way."

"Yep-way. Dem bullets flyn' ever which way."

"And you came back today? You must be brave too."

"Dese my fam'ly here. Where I gonna go? Don' mind braggin a touch, though the Lawd don't much like the prideful. I runned off with other folk and hunkered down. Might be they was just too much for dem crazies to hunt us all one by one by one."

"About the woman—"

"Dat poor woman. I can't say I saw her fall, but I seen her lay'n there after. Poor woman."

"Do you know what happened to the other woman?"

One question too many. Her eyes became knowing, despite the alcohol fog. "Mister, how you know 'bout a…?"

"Oh, I heard a couple Coast Guard boys." I handed her a twenty. "I'm just wondering if those crazies dragged her off, or maybe—"

"I think you talk too much, Mister Navy." She tucked the twenty up her sweater sleeve.

"Not me, ma'am. What Navy?"

"Dat Mister Crazy mo'fecker shootin folks. Mister Navy Peacoat, but no Navy haircut. Him raggedy down to the lapels. Where's yo Peacoat, mister?" She walked away faster than she came.

"I'm just worried about the other—"

She stopped to glare from the corner of the building, then disappeared.

"What now!" Pedersen yelled at his phone.

"I'm not asking, I'm telling," I said. "You have a witness. An old lady who spends her days in the Tavern on the Point. She witnessed the shooting. Not sure about her memory. Said the shooter wore a Navy Peacoat, but he had long hair. There are plenty of those coats around, especially this part of town. Maybe it's something worth checking." I hung up before he could thank me.

Back across the city, the West End Marina, that place we had in common, I wondered at the value of breaking into vacant yachts looking for a friend who didn't want to be found. Then I thought I recognized her car, a dirty blue Impala parked amid a herd of shinier vehicles near the rear of the lot. Approaching the license plate, "HUMMRLV," I nearly turned away before seeing her calling card. A large letter "V" had been drawn with a finger in the dirt of the rear window.

"Alive," I whispered to no one. *Not too wise maybe, stealing a license plate—Of course, here I am driving a stolen car.* Checking the Impala's interior gave no clues to her whereabouts. I honked her car horn. She wouldn't recognize the Tahoe.

I hiked for over an hour along the boat docks and loading ramps. I talked with a number of sailors and hobby fishermen. I checked the shops and restaurants. Outside a coed privy, I offered a twenty to a homeless woman wrapped in a soiled blanket. She eventually unwrapped and stumbled inside, but returned with a head-shake. My buzzing phone interrupted my search.

"No, we haven't heard from her." Patty never led a conversation with small talk, which I appreciated. "Regarding your investigation, I have another bulletin before it hits the newsstands. A maintenance worker found a body in the stairwell of the same building where they found Pasternak. This one also with the Russki tattoos. Two pistol shots, sometime late last night, but we won't know the caliber until they dig them out."

I hung up without reply when I heard rubber soles on the damp concrete behind me. Alya stopped with ten yards separating us. For a moment, neither of us could speak or move to bridge the distance.

"Did you bring police?" She cut the impasse.

"How long have you known me?" I said.

She sobbed and ran at me and grabbed me in her arms. A moment's touch. Then, before I could hold her, she pushed away and hugged herself.

"Time to go home," I said.

"Just home?"

"To my home for now. Pedersen knows you are innocent, but we won't tell him where you are for now. Leave your car here. We'll come back for it once this garbage is behind us." I led her to the Tahoe.

"Nice car."

"I assume you took *your* new license plate off a Hummer. Maybe ask Ms. Gunston sometime to explain the less delicate meaning of that word."

"You assume I do not know."

I found street parking near the Hemmings building; police would not be searching for the Tahoe yet.

"We did this before," she said. "What did you tell me about making same mistakes twice?"

What did I tell you about leaving the apartment without me?

Inside. I asked if she wanted to lie down, then I asked if she wanted a strong drink. She asked for tea. While I put the kettle on, she settled into the wingback chair beside the fireplace.

"You are really not going to call your detective friend?"

"Not until you feel ready." I wondered if she would fall asleep in the chair, and I waited quietly for the kettle to boil.

"That woman," she said, "police woman, Calhoun, she told me you were in car accident. She said your Pedersen asked her to bring me to hospital. She lied." Alya massaged her scalp. "I need bath…She is dead, is she?"

"Yes. But don't talk right now. Rest. It's been a stressful few days."

"I need to say. In car, she put on zip tie cuffs. Men were waiting by the river."

"One with long hair, wearing a Navy Peacoat."

"Long dark blue coat, anchors on buttons. How did you know? Other man short hair. Russian tattoos. Calhoun only said, Where is the money? Long coat shot her twice."

I set her cup on the small table near her hand. She stared at it as if reading invisible tea leaves.

"Russian grabbed his arm. More shots in dirt, and I ran. Papa would say, You run and shoot, you will miss everything. Long coat missed me." She lifted the cup but with a shaky hand, so she returned it to the table. "Sailors running to gunshots. I stop one, show zip ties and said, men try to kidnap me. He cut zip ties. He asked questions, but I ran again."

"Try to relax. The Russian is dead. They will find the other."

She did not react to the news, but used that moment to mask her eyes with the teacup.

"What else would you like to tell me?" I said.

"Nothing."

"Please. I need to know the rest if I am to stop this. You've told me about your childhood, your father." I had never seen her cry, but I recognized the trembling struggle to hold back.

"You must know someone back home who knows where you are. Someone you have contacted since you've been here."

"No one." She almost stood, but exhaustion dropped her to the seat.

"Someone here, in this country, knows you are Russian."

"Everyone who has heard me speak."

"Trust me. Help me to help you." We reached that point where she would tell me, or she would shut down and lock me out. I gave her an understanding smile and returned to the kitchen. "Would you like me to warm yours?" It was the right tactic.

"*Nyet. Spasiba.*" She became quiet.

"The *stick*. Because you keep asking, it was a gift from a friend. I was still with the department. I was chasing a perp when I broke my leg. After losing the crutches, an overly-dramatic friend presented me with the fancy walking stick. It used to be a theater prop. She was an actress. She said, I should carry it because I'd rather break my leg than use my gun."

"And she had prop blade replaced, or did you?"

Now I fell silent. She was holding her face, so I listened to her breathing and allowed her time.

"It came from me." She inhaled deeply.

"What?"

"I never send my whole name. I send only…"

"Oh, Alya." I returned to the settee, close enough to the chair for her to read my concern.

"Last year. Christmas. I send package to Misha. Just chocolates, cigarettes, warm socks for winter—I only sign Alya. I never had to give—"

"The postmark, Alya. A New Orleans postmark."

"I did this…" Tears finally appeared.

"We did this. I should have made you change your first name when you moved in. I should have talked to you more about this. Who is this Misha?"

"My friend. Best child friend. He—He went to prison before we—He would never betray me."

"Alya, everyone changes in prison. Life is harder than you can believe. If someone there, someone powerful, wants to find you bad enough, there are ways to change another person's loyalties. From what you have told me, your father might be one of those people."

"If Misha sent postmark to Papa…"

"Your Papa has friends here who could find a Russian woman your age, description, no known family history, calling herself Alya. They may have been looking for you for a long time."

Two days later, with her permission, I called Lt. Pedersen. He promised to keep Alya's location a secret from his department for as long as he could. He told me about Calhoun's mailbox key and the notebook detailing her intentions.

"She was desperate," he said. "She needed to pay off debts quickly. Her sister…Then she learned about a large cash reward offered for Alya."

"Everybody needs something."

"By the way, the man in the blue Suburban watching your place, the phony surveillance, she mentioned him as a paid friend, a cop from another department. He's in custody now. And she verified what we already knew about those who would murder her in the exchange. The notebook was her way of reaching out from the grave should things turn sour, as you no doubt figured."

Quid pro quo, I gave him information on the Russian-prison connection without mentioning Alya's father specifically. Just that someone from her past had dangerous friends searching for her. I filled in more of what I had learned from Warden Moran. He needed more questions answered, but I made an excuse to hang up.

The following night, Alya opened the door to Pedersen's knock. He crossed to the dining table and dropped a copy of The Delta Tribune.

SHIP CAPTAIN MURDERED, PORTNOLO

Tuesday, 11:35pm. Port of New Orleans (PORTNOLO). Harbor Police had received an anonymous call of a body found half-submerged beneath the Crescent City Connection Bridge, W. (CCC)(US 90 Bus.) A preliminary identification was released Wednesday. Captain Maxin Gusev, of the cargo ship Aurora, out of Riga, Latvia. Details of the death are as yet un-released, however, one EMS worker at the scene spoke of an apparent knife wound to the throat. This is yet to be confirmed by authorities...

"Would you like a drink, Lieutenant?" I said.

"I assume, by your offer, that you know something but will refuse to say anything. You know there are limits to what I withhold when it comes to a murder case." Pedersen slammed the door on his way out.

"Maxin was nice man." Alya edged away from the paper. "When he finds me hiding on ship from Latvia, he gives me job to pay for passage to America. He protected me from other men working on ship. When we land, he gave to me money for food. Sad, nice man."

Three nights later, Pedersen returned with another newspaper. His sarcasm deepened when he learned I was not there. Alya relayed the meeting to me later:

ANOTHER RUSSIAN IMMIGRANT DEAD

A New Gang War?

...Lower Ninth Ward, where the body of an unidentified young man was found by a local dog walker Sunday, near 5a.m. Authorities have reported the man carried a forged I.D., and that he might have been in the country illegally. Tattoos on the body are said to be associated with the Odesa and Volgograd regions...and cause of death, a .38 caliber bullet dividing the trachea two inches below...

"I am afraid you came at a wrong time," she said. "Mr. Vagelle is out of the country."

"I don't believe it," Pedersen said. "Since when?"

"I do not lie about this."

"I know. Sorry. So, he's not out of the city, he's out of the country?" He opened the paper and a police photograph fell out. "I believe you recognize this man. He has been identified as one of those who killed Detective Calhoun. Your boss will know him as a vagrant we first saw hanging out near Lafitte's after Sasha's murder. He calls him Ragpile."

"It is him. But Mr. Vagelle has no cases about Russian killers. And he does not talk to me about them. He has other business to see to. He has been very busy."

"If he has a flight itinerary, I need to see it."

"I am sorry, Lieutenant. Mr. Vagelle is specific. He said if you demand to see travel papers, you should come back with warrant."

"That son of a—" He spun for the door, then stopped and apologized through his teeth.

"Mr. Vagelle also said that I should offer you a drink."

"Sometimes I hate your boss." But he returned to the table and accepted a tumbler of Mr. Vagelle's Widow Jane bourbon. He stayed late, and it was a pleasant conversation. When he searched me for information, I recognized it, and changed the subject. I believe he understood.

Kaliningrad. Set into the deep recesses of Vistula Lagoon, hiding as much from the Baltic Sea as from her neighbors, Poland and Lithuania, her citizens could feel the draw of old Europe, despite their satellite kinship to a distant homeland.

Late autumn, gray skies above skeletal trees, wet cobblestones reflected the dull afternoon light. In Victory Park, a leather-skinned accordion player filled the plaza with exuberant traditional music, while the few passing tourists remaining in the city dropped rubles into a battered hat.

On the well-dressed side of the Pregolya River, the newly anointed "Fishing Village" might catch the eye with brightly painted, recently renovated hotels and shopping centers. Visitors, old and young, carried their shopping bags, laughed, took photos of friends in front of the dramatic architecture inspired by quaint, century-old German villages that had been destroyed in 1943. A city doing everything possible to divorce itself from its Russian parentage.

But this was a business trip, and my business came with specific requirements, the first of which included a utilitarian location. A quiet bistro apart from the crowds, not too isolated. A small table against the back wall and a view of the river. I warmed my hands on a coffee cup while contemplating, across the Pregolya, the less attractive view, the old, ten-story, Soviet-era, Khrushchevka apartments.

A handsome elderly couple, the only other patrons, finished lunch and went about their shopping.

The door closed and immediately reopened. Two men entered like movie cliches, Mutt and Jeff, black leather jackets, pressed slacks, patent leather shoes. They took a tall table closer to the door and scanned the narrow room as if the candle stands might disguise cameras. The proprietor approached. Mutt, the younger, bounced from his stool and whispered something I couldn't hear. The proprietor spun, lowered his head, and returned to the kitchen.

Out front, a black BMW pulled against the curb. The driver climbed out first. Then a grizzly spent several seconds unfolding from the passenger seat, and the car rose on its springs as he did. He turned to watch the street, and the driver opened the rear door, releasing another thick-shouldered bodyguard carrying a large something beneath his longcoat—my guess would be easy enough. Then the grizzly opened the far door and *Papa Elin* emerged. He was younger than I'd expected. Well-groomed, sandy hair, touched with silver. A weathered face held empty eyes. He entered the café behind griz and longcoat, while the driver threw the lock and remained in the doorway. All turned to me, naturally.

Papa tipped his head, a signal for longcoat to show off his "Vikhr" submachine gun, popular with the new *Spetsnaz*. Mutt and Jeff stood away from their high table and drew their Makarov pistols. Just to further the cliché, Papa pulled a gold-plated *Soratnik* (meaning "Companion"). It all reminded me that Papa had been released recently to the outside world.

Be careful of preconceptions. Watch the young ones. Those with the most to prove are more likely to prove their volatility. I recalled *Seneca the Younger,* and *"the cruelty of weakness."*

I stood slowly and lifted my arms from their sides. Griz smiled and did the honors. He ripped open my shirt, ran beefy fingers over the rest of me and, as a parting gift, slapped a hand up for the groin search. I flinched, but I had readied myself for it.

"Ivan, *pazhalusta* (please)," Papa said. He wagged his Soratnik at my table, indicating I should sit, then looked me over before deciding he should sit as well. He laid the gold-plated Soratnik on the tabletop pointed toward my sternum and waited for my reaction. His trigger finger tapped a heart's cadence as he spoke.

"I would have thought you might pick someplace more busier. There is a square popular with tourists, and you could look up at white Cathedral and pray for a last request."

"I prefer the calming waters of Pregolya," I said. "I chose this spot with you in mind."

Mutt sniggered. Jeff did not react. *The young ones.*

"So you are thinking of my comfort. Meanwhile, I am thinking of your balls. Do you have iron balls, Mr. Vagelle?" His face told me it was not a joke. He spun the Soratnik on the tabletop, his Wheel of Fortune, and it stopped with the giving-end exactly where it started. "Here you sit in my country, alone, unarmed, not concerned with any one of my friends walking in, putting a bullet in your eye, and walking out," his wheel spun again, "while I dine with politicians at the most expensive restaurant in the city, waiting for reports of your demise. Demise, it is the correct word?"

"It is," I said.

"Do you have American Seal Team surrounding the café while we talk? You have ultimatum for me maybe? I think not. So maybe you do not have iron balls. Maybe you have a death wish. I like Charlie Bronson. I watch many good American movies. Tell me, Charlie Bronson, why you are so confident I would be here today."

"Because I mentioned the right name."

"You wrote several names in your note."

"But only one that matters. You have gone to much expense these past years hunting for her. I calculated the importance of my death over whatever information on Alya you believe you can extract from me before—" I waved to his platoon—"*your friends* put bullets in my eyes."

"I like this kind of movie, Charlie." He clapped. "You believe they cannot get information without my presence here? And once they have it, they would not kill you anyway?"

"They could get nothing. And I knew you had no reason to assume anything before seeing me." I did not look at the spinning pistol, as I knew where it would stop.

"So, you met a Russian girl named Alya. And she sends you to my door to die for her?" He turned with an expressionless laugh for his heavily armed audence. They had been trained not to laugh with him.

"I met Alya," I said. He studied me like a museum statue studying its gallery. "She does not know I am here."

"In Russia we say, killing a madman is a sign of weakness. Laugh loud, Charlie, so we may all see how mad you are."

I mirrored his emptiness.

"Okay, I am getting bored, Charlie. I wasted many minutes in traffic getting here and your clock is ticking. Your next words should have meaning."

I nodded to the red dot on the window beside our table. The red laser light pierced the glass to land on his jacket lapel. His empty eyes filled with hate, and his finger stopped tapping, and his hand encircled the grip of his gold-plated *Soratnik*.

"You think you can move away fast enough. You cannot," I said.

Each of his men stepped back and leveled up their weapons. Mutt's gunhand lept forward, shaking, and I threw a salt shaker, forcing him to swat it aside. I lifted both hands in surrender. More red lights pierced the windows and decorated the café walls.

"Stop," Papa Elin said.

"I think you would not have come here today without investigating me a bit," I said. "Maybe you knew me before my note. Back when you first learned of your daughter's present life. You may have even learned something useful."

"I should have learned enough to have Ivan throw you in the Pregolya River the day you got here."

"You may have learned my life means nothing. It hasn't for a long time. You, on the other hand, believe you have something to live for. I believe this is leverage." I pointed to the red dots. "These are just to give me the time I need to finish what I've traveled eight-thousand kilometers to say."

"You think I fear death?"

He likes macho movies.

"Mr. Elin, you are an important man to some, and gaining in importance now that you are free from Vladimir Central

Prison." My knowledge of him did nothing to dampen the hate in his eyes.

I whispered out of range of his men, "You got your early release by performing favors while you were inside. You knew of Sergey Breza's power, his networks inside American prisons, and you knew of certain mafia heads in Moscow growing ever more nervous of that power. Just as you had grown your status in Vlad Central. So, you put out the contract on your competitor, and bumped up your status even more with your bosses. Everyone wins. Bosses pay large bonuses to Moscow politicians who set you free."

"Tick-tock, as you Americans say." He tapped the *Soratnik* on the tabletop.

"Everyone wins, except a young Russian woman in New Orleans whom Breza located, thanks to you and your friend Misha. Now you are in Kaliningrad, meeting *important people*, thinking to expand your influence. Maybe Moscow leadership grew too crowded while you were locked away. Maybe this distant Russian island of a country, surrounded by the E-U, far from Moscow's tentacles, seemed the perfect place for an ambitious partner to corrupt an unwary establishment."

"So, Charlie, you have proven that you know things. This is why you come all these kilometers to die? I should care that a dead man knows things?"

"I did not come here to threaten. The red lights are a precaution, nothing more." He looked at the window, perhaps wondering where the shooter was.

"I'm not here to start a war. My wish is that nobody dies here today. That I board a private jet this evening and return to my quiet home, share a drink with my friend, and never step foot in this province, or your Russia, again. I sincerely wish to never see you again."

"You also knew your red lights would anger me. It was a bad chess move."

"Possibly. But there is the matter of *my friend*. Her life has been threatened, she has been injured and arrested, whether by your direction or because of you. I believe I know why, but that is also of little consequence."

"You think you know why I have searched for her?"

"To keep your enemies, like Breza, from using her against you. But they have. Breza's slave attacked her out of revenge for his suffering in prison. Then the men you sent to bring her home nearly killed her."

"And you killed them?"

"You are a businessman. In your business, you know the value of a promise. I have traveled all this way for a simple promise from you. Nothing more. All I ask is peace between us. You control your kingdom, wage your wars, and you leave my tiny slice of the world to me and mine. We have no significance in your world."

"So, you believe I cannot lie to you. What can you do to me with your red dots once we leave this bistro? You have been more than an inconvenience, Charlie Bronson. I have gone to large expense over this. I have reputation to consider. What would my friends think if I let you walk free after making more threats?"

"They would think you are strong enough not to worry over mice so far away."

"You say you believe you know why I have involved myself in Alya's life again after so many years. I say you do not know as much as you believe. She is not everything that you believe."

"This is about you and me now. No one else. This is about what brought you to this table this morning. Your curiosity. You wonder who could come into your apartment, past all your security, past the alarms and cameras, and set the envelope on your nightstand."

He took the small gift from his top pocket. He turned it in his fingers. The wedding band, plain gold with an engraved promise inside. The only item Alya thought to take when she fled Moscow. Her mother's ring.

"If I wanted you dead, you would be dead," I said. "Again, not a threat, just a statement of the obvious. I understood you needed a calling card of sorts, something to make you aware of the gravity of your decisions here this morning, and the consequences. She is under my care now. I would like only your promise. Never attempt to contact your daughter and keep your people away."

The wedding ring continued turning in his fingers, reminding me of the turning of his golden Soratnik.

"And if I say you are not as powerful as you believe?"

"She will be escorted from her present home, relocated before the end of the day. And you and I both die this morning. And the world will turn without us."

"Are you sure you are not a Russian poet?" He surprised me with a faint smile. It failed to reach his eyes, of course. "I should be angry at all this…" He pointed to the red dots. "Maybe it will be the death of you one day. But not today." With a pinky finger, he pushed his late wife's wedding band across the table. "You take it back to her."

The red dots disappeared from the window.

Early evening, REGNUM News, the Press Service of the Kaliningrad Ministry of Internal Affairs, released a brief statement to the local media:

Following an anonymous call to police, investigators accompanied a Spetsnaz team into a vacant apartment in the Khrushchevka building across the river from the Bolshoi Café. What they found was an array of tactical laser sights, no weapons, secured to two window sills. All had been hardwired to a receiver set-up, all pointed across the river to the windows of the café.

The public announcement called it a dangerous prank, and issued a reward for information leading to the arrest of the perpetrators. The Ministry would not report on the slender remote they found affixed beneath the last table in the café. The trigger I had operated with a raised knee at the appropriate moment in the conversation.

By this time I was already in the air over the Baltic Sea.

Alya opened her door. Surprised at first, she touched my cheek then stepped back and invited me in. Her eyes glistened, and she turned to hide them.

"You said it was over. I came home." She kneaded her empty hands as a child might, expecting a scolding.

"You are okay," I said.

"It is strange with you in my apartment. I am always in yours. I am glad I cleaned after police—" She went to the kitchenette. "I buy your favorite Widow Jane, in case you ever visit here. Would you like?"

"*Spasiba*," I said.

Laying my coat over the arm of her sofa, I surveyed the room. I wandered to the windows overlooking St. Charles Avenue. Sensing her at my shoulder, I accepted the tumbler of bourbon. She sipped her sparkling water.

"You do not wish to sit?" she said. "You had a long two days traveling."

I turned the amber liquid. I breathed the bourbon's aroma, the smells of her clean apartment, her shampoo. It all wearied me. "You've had no more trouble with the police? I didn't care to talk with Pedersen until I checked with you."

"No. He is nice man, when he is not arresting me." Her welcomed humor; I tried not to see her father in her eyes.

"I talked with Patty from the plane. They found the second of Calhoun's killers. Long hair, Navy Peacoat. She tells me he'd been shot with the same .38 handgun that killed Calhoun. They also found evidence that Peacoat killed the ship Captain."

"Yes. He was looking for me?" She lowered into the plush cushions of her armchair.

"I shouldn't have started this tonight, so soon. I just wanted to tell you, I believe he was the last of your troubles, so you can rest easier."

"*Da* (Yes)."

"Thank you." I finished the drink and set down the glass. "I'm exhausted. I should go."

"Not so soon. Please sit. Tell me about your trip. I very much…" She looked almost fearful of my leaving.

"I'm too tired to talk." I dropped onto the facing sofa. "But you tell me, how are you? After everything. Have you talked with the shrink?"

She said she would be okay as I fell asleep.

I don't know how long I slept, but I woke to the dark with traffic lights drifting across the ceiling like an extended dream. She had given me a pillow and blanket at some point, and she slept snug in her armchair beneath her own. I watched her.

I got up quietly, took my coat, reached into the pocket and retrieved the small manila envelope. I laid it on my pillow. Thinking to rinse the taste of the drink from my tongue, I halted in her bedroom doorway. By the light filtering through the blinds, I could see her nightstand beside the bed, and her .38 snubnose next to the lamp.

I recalled her Papa Elin's words, *"I say you do not know as much as you believe. She is not all that you believe."*

I would never ask where she found her snubnose. And she would never ask me where I found her Mama's ring.

One loyal friend is worth ten thousand relatives—Euripides

"You like, too much, the dead philosophers, I think," she said.

Four

Acheron's

Angel

The great egret, broad, pristine wings, drifted low on warm currents like an angel through the gloom.

She caught the sunlight, emblazoned for a moment, before cypress shadows darkened her again. Black water reflected her white grace. She swept the air again, tilted to one side, and with a single feather, sliced the untroubled surface of the lake. Ripples designed to attract a meal. The gator splashed, clamped onto the wing and rolled back beneath the surface.

The tropical storm had passed, plowing northeast across what remained of Louisiana and onto Alabama, Arkansas then

Tennessee. Here in the Basin, the river had already returned to its tranquil and routinely predatory ways. A fragile tranquility easily ruptured as our light aircraft descended, clipped the treetops and tumbled into the wetlands.

Green water rose throughout the cabin. Choking as it filled my nose and throat, I snapped awake, or something akin to it. I raised my head above the muck and spit. Sight remained clouded. Objects defined themselves only as my physical pains prioritized, and survival instincts forced my concentration. The ache at the back of my skull had a pulse of its own.

An uneven gravity pulled at me as, below the waterline, the seatbelt dug its grievance into my right hip. Disoriented by shafts of sunlight falling from above, I recognized the tilt of the fuselage. Struggling with the seatbelt clasp became more of a struggle, as I had sprained my left wrist. The catch eventully worked free.

That freedom settled my mind, so I breathed deep and took stock. The water remained level long enough to assume the cabin would not fill. Across the aisle slumped Detective Hayes, who had invited me on this junket. His face had been submerged for too long, making resuscitation unlikely. Likewise Trooper Daniels floated facedown. Trooper Gomez had died with his face above water, but his throat cut. I could not see their prisoner, the life I should've taken back when it meant something—when he threatened to shoot the child—when I chose to incapacitate rather than kill. A decision that had now destroyed more lives.

Some would call it my own narrow, self-righteous vision.

The seats across the aisle remained above water. Hayes had drowned upended. I checked his pulse anyway. I pulled his gun belt free and buckled it bandolero-style over my head and shoulder, mindful to keep the holster high and free of the marsh water. I checked his pockets and found the backup clip. I buttoned that into my shirt pocket. Then I half-swam toward the cockpit.

There I found the prisoner, broken by his impact with the windshield. Another bad guy over-estimating his abilities. He had died beside the equally dead pilot with the exit wound in his chest. Dragging the killer off the partially submerged instrument panel, I threw him behind me and let him sink. I found the radio, but that had died of bullet wounds as well.

I teetered. My previous movements had rocked the plane and it shifted in the silty riverbottom. The swamp began to rise once more. I pivoted and battled through the resisting water back to the cabin, where I released the hatch above, and let the sun blind me in return. Insects attacked mercilessly.

The Atchafalaya Basin spread well over a million acres of swampland, backwater lakes and bayous. Twenty miles wide but a hundred and fifty miles long, many have found their way in here and never found a way out. And I had no idea where we had crashed.

I climbed free of the wreck. Slogging through black brine, I clawed at the duckweed, the low Spanish moss, and bracken, each step searching for solid purchase. *Never stand still.* Once a quagmire takes hold, struggling saps energy. Predators appreciate a floundering prey. Hauling toward a broad-kneed cyprus and tupelo, I found somewhat stiffer soil near their roots. I could rest here, but not for long.

I felt for the lump on the back of my head and my hand came away bloody. No small concern—not the loss of blood; it wasn't that bad—but the knowledge that smell is a gator's strongest sense. A single drop in ten gallons of water, he can smell a carcass over four miles away, and there were some two million gators in this swamp.

I tore a sleeve and used it to wash the wound and the blood from my neck. I tossed it into the branches. Then I packed the wound with moss and wrapped my head with the other sleeve, hoping to disguise the smell as much as possible. A narrow strip of shirttail tightened my aching wrist. The detective's Glock passed inspection. Then I checked myself for ticks.

Stay with the Cessna, was my initial, most practical, thought.

A search party would spot that before it ever found me, and despite the interior soup, it would be my strongest shelter from the elements at night. More realistically, with the baking heat of day and the rot of human flesh inside, that pot would become toxic within six hours.

I could still see thirty percent of the plane and its left wing above water. As I rationalized returning to search for anything salvageable, I noticed liquid rainbows on the swamp. At least one of the fuel tanks was draining.

Swimming through gasoline would do nothing for my health.

Fantasies of a signal fire snuffed themselves out as well. With multiple fuel tanks, a Cessna explosion would certainly attract authorities; but with all that dead vegetation amongst the green, a wildfire could easily destroy three counties, and me.

There will be no rescue. My inner realist reined in the fantasies.

I had no idea the time of the pilot's last transmission. I knew we went down east of Lafayette, but for all anyone else knew, we might as well be vacationing in Havana. Ultimately, I understood the dangers of sitting still, especially without the means of making fire. Dehydration, insects, and bacteria from drinking or eating anything the swamp offered up—I estimated, if lucky, I had maybe five days.

A young copperhead came out of the scrub to investigate the lazy intruder. Time to move.

Do not spoil what you have by desiring what you have not, said the great philosopher.

I had skills. That's about it.

Day two announced itself with a pounding of rain, which brought temporary liberation from mosquitoes and relieved my thirst. I stripped to my shorts and scrubbed my clothes then scrubbed myself.

By the morning of the third day, I devoured a raw mud turtle from its shell. My stomach couldn't keep it down, but I decided to keep the shell for the next rain. If I lasted that long. By mid-afternoon I skinned a large water snake. That came up as well, so I wasted a bullet on a middling catfish, and wasted an hour plucking through the infinite bones.

On the morning of the seventh day I came to a house.

A house, if it stood here for more than twenty years, had to be planted on sturdy soil. If it survived the floods and the storms, it was built on raised ground. If it was constructed of anything but log and peat, if it had a stone fireplace in this land without stone, it must have a road. And if it had a road, I had a way out. Or, I was delirious and hallucinating all of it.

I took to a knee. Not to pray, I didn't believe in it, but because I could no longer stand. No physical strength remaining, I had been moving forward powered by nothing but will. My mind had long since surrendered of purpose or character, and seeing this house threw a switch signaling a termination of other motor skills.

Not a mansion, but neither was it a shed. It had a proper door and three shuttered windows across the front. There might have been a grass roof, but as I forced my focus I detected slate peeking from beneath the sod. The chimney had a break in it, a few stones missing, but it had once been sufficient for family life.

A fat gator, resenting my intrusion, deserted the porch and vanished into the tall grass. The yard absorbed its stillness. No further signs of life. I wished to announce myself to the house, but my throat felt caked with moss. In time, I pushed myself up from the soggy earth.

The door swung freely, a surprise. I expected hinges with decades of corrosion, or animal droppings cementing the base, or anything restricting its movement. A familiar, sick odor answered me from within. I called out anyway, choking on my words. I knocked on the rotted doorframe. I stomped the threshold. Living in seclusion either plays with, or attacks, the mind. After the week I was having, the last thing I wanted to hear was the shotgun of an old hermit protecting his home from *visitors*. All I heard were the sounds of small creatures scuttling for the corners, so I entered the gloaming with my gunhand behind me.

No electricity, naturally, so I crossed to the window. Shattered glass crunched beneath my shoes and I unlatched the shutters to admit a flood of daylight into the room. *The crime scene.*

Old blood, now brown, had been painted or thrown at the walls, dragged across the floor from end to end. Someone had written in the brown graffiti with a hairy brush the size of a head, but if the strokes formed letters they were indecipherable. The hand-made furniture had been likewise desecrated, as was the splintered, framed photo canted against the baseboard. I dizzied with the visual chaos. I saw no bodies.

Rushing back to the porch, I grabbed my knees to steady them, and staring at the grass helped me breathe. If I had a drop of anything in my stomach, I'd have purged it.

Once upon a time, as the fable goes, I had strolled through many a crime scene. It used to be my job. But I had never walked into a scene like this. This was a work of art. Almost joyful. The closest I had witnessed to perfect madness. Or evil.

Or perhaps mine was the diseased mind. Perhaps this house, all of it, was an illusion born of my tortures, my weariness. Born of the swamp disease and lack of food, or bad food, bacteria in the water, insects, lack of sleep. Perhaps my mind had finally succumbed to fantasy and given up. I was open to suggestion.

Sunlight played across the lawn as a fetid breeze nudged the surrounding cyprus giants, and their shadows slow-danced through the green. If I had the energy, I might flee this nightmare, race into the swamp to lay in a bed of water hyacinth and hydrilla, to willfully accept my nearest neighbor, Death. But no...

I re-entered the house.

I kept my eyes to the painted floor. I tried to convince myself it was animal blood and a butcher gone mad, but the sicker voice in my head said otherwise. Splashes and slashes of the crazed brown paint. I followed toward the kitchen, but was halted by the design. A long brushstroke crossed my path. I turned with it, then I saw the handprints. The *forgotten investigator* within me forced a more intimate examination. Adult handprints, long and thin fingered, had slapped the floorboards repeatedly. Had clawed the old wood and dragged splinters and left broken fingernails between the boards. A sharp blade turned in my chest, but I refused to sit now. I continued along the brushwork, down the blunt hall to a bedroom.

I stood in the doorway. The shutters here had remained open to a divine daylight, and the woman in the bed glared back at me with empty eye-holes. I guessed it to be a woman because of the white nightgown, but the corpse was unidentifiable as such. Dusty brown, like desiccated pear skin, stretched with nothing between it and the bones of the face. The same with the flesh of exposed arms and legs. Fingers and toes had been broken into bone hooks. In a distant past, she had been bathed, the nightgown and bed sheets as unspoiled as a Macy's display, but she did not look at peace.

She rose from the bed. Her lipless grin opened and her jaw disconnected from her face and she extended her broken claws—

But no. Again, an illusion manufactured by my fevered mind. She yet lay dead, breathless and staring without eyes. No Medical Examiner necessary for this autopsy, the means of death was obvious thoughout the house.

The oak dresser had been beaten with a hammer by a madman. The second level handles fingerprinted in brown. My *investigator* tugged on them, somehow knowing—I spun away and fled the room. The infant had died mid-scream, a tiny visage that would follow me to my own final sleep.

My namesake, Nicolaus, had been a remembered philosopher. A contemporary of Herod the Great, he tutored the children of Marc Anthony and Cleaopatra. He wrote of the psyche and the soul, and he connected the two through science and art. Most of his scribblings had been lost to time or ravaged by barbarians, but other philosophers would be born, thousands across the centuries. Each built their house upon the teachings of their forerunners, challenging both psyche and soul, changing many gods into one, one into none, until all that remained was "self." A mocking of the concept of *soul.*

Little more than two-thousand years later, my mother named me, and I would never know why. There were no gods. There was no soul. Human psyche fluttered as fragile as dragonfly wings.

I had abandoned my profession, my search for justice in an insane world, and because old habits die hard, and I was good at what I did, I played for years at advising others. The "Consultant." A spectator on the soul of man that had never been relevant. The world directed me and eventually brought me here to stand in the house of the *artist,* and his work was a portrait of my world.

I entered the kitchen. The artist's canvas continued. The remains of a man, stripped naked and as devoid of humanity as those in the bedroom, his back showed the effects of a twelve gauge followed by carnivora. He occupied the hardwood chair, his face hidden in a plate of dead worms and animal leavings.

The table held a nest of snakes and a partially devoured, twenty pound, nutria. A last supper.

Mindful of where I stepped, I escaped to the backyard. Scattered pools lay where the earth had submerged reflecting bits of sky. A box, I guessed to be a privy, stood beside a poorly constructed shed, and a ghost. He jumped to his feet when he saw me, his eyes large and glaring either in fear, disbelief, or something I could not imagine. He appeared to be about fourteen.

Quickly, I holstered the handgun and lifted my open hands.

"Hullo!" I coughed and tried twice more. "Don't run."

He did not run yet. Nor did he answer.

"I mean no harm. I am lost." I did not dare approach for fear he would bolt, and I would be compelled to give chase. I hadn't the strength for it. My hands lowered, clear of my sides. Neither of us spoke, and I believed I felt the sun move across the sky.

Eventually, he backed away and lost himself in the undergrowth. Every impulse urged me to pursue, to catch and grab hold, to demand answers to who he was, how long he had been here, had he witnessed the horrors taking place in this house, to force him to get medical assistance…but he was a phantom.

I tried not to think on him. Already I began to doubt he was anything but imagination's sunlight and dust. I needed to think rationally again. Survival became important again. Harrowingly, I understood the need to revisit that kitchen. I might find some essential tidbit there to keep myself alive for one more day.

But first, I would check the shed.

The strongest odors lurked within these walls; the tight room repelled me. *The boy's room.* He must have lived in here for years. The smells of human filth, peat, animal remains, all hung confined in this poorly ventilated box. Uncured mammal skins hung from the walls. Other things. Standard shed items. A wheelbarrow missing its wheel, a shovel, a rake, a log-splitter, hoses posing as uncoiled snakes, and more. Blankets heaped in a corner, *possibly a bed.*

I controlled my breathing and crossed the doorsill. I found a hatchet beneath the blankets and inserted the handle behind my belt. Beside the door, squatted a kerosene lantern, long dry, but I took it along with an aluminum bucket and the shovel.

The sun had passed the roofline. I could not stay the night in that house or the shed. That house—I needed to return to that kitchen and search before sundown.

I watched the floor for movement, so I failed to see the coyote until it growled at me from the living room doorway. I eased the Glock from my holster and waited, avoiding the waste of a bullet with my confusion. When I stepped forward, he turned tail, and I heard claws leaving the front porch.

He could have been a meal, I admonished.

I opened the pantry to more rot and decay. Every can had been opened, emptied, and thrown to the floor in a heap. Someone else in survival mode. I should have brought the shovel. Using the hatchet as an extension of my arm, I rooted through the waste, but found nothing other than an unopened jug of cooking oil. I took it.

I rummaged the rest of the kitchen and found a wicker basket to collect items I deemed important. Cutlery, a cookpan, a box of matches found fallen behind a drawer. I strolled through the rest of the house. I avoided the bedroom dresser, but in the closet I found dusty, otherwise clean, men's overalls and a white long-sleeved shirt. They joined my basket collection.

Returning to the yard, I fought the wheelless wheelbarrow across damp soil, stopping midway to the house. I gathered dry wood from the kitchen. With the hatchet I splintered what I could—kitchen drawers, shelves—and I packed the wheelbarrow with kindling. I tested a match. Then another. Frustrated, I lowered the head of the shovel into the shavings and struck it with the hatchet. It sparked. As the wheelbarrow blazed, I ran back into the kitchen and hauled enough wood to satisfy Prometheus. I then set a kitchen chair beside my modest pyre.

Renewed energy boiled my blood. I boiled swamp water in the aluminum bucket.

I filled the kerosene lantern with vegetable oil. It wouldn't start a fire, but it knew how to burn. The Romans had illuminated their homes with it for generations. Into the night, I strained water, filling as many pots and bowls as I could. I washed a cloth in it, stripped myself then scrubbed with the cloth, ripping new sores and insect bites. I'd lost my head-wrap days ago, but I scrubbed my hair, reopening the still painful head wound. Infections could be managed if I found a doctor in time, or so I convinced myself. I fed the blazing wheelbarrow and stood naked near the flames to dry.

An out of place movement in the dark, the boy watching from the treeline. I pushed nervously into unfamiliar but cleaner clothes. I steered wide of the gunbelt hung across the back of my chair.

Breaking the handle from the rake head, I wrapped the end with cloth. I soaked that in vegetable oil and held it above my fire. I speared the earth with my long torch several feet beyond the flaming wheelbarrow, then I sat in the chair and pretended to ignore him. I held my hands out to the flames, indicating comfort.

I knew, like the boy, animals would be curious about my fire, so I stayed awake. Near midnight, I killed a rat with the shovel. I skinned and cooked him. Though my stomach tortured me, I ate only half and left the remainder on the skewering branch. I stuck that in the ground beside the torch. Once I had returned to the chair, the boy came forward.

He never spoke.

As the sun reappeared to tint the sky through the fat bars of cyprus, I buckled on the gun belt and reseated the hatchet at my waist. I ran the other belt through the handle of the oil jug, as well as another jug I had boiled clean and filled with new water. I slung the rig over my shoulder and carried the rake-torch as a hiking stick. Then, circling the house in ever-widening arcs, I hunted for the road.

I discovered a stretch, some thirty feet of gravel and broken tarmac pointing to the sunrise. The patch soon disappeared beneath a shallow pool and fern, but I picked it up again on the other side.

And so it went, my long hike, searching for signs of a continuing road, finding bits and pieces until another day had passed and I came to a ramshackle wooden bridge. I looked back only once to see sullen smoke still billowing, expanding its mass against the sky.

The road continued on, but I spent a night on the bridge because it was easier to defend and cleaner than lying in foliage.

The following day, I came to a pair of fishing shacks. An old man, with Cajun-broke English I barely understood, took pity and fed me on crawdads and gator meat. He offered a ride in his pirogue.

"Dere come trouble, dat." He raised his chin to the western sky. "Mi'be w'all come to prayin' awn rain 'fore long."

Too sick to answer or even look back to the gathering clouds of soot and ash, I simply nodded. He didn't need conversation. He needed someone to talk *at* and he continued for the remainder of our voyage.

I managed a thank you as he dropped me at a larger riverside camp with commercial airboats. A kind young father and son team helped me aboard theirs. They delivered me to a market fronting the Interstate.

I spent three nights on clean hospital sheets, fed through needles and tubes. On the fourth morning I woke with my assistant, Alya, at my bedside. The black giant, club owner, Bobby J., had been shoehorned into a second chair.

"You are going to be okay," Alya said. "It seems I say that to you too often, Mr. Vagelle. One day I will have it scribed into your headstone."

Bobby J. laughed.

They asked about my adventure, but I said I was too tired. I pretended to sleep, but sleep was unapproachable for the remainder of my hospital stay. Though they were the only two people I might consider friends, I would never tell them about the house, or the horrors, or the boy, or my final morning there.

Waking in the chair alone by the dwindling fire. Walking into the kitchen to see the boy bent over the corpse at the table, chewing the dessicated flesh from his father's back. Upon hearing me at the door, he glared with feral eyes and a grin filled with human meat. Then, as if to prove who he was, he took up a steak knife and plunged it repeatedly into the lifeless form, checking for my expression, still grinning, until I walked back outside.

I heard him coming on the run. When I spun, he had the knife in his fist, and the grin held firm, and I put a bullet through his chest from four feet away.

Charon the Ferryman, of Greek mythology, transported the souls of the dead across the River of Pain, the River Acheron, to the distant banks of the Underworld.

—Homer.

I will see that boy, if that's what he was, for the remainder of my life. And whenever I do, like my philosopher namesake, I will contemplate the nature of evil or madness or both. I will still deny the existence of God, but I will believe in the Devil. I will see his mother gowned in white, laid on clean linen, and the infant in the dresser drawer. At times I almost cry.

FIVE

A DANGEROUS COUPLING

Beginnings

"Do not touch me, please."

"Wouldn't think of it," I said. She appeared to be in her late teens. Huckleberry haircut self-inflicted. No makeup. In need of a shower and a bath, and another shower.

"Why?" she said.

"Why what?"

"Why you not think of it?"

"I—well, besides the blood on your jacket and pants—"

"I have no blood on pants. These are trousers. It is rude for you to speak about pants and I wish you to go away now, *spasiba*."

"I think we started this all wrong," I said.

The West End yacht cemetery reached inland from the marina to *as far as the eye could see* after the sweep of that last Cat 4 hurricane. Three weeks prior, this frontage boasted seafood restaurants, condos, shopping, parking lots and any number of major thru-roads. Now it resembled Poseidon's temper tantrum—a gumbo of yacht wrecks and dock planking, rooftops and construction debris, the air thick with the malignance of sun-rotten fish and toxic algae. I had come to this neighborhood at the request of a client who had lost his wife's beloved Shih Tzu in the storm. He was willing to pay the price of a new Mercedes if I found the animal, dead or alive. Back when the storm proved imminent, the dog had been abandoned, or so he believed, aboard an eighty-foot party yacht ironically named *Sundance.*

I had yet to find the *Sundance,* but I meandered along what used to be Lakeshore Parkway reading the yachtmen's stern wit—*Envy Me, Shag Master, The World Is Enough, Miami deVice, Disco Volante.* Then I noticed a tendril of smoke curling from beneath another millionaire's insurance write-off crashed to starboard. Being the conscientious citizen, I thought to snuff out what might be the beginnings of a blaze, but as I circled the hull of the *Flushed Buster,* I found this young *person* sitting on a bait box, cooking a can labeled "chili" over a bent and rusty barbecue grill. She jumped to her feet when she heard my approach.

"Don't eat the fish," I said. "They've been out in the sun too long."

"Is that joke?" she said.

"I was going to ask if you've seen a small dog, but now I'm wondering if you've eaten him."

"Why, because I am Russian?"

"Because of all the blood."

"*Nyet.* I do not eat dog."

I scanned the setting, wondering what to do with her.

"You are not going away, are you?" she said.

"I'm thinking about it. Can I ask if you are okay? Is the blood yours?"

"I am okay."

"So, you know my next question, right?"

"Are you police?" When I did not answer, she said, "He is in next boat. You are going to make trouble for me."

"How many days has he been dead? Two?"

"How do you—?" she looked down at her jacket. "*Da,* blood is dry. If three days, I would be gone. I get it." She examined me as well. "I could outrun you. You are skinny too, but you are too old."

I determined, nearing thirty, I probably looked old to her and, yes, she probably could outrun me. If I still carried a badge, I would be required to detain her, or attempt to. As it was, I gave her a wide berth and strolled to the next up-ended yacht, the *Out On Bond.*

I pulled myself over the metal railing and walked along the curve of the gunwale. I noticed the red spots before reaching the tilted cabin door.

Fumes kept me back. The interior glistened, half-filled with seawater. One shirtless denizen floated facedown, his tortured hide acrawl with miniature crustaceans. Basic cotton, pink-stained, woman's briefs floated beside him. A second man, fully naked, appeared to have been trapped beneath a foldout wall-bed, his torso submerged. The stench of human stew, considerably worse than the fish-strewn Parkway, helped my decision. I had no reason to check for life. Nine-one-one could do the dirty work.

Stowing the cell phone after my call, I followed the handrail around the deck, mindful not to touch, or step in, anything resembling evidence. I found what appeared to be claw marks in the thick teak varnish. Then I found the claw, an eight-inch fillet knife with blood baked to the blade and handle. Four feet farther along the boards, a bloody handprint and a bare footprint, possibly feminine. When I reached the spot where I had climbed aboard, I looked down at the girl looking up.

"Satisfied?" she said.

I lowered myself over the railing and dropped to the road. She stepped back reflexively.

"You called police," she said.

"Yes. Your friends inside have become a health hazard." To relax her, I occupied my hands by cleaning them with my handkerchief, and when I ran out of things to do, I stuffed them into my pockets. "We need to talk about this."

"Until police," she said.

"Until I know what went on here.

"I will not be touched." She turned her back to me, and I followed at a modest distance until she returned to her bait box stool and began, once again, on her can of chili. She spoke between bites. "When I hear sirens, I go. If you try to come close, I go. If you talk again about *pants*—"

"You'll go. I understand. So let's talk fast. You haven't been in this country long."

"Cargo boat. Five days from port when they find me hiding. The Captain, he was not bad. He give me job—"

"As much as I'd like to hear the full story one day, we'll need to shorten it before you hear sirens." To keep from appearing the Inquisitor, I let my gaze pick at the surrounding debris. A blanket draped evenly, drying over another yacht's railing. She had spent the night nearby, or intended to. "Let's talk about the boat next door with the dead bodies. What happened?"

"People hide from storm in a school. Many people close together, getting to know strangers. I do not like close people, so I sat away…apart. Some men sat apart, too. But we talked. They were nice. They ask me about my home country. I lied some. I did not want to make friends."

"You show good instincts," I said.

"*Da.* But not always. Still, everyone friendly. I talk with mothers and children. I say I am not staying long. I say I was going to Texas or California or something. The three men started talking about Hooston, in Texas. They said they have nice boat, and they can at least take me to Hooston. One man was young, *pretty,* and I make mistake. I let them take me to Hooston." She flinched as a rat skittered through trash.

"And the hurricane was delayed south of Cuba," I said.

"The men talk about storm with delay. If we leave soon, going west, we could outrun worst of storm before it makes Hooston. I said I do not like small boats. They promised me big boat. I could have cabin to myself."

"But the boat was not big."

"When I get here, I see boat and I say it is not big enough for four people. And young man grabbed me and dragged me. I screamed. I do not like being touched." She stood and threw the empty chili can into a pyramid of waste.

"I believe you." I walked wide around her, not looking directly at her, but I wanted to see her eyes as she talked.

"Second man, big man, has fishing knife on belt. He grabs me and two of them carry onto boat."

"What about the third man?"

"He is surprised. He argues them not to. When we are on deck, he pushed younger man. Then big man punched him down. They pulled me to cabin."

She poked a stick into the grill's embers. Nothing cooked there, a mindless task. Her eyes flicked to me and away, gauging my temperature. "When big man is taking trousers down," her head hung forward, but she tracked my attitude, "I grab his fish knife from his belt and cut him. I run out." She lifted her face, perhaps more assured of my intentions. "What is your name?"

"The third man had run off. You slipped on the deck and fell and you dropped the knife. But you came back here after the storm. Why?"

"I hide where there are no people. When storm passed, I see all boats crashed on the road and in trees. I think the men have ran away, or they are dead. Maybe I can find clean clothes or food to take with when I leave this misery city."

"My name is Nicolaus," I said.

"Like the Tsar."

"But spelled like the Greek. You haven't found clothing, obviously. But I now hear sirens."

"You will not try to stop me, Nicolaus?"

"I'm gambling. If you were a killer, you would not have said you could outrun me. And when I came out of that boat, you would not have been waiting. You'd be gone."

"I think you are pretty smart."

"If you see a small dog, his name is Bruno, or a yacht named Sundance, make another small fire for me. For now, I need to meet the police."

She saluted with her back to me. She left my sight by the time police cars skidded to a stop.

I gave the on-scene officer, Sgt. Pedersen, as much information as I could, which wasn't much, considering I didn't mention the girl. I gave him my card. He asked for other I.D. He was familiar with my name and profession, so I told him the truth, that I found the bodies while hunting for a missing Shih Tzu. He believed me, surprisingly. He asked me to stop by the precinct and fill out paperwork within twenty-four hours. I didn't wait around for his crew to carry off Laurel and Hardy, the cabin swimmers, so I continued my search for the Sundance.

The following morning, I returned to the West End for a leisurely drive-by hunt. I'd give it another day or two, then hire a P.I. firm I did business with on occasion. I hated this sort of grunt work. It reminded me of being a rookie on the force, but for what this client was willing to pay, I could sacrifice the percentage.

Aiming south, I angled as close to the waterfront as I thought practical. Floodwaters made it difficult to determine where a jetty ended and my drowning in a car began. Even the city clean-up crews and Coastguard were keeping a distance from the deeper destruction. The more experienced clean-up specialists, the criminal class, took better advantage of the chaos. They swarmed a bent tower of wrecked sailboats ready to strip ornaments, anchors, and the sails themselves, if only to decorate their respective caves. Trophy hunters. To the landward side of the road, a broken hull cruiser, aptly christened the *Gilligan,* had crushed a late model Corvette. On deck, two half-naked rough boys danced, one swinging a pirate's cutlass, and another defending with a stainless steel stanchion. But I wasn't one to interfere.

Two miles later I saw the smoke, a climbing wisp from the midst of more maritime destruction. I turned in at the party-yacht balanced atop a fast-food shack. There she was, *Sundance.* I took the cane from the car's rear seat and approached on foot.

My young friend sat at a round, concrete picnic table, feeding burger scraps to a small, raggedy dog who displayed remarkable patience beside the paper plate. He threatened me to keep my distance.

The girl glanced to verify it was me, then she returned to their lunch. Good to see she had cleaned up some. She had found bloodless clothes. Long cuffs of the men's dress shirt had been rolled for work, but she forgot to remove the price tag from the collar.

"Say *dobroye utro* to your Bruno," she said. "His name is on collar."

"I assume you cooked that meat?" I said.

"At least I am not eating dog." She rubbed Bruno's ears and checked my expression. "The power was on when I got here. Refrigerators work. Oh, and it should not be *breaking and entering* if palm tree is already breaking window. *Da?*"

"You've heard the phrase breaking and entering before. Your English is good," I said. "You learned it in Ireland or England?"

"My Papa did business with Irish. He made me to learn. How could you know?"

"In this country, *pants* are what we wear on the outside." I circumnavigated the table, contemplating the hamburger shack wearing a yacht. "We have other words for our underwear."

"Oh." She thought long on that. She followed my gaze. "I knew this boat name when you said it yesterday." She pointed to a business card laid on the second concrete bench. Bruno flaunted his teeth when I took it.

The card was white, soiled, but with a pencil scrawl: *"Sundance—slip 67."*

"When I meet him," she said, "pretty man says I should go to party. Meet him at this number. Then he and friends have other ideas. Now, his party is over. This number is gone, but I find boat up there one week ago. You carry a cane you do not lean on, Mr. Greek Nicolaus. You want to hit something?"

"I'm impressed you would climb up there looking for the dog."

"Dog was already down. He eats fish."

"The cane belongs to Bruno's owner. The dog likes chewing on it and he suggested that if the dog smells it, getting him into the car might be easier." I neared the table, intending to check Bruno's collar, but he bared his teeth again with an ugly noise.

"He does not like being touched either. Especially when eating."

"I see." I laid the cane on the table drawing Bruno like a magnet. I extended an open palm. He sniffed at a distance, still grumbling.

"Bruno's collar has small tracking thing," she said. "It does not work?"

"The storm left many service areas down. Or it may be he was hiding inside where the signal did not work." I had wondered about it. A wife so worried over losing her pet. A husband who made millions in the tech world. Chip implants were commonplace and inexpensive these days. "You know my name. What's yours?" I said. "You can lie if you like."

"Alya. It is real name."

We both heard the car before we saw it. It maneuvered around and between stacks of trash and broken boats, a black Mercedes I had seen before. Alya shot me an accusing look.

"I did not know they would be here," I said. "I don't like this either. Take Bruno. Stay back."

I took the cane and walked to the car as three men emerged. One was my client, or the husband of my client. Mateo Pérez, a thirty-year-old computer wizard with enough money to afford two large bodyguards and a four-million-dollar rooftop boat. Enough money to wear a three-piece suit to retrieve a Shih Tzu.

"I did not expect you." I offered a smile of greeting. "I would have called, naturally."

"You found her," Mateo said. "I knew I had made the right decision. Who's your friend? I would expect you'd like them older, but these days, who knows—"

"If you came here for the dog, I assume you brought payment," I said.

Bodyguard One held his hands behind his back. Bodyguard Two approached, extended a hand, and nodded for the cane.

"Let's see, how much was that reward?" Mateo said.

"Seventy-five thousand." I kept my eyes on Bodyguard Two. "You came up with the number, if you recall."

"You wouldn't have taken the job for less."

"I almost didn't take it anyway. I told you this is not my line, but I was softened by your wife's tears."

"Either way," Mateo said, "have your girlfriend bring the dog here. He looks more like a wharf rat than my Bruno. Max, get my checkbook from the car."

"We need to return to my office." I watched Bodyguard One lift the back of his jacket. "I have a nice bourbon there. You can sign the receipt and, like we agreed, *no checks*. A sharp young man like you should remember business details, Mr. Pérez."

Bodyguard Two came forward for the cane. I hooked it around his support ankle and pulled him off his feet. As he landed, I cracked him above the left ear, drew the Wesson from my belt, and Bodyguard One lifted his hands. At my direction, he lowered his Glock to the pavement. I pointed the Wesson at his employer.

"Now, that didn't go well, did it?" I heard Alya's steps behind me. "Girl, you don't take direction well. See what's going on here?"

"*Da*, I see. And I am not *girl*. I am adult," she said. "I was going to throw Bruno at him."

I tried not to turn and glare at her.

"Fuck the dog, fuck your bourbon, and fuck your money!" Mateo said. "If you had the cajones to shoot, you'd have done it by now."

I shot him beneath the collarbone.

He went down screaming. Bodyguard One waved his empty hands. Bodyguard Two choked on the cane pressing into his larynx. Bruno barked, and I heard Alya move away from me.

"You really think I believed you'd pay seventy-five grand for your wife's dog? Girl?" I didn't look to see if she'd run off. "You're safe. Do one more thing for me, please. My cell phone is in my right pocket. If you dial nine-one-one, I'll buy you a burger."

She snorted.

Alya disappeared before the arrival of police. With Mateo and his pals literally sitting on their hands, I sat on the concrete bench at the concrete picnic table with their handguns between my feet. Bruno gnawed on the end of the cane I held in my left hand. I still held the Wesson in my right.

Sgt. Pedersen arrived first, as he was only two miles up the coast revisiting the previous day's crime scene. Paramedics pulled in behind him. As he left his car, I laid my Wesson on the table and showed my empty hand.

"What the heck are you up to, Vagelle? Tell me this is related to yesterday."

"Remember the Shih Tzu I was looking for?" I tipped my head to Bruno.

"So, are these clowns connected to the cabin guppies up the road?"

"Sort of." I handed him the business card.

"I'm assuming you did not take evidence from the crime scene. The gun on the table is yours? And all the rest belongs to them."

"Correct."

"The one needing bandages, that was from you."

"Collateral damage."

"He'll probably have a lot of lawyers. Who's that? Miss!" he called. "Did you witness what went on here?"

"*Nyet!*" Alya waved from the door of the hamburger shack. "*Ja ne govoru pa Angliski!*"

"Russian?" he said. "We have a translator back at the station."

"*Nyet! Nyet! Litva!*" She began to panic.

"Lithuania?" I tried not to smile.

"We may have to call someone for that," Pedersen said.

"If you can stick around for a bit…" I said.

We waited for the EMTs to take the wounded millionaire to the ER. Two radio cars drove off with Bodyguards One & Two. I put Bruno in the backseat of my car and Pedersen walked beside me to the hamburger shack. Alya backed for distance.

"You sure you don't speak English?" Pedersen said. She played dumb.

"I don't think we'll need witnesses or lawyers." I pointed the cane to the yacht. We both stared upward for several seconds. "We just need to find a way up."

"How important is this?" he said.

Alya signaled for our attention and gestured to the yacht.

"*Da,*" I said.

She waved for us to follow, which we did, of course. At the back of the burger shack, a length of black wrought iron fence, that must have blown in from a fancier neighborhood, leaned like a ladder from pavement to gutter.

I indicated my thanks, but Alya turned and climbed like she had trained for the NOFD.

"Not sure how sturdy that boat is up there," Pedersen called. Alya jumped up and down in the stern of the yacht. "Sure, you no habla English!"

We followed up, one at a time. I began searching, and taking my cue, Pedersen followed suit. We tore open cupboards, closets, consols, and appliances. We turned over mattresses, searched medicine cabinets. I broke open food containers. I even checked scuba tanks and unscrewed the backs of televisions. Pedersen found a couple miniature baggies of white powder in the tip of a slipper.

"Your boy won't even get a traffic ticket for that." With the interior torn apart as much as we could, he said, "I'll send out a crew and have them rip up the floorboard, gunwales, and hull. If there's something on here, we'll find it."

We returned to the rear party deck. Alya lounged on red leather cushions that encircled an ugly Aztec-tiled dance floor. I sat, and Pedersen joined me.

"No accounting for taste." He must have noticed my expression. "You've worked with a friend of mine, Lt. Murphy. He's had good things to say about you."

"Should be a nice sunset from up here."

"So, okay, I get that your client is a sleazebag. What made you think he'd keep anything illegal onboard here?"

I turned the cane in my hands, a K-9 chewtoy with a gold band beneath the top hook. I felt the weight of it. Tapped it on the dance floor. After consideration, I unscrewed the hook. Within the shaft I found a notch, and from within the notch, I extracted a chip. I gave it to the Sergeant.

"And on this we're going to find incriminating evidence of what? Top-Secret government files? Illegal cash transactions?"

"More likely a GPS or simple locator chip," I said. "When he and *the lads* drove up almost immediately after I found the dog, I knew. Mateo gave me the stick, not to control Bruno, but to signal back to him. It doesn't take a tech genius to hollow out a cane and install a small battery and locator. Your lab will most likely find it corresponds to the tracker on the dog's collar. After the yacht was lost, even a weak electronic signal could be sent whenever someone—me, for instance—got the stick within proximity to that collar."

"That's some figurin', pardner." He turned the chip in his fingers.

"When *you* found dog. I like that." Alya's attention was elsewhere. She drummed her fingers impatiently.

"No habla English," Pedersen mumbled.

"It's why he told me to find the dog 'dead or alive.' He didn't give a damn about the animal. He said as much when he got here. They could not find the dog, or they forgot him with the storm bearing down, but he knew the dog was on the boat, and I was searching for his boat. This is what he needed to find. He needed it enough to go to a lot of trouble and money, no matter how wrecked it was by the hurricane."

"Might've been easier to hire you to look for his yacht. Well, maybe CSI can tear something out of this gal." He noticed Alya's shock. "No. Sorry, not you. We refer to ships and boats in the feminine. Like, *she's* a good sturdy craft."

Alya rose from the bench, head bowed. Then she entered the galley with certainty. I heard dishes and silverware, and she came back clutching a dinner knife, mischief in her eyes.

"Hang on, now!" Pedersen stood slowly.

"Your crew would have done this sooner or later," I said. "Watch her."

She held up a palm for us to keep our distance. Moving to the first bench along the gunwale, she slapped the red leather cushion. She kneeled, licked a finger, and dragged it along the base of the bench. She held the finger near enough to see the powder.

"Now, aren't you embarrassed?" I said, and Alya pierced the cushion with the dinner knife. And again. And her expression changed when all she found beneath the torn red leather was yellowed foam cushioning. She repeated with the next cushion, then turned to me confused. Pedersen turned to me confused.

I crossed to her, and my smile confused her more.

"You are very smart," I said. "Very close." I kneeled beside her and extended my hand for the knife. My fingers touched the floor tile face of an Aztec deity. Then, with the tip of the knife, I scratched respectfully at the protective glaze finish. Beyond the finish, a thin coat of wax gave way to the sculpture beneath— the dance floor deity carved in deep tiles of compressed cocaine.

Pedersen was on the phone before I stood up.

The following week, Alya delivered Bruno to Ms. Pérez, who was so thrilled to get her dirty animal, she asked the girl to wait, dispatched an employee to the bank, then handed the girl a gym bag containing the full cash reward. She would not post bail for her husband.

That evening, I opened the bag on my dining table.

"I took five dollars for slice of pizza," Alya said. "I never had slice of pizza."

I was so shocked Alya had returned with seventy-four thousand, nine hundred and ninety-five dollars cash, I gave her twenty percent commission, making the shock mutual. I called out for a large pizza delivery, then asked her if she wanted a job. She asked if I could help her open a bank account.

Six

A Sharp-Edged Seduction

Three a.m.

The scream ripped at the alley's blackest shadows, only to be swallowed by concrete and steel. But screams here were too common, and this one would go as unanswered as the rest.

By sunrise, a sticky summer heat rose from the pavement in what neighborhood kids referred to as "ground ghosts." Weather soothsayers had forecast the mercury rising upwards of a hundred and five, but this ward wore the nickname The Devil's Skillet like a blue ribbon. Fifteen city blocks of a geological low-spot bound by city on all sides, the heavy air would find no escape. It was the kind of heat that made babies cry. The kind that took the breath from an old man's lungs before he reached the fifth stair. The kind that started fistfights out of handshakes. That turned lazy sex into a violent argument.

"When the Himalayan peasant meets the he-bear in his pride, he shouts to scare the monster, who will often turn aside. But the she-bear thus accosted rends the peasant tooth and nail. For the female of the species is more deadly than the male…"

I knocked on the consultant's door. With no answer, I fished the bottom of my satchel for his latchkey to let myself in, but the door opened to my touch without turning the lock.

"Mister Vagelle? *Dobroye utro,*" I said to the silence.

Crossing to the dining table I laid the morning paper, the bakery bag of bulochki, and a manila envelope, yesterday's mail. I felt into the satchel for the Kipling I had borrowed; he knew I liked the poetry. Tucking stray hair behind my ear, I turned to the bookshelves, then turned to ice. I dropped the Kipling. Beyond the settee a young woman slumped beneath the open window, throat to lap a crimson mess.

My hands failed to muffle my cries as I fled the room. The floor rolled, and I sagged to my knees on the landing. As soon as I could steady these hands, I grabbed for my phone.

Mr. Hemmings, the landlord, and Dr. Maiwand, the second-floor tenant, heard and rushed up the stairs. The doctor comforted me as he could, and checked my pulse while Hemmings entered the apartment. When the landlord shrieked, Dr. Maiwand decided I would be okay.

"Alya—Wait here!" He hurried inside. I would not have followed anyway.

Police drove me to their station where a tired-looking sergeant wrinkled a lip and led to the interview room. A female officer brought a bottle of water. She closed the door, and sat with us while I answered questions, mostly concerning my boss. Two hours later, a feverish noon sky greeted my release and sapped any remaining energy without mercy.

Mr. Vagelle's phone went straight to the automated, "mailbox is full," and I texted several times without response. He should be easy to find, but not until evening. I returned to my apartment, showered, and flopped naked across the sheets to cool off. Sleep came to me in fits.

I woke, dressed, ate an early slice of dinner at Nero's Pizza, then I headed into the *Skillet* and Bobby J's Black & Blues Club.

I checked my watch as I entered. The giant proprietor, Bobby J., broke my mood with a full-faced smile and called from behind his bar.

"A bit early, Ms. K., but you can take a seat at his booth. I got a White Zin with your name on it." He held up a bottle he kept for my rare appearances, but I waved him off.

"No, thank you, Bobby. *Spasiba.* I am not sure I can stay. And my stomach is not happy with dinner. Maybe a sparkling water?"

"Nero's greasy pizza again?"

I moved to the curved booth in the club's far corner, the one Bobby reserved for my boss. No matter how crowded his place got, even on the four nights a week Mr. Vagelle did not come in, no one else sat at this booth.

Art posters of famous Jazz and Blues musicians decorated the century-old room along with signed, black-and-white publicity shots and framed LP covers. A wide variety of dusty, dented, or just well-abused band instruments added the color of precious metals to dark timber walls. Behind the bar, the exposed bricks supported a shrine to Charlie Parker. Bobby had once given me a record, so I might better appreciate his passion. I confessed I did not own a turntable, and that December I found one at the office, paper-wrapped in Christmas horns and holly.

By nine-fifteen, the bar filled with a growing chatter. The half-moon of scuffed tile and parquet along the far wall spawned a maneuvering of lights, microphone-stands, and speakers, around the more permanent piano. A piano scarred as if it had marched through the frontlines of a Cossack uprising.

"Yo, Bobby!" I heard. "Why that white boy gets his own table here night after night and some-a us gotta stand leanin' on your bar?"

"Because none' your business, that's why," Bobby said, bending his nearly seven-foot structure to within inches of the spindly man. "Now, Chuckles, you gonna have another Bud Light, or do I clear your space at the bar?"

Chuckles slapped another bill on the bar top to show he was not intimidated, but he turned his back and pretended to watch the band set up.

"Good evening, Mister V.," Bobby called. He poured a tumbler of Widow Jane as my boss approached. "You have a visitor." His head tipped my way, and he called for Sandra June.

The other bartender, the pretty one, picked up the bourbon and my second sparkling water. She hurried to the booth as I moved to the opposite side, allowing Mr. Vagelle sightline to the door. The night's mist sparkled on his short hair, adding to the illusion of snowdust. He moved steady and somber. His cane, which he seldom carried, lent support while he lowered to the bench. I took the hand-off of drinks from Sandra with thanks.

"He can't very well carry two glasses and that silly cane, now can he?" She winked. Her dark skin and makeup failed to hide a bruised eye. "Mr. V? If you don't mind, I have something—"

"And I need to talk with you, Sandra, but later, before we leave. I promise." He took her hand and whispered something I could not hear. As she wandered back to the bar, she checked her hand.

"Alya," he said. "Glad to hear they didn't keep you long."

"A detective told me not to worry," I said. "A Medical Examiner said she died before two this morning, and the bakery confirmed that I had bought pastries after eight. Actually, he said I was never a suspect. You were."

"Still, I wish you didn't have to see that." He avoided my eyes.

"I will not ask if you killed her."

"Good." He raised the tumbler, inhaled the aroma, then returned it to the table rings.

"I don't get it," Chuckles said loud enough for us to hear. "White man comes in three times a week, I ain't never seen him pay for a drink. He blackmailin' you?"

I watched their reflections in the poster glass above Mr. Vagelle's shoulder.

"You know that fireplug out front?" Bobby J. leaned in, forcing Chuckles to look up. "You need to go ask it all them questions as they pop into your head."

"What?"

"It wasn't a request."

The guitar player tuned his strings and crowd chatter eased somewhat. I sipped my water and watched the spindly silhouette in the poster glass walk off beneath the exit sign.

"That man worries me," I said.

"Jimmy *Chuckles?* I've never seen him when he wasn't complaining about something. I expect one day my friend Bobby will bounce his big fist off Jimmy's head and regret it when the little man never wakes up."

"*Nyet.* Not him. The man at the end of the bar wearing a leather jacket in forty-degrees Celsius. He keeps looking at you."

"Another regular, or should I say his boss is. The man at the table with three ladies and wearing more gold in his teeth than a Bulgari storefront. That's Joe Douglas. A wannabe high-roller but a low-level pimp. *Leather jacket* is his favorite bodyguard and drug supplier. He's also Joe's former cellmate, Dennis Wills."

"Okay." I swirled my glass to watch the bubbles. I watched Sandra towel a table while new customers stood at the ready. I watched my boss. "I understand I am only working for you for two years…" Surrounding noise distracted me, forcing me to concentrate on my English lessons. "You know me well, but do you trust me well?"

"You still have the key to my door," he said.

"I do."

"I gave it to you when we first met."

"*Da*. Okay, stupid question."

The singer came from the backroom to join the band. Not quite as heavy as Bobby J., but then, she was only half as tall. Carley Dame was no cartoon Blues singer in a sequined dress pinching a twenty-two inch waist. She must have hired two women to squeeze her into the razor-cut jeans before throwing on the "wife-beater" shirt that Brando could have worn as a dress. Her eyelash extensions lowered as her fingers made love to the microphone.

"Will you ever tell me what happened in your apartment last night?" I said.

"I will." He touched the bourbon to his lips without swallowing. Ritual.

Piano, drums, bass, and an eight-fingered guitar player they called "Thumbs." A sizeable band for a modest tavern, but whenever Carley began to sing about *The Sky Crying*, I understood why my boss liked the place.

Others came in off the street and crowded the corners. If New Orleans had Fire Department regulations, I would never know it. Sandra June handled the crowd with the skill of a preschool wrangler.

Mr. Vagelle studied the room, more brooding than his usual. He filled the gaps between songs by describing other patrons. A retired police chief, already in his cups, mumbling to an empty bottle. A table of realtors relaxing after their long day, one he suspected of wire fraud and bribery. A slumlord politician out with his wife. A barber with eyes that made me think of Sweeney Todd.

My stomach still teetered a bit from this morning.

Carley's first set neared its finish, a smooth blend from Etta James to Nina Simone, and she rose from the pianist's bench. Thumbs took serious interest whenever she flirted with the piano player, or bass player, or drummer. She enjoyed spreading the love to everyone but Thumbs.

Mr. Vagelle tapped the table. "Sorry, I need you to make room on that side of the bench."

I followed his gaze to the door, and the woman entering. As sturdy as a Volgograd statue, she wore a gray pants suit, her jacket over her arm, and a black, all-business, blouse. Dull-brown, collar-length hair pinched by a plain rubberband. Some hairs had escaped, indicating a long workday not yet ended.

"She looks like a party. Should I leave you two alone?" I said.

Sandra June met her, handed her something I could not see, and a number of men followed her to our booth with their eyes. She sat across from us without prompting. Up close, delicate age cracks betrayed her former beauty. Mr. Vagelle introduced her as Patricia Gunston, of the Gunston Detective Agency.

"We have spoken on the phone," I said.

"I'm just a glorified office clerk and full-time bookkeeper," she said, and smiled for Sandra June as a bottle of Parish Beer appeared before her.

"Hardly that," Mr. Vagelle said. "You seem to be managing your detectives and caseloads well enough on your own. How's your brother? You still sending cigarettes up to Dixon Correctional?"

"Keeps his roommate off his back, literally. Truth be told, I'd been running day-to-day ops for years while Mack was learning how to defraud our clients and the company."

I wondered if Mr. Vagelle had put her brother away, and if I should slip my hand into my satchel for the snubnose.

"Don't worry, dear. Your boss got my brother convicted, but I'm the one who hired him. How you holding up? It must've been tough walking in on that horror show this morning."

"Still a bit shaky, if I am honest," I said.

"So, Patty," Mr. Vagelle said, "do you have anything for me?"

"So far, the boys haven't come up with much. A rumor that Joey D. tried to recruit the girl when she showed up eighteen months ago, but no evidence linking the two. Besides, he's been holed up with *his ladies* the past few days out at Residence Inn. A blow-party for four."

"Celebrating a recent windfall?"

"No doubt. Not much on his bodyguard either, but I can't see him having a beef with your girl. She danced for a short time at the Belly-Up, but she wasn't *horizontal refreshment*, as they say. No drugs connection, no record with vice."

"So, you were able to confirm her I.D. for me." His eyes were on the room, but as he once said to me, *I don't hear with my eyes.*

"Laurel Smith, at least that's what her fake driver's license says. Confirmed by the manager at the Belly-Up once I described her tattoo."

"A small, black, double-heart tattoo below the right ear," he said for my benefit.

"The cops, they aren't ready to share everything with a lowly P-I. Also, rumor has it, she played for the other team, and Joey D. can't make money with that." Patty raised an eyebrow for me.

"But it's just rumor," Mr. Vagelle said. "I'm sure you checked on Joey's competition, at least here in the Skillet. Do you happen to know of any legitimate love interests for Laurel?"

"Nothing. More hearsay. She may have once shared a flat with a certain Blues singer." Patty nodded toward the stage. "That's where the previous rumor comes from, but she's been living alone for the last six months in the French Quarter. She's a—*was* a lonely gal."

"Excuse me," I said. "How much do you know about our waitress here? I noticed a pretty fresh black-eye under her makeup."

"Assume it's unrelated," Mr. Vagelle said. "Sandra June is a fighter, Mixed Martial Arts, and fairly proficient from what her father tells me. Last night was her dojo night."

"But a good question," Patty said. "Look me up if your boss ever shows you the door." She slid a business card my way.

"Anything else to the business at hand?" Mr. Vagelle said.

"There might be a sibling in the picture somewhere. But the girl was un-officially orphaned very young."

"I need to know how you came by this information."

"Investigators found several letters in the dead girl's apartment. No envelopes. That would be too easy, right? And the contents pointed to a familial relationship. Oh, one more thing. As of this morning, you're still chief suspect with Detective Pedersen."

His tovarisch (comrade), I thought.

Mr. Vagelle took his first real sip of the bourbon. Something in the timing made me think on it. Patty downed her beer and stood. She opened her wallet, but Mr. Vagelle waved her off.

"I've got it, Pat. You're still on retainer."

"You'll hear something when I hear something." She tipped a smile at me before pivoting away. It felt like a goodbye she had seen in a movie.

The music started again with *Misty Blue.* Perfect timing. Carley re-emerged from the back with a blown kiss for piano man, followed by an obvious glance for Thumbs' reaction on her way to the mic stand.

Mid-way through the second set, a bone-thin blonde drifted in from the street. Her hair had not seen a brush this year. She swerved, ruffled the crew cut of the retired policeman as she passed, but continued to the *high-roller's* table where she fell onto the lap of Joey D.'s purple-haired lady-friend. Purple-hair did not know how to react without first checking with the gangster, but he ignored her.

Mr. Vagelle's eyes stayed with the singer, but flicked to the bodyguard twice.

Before long, purple-hair grew impatient and shoved Blondie to the floor. Blondie squealed, tried to rise, but got slapped back down. Wills hopped off his bar stool, but Joey D. had already grabbed purple-hair's arm and spun her back into the chair.

Then Bobby J. materialized.

"You said you wouldn't bring this shit in here," he said. "If you can't control your girls, take it on home."

Wills tried to position himself between his boss and Bobby J., but the big man backed him down. Eventually, Joey D. made a drama of marching his carnival out the door.

"Don't need this punk-ass shit—I bring a lot of money to this—I can make it so's the money stays outside, mother…"

Wills grabbed Blondie and steered her through the crowd following his boss's crew. Bobby J. returned to his bartop and Charlie Parker. The singer kept singing.

"I know your streak of dangerous curiosity," Mr. Vagelle said, "but you need to give that crowd a wide berth."

On cue, the old cop pushed up with a loud screech of chair legs on tile. He followed unsteadily to the street.

"Come have another drink, Mack," Bobby J. called. "On the house."

Either Mack did not hear, or he was suddenly no longer thirsty.

"Old cops die when they can't give up the job." Mr. Vagelle lowered his eyes to the rolling amber in his glass.

A long day. I had grown too weary for the music despite the fun floor show. Near midnight, I made my way to the ladies' room. The afternoon nap had done little for my nerves, and I shrugged off my worn reflection in the mirror before entering the last stall.

I was not there long when the music beyond the walls came to another break, followed by applause. The door opened and wooden heels clacked into the restroom. Through the quarter-inch crack along the stall door I could see our entertainer inspecting her reflection longer than I had been able. Unsuccessful in her attempts to reset falling eyelashes, she cursed repeatedly, hung onto the sink bowl, paced in a tight circle, then tried again.

The door banged open and she jerked upright in response.

"What the hell you doing in here? Get out! Now!" She moved out of view, but I heard the slap and she reeled back.

"You disgust me!" A man's voice. Then the door slammed.

I emerged from the stall, concerned and sympathetic, while Carley held a bloody tissue to her nose.

"Are you okay?" I said. "Who was that?"

She spun, shocked by my presence, her eyes simmering.

"Who the fuck are you?" She spit blood at the sink. "You spying on me? Hidin' in the shitter? Damn you! Damn all of you!" Ripping free the rebellious lash extensions, she hurled them into the sink and stomped from the room. The slam might have unhinged a weaker door.

Eventually, I returned to the table where Sandra June sat across from my boss, tying her straw into knots, her anxiety poorly masked.

"We'd only met—We met two months ago," she said. "We were strangers, but I knew her as if—" She noticed my arrival.

"And she felt much the same," he said. "She explained about your relationship, hoping I could tell her all the things she wanted to know about you. I'm sorry she left without answers."

"I can't understand. Why does something like this happen? How?"

"I'll try to help you find out, but I need you to do something for me. Say nothing about her to your father. Not yet."

Her eyes went to Bobby J.

"It would only confuse him. And I need space to find the answers for both of you."

She pushed up and checked my expression, but I had nothing for her. She threw her towel at the bar on her way to the door. Seemed everyone was throwing something tonight.

Bobby J. scowled.

Mr. Vagelle had called a cab while I was in the ladies' room, now he walked me to the curb and climbed in after me.

"Tonight I'll see you to your door. Too much volatility, even for this neighborhood."

Police lights threw colors across the windshield, no sirens, and *my escort* turned his face away as they passed. They slid against the same curb we had left behind.

"Searching for me, of course," he said. "Pedersen knows more than a few of my habits."

"Oh, and here I thought you were being Mr. Gallant."

As I stood on the curb in front of my building, he insisted I take a week off. "My home will be yellow-taped. And as indomitable as you believe you are, you need to put this morning behind you. Rest. If you need to talk anything through, please call me."

"Good night, Nicolaus."

No sleep. I lay atop warm sheets in my standard summer PJs, which amounted to the long t-shirt and men's boxers abandoned by a former friend who thought he would spend the night. A memory less comfortable than his clothes. Most nights I could put myself to sleep by watching the city lights glide across my ceiling, but this night *Mr. Brain* refused to shut down his internal slide show. Too much blood, shocking and unexpected, reminded me of distant things.

Mr. Vagelle had not helped, being out of character all evening and too concerned for my safety. Not that he was normally uncaring, just the opposite. But then I had never seen him too close to anyone. Whenever I thought I had him figured out, his mask would slip and confuse me, so I stopped trying.

Bobby J. understood much of Mr. Vagelle's moods. Theirs was a deep history. My boss could come into the club any night expecting solitude, a soft bourbon, and softer Blues. He once said the combination massaged his thoughts and muffled the external chaos, but his few close friends understood the meanings ran deeper. I was not that close yet.

Tonight, habits were altered. *Too much turbulence from every corner. Blame it on the heat. Blame it on the dead woman in his apartment. Blame it on blood.*

He controlled his body language well, but I have studied him. His mannerisms shifted slightly when Patty P.I. entered the bar. Then he chose to share my taxi ride. He knew I could take care of myself. I had witnessed enough evil in my life—enough to keep the snubnose in my purse and the mini-Mossberg on my nightstand. I understood I was just his sort of employee, someone he need not worry over. At least not too much.

No sleep tonight. An hour before sunrise, my stomach complained again.

A minor benefit to living in the heart of the city, with all the lights outside my windows, I was used to prowling the apartment without turning on a lamp. At the rear of the refrigerator, I found a lonely cup of yogurt. I spooned the first of it when I heard the slow turn of my doorknob. My brain raced ahead—

The snubnose in my purse on the sofa—too far. My Mossberg on the nightstand—even farther. I grabbed for the knife rack—my only option—and I lowered myself into a corner at the sound of the doorjamb splitting.

My immediate thought was, *he'll head for the bedroom first.* I was right.

Soft boots turned away and I peeked from my bunker in time to see his back round that corner. Without pause, I sprinted for the open stairway. But my knees had grown stiff from crouching. I was two seconds too slow. He heard me.

I made the threshold as he latched onto my baggy shirt and flung me back into the room, kitchen knife continuing into the hall without me. My ribs slammed across the end table. The lightbulb popped as the lamp hit the floor. He grabbed my hair, and I grabbed my hair as he dragged me, suffering, to my knees. My vision swam with the sudden pain.

"Where is it? What did she leave?" His voice dragged along a sandpaper throat. A voice like my Papa. But not Papa. "I know who you work for. I know she gave him something. I want it."

Even if I could speak, I had no answers. I pushed my knees across hardwood and glass fragments to keep up with his pull toward the bedroom.

The night splintered as he howled like a coyote in a bear trap. I dropped. My head struck something, and the sound chased me back to the time with my Papa hunting roe deer in Kurgan. *And the coyote's screams of pain. And Papa telling me I should put the animal out of misery. I begged him to never take me hunting again. I begged his look of disappointment just before he pulled the trigger.*

Teary-eyed, I could barely see enough to understand there was a third person in the room. A long stick thrust from the moving shadow. Another hard grunt from my attacker and I realized the stick was a cane, and that cane had produced a blade. The blade sliced beneath my attacker's arm.

Mr. Vagelle's cane.

The villain recoiled, startled by the sting.

I scrambled on hands and knees to the bedside as my rescuer's next swing of the cane drew a deep line across the man's jaw. I fired the Mossberg but missed everyone. The bang stunned my rescuer for just a breath, but long enough for the attacker to lunge, bulling him into the door's edge. He raced past, out of the room, and down the stairs.

Mr. Vagelle grabbed me. Instinct.

"I am okay! Get him!" I failed to quiet a moan, as misery chewed at every nerve.

"Shush." He backed off and stood long enough to flip the light switch and return. "You are the priority." He slid a pillow under my head, then phoned emergency.

His neighbor, Dr. Maiwand, looking like he had dressed in a hurry, arrived moments after the ambulance. His shirt hung crooked; he had missed a buttonhole. But he was sharp-eyed and attentive as the Med Techs checked my vitals and asked questions about my health and my pains. I cringed with every touch. They looked confused.

"It's not physical," Dr. Maiwand whispered. "It's a mild haphephobia."

"I'm sorry," Mr. Vagelle said. "I had to tell our neighbor. You understand."

I nodded.

"I would accompany you to the hospital but—Our doctor friend will be my stand-in. He knows much of our situation. He also knows the Emergency Room staff by sight, and Ms. Gunston will meet you both there. They will not leave your side."

EMTs lowered me onto the gurney.

"How are you here?" I said. "You were outside my apartment all night?"

"I suspected, but didn't know what. With Laurel dead in my apartment, the killer had to return to find out what she'd told me. When he couldn't find me, I guessed he might come to you for answers. I should've stayed closer."

"I will be fine."

"I'm sorry."

"I have been slapped before."

"I need to get you a shooting instructor."

A small laugh, and my side felt the electric jolt of it.

"Okay," the Med Tech said. "We need to get her to the ER. She may have a cracked rib, at least."

Mr. Vagelle stayed with me down the stairs.

"Officer Pedersen," he said. "A few moments, please, before you arrest me. I need to see Ms. Korikova safely away."

"You ain't under arrest," Pedersen said. "Your pal, Bobby, and others, alibied you at the club for the last two nights. But we need you to answer a shitload of questions, so you will be coming with us for a bit."

"The up-side to your nightclub habit," I said, and tried not to laugh again.

Mr. Vagelle touched my hand, then quickly withdrew. He nodded to Dr. Maiwand, who climbed into the van beside the Med Tech. The doors closed. Then the sedative put me to sleep. Thankfully.

Daylight streaming through hospital blinds, I became aware of voices and a tall white coat alongside Dr. Maiwand.

"We're awaiting test results," white coat said. "You do have two cracked ribs, but hairline. Nothing dangerous, if you take care. We took glass shards out of your right knee. Did you fall on a lightbulb?"

I nodded.

He had ordered a full-body scan and blood tests, but did not expect to find anything too serious.

"We think that returning to your apartment might not be wise at this point, yes?" Dr. Maiwand said. "Vagelle will be in touch but, if you don't have an alternative, he asked Sandra June if she wouldn't mind putting you up for a few days. Just while you recover, and he's looking into our problem."

Patty P.I. stood in the doorway with—*the bartender? Was that Sandra June?*

"It's really no imposition," Sandra said. "I have plenty of room." And before I could object, "I would offer even if your boss had not already paid me."

"You'll be in good hands," Patty said. "Trust Nicolaus."

"Well, I guess it has been decided for me," I said.

By late afternoon, I had substituted the crowded hospital room for Sandra June's crowded apartment in the city Skillet. She cleared her things from the bedroom and insisted on taking the pull-out sofa bed in the living room. Patty P.I. had picked up necessities from my apartment, and she and Dr. Maiwand helped move me in.

"The police still hold your bedroom handgun as evidence," Patty said. "But I notice you have another in your purse. Good for you."

"And I'll be here," Sandra June said. "Dad gave me time off work."

I argued that I could survive without a twenty-four-hour bodyguard, but she stood her ground and the medications kept me from debating.

I slept off and on until mid-morning the next day, and a knock on the apartment door. Voices urged me to pop a light pain pill and struggle out of bed and into my clothes. In the living room, Dr. Maiwand and Patty had been met by Mr. Vagelle.

"I'm told you'll be okay." He led me to the sofa.

"Pain is manageable, thank you. Sandra is great."

"I've known her a long time. Ms. Gunston, did you mail that package for me?"

"This morning," Patty said.

"It's been a complicated twenty-four hours. The rest of you probably haven't heard, but there's been another knife attack. Carley Dame was admitted to the ER early this morning."

Sandra June covered her mouth in horror.

"My God! What's happening?" Patty said.

I thought to describe my run-in with the singer after her assault in the ladies' room. I mentioned the guitar player's obvious frustration as Carley flirted with everyone but him.

"That's a mistake," Sandra said. "The flirting, it's all part of her act. Thumbs has problems with her. Everyone around her knows her temperament, but it's nothing to kill over."

"There is another connection," Patty said. "Carley had befriended Laurel, the first victim."

"According to Detective Pedersen, it was possibly the same weapon in both attacks." Mr. Vagelle turned to the fridge, then brought me a sparkling water.

"Last night, I could not answer his questions," I said. "But he knew I worked for you. He is searching for something, but does not know what it is."

"He failed with you. He must have learned about Laurel's earlier friendship with the singer, but he failed with her as well. She'll live. But I fear he may work his way through her entire address book."

"How is he getting all this information?" Patty said. "It took my three investigators—"

"The person behind him knew her better than anyone in this city. Maybe better than Sandra." He crossed to the window. He once taught me, *When the questions are as difficult to come by as answers, focus on the unrelated object. You will be surprised what your peripheral vision picks up.*

"But I met her for the first time two months ago." Sandra's eyes glistened.

"Yes, but you have known her for several years." His voice was gentle, but the words pointed. "She kept many of your letters with her when she moved here from Atlanta. You were the reason she came. She wanted to meet her big sister."

"Okay, but—is that why he murdered her?"

"Indirectly. But more accurately, she left Atlanta in a hurry without telling anyone why she was leaving. She changed her name because she didn't want to be found. It all left the wrong impression with the one she left behind. A wealthy, corrupt man who assumed she took the proofs of his corruption with her."

"With what intention?" Patty said. "Blackmail? He hired his assassin to retrieve whatever he *assumed* she had taken?"

"Then Laurel's second big mistake was coming to you," I said. "The killer saw her visiting a consultant."

"She first came to me suspecting she had a stalker," he said. "Her ex-. She mailed evidence to me for safekeeping, making me promise not to open it unless something bad happened."

"The manila envelope I left on your table that next morning," I said.

"When she returned two nights ago, I can only assume she was running from him. I don't know how they got into the building without Hemmings or a front door key, but he caught her on the stairs, dragged her inside and finished her. I wish I'd been home. Pedersen doesn't yet know what he's holding. To him, it's just more crime scene evidence in a baggie."

"But you have to tell him what you know," Dr. Maiwand said. "You can't let the man get away with this."

"He will get away with nothing, doctor." Before he could turn his back to the room, I recognized an ancient darkness overtaking him. "Naming him to the police today will do nothing to stop the assassin from moving forward. The package points back to the man who ordered the murder of that beautiful young lady. She came to me for rescue. And now he is responsible for the attack on my—on Alya. I will make him regret he did not kill me first."

"So, the envelope you had me mail was to this person?" Patty said. "The man behind the killer? You are baiting him, am I right?"

"When he comes for me, he will stop looking for others to kill." Mr. Vagelle walked out before I could respond.

Dr. Maiwand dropped by several times to change my bandages, or just check on my recovery. The painkillers made his touch bearable. Patty visited once a day. Sandra used the opportunity to take some air, run errands, pick up groceries. Claustrophobia is not one of my problems, but I felt increasingly trapped by my fear of missing word from Mr. Vagelle.

Chuckles carried a long-standing resentment for him, but he loved easy money in exchange for information. My boss knew how to use him. Between visits from friends, I learned more of these relationships. Pieces began stitching together with what I already knew.

Chuckles was not just the local clown. He had survived for years because the grapevine understood, as long as he did not bite the wrong hand, he could always be tapped for the latest rumor. Chuckles would be in the loop if an outside contractor came to town spreading word, offering cash for information on the whereabouts of a young lady with a double heart tattoo below her ear. He never saw the tattoo himself, or Laurel up close, but after she was killed he knew who received the big payout.

Patty said Joe Douglas failed to recruit Lauren when she started working at the Belly-Up. He had seen her up-close. Patty also mentioned Douglas holed-up in a motel the day after the killing, partying with his ladies after a "possible financial windfall."

Chuckles kept close tabs whenever new money changed hands in his neighborhood. Douglas was an ambitious thug and, just like the Russian *Bratva,* gangs here had no respect for a snitch, but he also understood their usefulness.

If the young lady was worth a contract killing, there must be someone powerful behind it. Mr. Vagelle told me, during our taxi ride from the club, he made sure Chuckles was within earshot when he let it slip that power and influence might be gained for "a well-performing gangster, provided he could prove himself valuable." Even I knew where Chuckles would take those words.

I touched for the pain beneath my breast. Two weeks was too long. I felt well enough to leave the apartment, as long as I wrapped my ribs tight and avoided wrestling bears. Of course, I had not fully healed, and Mr. Vagelle liked to warn me of my *dangerous curiosity.*

Following a lengthy phone debate, and a little fib to end it, Bobby J. told me where I might find one of Wills's lady friends. The one I thought might be on the outs with her clique.

I found her sleeping face-down on a bartop. She made a passable show of consciousness when I bought her a tall drink and let her see I had more in my wallet.

"Joey's been okay by me," she said. "Almost never beats his girls, long's they stay in line. Now, Wills, he's different. He even likes his good times rough—Sorry, I can't say more."

"No worries. I hope I never get the chance to talk with him."

"So why'd you wanna to talk with me? You said something about that one got her throat cut?"

"Actually, I am just looking for my boss. He went missing and he owes me a paycheck. I need to know if I am out of a job."

"Ain't it the same ol' story. Pro'bly holed up with a piece of perfumed uptown-go-down."

"I heard about some out-of-town *bad guy* going around cutting on a few of you girls. You hear anything about that from your Joey?"

She hesitated, most likely wondering if I had already asked too many questions.

"Might be. Last I heard 'bout some out-o'-towner, Joey's throwing a get-together for him with the girls on the riverboat *Laveau*. A late-night deal. Hey, that's tonight! He rented the whole casino boat just for us. Some high-level muckety-muck. Should be a real kick. You wanna come?"

Of course, she had no details, but I suspected what Joey's game would be. In all his ignorant ambition, he had invited a hitman to a party. He would tell Mr. Hitman that what he knew about life was extremely valuable to his employer. The killer would understand only one option, and it would not be a bonus for Joey D.

A valuable lesson growing up with my Papa. "*Zatknis* (Shut up)—and keep head down."

Unfortunately, my new drunken friend gave me a two a.m. time for the show. I had no idea what I could do about any of it. Maybe pull a fire alarm and tiptoe away, but the show ended long before I got there.

I witnessed the assassin's speedy exit, but the locks to the riverboat moorings had been broken, possibly as a failsafe to his getaway. I stood open-mouthed as the floating casino edged away from the dock, heading for innocent bystanders on the water.

An out of place sound—shoeleather slapping the wet dock—then a tall figure sprinted from the shadows. He raced for the gangway, passing under a sodium lamp. Then I recognized him. My boss.

He launched himself from the dock's edge as I never thought possible for the man who carried a cane. He came down on the boat, but something went wrong. His leg buckled under. I watched as he struggled to rise. But he pushed forward, limping towards the bridge deck.

Helpless. Nothing I could do but call Harbor Police.

As a taxi carried me toward my temporary home with Sandra, frustrations blinded me. Mr. Vagelle had taken the noble action. He gave up pursuit of the killer for the second time. This time in order to save innocent boaters' lives.

Again, I could not go back to sit idle on Sandra's sofa. I relived the night the assassin broke into my rooms and assaulted me. I asked myself what Mr. Vagelle would do next. And before we turned the final corner, I understood. I knew the killer's next stop. He would expect the *consultant* to be home.

This time, I was there when he walked in.

I left a light on and the door open and I stood beside the ottoman in the middle of the room with my snubnose pressed along my thigh. Naturally, he needed Lauren's thumb drive before he could kill me.

"Is it here?" he said.

I nodded.

"I will get it from you. I have a knack for getting answers from hard-ass women."

"You abducted a young fifty-kilogram woman. You beat her, and she still got away from you and came here for a second time. You need to rethink your sales pitch, *Mr. Hitman.*"

After the night he had, and his previous failed attacks, he had wound too tight. His eyes said everything, and my taunts popped his spring. He charged like a bull. Like I knew he would. Like he had charged Mr. Vagelle in my apartment. I simply side-stepped, kicking the ottoman in front of his shins.

"But the she-bear thus accosted..." It ended quickly after that.

Sandra June was good company, though she fought severe bouts of depression over the loss of her newfound sister. Anger resurfaced if we lingered too long on it, so I avoided the topic as I could.

Detective Pedersen and Patty P.I. met us in the hospital corridor. I expected bad news.

"Between you and him," Pedersen said, "they should put a new orthopedic wing on the hospital."

"Is Mr. Vagelle okay?" I held my newly bandaged ribs out of habit now.

Two uniforms rounded the corner. A Sgt. Russo grinned for me, and called Pedersen aside. While Patty asked about my healing, I overheard the sergeant, "Right about now your men are pulling Jimmy Chuckles out of the harbor." Pedersen stiffened, and whispered something that sent the patrolmen away.

"Is Mr. Vagelle—?"

"I'm told he managed to get the riverboat under control," Pedersen said. "He prevented a catastrophe. Harbor police quickly took over, but they found a bad scene. Looked like a gang shooting. Ms. Gunston tells me you're familiar with those punks, Joe Douglas and Denny Wills. We found their bodies lying across a craps table."

"How are the ribs?" Dr. Maiwand said as he passed the nurses' stand. I wished everyone would stop asking. He led us to Mr. Vagelle's room. He motioned as if to pat my shoulder, but stopped short. "Your boss will be fine. He will need that cane of his for a time. He just had a pin put into a cracked ankle."

Seeing Nicolaus in the hospital bed, attached to tubes and machines, shortened my breath.

"Is he dead?" were the first words out of the detective. "I mean the killer."

"Hello. I am awake, thank you," Mr. Vagelle said.

"Dr. Maiwand said you are okay." I touched his arm, then pretended to check his IV instead.

He watched me, then said, "I made two miscalculations."

"I heard that word before."

"The first was, I *also* got the wrong time for the party. How are the ribs?"

"Also? You mean you knew I was there?"

"They told me after, but I could've bet that you would be. My second miscalculation was that I never expected Chuckles had the nerve to sneak aboard the riverboat. I suspect he was the first one killed and thrown overboard. I regret that."

"But you are okay," I mumbled.

"Can you tell me what was in the envelope you asked me to mail to Atlanta?" Patty said.

"There were two small items in the manila envelope Lauren had sent me. One, the thumb drive, incriminating files she had lifted from her boyfriend's laptop. The District Attorney. The other was a campaign button for the upcoming governor's election. She'd sent it to identify him in the event of her death. In your envelope, I placed a copy of the thumb drive along with the button for proof that I was Lauren's confidant. And I included a brief note on my personal letterhead."

"I have your files. You'll be hearing from me," Patty said.

"Something like that."

"You made sure you became his top priority," I said. "But his assassin put his own priority first, after Douglas's party invitation."

"Damn-it, is he dead?" Pedersen said again.

Throughout the discussion, Sandra June may have been listening, but I believed her inner monologue spoke louder. She attempted to hide her growing anger, but I imagined what she held inside. After all, I never had a sister.

An *anonymous caller* tipped the police on where to find Horace Greenwald, a.k.a. "the assassin," wrapped ankles-to-head in silver duct tape and dropped in a dumpster. Also taped to his chest was the knife used to kill Lauren and Jimmy "Chuckles," and wound the Blues singer, Carley Dame. His arms were taped around a bent brass fireplace poker, wiped clean of prints, but obviously used to break Greenwald's ankles, tibia, three lower ribs, and a number of facial bones. Though his assailant would never be *officially* identified, I did find a clumsily wrapped package on my doorstep containing a new roll of duct tape and a Post-It note: "In case you've run out—P."

Detective Pedersen wrote his report, filed charges, and logged all supporting evidence, including the thumb drive. The assassin would never be lucid enough to stand trial and was committed by the court to a permanent care facility.

Mr. Vagelle asked me to accompany him to the club one evening near closing. We sat with Bobby J., and told him a long story about the sad death of his *other* daughter, the one he never knew, the one his ex-wife put up for adoption before they were married.

I found it difficult to put the giant through such pain, but when his emotions leveled off, he told us Sandra June had made hints to him.

She left town shortly after I moved back to my own apartment. She would keep in touch, she said. On his birthday and holidays, Bobby J. would receive long letters from his surviving daughter, ensuring him she was doing well in her new life, sometimes in Colorado, sometimes Wyoming.

Mr. Vagelle and I settled into our routines. I went back to being the consultant's assistant. He returned to his often busy, distracted, somewhat secretive self, but not quite as it was before. Often, a warmth crept into his tone. Perhaps a new respect, and he would follow it up with, "Remind me to buy a new fireplace poker." Sometimes, for no reason, he would take me to lunch or a night at Bobby J.'s.

Quitting work late one night—research on his latest, less-than-trustworthy, client—he shared a bottle of expensive Cognac and the latest edition of the Atlanta Star:

TRAGEDY BEFALLS ATLANTA D.A.

Esteemed District Attorney, Charlie Dorn's body was found by his fiancée this morning, August 2nd, at 3a.m. Ms. Lori Jay reported that she had been awakened by a muffled cry. Leaving their bedroom to investigate, she said she could see his lifeless shape at the bottom of the long flight of stairs, "...with his head turned around backwards." She immediately phoned the police. Ms. Jay could not be reached for further comment.

Although identity could not be confirmed, one reporter grabbed this shot of a woman, thought to be the unfortunate fiancée, rushing through Concourse-B of the Hartsfield-Jackson International Airport late this afternoon.

The blurry, turned-away face in the grainy black-and-white photo might as well have been Angelina Jolie, but for the exposed side of her neck and, with closer scrutiny, two small heart-shapes freshly tattooed below her right ear.

"She seems to have found a practical use for her Mixed Martial Arts," I said.

"I wonder," Mr. Vagelle said. "I wonder if her father ever noticed that the postmarks on her letters to him were not mailed from the wild west. I don't have the heart to tell him."

SEVEN

A CRIMINAL
OBSESSION

"Never again, bitch"

Mutt waited with his back to the street, a small bag of "personal possessions" on the concrete between his feet, hands clasped behind him, a pose he was familiar with. His eyes held on the cloudless sky. He would not look back until the bus arrived. He would not look back to the closed gates of "The Farm." Angola Prison.

"Never again, bitch," he whispered.

He heard the bus brakes behind him. Saw the sign above the windshield as it slowed, "Baton Rouge." There was no direct

Greyhound ride from Angola to New Orleans. He didn't mind the stopover. He wondered how many others had mumbled that line, *Never again.*

"So, you getting on or what?" The bus driver called. He had a lot of meat on him.

Mutt said nothing, climbed aboard, and paid the fare. His instinct said there was a familiarity in the driver's look, or maybe he just had that "former inmate" stare so many walked out with. It forced him to look away. He missed his connecting bus, Baton Rouge to New Orleans, because he dozed off in the terminal.

Terminal—there's a word.

No worries, there would be another soon. He fell asleep again on that bus and woke up three times before reaching the New Orleans Station in the Warehouse District. He checked into his *fleabag* near two a.m., Thursday. He wore the complimentary disposable shower cap to bed because, of course, real fleas. As he settled in, he made a mental reminder to keep his appointment with his parole officer Monday morning. He was on the road to model citizenry. But before that, he had plans for Friday night.

Friday, he entered the "Stable," formerly "Godiva's Stable" back before half the neon got shot to hell in a drive-by of creative vandalism. A neighborhood landmark from the outside, a cliché strip joint within. The owners had preserved that cliché since World War Deuce, with at least one dancer old enough to have danced for Audie Murphy.

From his swivel stool at the bar, Mutt watched the old broad carry her drink tray around the room, his imagination straying into Fantasyland and his own mommy issues. She stopped at a table in the far corner with barely enough light to recognize a face he'd come here for, "Dane." Across from Dane, his back to Mutt, sat another familiar shape that might be "Pug."

Alya—Two Years Ago

It was an important year. The year of my leaving.

I was nineteen when *he* first found me. I had been living amid the boat wreckage, what he called "the West End Yacht Cemetery," after that year's hurricane. A wanderer without caring, having escaped my native Moscow, my Papa, Mama, and my childhood crimes and nightmares, I somehow managed to land here beside a volatile Lake Pontchartrain with no thought to my life other than scavenging enough to see tomorrow. *At nineteen.*

Nicolaus Vagelle found me while searching for something else. I later learned he made a good living doing just that, mostly for wealthy clients who could afford a high-valued bloodhound. Then, when he learned a bit about me, he decided I needed a job and a place to live, and he gave me both.

Mr. Vagelle proved to be an unusual man.

Ten years my senior, he looked even older from a distance, with his premature white-dusted crew cut. He was thin-waisted and as tall as a grave is deep, everywhere but New Orleans. Sometimes, he reminded me of a predator bird, or maybe a seventeenth century *palach* (headsman). But only sometimes, back before I learned to understand him.

His office was his home, the third floor of a narrow four-story building, many blocks removed from the touristy French Quarter madness. I assumed he must be wealthy, until I saw the state of his apartment—tidy but cramped, workspace-living-dining room, a cabbage soup of inexpensive furniture with one very expensive painting above his fake fireplace.

This unusual man asked nothing from me in return except for light housework, answer his phone, continue my English lessons online, run errands and, once he learned my skill with numbers, he asked me to help with his books and billing. Over time, he taught me something of his business. For this, he found an apartment for me less than five miles away, gave me enough money to open a bank account and handle other expenses. More than I expected to make in my lifetime, *legally*.

We soon developed an unusual relationship. After several weeks, maybe to relax the concerns of a nineteen-year-old, he let me know he was not sexually interested *in anyone*. He called me "girl" on occasion to prove his point, until the day I cornered him, fixed his eyes, and said, "I am woman! Stop that!" Once those clouds drifted on, he sat with me over breakfast tea and explained his discomfort.

"I would like you to get into the habit of calling me Mr. Vagelle. I will call you Ms. Korikova. This doesn't mean we are not friends, but it will remind us that this is what we are and, as we work closely together in this tight space for so much of the day, it will also inform outsiders and clients. My office needs the appearance of propriety."

"And because I might not be able to resist your old man charms," I said, and he wrinkled his brow until he recognized my sarcasm. "I will look up word."

"What word?"

"Propriety."

Unfortunately, it took less than two years in each other's company before I felt a growing distance, a strain to the friendship. Our five days a week became four, sometimes three. He began spending more time away from the office when I was in it. Then one morning a courier brought a large envelope addressed to me, sender unknown. It contained papers, city and state documents, a driver's license, applications for citizenship, with what must have been a forged birth certificate, visa and work papers. Mostly correct personal information, except for my real last name.

"I have another job for you," he said, as I studied previous case details at his corner desk. "I will supply books and other materials, but I would like you to study for your GED. I am thinking of your future."

"Da, Papa."

"That was unnecessary."

"You used to not mind so much my jokes."

"Also—"

"What is ged?"

"Also," he pushed from the wingback chair, considering his words, "if you can, we need more work on your English. This is not a criticism. Yes, you do very well for your short time here. But I'm afraid, with some of the people I do business, your vocabulary might be…a distraction."

"What is vocabulary?"

"Exactly."

"You do not like accent."

He turned for the kitchen.

"Ya ponimayu," I whispered, and he paused.

"I know *you understand,"* he said, his back still turned.

"Your Russian gets better too."

Within four months a GED certificate dropped on my desk. The same morning NOPD Detective Pedersen dropped in with his news. I had met Pedersen back when I first met Mr. Vagelle, and I soon found he was a regular, if not a friend, within these walls. He helped himself to the tea kettle in the kitchen while my boss took the old wingback chair and waited.

"Remember Mutt?" Pedersen said.

"Horace Mund," Mr. Vagelle said for my benefit. "You know I do, Detective."

"Horace?" I said.

"And you know he's coming up for parole in a few years." Pedersen stirred more sugar than any teacup should allow.

"Ms. Korikova, you may want to take notes. I predict a complicated discussion."

"Not complicated, Vagelle, but something I figured would tweak your interest. One more ex-con on the street with a hard-on for—um—sorry, Alya. With a grudge against you."

"Horace Mund, also known as Mutt, a career criminal who has made a lifetime specialty out of getting caught."

"These days he's serving a dime for his part in a failed bank holdup. He was the inside-man, friends with a bank teller who was supposed to cut the alarm wires to the cages before his crew charged in."

"A dime?" I said.

"Ten years," Mr. Vagelle said.

"He learned bank security is a bit more complicated these days." Having tasted his mixture, Pedersen returned to the kettle and added tea to his cup. He talked over his shoulder. Mr. Vagelle had once called it *avoidance. Typical of a detective schooled in interrogation, uncomfortable with similar analysis of himself.*

"Ten years equals a dime." I scribbled abstract patterns in the borders of my notebook.

"And knowing Mutt," Mr. Vagelle said, "I assume the detective came here to tell us the convict is already planning to get caught screwing up the day of his release."

"Pretty close." Pedersen stayed in the kitchen, leaning against the sink, eyeing the cupboards. "Mutt's snuggle-buddy these days is a Kaspar Berk—"

"*Not* a career criminal, but a Nazi who beat a man to death while working as a strip club bouncer."

"Snuggle-buddy?" I said.

"Cellmate," Pedersen said. "Berk may have a swastika on his neck, but it was a first offense reduced to Second-Degree Involuntary Manslaughter."

"There were extenuating circumstances." Mr. Vagelle's face had lost expression as his vision drifted somewhere beyond this room.

"Well, as the new story goes, Mr. Nazi seems to have been propositioned by his snuggle-buddy to team up for another of Mutt's schemes once they get shed of Angola. But snuggle-buddy wants no part of it 'cause he's looking forward to reuniting with his Mrs. Nazi once he gets paroled, and he announced to the world he ain't never going back inside."

"The road to Hell being so well-paved."

"Yep."

"So, how did you find out?" I said.

"Mr. Nazi told Mrs. Nazi. He imagined she might be extra-lovin' if she knew how much he was sacrificing for her."

"This is complicated." I continued my scribbles.

"Nah," Pedersen said. "All them players don't mean nothing. What matters here is Mutt. And he's making big plans for three years from now."

"But he never told Kaspar Berk what those plans are, right?" Mr. Vagelle said.

I answered the door two days later to a short, round, three-piece suit with shoes like black glass. Pinched eyes squinted up from a round face that got rounder when he smiled. He carried a spotted cowhide briefcase with its fur rubbed thin along the edges. I wondered if his initials had been branded underneath. I accepted his card—poorly drawn Justice scales, a phone number, and *Baron J. Daggett, Defense Counsel*. I turned quickly to avoid shaking hands.

"Mr. Vagelle is expecting you." I invited him in and directed him to the settee fronting the fireplace.

"Daggett." Mr. Vagelle closed the bedroom door at his back, and the round man rose from the settee with a soft grunt. "Please sit."

I moved to the black L-desk by the corner window, and picked up the pen like I was an actual stenographer.

"I hope you are not wasting my time, Vagelle," Daggett said.

"I'd enjoy wasting your time, as you once wasted mine. Promises made, and then a bounced check. Remember?"

"I was young. My client's family stiffed me on payment—"

"Your client did not hire me. You did. But we'll leave that for now. If you thought I was wasting your time by mentioning Kaspar Berk, you would not have rushed over here to meet me."

"You said there might be a lot in it for my client and me."

"Okay, here's the deal, Daggett, with no dickering around. Take my offer or don't. I have other avenues to approach this, so if I even sense a headache coming on, you're through."

After failing the stare-down, Mr. Daggett turned his attention to the landscape above the fireplace mantel.

"I'm listening," he said.

"Just to be clear, I don't give a shit about the Nazi you represented." Vulgarity was a surprising approach for him. "You lost the case and blamed it on my work, while Judge Rosenbloom stared at that neck swastika seated beside you for three days. It's long ago, but I have a good memory for bad clients. Today, however, I have an interest in his cellmate."

"Mr. Mund?"

"Mr. Mund. So I need your former client to do me a favor."

"Oh, sure," Daggett said. "Inmates are in the *doing favors* business this year."

"You will persuade him."

"My motivation?"

"What *you* will get from it, I will forget your debt to me. Ms. Korikova will even give you a five-star rating on Yelp. And I will hand you the exculpatory evidence to get Berk his early release. You will, of course, convince his family that through *your* diligent labors *you* have accomplished this, and they will pay you the full reward you claim they stiffed you on back when you lost their case. Our ledger, yours and mine, and your conscience, will be clear, and your wallet fat." His glance said the round man had little conscience to concern him, but he had once told me, "*Always convince a con man he is receiving something extra. Even if it amounts to nothing, he will consider break-even a win.*"

The lawyer regarded the cowhide in his plump fingers.

"And if I get Berk to do this thing, you will not show up later and ask for any percentage of the family remittance? I owe you nothing? You will put this in writing?"

"I don't repeat myself." Mr. Vagelle shot me a glance. "It might begin that headache I mentioned."

"You did not say what this favor is."

Mr. Vagelle removed a hand from his pocket and revealed two small black bugs.

"You will tell Berk, for his early release, all he needs to do is wedge one between the bedframe and the wall without breaking it. It's small enough to be overlooked by most routine inspections."

"You seriously expect these to transmit all the way from Angola?"

"Not your concern. The second, drop that into the cell's air duct. If one gets found, they'll not look for number two. He tells no one, especially his lady-friend, especially Mund. No one. Tell him twice. Tell him if he slips up, I will know, and I will make his life and yours increasingly uncomfortable. You know I can."

"After which, you will give me the evidence I need for him."

"Time to go, Daggett. We both want him out of that cell as soon as possible, but only after this is done." He opened the door for the sneering attorney.

"You know how much I dislike you, Vagelle."

"Not as much as if you leak this conversation outside my room."

The following week, Mr. Vagelle sent me on an errand. An hour's drive up to Baton Rouge to be met by Jazz Lamonte, Executive Assistant to the Warden, who had agreed to make the drive south from Louisiana State Penitentiary. Lamonte would meet me at a coffee shop on the LSU campus across from University Lake. Mr. Vagelle suggested I take his Mercedes to make the long ride a bit more comfortable than in my long-suffering Impala.

"So how did you recognize me?" Lamonte said from between shoulders that might bench-press the Mercedes. He grinned over the rim of his delicate paper cup. "I'm sure Nick told you we go back a long way."

"To be honest, Mr. Vagelle does not speak much about past. I have only worked for him a short time."

"Ah, well, that doesn't surprise me much. Always a decent guy back then. Reliable. But not much of a romantic, as you've no doubt noticed."

"I know what you mean." *Too well.* And somehow, the way he said it, I felt a breath of sadness pass through me.

We drank our coffees and avoided small talk about my boss. He asked about my background, and I lied some. I did not ask about his work. Eventually, he said something about my errand, and I removed the pocket recorder from my satchel. I nudged it across the tabletop.

"Wait." He reached for my hand, and I instinctively pulled away. "Nick said he couldn't send this by email or mail, or meet with me personally. For my sake, he said. This place is too crowded for his cloak and dagger shtick. Maybe we should take a little stroll along the lake."

Mr. Vagelle did warn me about Lamonte and his *romantic* ways, but I said, "Sure." I did not ask about his word *shtick*.

We faced a warm spring breeze, but not too warm, and university grounds were the right color beside the blue of the lake. Young people strolled, or jogged, or lounged on the grass. A convoy of standing kayaks paddled along the far shore like they had somewhere to go. Once we were alone, Lamonte played Mr. Vagelle's recording.

A brief pre-ramble, "old times" stuff like friends who had been apart for years. He did not mention the time he saved Lamonte's wife, as he had told me when I pressed him about who this prison official was in his life. That sort of *friend* did not need reminding, and mentioning the act was beneath him. The recording led into the favor, and the reason for our meeting. He told Lamonte about his deal with lawyer Daggett, and that he expected inmate Berk's early release. Then, without getting too specific, he described suspicions of Horace Mund, as well as the minor crime he wanted Lamonte to involve himself in.

"I would never ask you to betray your position with the prison. You should be able to distance yourself from all of this, and pass along a simple request for a prisoner cell swap. Maybe ask a friendly Associate Warden there to move Wilson Franks in with Mund after the Nazi vacates."

"Willie Franks? Bookkeeper?" Lamonte clicked off the recording, but I shrugged. He explained, "Bookkeeper is another short-timer. Should be out in a year, given good behavior. I don't imagine much of a problem moving him in with Mund. They're both low security risks. I might question why—" He continued with Mr. Vagelle's voice:

"I don't imagine much of a problem moving him. The problems will begin once they're both back on the street. You understand the reasons for all my cloak and dagger. I want you to be able to say, Sorry, Vagelle, no can do. I will understand any discomfort, and you can walk away, and we will remain friends. I mean that. If you need time to think about my request, send some innocuous message. But I need your answer soon. Give my best to Sheila and Robby." The recording ended.

Lamonte nodded, showed his teeth, and erased the message while I watched spindly-legged egrets strut the shoreline.

"He'd have made a great salesman." He handed me the blank recorder. "He knows he didn't need to use the psychology with me for such a small favor."

"He said you would say that." I thought I recognized a gator's snout cruising for egrets.

"Ha! Of course he did." He scanned the gray clouds low on the horizon. "I need to be getting back north. You should take time to enjoy this place before you head on home. Tell your boss I don't need time to think. I've got no problem with the request. We should get together for beers next time I'm in the Big Easy."

"I will tell him. Thank you." I caught him watching me walk away.

"Oh, and tell him I approve his choice of employees. You may be his first, but be careful on this job."

Back at the desk the following day, I finished typing the boss's letter of evidence to the courts to accompany a copy of his original deposition from back before Berk's lawyer got the judge to rule his paperwork "inadmissible." Also included in the folder were crime scene close-ups, witness statements collected *after the Judgement* by strip club patrons not wanting to be identified, but who may have been a bit coerced by Mr. Vagelle. Brutal hospital photos illustrated the stripper Berk had been defending, and the bloody table edge that ultimately, and accidentally, broke the attacker's C-2, 3, and 4 cervical vertebrae.

As I stuffed the thick folder into a manila envelope to await lawyer Daggett's call, I heard Mr. Vagelle's key in the doorlock. He entered and set a grocery bag on the dining table.

"I put on a pot of tea, but it must be cold." Beyond my window, the blue had deepened, and the clouds had warmed with evening.

He opened the sideboard cabinet and withdrew a bottle of Widow Jane.

"Care to join me?" he said.

"Did we have an important day?"

He poured two short tumblers and set the one at my elbow beside the manila envelope. He took the other to his wingback chair, lowered slowly into its embrace where he appeared to deflate a bit. He breathed the bourbon's aroma, then he told me how he appreciated all my hard work. That I had surprised him by becoming a better assistant than he ever anticipated. And he told me I should leave.

When he said he would pay for my tuition at LSU, with my permission, of course, I snapped back.

"You are employer! You are not my Papa!" My face heated, my sight blurring against emotions. My knees trembled as if I stood on the deck of a shrimp boat in the choppy Gulf. "You decided this without consulting me? Do you have so little understanding of others?"

Hustling around the room, I dropped the laptop and a few personal things into my satchel. Grabbing for my car keys, I spilled a few drops of his Widow Jane. He watched silently.

"I will not! I cannot live in a dormitory. I cannot shower with others!" A growing hysteria shook me in its teeth. "I know your shrink-friend explained. What were you thinking?" I rushed to the door with my life here at an end.

I did not flee, but measured my steps deliberately down the three flights, passing Dr. Maiwand in his second-floor doorway saying something I could not hear. At the first-floor, Mr. Hemmings peered round his own doorjamb with a similar expression. I shut the street door with, what I thought, dignity. I followed broken concrete to my car a block and a half away. The cage door closed on the outside world and I tortured the steering wheel while my brain refused to assemble its thoughts. I focused on my breathing to clear my eyes.

The sound of my passenger door jolted me. Mr. Vagelle lowered into the seat. More confusion came in with him.

"I do not often consider my words," he whispered. "You are right to be angry."

"Of course you do. You always consider words you mean to say. I need to go."

"As soon as you calm and I have explained my actions as best I can." He paused. I could not respond. "Apologies are difficult for me too, but you know that by now."

We heard cars approach and pass. We heard muffled conversations, saw pedestrians moving like fish in a bowl going nowhere special. But they were outside the bowl. We were the captives barely recognizing their existence.

"First, I had no intention of sending you to a community dorm. You know I understand your fears. You know I have made sure of your safety here. One reason I had not mentioned this is because I was waiting for a response from a friend. He keeps a winter home in Baton Rouge. This week, he has finally gotten back to me to say the house is yours for as long as you need it."

"I do not *need* university." I still refused his gaze.

"I came up with this idea when I saw how quickly you got your GED. You are fast and smart, and I wanted more for you."

"I think you wanted to be alone. Is okay. Me too."

"I never lied to you. But I am not telling you to go away. I know you are an adult. You make your own decisions. Yes, I want this education—for you. Hear me, please. You have been with me for almost three years. Everything you know about the world here has been through my eyes. I wish for you to have more of a life. Be around people, younger people. Make friends. Experience something apart from my tiny slice of the world. My world is…dark. You are not."

You do not know my life before you. I stared at the streetlight reflected off the wet hood of my car.

"Do you know the meaning of your name? *Alya* comes in many languages and it means light, or air. You need to be out of my shadow. I am not throwing you away. I hope you can visit often, and if you return to me in a few years, if you decide you want your old job back, as long as I am here, you are welcome."

Still, I could not speak, even when he opened his door and stepped to the curb. When I looked up, he was gone.

I passed the following week rarely leaving my apartment. I needed my thinking time. Once I had chased these new demons away, I understood he was right. *He usually was*—a thought that felt like sandpaper to my nerves.

As I continued writing my journals, "a coping device" suggested by Mr. Vagelle's "shrink-friend," I suspected my solo trip to the campus at Baton Rouge might have been a set-up. I recalled Jazz Lamonte's suggestion, *"You should take time to enjoy this place before you head home."* Likely, Mr. Vagelle had mentioned his plans for me, a gentle manipulation that, in reality, I did not mind much. I remembered Lamonte's last words to me, *"be careful on this job."* And I began to think sending me far away might have had another motive.

The Present—"Road Dogs"

(Prison slang for close friends.)

Are they the only two left from the old crew? Strange to see both of them together in the Stable after so many years.

Mutt took his beer glass and dropped two singles on the stage for the overly energetic dancer as he passed. Dane saw him coming. He almost smiled and Pug turned to look.

"Son-of-a-bitch," Pug said. Heard you was gettin' out. How's freedom taste?"

"Slightly sweeter than inside." Mutt slid into the booth without invitation.

"How long?" Dane said.

"Two days."

"Shit." Dane waved old Doris back to the table. "You need something better than that stale crap you're drinking. Hey, Doris. Bottle of JB for our friend here."

Doris let me count the wrinkles on her forehead.

"Mighty white of you, pal," Mutt said. Neither of them was white. "You must be doing okay for yourself, springing for the *quality stuff.* But I always figured you'd make good. You're the only one of the crew didn't get sent up for what we pulled."

"Tried to pull," Dane said."

"Shut-it," Pug said. "We don't talk 'bout dat shit here. All dese years later, de Feebs are tattooed to our asses from de time we make our mornin' flush."

"More than ten years later? Did Batman stop all the crime in this town while I was up-Farmin'?"

"Every time one of us gets released, de smell of pork fills de air for at least six mont." He eyed the lonely men at the dark tables. He squinted into a darker corner, seeming to land on a lean figure in a stained white shirt and a Saints ball cap shielding his eyes, possibly asleep. "You're here, so it's eggshells for awhile, bruh."

"Hell." Mutt took a sip, curled his lip, and pushed the beer aside to await the celebratory bottle.

He angled his seat for a better view of the young dancer as she snaked her way up the brass pole. She might have begun her diet in Ghana. He tapped his pocket, wondering if he had any singles left there. "So many years surrounded by zombie convicts, I've been in desperate need of conversating. Something more than who got shanked in the shower last week."

"I get dat," Pug said. "I didn' get de full ten, like you, but I get it."

"Do you guys ever get together where brothers can relax? This used to be our place. It's why I came here first—Don't look at me like that. I'll let you search for a wire 'fore we sit down."

"Nah. That ain't it," Dane said. "We know you got out after a full dime, so they got nothing to hold over you. Besides, none of us walked away from the job with anything but more lines on a Yellow-sheet."

You didn't even get that, Mutt thought.

"Hey," Pug said. "How 'bout next week we meet up over at de Shep's Garage? Still looks like a warehouse, but he got a full bar in dere now, two hot waitresses, and a fifty-cent pool table. Nobody gets in dere without Shep knowing him personal."

"Remind me the street, and what day, and I'm good with it."

Doris finally appeared with his bottle. Dane paid and stuffed an extra Hamilton between her saggy tits, then he and Pug pushed up from the table.

"Hey," Mutt said. "Ain't you going to help me christen this thing?"

"It's yours," Dane and Pug said in unison. "I got work tomorrow." Dane slid a business card onto the table. Dead Dog Deals, Used Cars. "We'll do it next Friday night. Call. I'll give you directions."

"I thought *Dead Dog* never made it out of the bank?" Mutt said.

"He didn't. I named my car business after him out of respect."

Or because you thought it was a cool name, Mutt thought. *You never liked DD that much. Nobody did.*

After they left, Mutt cracked the seal on the JB, asked Doris for a fresh glass, then he slid the curve of the bench for a full view of the stage and the starving dancer.

The girl can move, though. I'll leave her a couple bucks on my way out. Tell her to go buy a milkshake.

He barely noticed the Saints ball cap had disappeared. His eyes landed back on the bottle, and growing bored waiting for the glass, he drank from the neck. Thoughts traveled back to the conversation. Dane and Pug—"they were always the smart ones." He thought about the lives of the other dogs. *The Dogpack. With Dead Dog now really dead.*

Memories grew clouded as the bottle grew lighter.

As the fog lifted with morning splitting the drapes of his fleabag, he sat up long enough to taste the "hair-of-the-dog." A taste was all that remained at the bottom of the bottle. He fell back onto the pillow and contemplated the immovable ceiling fan and his headache. He rethought then reassembled then reorganized the brainstorm he'd memorized during his lengthy government stay. By noon, he called the number on the business card.

He flirted with the receptionist, then he set up the meet with Dane.

"Glad you got back in touch," Dane said. "Listen, if you need a low-paying job 'til you get on your feet, I'm sure I can set you up with something here. Won't be much, but it's something to tell your parole officer, so he doesn't keep hounding you to find work."

The following Friday night Mutt wandered through the lot behind Shep's Garage—a mini warehouse turned private tap room. He noticed a bus parked at the mouth of the alley with its engine off, but figured it was the driver snoozing on his break. No working alley lights, the warehouse stood dark against the equally dark parking lot. At his knock a pretty teenager, almost wearing a skirt, opened the only door in the wall.

Shep called out from behind the bar and poured him a tall stiff one, on the house.

"Only one rule in Shep's. If you're packing, you need to check your piece with Tisha by the door. We're all friends in here."

Mutt lifted his tight T-shirt and turned.

"So what if Tisha's got her monthly and decides to freak and blast us all to the Great Beyond?"

Tisha glared like he might be serious.

Dane and Pug sat at a table with "Dobie," a fourth member of the Dogpack crew. "Bull," a fifth, hung his gut over the bumper of the pool table with his ass crack showing above where his belt should be. He sighted down the stick for way longer than needed to miss and drop the cue ball in the side pocket.

"Yo, Mutt."

Like old "war buddies" reunited over many drinks and lines of powder, the gang shared memories of old times. "Good" old times, according to their fantasies. Only Pug remained silent and expressionless. When he did speak, he mocked the others until Bull casually mentioned Pug's gang rape his first week in cell block. Pug nearly threw a punch at the bull-man, but Shep stepped between them.

That's why Shep checks their guns.

The conversation skipped forward to the "honest" work, as each struggled to reunite with civilian life. No one mentioned the *botched* part of the botched bank heist, Mutt's missed alarm wire, "Goldie" and Dead Dog shooting hell out of a bank guard and a teller, then "Hounder" pounding the bank president into a coma. Goldie and Hounder would be serving multiple life sentences. Dead Dog would be serving his time in a warmer place than Louisiana.

Mutt listened more than he talked. He needed to *feel out* his former partners, and he took his time. Before the end of the night, he let it drop that he was already bored with the "outside," but he left that note hanging in the air. Something for next time. Patience may be the most important lesson learned inside a cage.

Over the following two weeks, they met at Shep's twice more. The remaining member of the Dogpack, "Lab," joined them, and that made seven. "A Not So Magnificent Seven," Dane coined, and even Pug joined the short-lived laugh.

Shep's barrel chest had descended to his waist over his years bartending. Long before the heist, a sergeant on the NOPD, he got busted twice for selling "shine" out of his basement, and once for dealing coke out of the trunk of his squad car. Unsurprisingly, a little time behind bars is certain to thumb the ejection-seat on a cop's career.

Bull resembled his nickname. He'd started his own plumbing company, and he still couldn't keep his pants up.

Most considered *Dane* the brains of the crew. A college grad, he'd worked as a stockbroker before his life went to shit. With most of his buddies in lock-up, he had recovered nicely with his used car business.

Dobie was an athlete who spent most of his life running from the cops.

Lab was a decent mechanic, and the gang's getaway driver, who never had the opportunity to *get away.*

Pug considered himself the smartest, and never failed to report this to anyone within earshot. Mutt automatically assumed this to be the fuel behind the prison gang rape.

And here sat Mutt, the bank's "inside man." The screw-up—with a whole new plan. The Dogs had all run together for years—drugs, pimps, car thefts, convenience store holdups, drive-bys on the competition—before Mutt showed them how to improve their street-cred with a simple bank job.

He'd show 'em now.

That second night at Shep's he dropped more of his "need to get some of the old fire back in my life." He made note of the distracted grunts and nods of agreement from Shep and Bull, and he passed around his cell phone number. The third night, he saw more interest when he unloaded that he had a new fool-proof scheme that he'd spent ten years scheming over.

"Listen, I know you guys got lives now. Businesses to run. Girlfriends. Shep's got a wife, fer-cryin-out-loud. I'd never ask my brothers to give all that up. I figure I still know enough to put a fresh crew together. Been thinking on this a long time, like I say. My last cellmate ran with a pretty jacked crew of his own before they got busted. Name of Willie Franks."

"I heard-o' him, bruh," Pug said.

"In the *real world,* he's known as Bookkeeper."

"Dat's right."

"He got early release a couple years back 'cause he was just a contact for the fence on a run of *bling-store* stick-ups. But he still has those contacts, and I kinda set him up with a teaser on my new plan. Now that I'm out..."

Mutt let that soak in some. A few drinks later, as expected, Bull started badgering him on his "big plan."

"Listen. You're my *Road Dogs,* right? Long time. No one I trust more. But you know how it is. I can't be givin' up details until I'm setting with my crew and laying it out full."

"Close to the vest, that's the smart way to do it," Dane said, and they all understood.

That night Mutt struggled with sleep for the first time since Angola, as he juggled the finer points of the plan and all the personalities he was dealing with. All of a sudden, everything bothered him. His old *brothers'* new timidity. The humidity and a dead ceiling fan. The bed sagging in the middle. The shower cap made noise when he rolled over. Not nerves. He wasn't the nervous type, but his skin itched. He got up and showered and checked for flea bites. If he had the energy, he'd go down to the street and shoot whoever parked his bus beneath his window every night with the damned engine running. Damned city had become overrun with buses since he went away. Must be a God-damned union thing.

Stop this! You're no good without sleep.

Three days later, Dane called, saying most of the crew sounded interested in his getting a piece of the "old fire" back.

When he hung up, all the old confidence came rushing back, and Mutt made his next call. Willie Franks had the new twelve-man crew readying over the past two years, waiting for his call. He had the boats painted up, just like Mutt described, had the uniforms and guns, and all they needed was the date of the drop.

He hung up. Then he called to check on the shipment.

He went out, stopped at the first Walgreens he could find, and picked up a few personal items, including a rubber swimmer's cap, quieter than the plastic shower cap. He ate a big Denny's breakfast with an extra side of bacon and waffles, then went back to his room and passed out for twelve hours.

"You're all in?" Mutt said when he had the Dogs back at Shep's Garage.

"Except for Lab," Dane said. "He found true love, and feels himself lucky he got such a short sentence last time, just for being the wheelman. I had to do some convincing with Pug, too."

"Ain't never goin' back inside!" Pug said. "I kill every moderfocker on de south shore before dey put me in cuffs again."

Mutt thought on it and smiled like he understood.

"Drivers ain't that hard to find," he said. "So, here it is. I did the research. As I didn't explain to Bookkeeper, we, you and me, we got us a second crew to do our heavy lifting. Bookkeeper's old crew. On a date yet to be specified, a shipping container coming all the way from Paky-stan is carrying one million fake credit cards, fake IDs, fake Social Security car—"

"Wait, bruh!" Pug said. "All dis for some penny-ante ID shit?"

"Can I finish?" Mutt tried on his menacing face. "I learned that one fake driver's license sells for three bills. That's three hundred. We got a million of 'em comin'. Bookkeeper knows the brokers who buy in bulk. They'll pay ten-percent on the whole shipment. They know we don't want to sit on a million cards waiting to sell one at a time, so we take the small end."

Lab walked into the circle. "Ten-percent of a score don't sound like much of a split."

"Thought you had a girlfriend."

"Can't take that bitch-mouth some days. I need release."

"Simple math," Mutt said, "Listen to me. One million cards at three hundred a-piece gets three hundred million."

Two of them whistled in unison.

"Our ten-percent comes to thirty-million clean, walk-away dollars. You go ahead and divide thirty-million by seven of us."

"Never heard of a bank job bringing in that sort of dough," Dane said.

"I can live on that kind of take," Shep said.

"To make sure I'm straight with all of you," Mutt said, "I figured four-million-two and some change. I'll have up-front expenses, and I do expect a finder's fee, it bein' my plan and setting things up. But you will still walk away with, minimum, four-mill a-piece."

"Wait!" Pug said. "I get dat a million fake cards is easier to carry den dollar bills, but you said seven of us. What 'bout your new crew?"

"Bookkeeper is waiting for the shipment date from me. He don't know squat about you guys. Right now, as soon as I call him with the date, he's gonna run off with his old crew, take my plans, and cut me out of my percentage."

"I think...I'm still confused," Bull said.

"You're my brothers, ain't ya? We're just gonna let Willie Franks take all the risks. They're gonna highjack that container ship before it lands, while it's out in the Gulf. Big shoot-'em-up on the high seas. Then the seven of us are gonna slide in after they feel safe. Then we make 'em disappear into the bayou while we go look for his fence."

"But what about—?"

"Bookkeeper's givin' me his buyer's name in exchange for the time of the shipment. That's it. Easy-peasy."

"Ain't no shipping company gonna cry to the cops about someone ripping off an illegal shipment." Dane said. "Four mil' to just grab that haul after the other thieves make the steal? I'm kind of amazed you came up with all this, Mutt."

"Ten years is a long time to think about a thing."

"How big's his crew?" Pug said.

"A dirty dozen. But they'll never see us comin'."

Alya

I began my Christmas break driving south in the Impala, as I began each school holiday for the better part of two years. I had spoken to *him* regularly, and I always called in advance of showing up on his landing. He should have expected my routine by now. This was the first break he had not returned my calls, but I was not yet overly concerned.

I had made several friends in my time at LSU, but they would be visiting their own families, especially over Christmas break. My return visits to *The Hemmings Building* had begun to feel like "going home."

Halfway there I called the landlord, Hemmings, who always shouted at the phone as if he expected a police raid. When he heard my voice, he shouted to be heard over the cheers of this afternoon's TV game show.

"I ain't seen him in two weeks. No, I don't know where he is, or when he'll be back. He doesn't check in with me. Bye." CLICK.

"Thank you," I said to the dial tone. Who else to call? Dr. Maiwand, the neighbor? The police? I decided I had come too far to turn back anyway, so I drove in silence for the remainder of the trip. It allowed me time to think, to recall my previous visits, and eventually remember our "situation" when I moved out nearly three years ago.

Before trying the apartment, I followed a whim over to the private parking garage where he usually kept the Mercedes. I used my pass at the gate and followed the ramp to his fifth-floor parking bay. I braked at the turn, the moment I spotted the broken remains of yellow crime-scene tape and scorched concrete. *Not a recent crime.* Other cars would not have been allowed to park here until all investigating agencies determined garage safety after the explosion. I left my Impala running and walked ahead to parking bay E-7. Apart from the permanent stains it had been scrubbed clean.

I failed to control my sobs as Detective Pedersen answered his phone.

"I will never forgive you!" I yelled at the phone. "Why did you not call me! Why did no one call me! I—It is indefensible! You are evil and a coward and I—!" I dropped the phone, cracking the screen. When I heard the distant voice, I hung up, but my legs did not want to straighten. I sat with my back to a concrete pillar below the stenciled "E-7," outside the burn ring, and covered my head in my arms.

Three feet away, the phone rang, and I ignored it. It rang again.

A car honked from behind my Impala blocking the driveway. I leaped to my feet, balled my fists, and screamed

Russian at the driver until he backed hurriedly from the turn. My cracked phone continued ringing. A new caller, not Pedersen.

"Alya!" a woman said once I answered. "This is Patricia Gunston."

"*Da.*"

"Gunston Investigations," she said. "We met—"

"I do not wish to talk now!"

"It's about Mr. Vagelle. You need to know he is alive."

To disguise my breathing, I covered the microphone.

"Where are you now? We need to meet. I can answer all your questions. *Not* at your office. Can you come here?"

When she closed her office door, I still had the adrenalin strength to make it to her visitors' chair.

"I'm glad you are here," she said. "We tried to contact you, but—"

The door reopened behind me. Detective Pedersen entered with two coffees and a newspaper folded under his arm. One coffee he held out for me. I wished for the energy to leap up and punch him.

"We were under orders not to call you," he said.

"Not even with him blown to bits?"

"I did not lie to you on the phone," Patty said. "Nicolaus is alive. We just don't know where he is."

"He phoned me." Pedersen frowned. "Minutes after the explosion. It was brief. He's always too fu—always too damned brief. Everything with him, always a damned enigma. Can you take this coffee? My arm's getting tired." I did, and he perched on the corner of Patty's desk. "His only concern was that we not contact you. He said it like it wasn't a request. Three times he said it, then hung up."

"We're sorry you had to find out like this," Patty said. "Who could suspect the garage would be your first stop when you came back to town?"

"I have been trying to call him for days," I said to the coffee. "He knew I would be coming in for Christmas. I called his landlord, Hemmings, who said he had not seen him. I stopped to see if his car was gone. That is all."

"That landlord's a piece of work," Pedersen said. "Almost had to arrest his ass just to get access to Vagelle's apartment. Do you have any idea what your boss was working on?"

They waited for my answer. I waited until my jigsaw tumbled into place.

"I think you know," I said at last. "Remember the last time you walked in with me there?"

"Shit!" He lifted slowly from the desk. "Mutt has been out for how long?"

"One month and fourteen days," Patty said.

"Shit!"

"That's some salacious headline, even for the Trib." Pedersen dropped the newspaper on Patty's desk.

PIRATES OF THE CARIBBEAN

"Not sure how this relates," Patty said.

"It appears as if the cargo ship that crashed into Mississippi River traffic four days ago turned out to be a *ghost ship*. She'd been waylaid out on the Gulf somewheres. When the Coast Guard boarded her, they found a dead crew. Bullet holes sprayed machine gun style, and containers blasted open or broken into. They're still fishing for more bodies."

"Your man Mutt is a notorious screw-up," Patty said. "His style is more smash 'n grab liquor stores, until he tried his hand at bank robbery. And we all saw how that turned out."

"Or so we've always thought. Did you read the whole story? Coast Guard has been swarming our coastline since the crash. Two days ago, they found a floater off Pelican Island, Barataria Bay—that's *Jean Lafitte territory*. Someone that, to our knowledge, never set foot on a ship anywhere, especially a ship from the Middle East—um, the floater, not Jean Lafitte."

"I think she knows who Jean Lafitte was," Patty said.

"Floater's name is Willie Franks." Pedersen hesitated when he recognized the light in my eyes. "Uh-huh. That same evening, I got a call from an official up at Louisiana State Penitentiary. He told me a story about how prison guards found a bug planted in Mutt's most recent cage. Why do I think you know something about this?"

"This is the thing Nicolaus had been working on?" Patty said.

"Willie's stage-name was Bookkeeper. Ever meet him?"

"No," I said. "But *the official* probably told you Bookkeeper was Mutt's last cellmate."

"Alya, I'm praying to God I don't have to arrest you for being involved in any of this."

"All I know about it, this goes back to…the day you came to us with news of Mutt. That he was making big plans for his release. I knew Mr. Vagelle would do something, but then he forced me to leave. Sent me to university. He wished me out of his life…and his plans."

"Looks like he had good reason," Patty said. "And after the car bomb, he demanded we *not* notify you. He knew you would chase after him. He knew you would probably get yourself murdered in the process."

"And now you only visit on holidays." Pedersen directed his eyes anywhere but toward mine. "Sure, okay, let's say I believe you. I still have to file the report. And detectives less friendly than me will want to interrogate you." He stood and dropped his unfinished coffee into the trash bucket, causing a minor mess.

Patty P.I. grabbed her phone, called a lawyer whose name I recognized as friendly with my boss. The phone passed to Pedersen. Sixty seconds later, to me:

"The detective agrees that he has no reason to subject you to a police grilling at this time, and you can remain available in case his superiors decide otherwise. But answer no questions without me being present. You have my number. Do not tell him I said this, but you should lose your phone for a couple of weeks. Unless it's me calling."

Patty followed up the stairs, and Mr. Hemmings popped his head from his hole to shout. "He still ain't back yet! I ain't heard word-one from him! Christmas is coming and rent is due on the first!"

"Hello, Mr. Hemmings! No worries, I have my key." I jangled the key-ring. With Patty on my heels, I pushed on to the third-floor and I closed us in.

"We shouldn't stay long," Patty said. "No telling who the little man will phone first."

"I need to find him. I do not know how, but you already called everyone in his book. This is the only place left to look for answers."

"The police already swept this place. Pedersen knew he was still alive and probably kept them from tearing everything to pieces." She went into his bedroom and I heard her pulling boxes from shelves. "Okay. Let's ignore the obvious hiding places for now."

I yanked the drawer from the black desk. Checked beneath and behind. Turned furniture cushions. I heard Patty in his bathroom hamper. I heard the distinctive lid to the toilet tank drop back into place. She came out as I was emptying kitchen cupboards. I checked inside the teapot.

"Everything is too obvious to me," she said. "Do you know where he keeps his tools? Maybe a power screwdriver? I can look behind wall plates and light switches."

"Wait." I interrupted a thought. "Give me a hand." I crossed to the fake fireplace, opened the grill, kicked at the show-logs as an afterthought. "Here. I cannot do this alone." I took the corner of his expensive Thomas Moran painting. Patty took the opposite end. "This painting means a lot to him." We carried and laid the painting carefully, face down, on the dining table. But I was wrong. Nothing had been taped to the back.

"Should we scrape paint off for hidden messages—?" We both flinched at a knock on the door.

She jerked the door open startling Mr. Hemmings. He recovered by inches and led us sheepishly up to the fourth-floor.

"You know Mr. Vagelle pays me to keep the apartment above him vacant." He turned the lock there and nudged the door open for us. "If he has a thing he wants you to find, I thought maybe—"

I hurried in. The windows remained covered with hanging sheets diffusing the sunlight. A single recliner, covered with a similar dusty sheet, stood as the only remnant of furniture. I pulled the sheet, revealing a business envelope propped against the padded arm.

"I would like to kiss you, Mr. Hemmings," I said.

"I think your Mr. Vagelle might do something bad to me if you did," he said.

I tore open the envelope and dropped the contents into my hand. A driver's license, a credit card and a yellow Post-It with the scrawl, *"Snail Mud Dosgris Turtle."* My hope disintegrated.

"Let me see." Patty took the items in hand. "As Pedersen says, damned Vagelle, always the enigma. What the hell? There has to be a connection to these words.

"Snail Mud Dosgris…" Hemmings craned to see over Patty's shoulder. "Dosgris. I know this word. Wait. Yes! Two words, *dos gris*. Gris is French for gray. It's a bird! Grey back!

That's it! Dosgris Bayou and Dosgris Bay, two small lakes—and there is also a Mud Lake, and a Snail Lake, and a Turtle Bay. Ha! I win!" He clapped like one of his gameshow contestants.

"You are sure?" Not knowing what else to say, I forced my mouth shut.

"Of course I am. I know my geography. They are all fairly close together. Swampland, and just up from—"

"Barataria Bay," Patty finished for him. He looked to be falling in love.

"And this was important for Mr. Vagelle?" I said.

"If he went to the trouble of concealing this here…" She analyzed the Louisiana driver's license for the first time, then held it out to me. "Jonathan Lafitte. DOB…*1870?* I'd love to know what kind of car he drove."

"Jean, not Jonathan," Hemmings whispered.

"A fake driver's license," I said, "and the note of a water trail through the Bayou. Important enough to leave this."

"It's a treasure map!" He withheld a cheer.

"You can find Lafitte printed on just about anything in gift shops around this city. But if Vagelle left this for us to find, our treasure might be fake IDs," Patty said. "Reports said one damaged shipping container left a scattering of credit cards and IDs. The hijacked cargo ship from Pakistan."

Hemmings eventually returned to his hole on the first-floor, his chest slightly larger than when he had come out.

"I should do a few things before I go." I reentered Mr. Vagelle's apartment. Patty followed.

"And I should remind you, there are people looking for your boss who like blowing things up."

"You said the cops went all over this place. Besides, those animals think he died with the car bomb. Why else would he disappear and not tell me? Help me rehang his painting, would you?"

"As far as that second part, that's just a running theory right now. For all anyone really knows, they're following him, and not vice versa."

"How well did you say you know him?"

"Yeah, okay."

She held the painting in place while I set the hook. When she sat at the dining table, I went to the kitchen, opened a cupboard, found the large trash bags, then began emptying the refrigerator.

"Seriously? You risk life and limb to clean house now?"

"Smells like a boxful of rotten. Besides, work helps me think. You can go back to the office, if you like. I will be okay."

"Not on your life. I'm just stupid enough to get myself blown up trying to protect you from yourself."

"Oh, God, this is awful. No way I am going to wash some of these containers." I dropped full jars and sealed plastic with furry white food into the black bag. "Though I am sure he has eaten worse." I stopped and gazed into the bag. "I was not with him when—Did he ever tell you the story about surviving that small plane crash?" I returned to the dining room. I took the chair across from her and stared at my hands.

"I'd read some reporter's version of the story." She tried reading my expression. "He got it from police reports, follow-up to the investigation of police officers who had died in that crash."

"Atchafalaya Swamp. He would not tell me everything, but sitting at the foot of his hospital bed for those days after they brought him in, I watched first-hand what the swamp can do to a person. For weeks after he had come home, I expected some disease, or maybe his heart just giving up, or some ghost of it dropping him to the floor and stealing his breath away. His bones, his skin, his eyes bruised and bloodshot. His eyes…And when nurses told me some of what he went through to survive…"

"And now, with what we've found, and maybe he's out there down near the Gulf, same conditions maybe, you suspect he might not come back. In your heart you know there is nothing much you can do but wait."

"I am not good at this kind of waiting." I pushed up from the table and hurried to the corner desk. "I never was." I pulled drawers. "He found people who would help him get home. People who know the swamp." I threw loose papers, note pads, and an address book onto the desktop. I told her what little I knew about those friends.

At his request, I posted generous Christmas gifts each year to the Post Office box of the old Cajun who had delivered him from Death's front porch, and to Mr. Steele & Son, owners of a small commercial airboat company who had been kind enough to take the broken passenger the rest of the journey out. I found a phone number.

A woman answered in a language something like English. She yelled several times until a man took control of the phone.

"*Monsieur Vagelle?* What—?"

I asked if he knew someone near Barataria Bay, maybe a charter airboat operator he trusted. I explained Mr. Vagelle's current situation without much detail and that I feared for his safety. When he questioned who I was, I mentioned mailing his Christmas gifts each year. When he questioned the urgency of Mr. Vagelle's disappearance, frustration pushed me to mention the car bomb and his vanishing. I told him I had few clues to work with.

"*Non.* Bayou ees no good to *Monsieur Vagelle. Absolument pas.* We will meet."

I insisted that I only called for a recommendation. I knew he was much farther north, and I did not wish to put friends in danger.

A brief laugh then, "We will meet."

The following sunrise, Patty and one of her investigators joined me at a taxi stand on the edge of the Intracoastal Waterway, outside the town of Jean Lafitte. I had tried half-heartedly to discourage her.

"This is my problem."

"I do not have many friends," she said, handing me a protective vest. "I can't afford to lose him."

I had left all personal effects in the trunk of my car, save the belt pack with my wallet and snubnose Smith & Wesson. I wished for a bigger gun.

"And as our buddy, Lieutenant Pedersen, refuses to take us along with his *Vagelle Task Force,* I think you may need a small one of your own—What—? Or maybe not…"

We had been watching the road, but *my* task force came in on the growl and thunder of eight giant fans plowing over marsh water.

"Oh, my," I said.

They moved in quickly and cut their speed in unison, and the first of them sliced the long grass almost to the edge of the road. A large gator materialized in the wind-bent reeds and he slid the bank to disappear beneath the foam. The lead airboat pilot, an "older" man who might pass for the boatman, *Charon,* ferried a teenager and a woman in his passenger seats. All three wore matching camouflage jackets and ball caps. Every man and woman in the flotilla carried a long gun either nose-up or across their laps.

"Umm—" Patty widened her eyes for me. "I don't impress easy…"

"Miss Alya?" The man hopped from the boat to the grassy shore. "I am Roy Steele. This is boy, and wife, Cara." He pointed to the other boats as well. "These are family. We go now."

"Wait," I said. "I did not expect—I mean, I still do not know where we are going, which direction." I handed him Mr. Vagelle's wrinkled, yellow Post-It. "This is all I have from him."

"So you said." He glanced at the note. "We know the waterways here. We go in order. Snail, Mud, Dosgris, Turtle Bay.

We could begin at the last, but it better to know Monsieur Vagelle's trail. I go in first with you. Other boats follow not too far back. Less noisy this way."

"These are very bad men, Mr. Steele. They killed people to get where they were going. If your boy and wife could stay here, I might feel better."

"Miss Alya, you are brave woman to do this thing. This wife say you will shame her to leave her behind." He dropped his smile to show he meant business, then replaced it with another. "We go now, *s'il vous plait.*"

His son handed out goggles and earmuffs, and Steele pointed to his collar mic. They would communicate this way. Motors revved—this was no longer my expedition. I shrugged for Patty, and she grinned like we were launching a Disneyland tour.

For about thirty full seconds, the flight of the airboat and the wind pushing my hair pulsed within me. It flew quickly away on the wings of *why we were there*. Mr. Vagelle had not responded to my many messages and his mailbox was full. In fact, he lost contact with everyone, including neighbors, the bomb squad, his lawyer, and Lieutenant Pedersen—who had initiated all this three years ago. Missing for nearly two weeks, I now imagined we were hunting for his body, if alligators had not gotten to it. We saw plenty of those dinosaurs dozing in the sun, or mostly submerged in the brackish waters and algae blooms, or escaping the roar of the airboat.

Patty caught me lowering the goggles to wipe my eyes and was thoughtful enough to turn away.

Steele navigated the shores of minor lakes and ponds. He often veered away into the spider's web of tight canals and overgrown water passages to avoid the gaze of fishermen or touristing airboats out searching for the thrill of more benign predators. I looked back several times to check the following Steele *family*, but they remained well hidden.

"They will take other ways," Steele spoke into my earmuffs and he nodded to comfort me. "Don't you worry, woman. Family knows where is Snail Bay."

We broke free of cramped foliage into a large expanse and picked up speed.

"Is this Barataria?" I yelled to be heard.

"*Non.*" He chuckled. "This much smaller Mud Lake. Barataria will look to you like Gulf of Mexico. We will not go out there."

We hugged the lakeshore for so long I lost my sense of time. Too many small canals, too much foliage identical to the one we had departed. I thought of Mr. Vagelle's trial—alone, lost, wandering through an endless bayou of sameness. When next I looked back, I spotted two other airboats in distant pursuit.

"That brother and uncle," Steele said. He laid on more gas.

More of the intricate maze. He cut the throttle and we coasted into what he declared to be Snail Bay. Our trio of airboats brushed the tall shore grass. Ahead, a fourth airboat appeared almost out of nowhere and stopped. Steele stopped. The distant pilot waved for us to approach.

"Andre has found something," Steele said, and waited for the two behind us to join him before proceeding. His son and wife both cradled their rifles. Patty noticed and she drew the Glock from beneath her jacket. Her partner took note but did nothing.

"No worry," Steele said, and followed Andre's boat into the weeds. Twenty meters in, we coasted to a stop behind Andre's boat.

A small, wrecked boat, but my eyes raced until I found the bloody clothing and partial remains of a corpse. Then another. All ravaged by predators. I tore at my seatbelt and jumped to my feet.

"Sit!" Steele ordered. I did, pulling free of my headphones. "Not safe here, you."

"Dead, maybe three-four days!" Andre called. "No tall-man here! Both dark! Many guns did this, I think."

I cupped my face in my hands.

"You mark the mouth of this canal, you," Steele said into his mic. "Then radio Coast Guard."

Andre waved. We backed free of the weeds to the main of Snail Bay as the sun blazed straight down.

"Are you okay?" Patty said.

"I need to be," I said.

"We go now." Steele pointed to his ears and revved. I reseated the earmuffs and buckled in.

Airboats five and six exploded from the green and raced for the far shore so we could cover both sides of the Bay more efficiently. As we exited the northern channel, one of their boats broke left. The rest of us slowed to watch.

"Martin, he going to Saint Joseph Bay."

Seventy yards or more, another voice interrupted. "Someting…another boat I tink. Mostly under water. Is not airboat. Is (pause) small shark boat. Coast Guard colors. Bad paint, I tink. I see no bodies here." He circled repeatedly.

"Set a marker. Radio to Guard. We must go."

We watched from a distance as Martin dropped a small buoy with a tall orange flag. He followed it with a canister that released a growing column of black smoke.

"We go north now," Steele said. "Others still circle Mud Lake. We go to Dosgris. My brother there. Then up to Turtle. Long ride. We need to put in by dark."

Patty's man vomited over the side-rail. Steele's boy smirked and his momma shook her head at him. We had been on the water at least six hours.

A crosswind buffeted, and we set a cruising speed. Steele said his boats were not as well-suited for open waters, and our fuel was low. We finally drifted into a shrimping station outside Bayou Dosgris, where we stretched our shaky legs while Steele spoke with the Deck Captain. With permission granted, our family of airboats gassed up.

We continued round the jagged shores and into a lazy, curving bayou.

At the first turn-in, we braked hard. An airboat floundered near the shore forty meters off our starboard side.

"It's brother." Steele pushed the throttle and three of our convoy pursued until he yelled into his mic, "Stay, you!" then he checked our own speed.

"Finn!" Cara yelled.

We had not yet reached the half-drowned craft when we heard a POP. We all ducked and yanked our headphones. Yet another, louder pop from the weeds and dust erupted from Steele's seatback. He spun us a sharp turn to give distance. Now that we knew where to look, I could barely see the moss-blanketed hut set deep into vegetation.

Again, pop. We angled beyond the hut and could finally see hints of white and orange. Other boats, empty. Not airboats.

"Shark boats. Coast Guard colors. Not Coast Guard, I think." Steele circled back.

Two of our followers could no longer hold back but flew straight at Finn's untended boat. A third flew at the shooter's position. Steele yelled for them to hold. The two seated in the prow opened fire into the tall weeds. Chaos followed with the remainder of our Cajun navy charging forward. Some circling, some in a dead-straight attack.

"It's one shooter, I think," Steele said.

"Hang on!" Patty yelled. We bucked, then flew.

We curved into a tight alley of water. I spotted two uniformed bodies, one in the weeds, another face down in the slop. By the time we reached the decaying boards of a dock, the firefight had ended. Three men had abandoned their airboat and, like trained commandos, hunched their way up the boards toward the hut. Others landed, but Patty held me back. I wanted to fight her.

Steele finally waved us forward.

Behind us, two airboats unloaded. Warily, they boarded the wrecked Coast Guard shark boats. They searched the surrounding bog while we joined Steele and his people, and a foul odor, beneath rotted moss-laden timbers—the hut's doorway. Long-dead corpses released their rot into the natural steam of the day. Bodies torn apart, limbs and more had been left as a reminder of the hungry inhabitants of this bayou.

The Steele family surrounded the opening. Every rifle pointed to the gory pirate propped there with one leg broken at the hip, the fingers of both hands crooked unnaturally. The youngest Steele crushed the pirate's fingers under his boot and grinned demonically as the pirate screamed. The others simply watched. I knew better than to interrupt a family's vengeance. Truth was, I did not want to.

"I recognize him," Patty said. When others turned, and the boot lifted, she said again, louder, "I recognize him. He's on a felon watch-list. His name is Oscar Moon. He goes by the name *Dobie.*"

"What does this mean?" I said.

"It's short for Doberman. A gang calling themselves the Dogpack."

"He knows Mutt?"

"Don't kill him. He should be questioned."

"You shoot brother? That airboat there?" Cara said to the pirate.

"Where are your friends?" Steele said. "Where do they meet?"

Mad pink eyes glaring up. Salt, like war-paint crusting on burned, black skin, cracked as Dobie bared his bloody teeth. He licked fresh blood from his lips and spit it at Steele's trousers.

Cara sent a bullet to his eye.

"Well, that is that," Steele said, as the noise of helicopters grew around us.

We remained on the dock and watched the water traffic gather. I could not count the boats. We answered Coast Guard and then police questions while watching the evacuation of the dead. We lied about Dobie's death.

"You're telling me he tried to shoot you with those broken fingers?" the officer said.

We all agreed.

Near sunset a Trooper picked up a cell phone call. He handed the phone to Steele, who walked down the planks for privacy. Then he came back to hold his wife. When Patty's phone rang, he nodded to her like he knew she should answer it.

"Oh. Oh, thank God." She lowered the phone to her chest. She then held the phone out for me.

"Alya. I am alive. I am fine," Mr. Vagelle said in my ear. I dropped her phone. I nearly dropped my butt to the dock.

"She will be okay." Patty had retrieved her phone. She listened, and when she hung up, she kneeled beside me.

"He will call you this evening. He has explained everything to Steele, and they will take their family back north tomorrow. We should get a ride into the city with Captain Scoggins." The Coast Guard Captain nodded.

"That son of a bitch!" I said. When Scoggins scowled, I pointed at the phone and said, "No, him."

Road Dogs

Twin shark boats, or something similar, bearing all the colors and markings of actual U.S. Coast Guard patrol and rescue, broke from the wide channel and sped over open water north of Turtle Bay. Each boat carried eight large canvas bags. Each bag had been stuffed with treasure, counterfeit plastic cards from *Paki-stan*. Each boat was helmed by an English-speaking Mexican, good boatmen. The sole survivors of Bookkeeper's *pirate* crew. They also carried passengers.

Dobie's dead. Mutt sat in the prow of the lead boat. He had been listening to the *official* radio calls from Bayou Dosgris when he heard Oscar's name. He instructed the pilot to change course, veering away from the right bank shallows. Near the center of the bay, he signaled both boats to stop. Burning clouds, the sun left its remaining fire ahead of him. Twilight's last.

"You a good swimmer?" Mutt said to the pilot.

"*Sí*, I'm okay." As the words left his lips, the man tensed. He would've almost given up hope of surviving until these words. The other two Dogs looked like they might shoot him for fun.

"You have two miles either way." Mutt lifted the nose of the AR-15. "In you go!" He smiled like a best friend. When Mutt dropped the smile, the man understood and lowered over the rail into the water.

"Por favor, señor."

"Maybe it's too easy. Let's make it more of a challenge." A short burst of rifle fire. The swimmer screamed and submerged, and resurfaced, crying, arms padding hard, his lifeless legs bleeding black into dark water.

The second pilot jumped off his boat seconds before that party sprayed fire into the bay.

"Enough!" Dane yelled. You'll bring the choppers down on us with all this racket. We still got a long stretch ahead."

Mutt agreed, though he resented anyone else taking control at this point. It was his operation. But then he understood the value of a subordinate mask. For now.

Lab took the wheel. Shep took control of the other boat. With an unhurried cruising speed, they continued to avoid the lights of lake traffic until they crossed the Intracoastal into Lake Salvador.

"We made it!" Bull shook his fists at the night sky.

Shut-up! Mutt thought.

Alya

Two hours of added questioning at the Sheriff's Department, they finally told me to go home. *Home where?* But as I left the front desk, Patty P.I. met me at the double doors. She coerced me to dinner at her favorite restaurant, on Gunston company expenses. We both opted for prime rib.

"I've smelled enough fish for one day," she said.

Near to falling asleep in our plates, the conversation smooth-danced around the hellish afternoon as we avoided the weightier subjects. She had heard from Detective Pedersen. With his *Vagelle Task Force* unsuccessful in heading off the Dogpack, they had dispersed to stake-out their less-than-usual haunts. He assumed the Dogs were too smart to walk into police hands after all this.

Patty convinced me to stay clear of Mr. Vagelle's building, and she offered a spare room for the night, but I needed to be alone. "Decompress," was her word for it.

We said goodnight in the restaurant parking lot as an easy mist drifted past the streetlights. She almost hugged me, but checked herself. She understood my haphephobia. Knowing I could not make the drive all the way back to Baton Rouge, I planned for a hotel I knew far from the hubbub of the city. I ducked into the Impala as the rains began and I closed my eyes for just a breath or two before starting. My phone buzzed before I fell asleep.

"Mr. Vagelle." Tears threatened again, but I fought them off. I checked my mirror.

"Alya," his voice said. "I did not know you were out there until I heard about the gunfight. I called Pedersen for an update. He was pretty angry with—No, not angry. He's frightened for you."

I swallowed my reply.

"We all are," he said.

"You could not call?" Earlier frustrations had been replaced by the relief at hearing his voice again.

"After my car—I needed to disappear quickly. I threw my phone. You can't know how sorry I am. I thought you were still in Baton Rouge. No one should have told you."

"They did not."

He listened to me breathe.

"You were never there, were you?" I said. "In that swamp."

"After a point, I didn't need to be. I knew where this would end."

"Is it ended?"

"No."

"So many involved. I never understood how you could be so sure of the actions of everyone?"

"Not sure. Never that." I could feel him thinking how best to explain without giving me too many details on tomorrow. "A series of compounded, educated guesses. Occasionally, I get lucky."

"Stop that. I have never known you to rely on luck."

"Alya, yes, you know me. I plan for what I can see. I speculate, anticipate. I stay flexible enough to change lanes. I left breadcrumbs for our police friend along the way."

"Eight moves ahead. We are all chess pieces for you."

Silence returned, and we listened to each other not speaking.

"But sometimes I guess wrong," he broke the quiet. "You were not on the chessboard. I could never have anticipated your involvement. I would've stopped you. Someone should have. From what I'm told, you've emptied all of Atchafalaya to search for me."

"Glad you can find humor in this." I wiped my eyes again.

"My friend, I—no, I blame myself. It was my miscalculation again. I should have known your...your tenacity."

"You almost said pig-headedness."

"All our time together, I know your capabilities, which is why, when I knew Mutt would come after me, I sent you far away. But I brushed that aside as instinct, me being over-protective, as usual. Now—"

"Now you know I am difficult to control."

"As if I didn't know that before. Tonight, everybody in Louisiana knows your name. Cajuns will write songs about you."

"Patty said I should not go to your home."

"No. Please. This is not ended." Any lightness of tone evaporated to be replaced by the fat raindrops on my roof. "I have things to do still, to end this. I cannot end this knowing you may become a victim."

"I will go back north. To school?"

"I know where to find you. Soon. Now, I am in a hurry."

"Be safe." But he had already hung up. Maybe he feared that word, *"dasvidaniya."*

Road Dogs

Lab had found an old yellow school bus parked, he said, "in a car graveyard behind some cracker's fallen-down barn." Not your average yellow school bus, a short yellow school bus. Lab left it behind a wire fence at Mutt's pre-determined jumping off point close to where they abandoned the boats.

"A school bus?" Mutt said. "Some Trooper sees six ugly criminals bouncing along in a yellow school bus, they ain't gonna have questions?"

"And they got no reason to hold us," Lab said. "We unloaded the cards and such back at the storage locker, and it's why we left the guns. They can't take us in 'cause we'd all scream racist. Besides, it's the only thing I could find that'd hold all of us."

"Idiot," Mutt said. "We're all parolees, except for Dane. They could throw us back behind bars just for riding with other felons. They'd love to catch us all violating parole in a short yellow bus."

"Ease up," Dane said. "This is just to get us to our own separate cars."

"Then we all celebrate," Bull said. "We made it, baby. We're all about to be like richer-than-shit movie stars. First thing, I'm buyin' me one of them private jets and a pilot to go with her."

"He'll be broke by next Christmas," Pug said.

"We ain't got the money yet," Mutt said. "Tomorrow, I go looking for Bookkeeper's fence for all them cards. Won't take more than a couple days. But remember, it takes six padlock keys to get those cards back. There's millions in temptation back there, which is why the rest of you need to keep an eye on each other. *And don't lose your keys.*"

With those words, the short-bus party quieted. They might have grumbled about Mutt playing den mother, but they all understood him.

Lab dropped them one-by-one. Shep got out first, two blocks from his warehouse-bar. He walked home in the rain listening for footsteps behind him. Bull climbed out across the street from his plumbing company van, still cheering silently in his head, no doubt.

"Ain't nobody keepin' an eye on you for two days, Mutt," Pug pointed a finger before stepping to the curb. "But somebody will be checkin' dat storage box every day. It's best you know what you're doin' and be quick about it."

Dane stepped to the curb in front of an all-night diner. He turned a knowing eye on Mutt before the short-bus drove away, then he went in and had coffee at a counter next to a city cop. The best camouflage.

"Don't know why you had to park so far out." Lab turned onto Chef Menteur Highway and glanced at his last passenger. "Been too long a day to keep dickin' around."

"I'm not out of the can much more than a month. I figured if I get grabbed for being anywhere near you others, they'll start rounding everybody up and throwing the keys into Pontchartrain."

"Uh-huh."

"There's a bus stop near the park entrance. They won't be running here this time of night, but they've got a covered bench out of the rain, and it'll be easy for some Lyft-jockey to find me. Sleep good, Dog."

5:40 a.m. A maintenance worker arrived at the Bayou Sauvage National Wildlife Refuge, and an unusual something caught his eye. Half-submerged into Blind Lagoon, a yellow something. The back end of a school bus. He cursed, spat, called 911 then sped away to the maintenance garage for a tractor to attempt to pull a small school bus out of the muck.

The police needed a bigger crane. Divers swarmed the lake. They discovered one victim in the driver's seat. Not drowned, a bullet had found his skull at close range.

11:00 a.m. Two attractive young ladies met the police car in the parking lot behind a small warehouse. The police were responding to a hysterical 911 caller. Both ladies still crying, one mostly unhinged, said they came in early to open the bar, which was a surprise to the officers who did not know of a bar in this alley. One, the more coherent one, said they did this three times a week.

Police backup arrived, five cars worth, then eventually a SWAT team. The SWAT went inside first.

They stepped over and around bodies, counting six in all. The seventh man had propped himself at the end of the bar with a .357 in one fist, a .12 gauge in the other, and eight bullet holes in his red-soaked T-shirt. The body came with a face familiar to the police captain. The waitresses called him Shep. A crooked cop turned felon, now corpse.

It took a few short hours to identify the other bodies and track the gang tattoos and locate a survivor that had been reported to NOPD by medical staff at LSU Emergency. In days to come, he would tell all about the "young bitch" who ratted that Shep's garage housed a crate of stolen money and "at least eighty-thousand worth of meth, coke and GHB and such." The young lady, Tisha (no last name), was identified and quickly confessed that she had been paid by one of Shep's crew to make that call. She had forgotten the caller's name, but it sounded something like a dog.

A full search of the premises had come up with a hundred and fifty bucks in cash and a baggie of coke-and-Pillsbury worth something in the neighborhood of two bills.

Bull didn't go to work that day. Instead, he spent the morning in his apartment, at his kitchen table with the tools of his trade spread round him. A distant memory glanced off the image of Sally, his ex-wife—her voice ragging about his greasy overalls on her furniture, and oil stains on the kitchen table. He smeared one with his thumb out of spite. He sometimes missed her, but mostly he missed her cooking. He decided to send her a note once he was rich.

"That'll piss her off."

He sealed the cap on the second pipe and got up to stow his tools. He finished the sediment in his grease-printed coffee cup as knuckles tattooed his front door. He checked the time.

"Morning, Money-bags," Mutt said with a grin.

"You're early." Bull tried to return the smile. "Did you find your fence?"

"You gonna invite me in?" Mutt glanced over his shoulder. "Or you want your neighbors to hear us discussing shit?"

"Sorry." He led the way inside, and Mutt shut the door. "Everything's right there in the kitchen."

"We need to get to this soon as possible. We can't start anything else until our *problem-child* is taken care of."

"I don't know how that last one missed him. Wasn't s'pose to blow 'til he sat behind the wheel. Something screwy there. I know my business, Mutt."

"I know you do. The bastard's slipperier than a mud catfish. That's how I ended up inside. Long as you made two more like I asked, I'll personally drop both of 'em into his lap. One cajone per each."

Bull led him to the table to watch him grin again.

"Get me a bag or something to carry them in. I think I heard someone outside."

Bull turned and stooped to look under the sink as Mutt, wishing he had not seen that ass crack again, returned to the door and cracked it open. Bull came up with a grocery bag and froze, stupefied by the sight of a single pipe bomb on the table. His first frightened instinct was to check if the other had rolled off the table. Confusion growing, he turned to his friend. Mutt lifted the pipe and struck the fuse. Bull had time to see the Dog's smile widen before rolling it between his feet and sprinting for the stairway.

2:15 p.m. The minor blast shattered windows in four apartments and blew the plumber's door onto the landing. There were no injuries to the neighbors. When he heard the news, Mutt thought, *"You knew your business, Bull."*

11:55 p.m. Dane went home. He was on alert. While never to be confused with the Ritz, his neighborhood landed on the green, "okay-side," of most crime charts. And in this city without much green, that meant something. Still, he stayed cautious due to the news of the day.

Did someone from Bookkeeper's crew survive? Did they follow us?

He parked two blocks from his building, took the stairs rather than the elevator. The corridor appeared unmolested. His door had remained locked.

He'd purchased a light windbreaker that afternoon to conceal the compact Sig Sauer he now carried in an elastic belly-holster. He lowered one hand to its grip as the other pressed his key into the deadbolt. Easing the door open, he stepped forward into the expanding geometry of light cast from the ceiling bulb at his back. He first noticed the shape slumped on his couch, and the Sig came out.

"Pug?" He recognized details in the crease of light. "What goes here? You sleeping?" He crossed carefully into the shadows until he towered over his partner. He turned Pug's face until it opened an obscene gash across the throat, and what looked to be a credit card stuck in that gash. Pug's fist had curled around something, and Dane almost broke the dead fingers getting to it. He held it to the light. On the card, a cartoon Monopoly Man, and the words, "Get Out of Jail Free."

A muffled shot knocked him forward. He fell across Pug's corpse and slid to the floor. He managed to roll his back to the couch. As the shock faded, the punch to his spine began to burn, and he could feel the wet spreading down into his elastic belly-belt and lower. The dark room lost its solidity, but he could almost make out the man-shadow in the corner chair. Mutt was talking.

"So, let me tell you a story." Even as he spoke, his words began to fade. "It starts with a dumb convict…who gets caught. And gets…smarter."

Vagelle

"I had followed enough, Alya. I did not stay with the cargo to its conclusion. I learned most of what I needed from the bug planted in Mutt's cell. Jazz Lamonte came through for us. The day of Mutt's release, I watched him fall asleep in the bus terminal, then I boarded behind him for the ride south. From there, I followed him to his hotel.

"When he went out the next day, I bugged the phone in his room and, when Saturday night rolled around, I was at a booth on the far side of the strip-club before he walked in to join his pals. I learned of their private meeting place, Shep's warehouse-bar, from his phone call. I found out the rest of his plans from there."

Road Dogs

Payday. Mutt was on a high, walking into the Baton Rouge Greyhound terminal for the second time in as many months. This would be his last. No more buses, ever. As of this moment, he was strictly first-class. And, as of today, there would be no more Mutt. He was Horace Mund. And tomorrow he would change his first name. What was Mom thinking?

Settle down, he scolded himself. *It ain't over 'til Brazil.*

He had arrived one hour early for his meeting. *Watch this prick walk in. Watch the other spectators when he does. If anyone makes eye contact, bolt.* He took the chair nearest the fire exit—his pre-planned getaway.

Of course, he recognized *the Bug* (prison slang for a staffer not to be trusted) the moment he cleared the door. Jazz Lamonte. Warden Michael's Executive Assistant from Angola. He'd been Bookkeeper's fence all along, sitting back, biding his time. The beast might have been surprised when Mund called, and not Bookkeeper, but he didn't show it now.

Jazz smiled—*We're all buddies here*—beneath dark aviator shades. He bee-lined for his target, while Mund watched the others on plastic waiting room chairs.

Mund rose by inches. They did not shake hands. Jazz spread his unbuttoned shirt and turned for the pistol inspection.

Vagelle

"I had a good idea who his old friends would be, but when I watched them come out of Shep's warehouse, I knew for sure. All the usual suspects, bad guys Mutt used to run with.

"The plumber, Bull, concerned me. I had an inkling Mutt would want me out of the picture before his big score went down, and there were a couple of obvious choices.

"Shep was a marksman in the military and in the police department before he stepped over the line. But Bull liked playing with explosives. He did his first long stretch at the age of sixteen when he accidentally blew up the family garage, killing his baby sister."

Road Dogs

Jazz led Mund across the room to an alcove resembling half-a-hallway leading to a dead end. The alcove housed short double-decker lockers lining both sides, and the only feature to the blank wall at the end was a medium-size universal dumpster.

Jazz tapped a finger as he passed each of the last five lockers on the bottom row.

"That's it?" Mund whispered.

"It's all I needed."

"Open."

Jazz pulled a key ring with five miniature locker keys and opened each locker in turn, closing and locking each before moving to the next. Each locker held a hefty duffle bag, open, displaying its contents.

That's a damn lot of green! Mund did his best to keep a straight line to his mouth. He hated walking away.

"Your turn." Jazz returned the key ring to his pocket.

"After you." Mund gestured for Jazz to go first. *He's too damned big to let behind me.*

Poker-faced, *the Bug* led to the street, and around the corner, to a bus-lined parking lot.

"The alley, just past there." Mund gestured to a mud-spattered minivan outside the gate. "You bring your bus around."

"You're one careful man." Jazz moseyed away.

"Remember that." Mund backed across the alley, never letting Jazz out of his sight until he unlocked his minivan's driver-door. He waited within arm's reach of the shotgun on his floor mat.

Vagelle

"I knew his psychological profile. I figured Mutt would want to make a big statement with my death—the man responsible for sending him to prison twice. And naturally, he had used Bull's infatuation with explosives in the past. They'd met when Bull was doing his second stretch for DWI with a trunk-full of gunpowder.

"I hired one of Patty's P.I.s to keep tabs on the bomb-maker, and her man eventually called to say he saw Bull going into my garage. I instructed him to back off and let nature take its course. I called Pedersen with some excuse to keep foot-traffic away from the garage. I didn't tell him the full reason. He would never have let me go ahead with my best play to have Mutt

*think I was out of his hair for good. Then I fell off the map until I read
about the cargo ship in the Gulf."*

Road Dogs

Jazz pulled the door of a bus alongside the rear hatch of the
minivan. He climbed casually down the steps and leveled a Colt
and watched Mund's cocky smirk vanish.

"If I wanted you dead, you would be dead," Jazz said. "Now
close that door and you can come back here with your hands
empty. Open the hatch so I can see what you have to sell."

It took a few seconds for Mund to realize his play was over,
and he'd be shoveling coal in Hell before he had time to grab
the shotgun. As he opened the hatch, Jazz threw him face-first
over the bumper and frisked him for a hidden weapon.

"Now you can do the unloading," Jazz said. "I'm done
playing nice."

Opening each bag for a quick glance at the cards, at Jazz's
direction, Mutt carried one at a time up the bus steps to lob them
down the aisle. He cursed with each bag opening. He cursed as
he climbed the steps. He cursed with each throw. With fists
clenched and his face burning, he watched Jazz retake the bus
driver's seat.

"I've an urge to put one in your eye," Jazz aimed the Colt,
"but your miserable existence ain't worth doing life in Angola if
I get caught."

"You gonna leave the locker keys?" Mund said, mostly to
himself.

"Take your ten percent, doggie. And if I ever hear you're back visiting Louisiana, I'll rip your beady eyes out and feed you to the gators." He pitched the locker keys over the roof of the minivan and watched the doggie chase.

Vagelle

"With that Pakistan shipwreck, I knew the second crew, Bookkeepers clan, had managed their part of the play. I stayed away to let them deal with Mutt's Dogpack. With crew number-two in the dark, I had no doubt who would come out ahead.

"I let our friend Pedersen in on the entire story, but the final landing in Lake Salvador was Mutt's spur-of-the-moment change. Pedersen had patrols spread all over the Intracoastal but missed the exchange from boats to bus.

"Still, I knew where Mutt was going. I had his fence. And my further suspicions were confirmed when I heard the radio call with the school bus dredged out of the lagoon and a convict behind the wheel.

"Mutt needed to act quickly with the rest, to catch them by surprise, and while I called Pedersen with my suspicions, it was too late for any of us to stop him."

Road Dogs

2:00 a.m. Mund's boot nudged a brick to prop open the door and re-enter the terminal waiting area. Most of the sparse crowd appeared to be napping. He pushed a dolly carrying a dumpster and wore a maintenance uniform with "Bob" sewn above his right jacket pocket and the company logo patch above his left.

One teller in a cage lifted his head but shrugged him off once he'd seen the uniform.

Maintenance Mund pushed directly for the alcove and past the walls of lockers to the back wall with the old dumpster. He did not look back. He pretended to shuffle the dumpsters, then slid the dolly back under the empty can that he'd come in with. He pulled the locker keys. He systematically opened the last five bottom lockers and transferred their contents, one at a time, into the clean dumpster. When he straightened, he was looking down into the curious eyes of a dirt-faced white-boy of about kindergarten age.

"What y'all doin'?" white-boy said.

"Gettin' rich." Mund smiled so big it chased the boy away.

"Junior!" a woman yelled from the seats. She woke a young couple sleeping entwined on a bench nearby, and Mund decided to speed the job along.

Pushing the dolly through the outer doors, he kicked the brick from its post beside the doorframe. He speed-walked to the curb and loaded the minivan from his can of thirty million dollars, green. There, he lowered the rear hatch ceremonially, as if sealing King Tut's tomb. He checked the sidewalk, both directions. *A sweet two-in-the-morning empty sidewalk.* He gazed up at the stars. He took a back-step and a deep breath.

"F'kin' Angola—I told ya ain't never goin' back."

Then he stepped off the curb and turned the fender of his minivan, to be slammed by the headlights of a traveling city bus.

Horace Mund felt the cold beneath him, but not much more. He couldn't move a hair. He knew he was dying, but he didn't know the how of it. He heard a bus idling. His vision cleared enough to see the enormous shape looming, bending to check for life. He wanted to say something like, "You sure look familiar to me, fat man."

"You look to be dyin'." The man leaned close enough to smell the onions from a taco dinner.

"You look…like…"

"Like I had a face-job. Federal boys give me a new identity to go with it. After I turned State's evidence. Remember the bank?"

Mund did not have the strength to choke on the onion smell or to say, *"Dead Dog. You ain't dead."* But the enormous bus driver read it in his eyes. Dead Dog left his field of vision, but somewhere in the confused surroundings, Mund heard his minivan open. Then, some thousand years later, he heard his minivan drive away. And then the bus drove away.

Dead Dog knew it as his "moment of victory." Though he had never in his life known what joy felt like—he had never smiled, as he could recall—the word was a curiosity to him. He had seen it on display many times from others around him. He had even recognized it in Mutt, though rarely, and usually while pulling a trigger. Sometimes he could imitate the expression, but he could not understand it. Dead Dog understood winning. That was a thing to strive for. A thing envied by others. He understood envy in others.

He had won big the day those others went off to Angola and he did not. The Feds showed their thanks.

He worked hard, his ass to that driver's seat. He worked for years, and he counted weeks and months, and he had purpose.

He knew Mutt. And he knew the dog would give him his moment of winning. The only thing he lacked was the witnesses, the others to give him their envy. It was why he tried talking to the dying Mutt, to tell him who he was, and to see the look of recognition. But he could not tell if Mutt understood, with his brain already dying.

Oh, well. Dead Dog had a minivan full of green forgetfulness to make up for the absence of envy.

He had watched Mutt climb the steps into his bus that first day of parole, and Mutt had not recognized him through the surgeries. And that was the win.

He had followed to the hotel, and for those days after, but he always kept a distance.

He had seen another following, a thin man he did not recognize, but the thin man did not act, so Dead Dog just stayed on his bus and parked in the shadows.

He had seen them all getting together, and he was savvy enough to know they had big plans. Plans he was no longer a part of. But this was *winning* again. They, all them others, thought they had won. But now Dead Dog won.

With Mutt pulling his last breath, lying in his dark pond, "Not-Dead Dog" strategized his future. It started with driving more slowly. It would take a loser like Mutt to let a Trooper pull him over for a thing as stupid as speeding. Then he would lose, just like all the rest.

The green light ahead turned yellow, and his foot left the gas. It turned red as he stopped. He tried to smile at his cleverness. If anyone were looking, they would see how smart he was. Then—*Those headlights* growing large in his mirror. No.

Not cop's headlights. Too many lights, too big, bus headlights. Dead Dog knew bus headlights. He glanced back once. Lowered his eyes on the duffle bags piled behind his seat.

"I have won!" He watched the bus picking up speed, the bus lights too close, the jolt and crush of the minivan a heartbeat ahead of the pain.

Nicolaus Vagelle abandoned the bus wreck and walked beneath the green light, angling for the sidewalk. This was Baton Rouge, and he needed a place to rest. Cell phone to his ear, he pressed speed-dial for Alya, his promise to call at the end of things. A promise he owed her after all she'd been through. She wouldn't be asleep. He understood her well enough. Her nerves would still be on a high-note from yesterday's excitement. He would continue his apologies. She would probably make him her Russian salad that he liked. Tomorrow, he would take her to the best restaurant in the city where they would celebrate the New Year. At some point in the evening, perhaps after too much champagne, she would say, "Does this mean I have to go back to college?" And he would smile and say, "Only if you want." And he would see admiration in her eyes. He would wish to say to her, "There is nothing to admire here. I am not what you believe. I am not a hero. I have done evil things."

EIGHT

A SPECTRAL ATTRACTION

Alya

"Any moment might be our last. Everything is more beautiful because we are doomed. You will never be lovelier than you are now. We will never be here again."

He had left the book atop his dresser. *The Iliad.* I would never have opened it, but for his devotion to the ancient Greeks…and the checkbook he had used as a bookmark. I was instructed to write a check for the landlord while he was out of town.

Sometimes he can be as subtle as a chest wound. Sometimes he can miss any sympathies in the next room.

The top, fourth-floor, apartment had remained vacant since the sentencing of its most monstrous tenant, Laine Baker, aka "The Shrovetide Ripper." Her execution made national headlines.

My employer, *the Consultant*, maintained the third-floor apartment/office, and the landlord, Mr. Hemmings, hinted to me more than once that Mr. Vagelle ensured the upstairs remained vacant with "regular tax-free donations to the Hemmings Family Trust." His words. *Ms. Ripper* was before my time there but, naturally, I had read the case notes and newspaper articles, so I was familiar with both the murderer and Mr. Vagelle's efforts to end her horrors.

He remained quiet about the case, and I quickly learned to leave certain topics alone. That was the initial reason for my silence whenever, over those past months of working late, I heard the wraith-like footfalls from the fourth floor. These old buildings were famous for the symphony of creaks and pops. The results of ancient plumbing and heating, or simply settling into expansive soil after the stormy season. (*Expansive Soil*— some New Orleans bureaucrat's verbal fog for a city built on swampland.) At least those were the reasons when I thought to confide my concerns to the young Dr. Maiwand, the second-floor tenant.

"I am not sure what to think, Doctor," I said. "I know about old buildings. I have certainly lived in worse, especially in Moscow. But I have heard these small noises from the top floor for months now. They were rare at first, so I shrugged them away."

"But since Mr. Vagelle has been out of town it has gotten worse, yes?"

"Some nights I hear creaking on the stairs, and sometimes…" Hearing myself speak, I realized how foolish I must sound.

"Go on."

"I should go home. It has been a long day."

"Sometimes?" he said. "What don't you want to say, Alya?"

"Okay. Sometimes, at night," I searched for another way of telling it and failed, "I think I hear a muffled crying. Not rational, I know. I do not believe myself, saying this. But I imagine other sounds late in the day. *Prizraki* (ghosts) roaming. I have even given up my glass of wine at the end of each workday to listen for it. I have worked here nearly five years, and I am not overly religious, and I certainly do not believe in the…"

"Paranormal?"

"Superstitions popular in much of this city."

"I am sympathetic," he said. "Truly. I have also been shaking off the beliefs of my Indian heritage since I was old enough to think for myself. But a child's upbringing is as hard to divorce from as centuries of religious inheritance. I, too, confess to personal experiences I have no rational answers for, but I've developed an overly skeptical response to many things, yes."

"I really must go," I said, taking up my satchel and umbrella. "Thank you for the cup of tea. You have a nice…*comfortable* apartment here." *At least comfortable for family visits*, I thought, noting Oriental rugs on two walls, the small painting of a serpent-crowned goddess, a framed slab of masonry on the sideboard with a broken corner and etched pictographs surrounding the Hindu god, Shiva.

"I also know your job with Mr. Vagelle has dragged you into many, well, *difficult* situations." He held the door for me. "Stress can play havoc with the imagination. Please, as I've said before, if you ever feel the need to talk, I am only one floor away."

"*Spasiba.*" I glanced up the stairs before turning for the street door and home.

Sleepless at three a.m., I had hoped to distract myself with city lights swimming across ceiling and walls, but tonight they added a sense of drowning to my unease. I got up, closed the drapes then fell back into the sheets.

The whimpering from the office walls came back to haunt me. Too much like a child. Too much like my own childhood.

Papa coming in drunk most nights. Violence. Mama's tears. Then Papa, shirtless, tattoos of stars and Russian crosses, and blood. Mama on the living room floor, holding him, burning the wound in his back with a hot iron. I learned the word prizhech'—to cauterize. He drank more, and hit Mama. Then the two men breaking our door, and Mama cutting one with a kitchen knife, and Papa beating the other with a stove poker.

My tears dried up by age ten. By twelve I was working for my Papa's *mafiya* friends. At sixteen I escaped to Lithuania. There, I once imagined I saw a ghost.

We lived in a large empty building. Several friends and myself. We stole, and we hid from *Policija* to stay alive. That winter without windows, I almost died. So cold, covered in damp rags, wrapped in a length of old carpet unable to move.

And my friends took turns keeping a fire in a can beside me and bringing me food. Until the night the ghost came to me.

Blanketed herself, hunched like a bear from the weight of many coats and a ragged nest of gray falling from beneath a torn hood, she found us, and the others ran off. Only I could not.

The witch-bear stood by my fire, warming herself. She bent down to steal my half-eaten apple and the open tin of beets, and when she turned to me, I saw a deathly face. A gray face. Sunken eyes, sunken cheeks, broken lips. The face of my Mama. Then she changed, and she was not my Mama, just an old *Baba Yaga*. She sat by me until the fire died. By morning she had moved on, but I always remember my Mama's face there, and I somehow knew Mama was dead.

I do not know how I got well, but I did. Then I managed to hide aboard a cargo ship.

I did not know if I believed in a God, but I had seen the work of fallen angels all my life. I avoided churches, reminded of my Papa's tattoos that meant nothing but pain and hate. I remembered old women leaving Sunday mass with their headscarves and beads. The pallbearers and slow processions in black. Or the parades here, in this New Orleans, with joy and music in the street celebrating death in a different manner. It was always foreign to me. All of it.

I will not believe in ghosts.

Near noon the following day, the storm fought to keep me from the office, or what I sarcastically referred to as "the Hemmings Building." The wind broke my umbrella and the rain turned to hail and assaulted me like flung gravel. I ducked into a bakery for a cup of coffee and a wish for the bombardment to ease a bit. I stabbed the remains of my traitorous umbrella into the bin beside the door.

The girl with cornrows and a Sophie nametag took my order and passed me a hand towel.

"Go ahead, it's clean," she said.

"You are my best thing all morning." I patted my face and dried my hands and added two glazed croissants to the order. I dropped a tip into her jar to return the smile. Taking a stool at the window shelf, I watched the sidewalk warriors and wished I could spend the day in here. She brought my order.

"Sophie, do you see the old woman across the road?" I said. "Leaning on that stroller piled with black bags?"

"Don't tell me you're a cop," she said.

"Oh, no." I forced a chuckle. "Just that I thought I saw her earlier. It is weird, but I think she keeps watching me."

"Enjoy your croissants." She returned to the counter and the next customer in line.

My morning smile evaporated, so I swallowed half my coffee, forgot my croissants, hooked my satchel over my arm, and braved the storm once more. Only a block and a half to go.

Up slippery concrete steps, then the street door closed behind me and I heard slippers shuffling away from Mr. Hemmings's peephole. Perhaps he did not want me dripping on him. Just as well. I shook myself. I turned for a moment to the etched glass of the street door. Through the veil of rain I imagined I saw the old woman, or someone built like her, wearing one of her black plastic bags, hunched in the recesses of a doorway across the street.

By late afternoon I refilled the teapot and turned on the flame. My focus had become scattershot (as Mr. Vagelle liked to call it) and I hoped for his early return. I considered leaving early and telling him to withhold my pay, but someone should be here to answer the office landline, should he call.

A soft knock at the door turned out to be Dr. Maiwand. I invited him in for tea.

"Oh, no thank you. I have a dinner appointment and just wanted to check up on you before I went out."

The kettle shrieked and I jumped. He came in and sat.

"I can spare a few minutes," he said. "You're still on edge from yesterday, yes?"

He had his doctor's reassuring manner, as usual, and by the time he left, my life was nearly back in order. I relaxed into the cushions of the settee and lost myself in the play of light and shadow on the Thomas Moran painting above the fireplace. Having studied it often over the years, I wondered if the golden waterfall was breaking free of the sinister clouds, or if the surrounding darkness was moving to smother the light.

My eyes opened to the dark. Stumbling to the desk, I fumbled with the elusive lamp chain and cursed when I saw the time. *11:15.*

Then came the tap-tapping on the planks above and my frustrations boiled over.

Enough!

I hustled down the stairs, knocked on the doctor's door. Still out. I descended further and Hemmings answered his door with a frightened look.

"You heard it!" I said.

"What! Is something happening?" He stretched from his portal like a squirrel expecting coyotes.

"*Izvinite (sorry)*. I thought maybe you heard it."

"Ms. Korikova, *maybe* you should call before pounding on someone's door. You scared the life out of—"

"There is someone on the fourth floor. I would like you to come up with me now."

"Impossible. That apartment is locked. It's always locked."

"Well, I say it is not. If you bring the key, we will check together." I started up without him. "Okay. I imagine I can find something to break the lock myself."

With a jangle of many keys, he raced after me.

The fourth-floor apartment did prove to be locked. The door came unstuck and the musty odor hit us, and Hemmings reached past me to flip the light switch.

"See?"

"Ha-llo!" I called upon entering. "Anybody here?"

The room had been cleared of furniture, with the exception of one old leather recliner peeking from beneath a half-fallen bedsheet. Hemmings shook the dust from it and re-covered the chair. I tested the windows, but they were all locked.

"We're four stories up," he said.

"Have you cleaned up here lately?"

"Of course not. No one comes in here. Your boss pays to keep it this way."

"So who sweeps the dust on the floors?"

He glowered in place, perplexed by the dust swirls on the hardwood. I walked carefully to the empty bedroom, then the bath.

"Someone removing the evidence," I said. Moisture sparkled on the sink, mirror, tiles, and walls. I heard street sounds then noticed the fifteen-inch window vent open above the tub.

"How long has this been open?" Hemmings peered over my shoulder. He squeezed past me and stood in the tub to close the window. "Too small, if that's what you're thinking. Nobody has come in this way. Maybe someone's pet monkey who likes to clean floors."

He locked the apartment and followed me back downstairs where we turned along the side passage to the rear of the building, the boiler room, then the service entrance. Hemmings turned a key in the alley door to prove it was locked. Despite the broken bulb outside the door, we had enough alley light to make out a beast-shaped man hurrying away from the dumpster. I also thought I recognized the shimmer of the old woman in black plastic limping into the distance.

"Well, at least something positive came of your paranoia." He locked us back inside. "I see I need to replace the bulb. Enough of this. I have better things to do. It's late and you should probably call it a night yourself."

Better things to do at eleven o'clock at night? I wanted to ask.

Returning to Mr. Vagelle's apartment, I checked the light on his answering machine. Still dark. I straightened whatever I had displaced during the day, rinsed my teacup in the sink, packed up my satchel, then locked the third floor.

Grateful the rain had stopped, the clouds ripping away from the moon, I made my way to the Canal streetcar line, then changed my mind and direction. If Mr. Vagelle was in the city tonight, he would be at Bobby J's Black & Blues Club.

"He ain't been in these past weeks, Ms. K.," the giant behind the bar called out when he spotted me. "But I got a White Zin with your name on it. You're welcome to take his booth if you think he might show later."

"You are great, Bobby, thank you."

The curved booth at the far corner remained on permanent reserve for Mr. Vagelle. A lot of history between the two. It served to remind me that, as much of a recluse as he was, my boss still had one or two close friends.

Blues music always comforted, and together with the wine my nerves began to untangle. I kept an eye on the door. At some point, Bobby J. squeezed into the far side of the booth with his glass of sparkling water.

"You good, Ms. K.?" he said. "You seem a bit *out of sorts* tonight, if you don't mind me sayin'. I mean, and as crazy as your job must be, you always carry yourself like you're the one chilled tomato in any fridge."

"*Spasiba*, I think." Then, after some encouragement, and my over-stating how I did not believe in such, I rolled out my story on the phantom of the fourth floor.

The corners of his mouth wrestled with humor. Then, after overstating how *he* did not believe in such, he started in on his employees many reports of apparitions and "other-worldly" happenings in and around his nightclub.

"One gets used to these things in the old district," he said. "Gets entertaining after time, until it keeps the kitchen staff from working nights."

Eventually, he needed to relieve his other bartender for her cigarette break. He returned to place a coffee cup in front of me and say, "You've had enough wine for the evening, my friend."

"Are you are cutting me off, you black Cossack?" *Over-performed outrage.*

"If he comes in, I'll insist he call you immediately," he said. "You sit here as long as you like. Chef's gone home for the night, but I might throw together a nice plate—"

"I'm fine, Bobby. Really."

"When you're ready, I'll call you an Uber."

It took ten minutes in the backseat of the Uber for me to change my mind again. Maybe it was the wine. I asked the driver to take me to Bourbon Street. I needed to be around people. That took less than fifteen minutes of strolling and sobering for me to decide I did not want *these* people this close to me, so I climbed into another taxi. I directed him to the Hemmings Building, but told him to let me out before reaching my destination.

What am I doing back here? The wine has me traveling in circles?

I stepped wide of a dark puddle and watched the glistening pavement. This sidewalk, its familiarity far from the tourist crowds, came with a counterfeit comfort after so many years. The psychologist might say this was the source of my upset for feeling chased out of my habitat. Not spirits of my own making, but a theft of my tranquility.

The dark windows of the Hemmings Building watched me from across the street, and I realized for the first time that the streetlight at the curb was dark. It reminded me of the alley. Then I realized I stood beneath the awning in the doorway where I had seen the *old woman*. I decided it was time to turn away from Mr. Vagelle's apartment and aim for my bed.

Walking in here at three a.m. should get a scream out of Hemmings. I smirked at the thought. As Mr. Vagelle once said, *His charm is in his predictability.*

A clang from across the street halted petty thoughts. More echoing sounds, and a distant angry voice from the *rooftop*. A wisp of light crossed the gutter and disappeared. Harsh noises, boots scraping tarpaper and gravel? I took a single step, but froze as a substantial human, not a ghost, fell from the eaves. It fell forever. The sound it made hitting the building's front steps sickened me.

Hemmings's windows lit up.

I stared long enough to convince myself the body was not imagined, then I fished into my satchel and found my phone. I touched nine-one-one speed dial while crossing the street.

For a moment, Dr. Maiwand and Mr. Hemmings loomed side-by-side from the top step. The doctor jolted from his stupor first and rushed to check the broken body for signs of life. Neither of us believed he would find any.

Hemmings said my name several times. His voice came from far away. An ache, a drum banged inside my skull, and the scenery turned. I tried walking away. But not far. A grip on my arms made me cower. Dr. Maiwand steered me to the neighbor's doorstep. He sat beside me there, not too close. He talked, but I could find nothing to say in return.

A familiar figure cloaked in her glistening black cape watched us from the corner but vanished with the sounds of sirens.

More sirens. Loud, with flashing colored lights, banging car doors, and a growing, confused morass of voices and movement. I was suddenly eighteen again and the constant movement of the cargo ship, buffeted by the ocean swells, lifted a bitter taste of sick to the back of my tongue. I vomited over the handrail into dead roses.

Dr. Maiwand called for the EMS. I recognized the patch on her sleeve as she rushed to attend, checked my pulse, and hung a blanket over my shoulders. I swallowed pills and water and held her ice pack to the back of my neck. More water.

Too many questions assaulting me, other voices crowded them, the most repeated being, "What were you doing here this time of the morning?" The doctor showed his credentials to the ranking police officer, said something, and the officer went away with a promise to return.

I woke to clean sheets in Mr. Vagelle's bedroom, fragrant steam rising from a bowl on the nightstand. Dr. Maiwand leaned against the doorframe.

"You probably don't feel like eating," he said, "but it's been hours since you put anything in your stomach except pills."

"Is Mr. Vagelle—?" I realized I wore a man's dress shirt beneath the blanket.

"I'm afraid not. But I knew he wouldn't mind."

"Last night, that man—"

"Eat. Have a hot shower. I knew you'd be out awhile, so I had Mr. Hemmings throw your clothes in the wash." They lay neatly folded on the dresser. "And the answer is no. A young lady on the Emergency team helped get you situated."

I thanked him in two languages. The thoughtful man had even left a bottle of Tylenol on the bathroom sink. As I toweled my hair, he called through the bathroom door.

"I need to run out. Another of my patients is having a bad day as well. I just turned off the burner for the teapot. Toast and soft-boiled eggs on the counter. But you know where everything is, yes? I'll check in this evening. Gotta run."

Breakfast and painkillers at four in the afternoon. The perfect remedy. I had not yet decided if I wished to return to my own apartment before nightfall. My Russian ancestors refused to allow my surrender to whatever had infected this building.

Detective Pedersen came to call.

"I am glad they sent a *friendly* interrogator," I said. We took opposing chairs at the dining table.

"You know better than that, Alya."

"Tea? Coffee?"

"Our doctor friend gave me your story, which is why I put off my visit 'til this evening. You look mostly recovered."

I poured his coffee anyway.

"He also told me about your upstairs *mystery guest* and all the late-night goings on. From what you had told him, it didn't sound like a heavy-footed man clomping around up there."

"Definitely not."

"The landlord mentioned a homeless man going through the dumpster out back. Said it might be our victim from last night." He seemed to never stop adding sugar to his cup. I looked away.

"He could have been the same size, but we never saw his face. And we never saw him actually going through the dumpster. He was already walking away when Hemmings opened the alley door."

"So, last night…?"

"I was across the street. Please do not ask why." I fought off the memory. "I have no answer, except I had a bad day and the phantom was on my mind. And I had a few too many glasses of wine. This building—I heard noises I thought to be coming from the roof. Maybe a scuffle. And voices. I saw a flashlight, I think. Then I saw the man fall, and I phoned your people."

"Well, maybe after last night, your ghost-visitor will have moved to another neighborhood."

"I am sometimes that lucky. Would you like me to go out and buy more sugar?"

"Just so you know, we've not yet ID'd the vic. He might have been homeless. Our team didn't find much on the roof, other than, yes, a possible scuffle and heel marks where he went over the edge. An open buck knife in the gutter that might match a superficial cut beneath the dead man's arm. A few items in the alley near the rear exit, like a broken flashlight, a ratty blanket, and a length of knotted rope—but it's an alley, so there's gonna be junk that might've been there since Noah floated onto Lake Pontchartrain."

I refuse to believe in ghosts.

I returned two nights later, carrying a small overnight bag loaded with necessities from home. Crime scene tape, that would stop no one, hung across the steps one-up from the third-floor landing. I ducked under and continued to the fourth floor with Mr. Vagelle's lock-pick set already in hand. He was much more skilled than I, but I was not pressed for time.

I locked the door behind me and, using the flashlight app on my phone, prepared for the night ahead. I removed the sheet and angled the recliner to view both the windows and the door. I took the snubnose from my bag and wedged it beside the chair cushion. I placed my water bottle on the floor, took napkin, fork, and a small Tupperware containing my chicken salad dinner, and settled in for what I mostly believed to be an uneventful night.

It was all an elaborate and hugely imperfect plan.

I woke to the sound of the old doorframe splintering and the lock hitting the floor. A light filtered in around the beast shuffling toward me, but I was already up with the pistol in my hand. At the size of him, it must have been the man we had seen in the alley. The man who had fallen from the roof could have smuggled a Saint Bernard with him beneath this one's shirt.

"Stay away—" my voice cracked. "I will use it."

He did not come closer, but circled to the bedroom and looked inside. I crouched, reaching my free hand into the bag for my phone. He poked his head into the bathroom while I *speed dialed* Emergency. Then he faced me.

"I have a break-in at—" I said, then realized it was a recording. But the beast was circling silently, casually, to the windows, one then the other. I backed for the exit.

The operator came on, said something, but I was more concerned with my gunhand jitters and pointing at the thick silhouette who ignored me.

A plastic rustled somewhere. I almost understood the beast was not interested in the view from the windows before the ceiling fell on me. The snubnose bid goodbye to my uncontrollable fingers and clattered to the hardwood as liquid filled my knees. Spinning as I fell, I believed I saw the eyes of an old witch before the already dark room flooded with even darker sleep.

The passage of time means nothing to the unconscious, but my half-waking dreams assaulted me with a spinning terror. A door slam. A child's scream. A witch's curse. The roar of the beast. I again became that helpless teen Alya, sick, in pain, bound and wrapped in the old carpet. This time it was ropes and twine restricting me.

Fear forced my eyes open, and the concussion drove a line of pain from the base of my skull to my brow. My hands and arms struggled against the ropes. I sat up just enough to spit the rag from my mouth and tried my best not to vomit over the edge of the tub or onto myself. *Not twice in one week, damnit.* I fell back.

Angry voices pushed in from beyond the bathroom door. I continued to squirm against the ropes, until I understood the damage I was doing to myself outweighed the chances of loosening my bonds. My arms strapped to my torso, my fingers already numb, my wrists burned. Ankles pinched tight, chafing at every squirm. I shifted my attention to the seductive chill of porcelain at my back. *Sleep,* it told me.

"What the hell do we do with them now?" the beast yelled.

The door banged open and a dwarf flew into the room—no. Not a dwarf, a boy. And he did not fly, he was thrown, and he hit the edge of the sink as the door banged shut. The boy labored to his knees. He sobbed. He might have been twelve.

Shocked at seeing me in the tub, he quickly wiped his eyes and face with the bottom of his T-shirt.

"You're the downstairs lady?" he whispered and sniffed.

"Can you help me?" I half-rolled to show him my ropes.

"She can die in that tub, for all I care," the old witch was saying. "But we need to get the boy away from here tonight, before anyone checks on that idiot downstairs."

"Shhh—" the boy said, as if I did not have the sense to remain quiet. He stood a bit wobbly, pried the lid from the toilet tank, and laid it on the floor. He reached in and came out with a wet kitchen knife. "I…lost my good Buck knife. I hid this in here. Grammy's not too smart, is she? Shhh. Hold still. I don' wanna cut you on mistake."

"We can't leave her to die!" the beast said. "She did nothing—"

"Shut up, fool!" the witch said. "She knows what you look like. What if the police accuse you of killing Jesus?"

The boy sawed at the twine wrapping my torso, freeing my arms, then went to work on the rope chewing into my wrists.

"I did not," the beast said. "I was not here that night."

"She saw you in the alley. She and that landlord saw you. Do you think police will believe you just because you say it wasn't you?"

The boy stung the back of my hand once and I flinched, but said nothing. He apologized under his breath, then worked the blade with added care.

"Now go down quiet," *Grammy* said. "See if the first floor is still empty. We will take the boy out." We heard the large man on the stairs. "Damned ape don't know the meaning of quiet," she said.

"I may be able to do this a bit quicker." With my hands free, I motioned for the knife and he let me take it. "What is your name?" I pulled up to sit on the lip of the tub and massaged my burning ankles. "I am Alya." I returned his knife. "You be careful with that."

"I am Jesus. Like my poppa." He looked away. "He died."

"I hear you up here at night. Walking. I have wondered, you come in through that tiny window?"

He looked at me as if he did not understand what I said.

"Boy!" Grammy said and opened the door. When she saw me free, her eyes blazed. "Boy! Get you here, boy!"

"No, Grammy!" The knife shifted in Jesus's hand.

"You gonna cut me now, Boy? You gonna cut your own Grammy?"

He sniffed.

"Get you here!"

A gunshot from downstairs shook us all.

Grammy lunged for Jesus, and the boy dropped the knife at the moment I grabbed the toilet tank lid. I was clumsy—blood had not returned to all my extremities—but the lid met with her ear and she went down. My knees folded from the effort.

Grammy crawled to the living room and the boy ran after her calling, "Grammy!" I followed drunkenly. She fell in the center of the room and her grandson stroked her arm. I propped my back against the living room wall, my eyes fighting to close.

I heard the distant sirens again, then I heard footsteps running on the stairs. A young woman entered the room. At first, all I saw was the revolver in her hands and the glistening rain slicker. Then I recognized Sophie beneath the hood. Sophie from the coffee shop. *A dream? No.*

"Jesus!" she said. The boy rushed to her and the pistol fell from her hands as she threw her arms around him.

I stumbled, then knelt beside the old woman. I checked the pulse at her neck. She breathed and moaned and touched her head.

"You!" Sophie said.

"Yeah, me," I said.

My boss, Mr. Vagelle, appeared as a *miracle* in the doorway. Behind him, Dr. Maiwand. I snorted.

"The cavalry," I said. "Late, just like the movies."

"It appears you've had a busy time in my absence," Mr. Vagelle said upon entering. Seeing my difficulty in rising, walking, and dropping onto the recliner, he rushed to my side. "Doctor!" Dr. Maiwand crossed the room.

"What happened to you?" The doctor took hold of my wrist and I shivered.

"A simple concussion. No worries."

"Oh, hell."

Detective Pedersen joined the party, accompanied by two uniformed officers with pistols drawn. He signaled them to stow their weapons.

"I get way too many emergency calls to this address. Take care of that man on the stairs," he told one. And get EMS to the boiler room. *Stat.*" To Mr. Vagelle he said, "I have a man standing by your Mr. Hemmings. His injuries don't appear life-threatening."

"Our friend Sophie found him on the way in," Mr. Vagelle said for my benefit. "She's the one who called the police."

"She must have a secret method for getting them to answer the phones. I am glad Hemmings was not hurt too bad." My fingers shielded my eyes from the painful light. "But how do you know more about what is happening here than I do?"

"I will tell you all about it when you've had time to recover."

"No!" I said. "You will not make me wait for this." I grabbed the ache at the back of my head. "Doctor, could you please find another ice pack?"

"When I heard the address on the radio call, I phoned your boss," Detective Pedersen said.

"Dr. Maiwand and I had just sat down to dinner after he picked me up from the airport," Mr. Vagelle said. "He explained your ordeal these past several days so, when Pedersen called, I expected you had found the trouble you were looking for."

"You know these other people?" I said.

"I am not oblivious, Alya. I heard what you heard, the child's footsteps above our heads. I imagined he needed a warm, dry place to stay, but I made the mistake of avoiding contact until I returned from my trip. I'm very sorry for putting you through all this."

"You never considered I might let my imagination run amok."

"Precisely. Of course, I knew Sophie from the coffee shop, and I knew she had a son. I couldn't connect the two until I heard of his father's *accident*. Then I hurried for a flight home."

"I ran away," Jesus said. His mother cradled him on her lap.

"Shut it, boy!" Grammy-witch leaned on an elbow. "Keep your mouth shut or I'll chop—"

"Grab her!" Pedersen signaled a patrolman. "Cuff her and drag her to a car, then drive it into the lake." Seeing the patrolman's open-mouth, he said, "Scratch that last. Just get her out."

Grammy went screeching, as one might predict. Once she had left the room, Sophie apologized to me.

"This is all my fault," she said. "I should have shown him the door years ago. The only good thing he ever gave to me was my little Jesus." She stroked her boy's head. "Bu-But I couldn't leave him."

"Momma," Jesus said, "I ran away because if he was out looking for me…"

"Shhh."

"…he would stop hitting you."

"When I heard he fell off this roof, I knew what happened," Sophie said. "I knew where he found my boy."

"Daddy tried—I mean, we were at the edge. I took his knife."

"Hush, child. You did nothing wrong."

"And the old woman?" I said. "That is your boy's Grandmother. She knew where to find him too."

"That night, outside, she saw her son fall. She didn't say exactly, but I guessed. And she blamed my Jesus. And she blamed you. You called the police while she watched. Then you said nothing to them about her grandson."

"Who is the big boy on the stairs?" Pedersen said.

"*Grammy* has more than a couple sons—all more afraid of her than the police."

"Pedersen," Mr. Vagelle said, "is there something you can do for her?"

"Please don't put me in the prison." Sophie wept. "Please don't take me away from my boy after all this."

"You and your boy will have to come with me," the detective said. "You shot that man on the stairs. You may not have killed him, but—well—it wouldn't look good for me to have you walk out the door just now. The gun—"

"My husband's. He threatened to shoot me with it."

"Detective," Mr. Vagelle said, "if I can convince our wounded *abductor* to drop the charges, after Mr. Hemmings files his complaint for the assault…?"

"Well, she'd still have a number of misdemeanor charges, but with extenuating circumstances…I know you have a good lawyer."

"Done." Mr. Vagelle winked for the boy.

Four nights of recovery, then I took the curved bench across from the "consultant" at his reserved table at the back of Bobby J's. The black giant set a tumbler of Widow Jane bourbon in front of Mr. Vagelle and an unrequested glass of White Zin in front of me.

"You're off the pain-killers?" he said. "Your drinks ain't on the house tonight, Ms. K. I'm making your boss pay for everything, for making your life hell lately."

"In that case," I said, "maybe I should order a round for the club." He returned to his bar with an evil grin. "So, do you think Sophie will see jail time? I know some judges would love to lock her up just for possession of the gun."

"She's already home and back with her son," Mr. Vagelle said.

Throughout the evening of soft Blues and a bit too much White Zin, I thought of the boy, Jesus, and his bravery. A part of me wished to tell Nicolaus Vagelle more. The other part of me decided not to mention the past three evenings, working late, hearing soft footsteps from the fourth floor. Jesus was back, of course.

I caught occasional side glances from him. Eventually, feeling defensive, I had to ask. "What?"

"Something…" he said. "I leave town for awhile and when I come home, half the neighborhood is beat up and, well, you continually surprise me. I believe if a bomb ever drops on New Orleans, when the dust clears, you'll still be standing."

"Me and the cockroaches."

NINE

AN IRRETRIEVABLE HEART

The Client

"Yes, I come with a high price tag. I am not in the Yellow Pages, I do not hand out business cards, and for my purposes, I'm mostly retired. Let me rephrase that. I work for myself and only when I feel motivated." Nicolaus Vagelle, appearing to study the expensive painting above his fake fireplace, stood with his back to the man on the settee. It was a mostly dark painting.

Our potential client sat with his feet apart, thick fingers gripping thick knees, knuckles growing pale.

"Also, regardless of how the press has colored my work in the past, I am not a private-eye. I'm a *consultant.*" His eye-flick to me, almost imperceptible. "Come to me with a crime, I immediately refer it to the police. I'm not a practicing psychiatrist, nor am I a priest, and your problems are not confidential unless I decide they are."

"Unacceptable, Vagelle. Discretion is—"

"Summarizing the contract, here are my rules." My boss turned to the visitor. "You hire me to look into your missing person, you pay me one week in advance. Regarding domestic problems, if I find your missing person, and that person does not wish to come home, I do not disclose my findings and I keep your entire down payment, no questions asked."

In this instance, my job might be described as "silent witness." I sometimes let my mind drift to the street traffic below, I sometimes pretended to scribble notes at the corner desk, but this speech was too familiar. I confess, silence could be difficult for me, so my scribbles became abstracts.

Mr. Vagelle had once suggested a female presence in the room worked as a psychological deterrent to an aggressive visitor. I responded with, "As long as you do not ask me to wear a dress." I said it in my native Russian, and it shut him up. That was early in our working relationship.

"You done with the speech? What guarantees can you give me for this large advance? How do I know you will not just take my money and go play golf for a week?" Unconsciously wrinkling his bespoke Briani suit, J.C. Landon was an executive accustomed to intimidating with a glance. He was in the wrong room.

Mr. Vagelle rolled the cuffs on his barely ironed, gunmetal gray, dress shirt. This, and his lean, six-feet two-inch, working-class attitude, acted as a scuff on the shoe to swaggering wealth. He enjoyed the gamesmanship.

"My guarantee is my reputation," he said. "And you would not have taken time from your busy day without first having me investigated."

"Listen, Vagelle—"

"I do what I say, Mr. Landon. Sign or don't. If you like, I can refer you to an investigations firm I occasionally do business with."

"I gotta say, you do come across as a heartless prick." Landon rose like a boxer anticipating the bell, but he opted for the easy exit line. "I'll take my business elsewhere."

"As you say, it's *business*. If it's *heart* you're looking for, St. Augustine's is only six blocks from the river."

The door slammed as Mr. Vagelle delivered his teacup to the kitchen.

"Would you care for my opinion?" I said.

"I know your opinion from your expression, Ms. Korikova. Were you watching his eyes?" His way of reminding me I was an apprentice as well as his imitation stenographer.

"Yes."

"Okay, then. What did you learn about him online?"

"James Carmichael Landon, born into old money. He turned it into a lot of new money." I scanned my notes, tapped the keyboard, and scrolled.

"Now, what don't I know?" He returned with two fresh cups of Earl Grey and set one beside my elbow. He carried his to the wing back chair beside the fake fireplace.

"Are we testy this morning?" Perhaps my needling might loosen him. Or not.

"Permit me a few minutes while the man's arrogance dissipates from the room."

"I can always open a window. Okay, here—part owner of LBRi, a conglomerate." The pages rolled. I jotted notes on my yellow pad. "Energy, transportation, agriculture, international real estate holdings, et cetera. The company name sounds familiar. Stock market manipulation? Three homes—one in Bel Air, California, one in Kilmore Quay, Ireland, one in Baton Rouge. A personal net worth near a hundred-twenty million. Would you like more?"

"Landon will turn around before his limo makes the second traffic light."

"So, no *golf* this time?"

Mr. Vagelle was wrong, words that seldom pass my lips together. J.C. Landon did not return. However, a Marie Honoré phoned requesting an appointment on his behalf.

Three minutes before her appointed time, Ms. Honoré, long black hair tied tight, black business suit with a calf-length skirt and black stiletto heels, opened her black leather briefcase and laid a number of papers on the coffee table identifying herself, and her power of attorney with the corporation. She raised the skirt, perhaps a bit more than was necessary, in order to sit.

I made a show of crossing the legs of my jeans.

A hint of tattoo extended from her shirt cuffs while she signed our consultant's contract. With the check pre-signed, she snapped her pen—more dramatic flair—and holstered it into her tidy briefcase.

"Anything else you would like me to relay to my employer, Mr. Vagelle?" Her voice hinted of Cajun-French and superiority. She had the discipline to hold her eyes on his without acknowledging my presence in the room.

"I'll call him in a week, if not before," he said.

Marie Honoré broke eye contact first, laid the check atop the contract and buckled her black briefcase. Rising from the settee, she might have continued into an Arabesque, but stopped short and pivoted militarily. The slit of her black skirt flashed to mid-thigh before the door closed.

"Quite a performance," I said.

Mr. Vagelle did not reply.

The eyes are the first, most reliable, lie detector. Pupils can enlarge fifteen to twenty percent with favorable input, and contract with disapproval to stimuli. All without pharmaceutical influence, of course. He had taught me much over our early years working together.

The missing person was the nineteen-year-old son of a Martin Boyle, whom Mr. Landon referred to as "a colleague."

Martin, Chief Operating Officer at LBRi, had died of a stroke the previous year. It was his wife, Cynthia, who asked our client to get involved in the search for her son. Jefferson, aka "Punter," Boyle had jogged off the university football field three weeks ago, helmet in hand, and simply disappeared. Family, teammates and acquaintances had all been questioned by police without success. The helmet was never found.

Mr. Vagelle asked me to deep-dive into Punter's background: police reports, traffic tickets, DUIs, high school and university records. He would check into family, friends, therapists—where wealthy families found *solutions* for everyday childhood problems—and anything else to get a picture of who Jefferson Boyle was.

"And just so we can rule it out," he said, "spend some time on newspapers and police reports of any classmates with a drugs arrest. Separate the buyers from the sellers for me."

"High school will be easier to track, but there will be more names."

"I'll give Pedersen a call, see if he can help us compile a list. Who knows, maybe the entire football team is on steroids." Detective Pedersen was the closest thing my boss had to a friend in the Department.

"I have seen the N.O.P.D. calendar. I think half of *Pedersen's* friends might be on steroids."

While I began my blitz on the headlines of six major newspapers, he phoned Patricia Gunston's Detective Agency. He put her on retainer to begin searches into Martin Boyle's and J.C. Landon's backgrounds, and whatever she might find on LBRi—private disputes, company turmoil, any gossip that may have avoided the paid press. The usual. He set the phone down slowly.

"Something she said?" I turned my eyes from the laptop.

"Or didn't say." He approached the dining table and touched the morning mail before deciding it was not a priority. "Patty's not one to shy away. When I asked her to check into our friend Landon, she let the name hang in the air for a few too many beats."

"In other words, you should have asked Landon for a larger advance."

"Of course, I wouldn't expect her to reveal any inside information if she had a working relationship with the company. The fact that she didn't come right out and say it is instructive." He gathered the signed documents from the coffee table and dropped them onto my desk.

"*Spasiba.*" I glanced twice. "Did you notice the date on the check? She forgot the zero in September Twentieth. It will deposit all the same, I suppose." The desktop scanner copied the check for remote deposit into his business account. I flipped the contract pages to verify she had dated her signatures correctly.

"She doesn't seem the type to make casual errors." He phoned his acquaintance in the N.O.P.D. to determine the state of the "official" investigation.

"According to Pedersen," he said afterwards, "with all of Landon's government friends in the loop, everyone but the Air National Guard and Interpol is out looking for Jefferson Boyle. Off the record, the case is in stasis."

"Or as my *Papochka* would say, 'As dead as Trotsky.'"

He told me to call it an early night and, "We can get into the heavy lifting tomorrow."

Two days later, as boredom tugged at my connection to Punter Boyle's high school social media brilliance, and I was about to make a second pot of tea before suffering his freshman year at university, Detective Pedersen phoned again. Our *heavy-lifting* had taken another form.

Mr. Vagelle's posture straightened, eyes flicking to me then away, and a hand swept over his frosty crew cut while he measured his options. He drew his fancy walking stick from its niche beside the fireplace, signaling his intent to travel. I knew the stick was for more than leaning on. He usually brought it out when events had become too serious to leave it behind. When he asked for my company, I was already on my feet and loading essentials into my satchel. The crime scene was an hour and a half drive northwest of New Orleans, *Paroisse d'Iberville*.

2

Iberville Parish. Moss-laden branches eventually gave way to ancient, gnarled, broken-backed oaks that might have descended from Slavic mythology and crossed the oceans to plant their feet beside abandoned Louisiana roads. Maybe they preferred the climate. Finding newer tire tracks in the soft earth, I followed them into the long-dead sugar plantation built in the mid-19th century. I parked my Impala behind a corral of county cars and vans fronting the antebellum manor house. As we exited the car, Pedersen approached.

"I'm sure you know this ain't my jurisdiction—Hello, Alya," he said, and I nodded. He waved for the attention of another plain-clothes officer. "This is Chief Deputy Dupré. I've filled him in on your involvement."

Dupré, one and three-quarters meters, built something like bear wrestler done in by vodka, wore cargo pants and chukka boots fitting the terrain, a tight polo shirt with a Sheriff's star sewn above his heart, and a bristle-top, Marine-style haircut. Not quite *plain-clothes*. He appeared to be having a lousy day, but he shook hands anyway. I gave them space. *I do not shake hands.*

"I'm familiar with your name, Vagelle," he said. "I know you've helped Pedersen in the past, like with the young lady murdered in your apartment several years back. But being the up-front kind of guy I am, I should warn you I'm not a fan of *private dicks*. And Lt. Murphy was my brother-in-law."

"Chief?" Pedersen said.

"He was also killed in your apartment, as I recall. Your address should be posted on the *Most Dangerous Places, Louisiana* list. According to the reports, you are more than careless with your friends' lives."

Mr. Vagelle's walking stick shifted in the dirt.

"How 'bout we keep this professional then?" Pedersen said.

"Yeah." Dupré led us across the sand and up the steps to the double doors. I expected crows waiting to attack us from the eaves. "I'm told you had no affiliation with the family until two days ago. Keep in mind that whatever you've been working on, it's now *my* murder investigation. I'll need to question you and your partner but, starting today, you are merely informed bystanders."

Mr. Vagelle wore a blank mask, a skill I might never perfect.

"Any details you leak to the public will be considered a serious breach of our *newfound friendship*. You may not wish to see this, Missus...?" He hesitated at the threshold.

"Korikova," I said. "I am here to accompany my boss, and I leave that decision to him." I imagined my *boss's* humor should I kick the Chief Deputy in the groin.

The interior presented itself like the war in the South had ended last month. I would not trust the staircase with the weight of a cat. Any resemblance to the *great room's* pre-Civil War glory had long since been stripped by time and vandals, gang graffiti a poor stand-in for classical art. We stood well back from the investigation team as lightstands around the perimeter helped our more remote viewing.

What remained of young Jefferson Boyle had been stripped naked, with his clothes folded and stacked neatly in a corner. His wrists and ankles were nailed to the rotted floor planks where he had been beaten—*or punted*—repeatedly prior to an impromptu heart surgery. Thick candles, spaced evenly around the victim, had melted out long ago. Or so we were told.

"Carter!" Dupré called. "How long 'til you zip him up?"

"Nearly there, Chief." The man with "Coroner" on his windbreaker did not sound happy either.

"I can't give you a closer look," Dupré said to us.

"Understood," Mr. Vagelle said. "Perhaps Mr. Carter will permit a viewing of the body back at his morgue prior to autopsy."

Dupré grunted.

"I'll wait to contact the people who initiated my search. You'll need to notify the mother. The father is deceased."

"The mother didn't hire you?"

"No."

"Seems we should have our little discussion sooner rather than later." Dupré dug the plug of a cheroot from his ammo pouch. "I make all death notifications. You can wrap up any business with them once I finish."

As we headed to the door, I nodded to a pair of complicated red designs painted on the main wall.

"A distraction," Mr. Vagelle said. "Someone studying voodoo on the Internet."

"How can you tell?"

"I recognize confusion."

Back outside, I waited near the front of the car as Mr. Vagelle leaned on the fender and pushed at leaves with the steel tip of his cane. He made a discovery and stooped for closer inspection. Taking a coin from his pocket, he laid it carefully in the dirt. He brought out his cell phone, snapped a close-up photo, then retrieved his coin.

"I guess you found something," I said.

"Take a stroll with me."

The air hung heavy, but I did not mind. We had a few hours of daylight left and, despite the crumbling surroundings, it felt good to breathe air this far from the city.

He kept his eyes to the ground except for when he took note of the house as we turned a corner. Twice, he pointed his stick at the dirt—at something I failed to see—and he signaled me to step wide of whatever it was. He took another photo, enlarged it on the phone, and held it for my appraisal.

"Partial footprint," I said. "Shoeless, obviously. Maybe an adult male."

"Now look at the print itself." He aimed his stick at the dirt. "What's your immediate thought?"

"First thought that comes to mind is more theater. Bare feet. A pretend clue to support all the fake voodoo inside?"

"And nearly as imaginative. Your second thought?"

"More likely the naked vic trying to run away. I noticed more than a few well-spaced boot prints behind us."

"Anything else?"

"This print was made sometime after the last rain. Which was three weeks ago?"

"Well done."

"What did I miss?"

"As deep and preserved as the print is, the ground was very wet at the time." His stick touched a single blade of grass that had been pressed then dried into the footprint. "The boy's been here awhile."

"*Da.* The coroner should confirm that."

At the rear of the house, he stopped again. A rot-walled shed, unpainted for at least a half century, listed forty degrees. Farther off lay a large, cannon-blast pile of gray timber that might have been a barn, once upon a time. He lifted his gaze to the treeless fields beyond, almost as if he had memories of before that war and the plantation workers bent in the fields. He did not confide his thoughts.

We rounded to the front. Chief Deputy Dupré had positioned himself on the manor threshold, the gristle of unlit cheroot pinched in the corner of his jaw. He waited until I opened my car door before descending the steps and crossing to his orange-and-black Sheriff's pickup.

Mr. Vagelle retook my passenger seat as I noticed a dirt-and-pea green van parked beneath oak shadows some distance from the herd of *official* vehicles. There may have been humans behind the muddy windshield. Hard to tell.

The Ascension Sheriff's Office, Donaldsonville. We were led to separate interview rooms, and I waited until a female sergeant could sit in with Chief Dupré and myself. She brought me reheated coffee in a paper cup, and I was thankful for it. Dupré scowled as if his strategy hinged on me coughing it up. I assumed Detective Pedersen would observe on a monitor somewhere.

I answered all that I could. I outlined what little we knew about the deceased, insisting more than once that we had no prior association, business or personal, with the victim, his family, or Landon's company. Dupré interrogated me like a suspect. He finally grasped my growing sarcasm and I found myself alone once he decided to grill Mr. Vagelle for a second time. I determined him to be a man with few friends.

I drove us back into the city in a less-than-happy mood. We spoke little. I dropped Mr. Vagelle in front of his building and turned down his offer for dinner. All I craved at that moment was a hot bath to cleanse a portion of the day's sins.

3

Iberville Parish Coroner's Office, late morning, I took a tall stool in a corner of the Examination Room as Mr. Vagelle approached the body. Detective Pedersen and Coroner Carter stood aside like mismatched bookends. Chief Dupré was notably AWOL, presumably beating confessions out of the victim's family members.

"We assume our boy had been dead two weeks when we found him," Pedersen said. "Thereabouts."

"Won't know 'til the autopsy," Carter said. "My guess is, apart from the obvious ten-inch copper spikes hammered through the wrists and ankles, many of his contusions or broken bones were hand delivered. From the amount of blood at the crime scene, I'd say the removal of the heart was the cause of death. Entry is clean enough to be the result of a surgical saw. I'll confirm later."

"Earlier, you said the heart had not been found at the scene," Mr. Vagelle said.

"Correct. Two shallow incised wounds from the struggle— you know about *hesitation cuts*. My guess would be the surgeon didn't like his job."

"Or was drunk, stoned, or..."

"Either way, the vic lost consciousness with the sternum cutting. Assumptions might change if I find needle marks and drugs in his system. But then, what would be the point of the ceremony? Curiously, his mouth is held open by a fifth, quarter-spike. To prevent him biting his tongue? But I should stop guessing."

"Too much crime scene theater. Any sign near the body indicating a receptacle used to transport the organ?"

"Nothing I found."

Mr. Vagelle touched Punter's hair behind the right ear. "I assume you saw this?"

"I did. I checked for a needle mark, but nope. Might be antemortem swelling from the first strike that brought him down."

"Skull fracture, maybe?"

"Likely. Certainly enough subdermal bleeding to suggest he did not die soon after impact. Chief Dupré said you were to see the body before I did any work on it, so anything I've come up with thus far is initial observations only. The boy took a beating, but likely didn't feel much of it. If your associate can leave me with an email address, I'll forward any corrections when I find them."

"I'd appreciate that." At the sideboard, Mr. Vagelle handled the plastic evidence bags, Punter's clothes. He lifted them to the light for closer examination. "Obvious overkill. Obvious staging."

"And who brings a mop to stage a ritual killing?" I said from my corner. "Of course, you all noticed the ammonia smell and sloppy cleanup at the scene."

"That ammonia may have preserved the body from predators for a time," Carter said with a nod.

"Sending a message?" Pedersen fiddled with his notebook. "Not for the father, he's in the ground. But this is very personal."

"That would be your department," Carter said. "I only report on what I can see."

Before I could drive us away, Pedersen crossed the parking lot with his hand up and circled to the passenger side. My boss lowered his window.

"We need to have a more private chat," he said. "I know a decent cafeteria on the way back, just before the Sunshine Bridge."

We reached the diner first and took the booth farthest from the door. We were the only customers. The waitress, busy stacking pies, called a greeting. Mr. Vagelle appeared deep in thought, so I answered her with a coffee request.

"Did you get anything from his clothes?" I said.

"As clean as if they'd come off the rack," he said. "Not a fleck of blood. Not a wrinkle, except where he'd folded them. Unless he was something other than an average, sports-minded teenager, he dressed too well for an afternoon of ghost-hunting old plantations. Those shoes were meant for pavement and tile, not dusty country roads."

Detective Pedersen flagged the waitress as he entered. He ordered his second breakfast of the day, I ordered my first, Mr. Vagelle said his coffee was enough.

"Well," I said. "My boss can sit here all morning waiting for the shoe to drop."

Pedersen toyed with his fork, absently eying the waitress.

"He used to be a good man, Chief Dupré. I worked a case with him some years back, but he seems to have a real hard-on for you, Vagelle. Pardon me, Alya." He cringed a bit. "Maybe it has to do with the death of his brother-in-law, maybe he's changed, I don't know. After you left yesterday, we stopped for beers. He couldn't get off the subject of *you*. When I felt he was grilling me, I instinctively tried changing the discussion. I eventually had to tell him I had a late date with the wife."

"You are married?" I said.

"No." He checked his reflection in a spoon.

"You're out on a limb, confiding in me." Mr. Vagelle gazed into his coffee.

"Like you haven't had me on that limb before? I've known you longer than him. And we were both friends with Lieutenant Murphy. You worked with him for years, and I know his wife still receives checks from an *anonymous benefactor*, so maybe I feel you deserve a bit of respect, if nothing else."

I waited, but Mr. Vagelle might have turned into a pillar of salt. Had he looked back on a thing that should have been avoided? Breakfast arrived on the arm of the cheery waitress. Pedersen broke his yoke with a corner of toast and watched it bleed.

"On the drive over here, he called me again. Asked if I knew where you were. I lied. Again instinct—" Pedersen's phone sounded the intro to a Dean Martin song. He answered, "You got me! Wait, Ms. Gunston, I just sat down to lunch and need to put you on speaker."

"Yes, Detective," the speaker said. "I'm calling about a case my company is working on. A couple of my investigators had a morning appointment with a Cynthia Boyle. It was supposed to be a simple review, details concerning her missing son, Jefferson. But my men were met with unexpected hostility by estate security and escorted off. We have since been informed of her son's death."

"You must know this is something I can't comment on at present," Pedersen said.

"Yes." She hesitated. "Then my men took their own initiative and paid a visit to the late Martin Boyle's company, LBRi, here in New Orleans. We've worked with the company in the past and still have a few contacts there. After some digging, they were told the violent nature of Jefferson's death. Also, the company has been aware of our present investigation, *and* who hired us. They suggested," she paused for effect, "the *consultant* might have had some earlier connection to the young Jefferson Boyle."

"All I can tell you—"

"They...*have access to a very large network of investigation specialists*—those are their words. They have engaged more than a few to investigate Mr. Vagelle and Ms. Korikovavich." Another silence.

"Ms. Gunston, at this moment my office is not conducting such an investigation. No evidence has been brought forward implicating either."

"We're told, by outside sources, D.C. sources, that evidence is inching its way through the pipeline. I'm calling to notify you that our investigation here at Gunston is on hold until further notice. I cannot endanger my license nor my employees. I already fear for the safety of my two *out-of-town* associates."

"Thank you, Ms. Gunston." He hung up and called to the waitress, "Hon, could you warm up a slice of that fine blueberry pie?" While toast-mopping the remainder of cold egg, he mused. "My diet starts tomorrow. I assume you are her two out-of-town associates. Did you tell her where you'd be this morning?"

"Ms. Gunston has a way of knowing things," Mr. Vagelle said.

"That call was intended for us," I said. "And for whoever else might be on the line. She knows my name is not Korikovavich."

"Precisely."

"It is all happening way too fast," I said. We bounced over chewed blacktop and I took the eastbound I-10.

"Almost makes one believe this set-up was organized well in advance." The thought seemed to change his mind and our trajectory. "I know it's getting late, Alya, but I'd like you to drive us over to the club."

"Ookay." When he used my first name, it usually meant the sky was about to fall.

"It's something I want to ask Bobby first, then I'll need to fill you in on a few things, so you're not blind-sided by events before I have all the answers."

"Sounds ominous, *tovarisch*. How should I prepare myself?"

"Wait until I talk with Bobby."

In our years together, one of the things that kept us together was the knowledge that, no matter how unsteady a case might make me, or others, this man I worked alongside always stood as the most rational person in any room. Then again, I had also imagined him standing in the face of an oncoming train with me wondering if I needed to dive in and push him off the tracks.

"Do you agree with Pedersen when he said this is *very personal?*" I said. "When I think personal, I think anger. Anger is not this tidy."

"An adequate analysis. This is unique. This is, I believe, a coordinated psychopathy."

I had witnessed violence my whole life, in many forms. I grew up searching to find scant threads of logic buried within the mess of it, and the absence of logic had always unsettled me. Missing logic usually wedded itself to that word *psychopathy*. Of course, the Russians use a different word.

"Going forward," he said, "remember the old lessons. When facing a juggernaut of a company, the more antagonistic, the cheaper their regard for us little fish."

"I did tell you who my *Papochka* was."

"Yes, but even he did not have *Landon money*. LBRi has thousands of employees, all looking to climb that money tree. They have dense security, private cops, their own investigators within the company, as well as many free-lance sources all dying to get on the inside."

"Makes you wonder why he needed to hire us, does it not?"

"Frankly," he looked away, "if things do turn the direction I now suspect, I'm sending you on an assignment far from here."

"Only if you jump off the tracks, too."

"That decision might be out of my hands now."

4

The sun would soon disappear beyond the taller city shapes. A fiery glimmer sliced through tattered clouds as we parked across the street from the faded yellow sign. Bobby J's Black & Blues Club.

"Ms. K! Wonderful! I got a White Zin with your name on it." Bobby raised a bottle he kept for my rare appearances. The black giant's greeting for me seldom varied. The flash of teeth and the throaty roar were enough to warm me whenever I walked in.

"*Pozhaluysta.* Please, Bobby. I need it tonight."

Mr. Vagelle took the hand-off of drinks. His usual tumbler of Widow Jane bourbon and my White Zin. He asked Bobby to stop by the table for a chat, and I led to the curved booth in the corner. The one reserved for him. No matter how crowded this place got, even on the nights Mr. Vagelle did not come in, no one else sat at this booth. Bobby's orders.

Famous Jazz and Blues musicians had decorated the cavern with their signed, black-and-white publicity photos and framed LP covers. An assortment of dusty and well-abused band instruments added the color of precious metals to the dark cave walls. A black-and-white Charlie Parker, eyes smiling beneath the glow of the spotlights, enjoyed his premiere status behind the bar.

The heavily weathered piano hunched silently a room away. We were too early for the headline entertainment, but the old Jamaican—Bobby only referred to him as "Ol' Jamaican"—sat at a table near the stage with his feet on a chair, his amateur sax filling the room with *Midnight Blue.*

I let the sounds soothe me, as Mr. Vagelle's gaze fell into the amber liquid with his thoughts. One of my skills was to know that whatever he had to say to me, he would say it in his time.

"Back so soon, my friend," the giant brought a platter of crawfish and fried clams, which we had not ordered, and a tall glass of sparkling water for himself. "I think you don't feed your partner enough."

Wishing I had passed on our diner lunch, I may have grunted my thanks. He pulled a chair to the edge of the booth, rather than squeeze his bulk into the curve.

"So, you are in need of a little Lower District counseling? Perhaps a trivia question on the Delta Blues? You're not here to steal my famous recipe for shrimp étouffée, are you?"

"Ooh, that sounds good too," I said, and he flashed that enormous smile.

"More serious than that, I fear." Mr. Vagelle snapped a crawfish. "You know my lack of education on college football."

"Yet another of my many areas of expertise," Bobby said. "We really must get you up to speed, Mr. V."

"You ever hear of a university player named Punter—?"

"Boyle, Jefferson Boyle. They call him Punter. A talented foot. Played varsity last year, and him just a freshman. Not like that team is overstocked with great players, but he stands out. Had a good career ahead of him but seems to be playing second-string most of his sophomore year. Hope he didn't break nothin'."

"Sorry to dash your hopes, big man. Punter's been taken out of the game permanently."

"Nooo." Bobby lost his smile. "That is a shame—But if it's you, in here, asking me about him, it wasn't like he was in a car accident or something?"

"It wasn't an accident. But I knew you'd know of him. You also know a little something about the sports bookies in this area."

"Nah, man. I don't see much percentage for getting all serious about a player who, like I said, found himself on a team that wasn't going too far anyway."

"Now that I know that, I agree." Mr. Vagelle raised his tumbler and inhaled the aroma.

"Shoot, that's a real shame. Too young—That reminds me, Mr. V." He hesitated, glanced my way. When I caught him, he dropped his eyes. "Last night…"

"Go ahead, Bobby. You can say anything in front of Alya."

"Well, it was last night after you'd left, maybe twenty minutes after, these pretty young ladies come in askin' 'bout you."

"Four of them?"

"You know 'em? And one of 'em was like, you know, a spoonful of cayenne sprinkled on raw green onion."

"I get it, Bobby." I smirked.

"Yeah, like that. But the kind of hot makes your eyes water. Anyways, the four of 'em struts in like they'd just bought my place. The hot one comes up to me there at the Charlie Parker, she leans over, and in her best Cajun accent says, 'Has Nicolaus Vagelle been in tonight?' And she says it like she already knows the answer. And it 'bout threw me, you know? All the years you been coming in here—"

"Understood, Bobby," Mr. Vagelle said.

"I mean, aside from Ms. K., you're kinda famous for being a loner, of sorts."

"We are not a couple, big man," I said with a conspirator's look. "No need to be nervous."

"Oh, I know that, Ms. K. I just didn't want to embarrass nobody."

"Thanks," Mr. Vagelle said. "But what else did she say?"

"Well, not much, actually. I told her she'd just missed you and I didn't expect you back for a couple days. And she says, 'We'll take that booth over there.' And she heads over to your booth with her pals. Like she knows where you sit. I say that booth is reserved, and she pretends not to hear. And I'm saying it again, and she flops onto the cushions, and one of her friends has her cell phone out takin' pictures. And I'm getting irritated—you understand. They're like taking over my joint, ignoring me. So, I slam my fist on the table. She finally gets up flappin' loud 'bout lawyers and, how dare I!"

"Sorry you had to deal with that, Bobby."

"Well, me and the cook, and a couple of my regulars—even ol' Jamaican here—we managed to get 'em out the door without injurin' no one."

I realized the music had stopped and ol' Jamaican stood close, listening in. The bush of gray hair and flare of his beard, he always reminded me of a brown Karl Marx in tropical-print shorts and docksiders. He head-bobbed to every word.

"I wouldn't even have mentioned it but, well, she used your name and all. I figured you should be warned."

"I'm glad you did." Mr. Vagelle asked to borrow my pen. He bent to the side like he would take a nap on the booth cushions, but when he sat up, he held a half-inch of black plastic pinched in his fingers. A bug. He dropped it into Bobby's water glass.

"Well, *sshugar* on that!" Bobby said. "Why didn't I look? I should'a known better."

"No worries, friend. You caught her." Mr. Vagelle took a clean bar napkin, and my pen, and drew a careful design. "With all the great trivia you store in that big head of yours, do you know this?"

"You seen it too?" Bobby said. "It was on her shoulder. And more, different tribe stuff down her arms. Yo, Jamaican! You ever seen something like this?"

"I believe..." with the effort of thought, his eyes grew as intense as Karl's. "Yeah, a Louisiana tribe...something seen in reservation gift shops up towards the western...St. Mary's Parish, maybe." He looked to Bobby for approval. Bobby sent him back to his playing.

"So, now we get to what you wanted to warn me about." I acted the coy ingénue.

"Yes," Mr. Vagelle said. "Last night, after you dropped me off, I came in, spent enough time here for a bowl of chowder and small talk with my friend. But I needed sleep, so I didn't hang around. As I left the club, a quartet of young ladies, passing loud and happy and what I thought to be under the influence, bumped into me. I didn't think much of it until one of them threw her arms around my neck and planted a long kiss."

"Is this going where I think it is going?"

"No. They all laughed at my embarrassment. But that's when I saw the tattoo. I smiled and started away, but she ran in front of me, grabbed my arm, and I recognized her. She lifted her long black hair from her face, she patted my cheek, grinned, and ran off with her friends."

"You have got to be kidding. The lawyer with the undertaker eyes?" Once my shock dissolved, I said, "Did you see the photographer?"

"Of course not. But now I know he was there somewhere."

"If that gal's a stalker, I should be so lucky." Bobby shook his head.

"Bobby, that *gal* is the stuff that regrets are made of."

5

"If she wanted you to see her, and to know she was setting you up, have you figured out her game?" I drove us wide of the rush hour confusion. "Something to do with establishing an earlier tie between you and her, obviously. If it is part of that *creating evidence,* why create a more personal relationship for you with someone inside LBRi?"

"Let's not forget the check dated some twenty days prior to them finding the body," Mr. Vagelle said.

"But why expose a piece of her strategy now?"

"She may be improvising. I doubt it, but I'm not sure yet." He suggested avoiding the front of his building, so I parked one block over. He stopped me from leaving the car.

"You understand, Alya," he said. "Changing dates, upsetting what might otherwise be obvious, merely confuses an investigation. It's more likely to confuse the police into thinking we've been lying to them. But let's assume they know our mindset, especially with Patty P.I. and her boys knocking on their door, we'd soon uncover enough red flags at that company to put them in the crosshairs."

"So, this is them forcing us to think defense before the opening move."

"It's the lawyer in her. She's letting the defendant see just enough of the evidence to frighten him. Maybe he'd pull the plug on the investigation before the lights came on. I predict a plea deal in our future."

We left the car in a crowded lot and took the alley behind his building.

"And Landon?" I said. "Knowing your contract has a quick expiration date, maybe he believes you will decide it is in your interest to let the contract expire. Inevitable legal battles with their corporation, and the District Attorney, and the Boyles, and maybe the Queen of England."

"Let's not carve our assumptions in stone. Not yet. Put all you've heard tonight together with Patty's warning this afternoon. The circus tents are in town, and it's an all-clown show." He used his key to the service entrance off the alley.

"A plea deal? Us?"

The landlord called to us on the stairs.

"Mr. Vagelle, if things are getting out of hand again, I'm taking a vacation."

"Let me guess, Mr. Hemmings," I said. "Men in black demanding admittance."

"Three times today," he said.

"Did they show you a badge?"

"The first one showed me a card for Gunston Investigations, but I didn't recognize him. He went away mad." His attention flitted to the door glass.

"Well done," Mr. Vagelle said. "If it was legitimate, Ms. Gunston would have come herself."

"I would have recognized her."

"Until further notice, I'm not home to anyone." Mr. Vagelle led up to the third floor.

"Now I *am* going on vacation," Hemmings yelled from below and his door sealed him in.

"Is she at least a good kisser?" I stood to one side of the window to see up the street. "Their stakeout is obvious."

They were not from Gunston, and they were not Pedersen's men. My money was on Landon and the company large enough to—*access a very large network of investigation specialists.*

"I assume they surveil my apartment as well," I said.

"If, as Patty said, they're still manufacturing evidence today, assume the authorities won't get their warrant until sometime tomorrow." He retrieved a burner phone from the desk. I took that as a signal for me to open my laptop. I checked network security software first.

"Memorable," he said. "The kiss. It was memorable."

I stifled my laughter.

"Yes, it's me," he said to the phone. "A-S-A-P, I need all liquid assets pulled from the joint account and moved to the safety deposit box. Withhold the usual for yourself." He stabbed more numbers.

I downloaded a file folder emailed from the Iberville Parish Coroner, apparently before Chief Dupré could stop him. I waved for attention and pointed to the monitor. The coroner's report listed his comments beside a photo close-up of a damaged open mouth:

Image D: Revised analysis. The short copper spike's suspected purpose was to keep the teeth away from the tongue. On further examination, it may also have served to direct our attention to a postmortem tattooing of said tongue. 'NO RED.'

"Alya, I have a new job for you. We need to find anything we can on Marie Honoré. And check on any association with the Chitimacha tribe."

"Again, with the tattoos," I said.

"The abandoned slave plantation, old spikes, torture, candles, the missing heart—At first, I thought maybe fake voodoo. Some street gang playing with the police. But, as you observed, street gangs don't carry bone saws and mops to an assassination. This tattoo changes all that anyway. 'No red,' makes it specific. The word Chitimacha translates to English as 'Men altogether red.' They are a tribe historically noted for their tattooing."

"Whoever murdered young Mr. Boyle enjoys melodrama. I hate to admit, I am still confused. I cannot see Lawyer Honoré murdering Punter like that. Or pointing the finger at herself, with you somehow in this together?"

"Yes. All too complicated. There are other stories here we can't yet see."

"This is not just misdirection to confuse a crime scene."

"Narcissists often enjoy the game to their detriment, believing they cannot be outplayed. Anyone familiar with the tribe knows there is no connection here, and let's presume Ms. Honoré has a calendar full of alibis. Until this morning, we have only had direct contact with two people on this case, and one misdated our payment by eighteen days. They are planting doubts, whether they are all colluding or not. It's weak, but…"

He moved into the bedroom to make more calls while I continued my research.

2:45 a.m. Satchel over my shoulder, I followed as he carried a medium suitcase out the service exit to the next block and my car. Our stakeout pals never thought to drive around the corner. Amateur work.

"Or meant for our eyes only," Mr. Vagelle said. "Like Chief Dupré's foreknowledge of our *alleged* pre-existing relationship with someone inside LBRi. Like her letting me know we were being photographed last night. Like investigators trying to get into the apartment today, and the looming, *Sword of Damocles*, warrant. They are goading us to run."

"And we are giving them what they want?"

"Investigators will find nothing here. Remember Sun Tzu. *Appear weak when you are strong.*"

"And retreat is just advancing in another direction. Do not ask who said that."

He directed me to take the Causeway, the taut double-ribbon of bridges stretching twenty-four miles to connect south to north shores of a vast Lake Pontchartrain. I once read of bull sharks in this lake. Why my mind went there, I could not say.

On the other side, Mandeville harbor hugged the water's edge where marinas paraded a daily pageant of stock portfolios and tax write-offs. We snaked through the adjoining neighborhood. I stopped, as Mr. Vagelle opened his wallet for the gate guard who nodded and pressed the magic button. The ornate barrier swung smoothly inward.

"How come you never introduce me to your wealthy friends?" I said as we walked up the promenade of hedges to the front door of what appeared to be five million dollars. Beside the door hung a dark coach light and, lifting the lid, he found a key behind the bulb. He opened the double doors into the set of Gone with the Wind, then typed a security code into the alarm panel. He told me the code.

"Instructions are help yourself to the kitchen. Your bedroom is second on the right, second floor. There is a connecting bath, of course. As we didn't get the opportunity to stop at your apartment, I'll wager the daughter has clothes in her closet still with the store tags. She's old enough to have something *professional* for you to set aside for tomorrow."

"So, avoid the plaid uniform skirt for school?" The foyer echoed a bit.

"It might open more doors for us, but yes."

I scanned our new, bright surroundings. "Scary."

"Sleep late. Another long day tomorrow."

"Just how many people owe you favors?" Halfway up the stairs I looked back, but he had vanished.

I fell asleep in a tub with a golden swan for a faucet and flower-shaped soap. Cool bathwater woke me near dawn and I made it to the bed. I woke again with daylight across my face. Unable to move from beneath my satin sheets and pillowed duvet, my Grand Duchess moment, the ceiling fan took on ominous shapes as I tried to remember an upsetting dream. I recalled the sad ending for Anastasia, the actual Grand Duchess. Then I sat up, and my stomach scolded me for missing dinner.

Predictably, Mr. Vagelle had breakfast waiting on a deck overlooking the shimmering lake.

"Indian burial mounds," I said.

"Excuse me?"

Setting the laptop beside my coffee, I looked out across the sparkling blue, then closed my eyes and breathed the bitter fragrance of the lake. Algae blooms had conquered the shoreline this year. I angled the monitor for his scrutiny.

"University, sophomore year," he said, "our young Mr. Boyle dropped his majors, swapped economics and business finance for an inordinate interest in archeology and Native American history."

"Subjects he never mentioned as a freshman." I switched pages on the monitor before buttering my toast. The teakettle still warm, my cup smelled of Earl Grey. "Suddenly, his social media pages exploded with photo essays on the Choctaw and Chitimacha tribes."

"As I see." He read further. "*Battles with early Conquistadores and battles splitting the tribe, battles with the American courts*—it might as well be his end-of-term paper."

"This year sports references disappeared, replaced with museum photos and any number of field trips to archeological digs and burial mounds. Besides artifacts and tombs, early pictures included his classmates, until one person became his primary model. His *teacher.*"

"Marie Honoré." Mr. Vagelle never smirked, almost never. "At the age of twenty-six, her legal history was impressive enough to get noticed by someone at LBRi."

"And her legs are impressive enough to get a hormonal university athlete to fall in love pretty quick. Two years ago, she decided to return to her roots and teach several specialized courses on Southern Tribal Integration, Legal Disputes and the Five Tribes, et cetera."

"Convenient choice of university."

"Punter signed up for every seminar." I enlarged a photo on his page: a paperweight on his desk labeled *Gift From TEACHER*, a twelve-inch glass box containing an ancient flat-head skull.

"Early customs included binding infant males in order to shape their skulls," he said.

"She had been planning something with this family for a long time. And she is detail oriented." Adding a drop of honey to the tea, I savored the mix on my tongue before swallowing.

"I was wrong before. This woman never improvises. Do you have an address for the Boyles?"

6

"First, we get the lay of the land."

"Translating into Vagelle-speak, the 'lay of the land' means storming the castle?"

We traversed the Causeway, this time to the south, and followed directions through the city to the belly of the Central Business District. The inescapable LBRi logo hung fixed in concrete above the doors to an architecturally modern high-rise, with its adjoining campus facing the river.

"Think we can get in without an appointment?" I said.

"Let's see how far we can get on my *joie de vivre.*"

I gave him a slow-take.

The marbled lobby shouted its wealth with six-story ceilings and twin chandeliers the size of dangling Range Rovers. We were greeted by one of three security guards who asked to examine my satchel. Fortunately, I had left my snubnose in the car. The guard asked if we had an appointment while escorting us to the three-man front desk. One desk attendant asked the question again, followed by a request for identification from us both.

"Mr. Landon will want to see me." Mr. Vagelle showed Landon's business card, and the attendant suggested we wait in one of the lobby's three seating groups.

Twenty minutes later, nearly hypnotized by the veins of a marble column, I returned to the desk and asked if Mr. Landon had been notified.

"I'm afraid Mr. Landon will be out of the office for several days. A business conference."

"So, who are we waiting for?"

The elevator doors opened as if they were awaiting my question. A three-piece suit carrying an underfed young man crossed the expanse to greet me. Introducing himself as Tyler Coombes, legal associate, he extended a hand. Mr. Vagelle arrived in time to intercept it. *I do not shake hands.*

"Yes, I am aware of your contract with Mr. Landon on behalf of Mrs. Boyle." He glanced at the card laid on the desk. "She is, of course, a major company stockholder now, and Mr. Landon, and all of us at LBRi, are concerned that she gets through these difficult times with as little inconvenience as possible."

"And my company is here for that very purpose," Mr. Vagelle said. "Perhaps we can meet with Martin Boyle's replacement, your company's new Chief Operating Officer?"

"I'm afraid that is impossible. I'm sorry you've wasted a trip."

"Not wasted if we can speak with someone in authority."

"About?"

"Our contract."

"I was not made aware of your relationship with Ms. Honoré until your contracts came across my desk this week."

"My *relationship.*"

"Mr. Vagelle, there seems to be quite a bit of confusion regarding you, Ms. Honoré, and the Boyle family, and the depth of your involvement with the family for some time prior to our signing those papers."

"*Involvement.*"

"There may be legal considerations, and I cannot go into the details at this time."

"Not finished manufacturing *details,*" Mr. Vagelle said, as if to me.

"Pardon me?" Mr. Coombes stiffened.

"I was speaking to my associate."

"You are in no position to take an aggressive tone—"

"Mr. Coombes, you have yet to witness my aggressive tone. As a matter of fact, given the circumstances, I believe I may have been too cordial."

The security guards inched closer from their stations around the lobby. The elevators doors parted, and Ms. Honoré made a regal entrance, stiletto heels resounding on marble. Her manufactured smile communicated arrogance, which my boss returned in kind.

"I believe others have informed you that your services are no longer needed." Her former Cajun accent had escaped to parts unknown.

"What, no kiss? I'm hurt," he said.

"You were hired to find a missing person. That person has been found. The Sheriffs' officer who found the young man has informed you your participation in the case has ended. You have no further business here and, as I'm sure you can see by our surroundings, our time is extremely valuable. You are wasting it. Have a pleasant day." She pivoted.

"The police did not employ me. Mr. Landon paid for my week."

"You will be sent a severance notification."

"And the mail should take three days and by the time I receive it, our contract will have expired. Unless I hear directly from Mr. Landon himself, I am still under contract with LBRi. I will advise him of our progress."

She spun back, her smile forgotten.

"I can't quite tell if you are heckling, or merely ignorant, Mr. Vagelle. You know our position and the disposition of the case, yet you refuse to comprehend."

"Oh, I believe you are intelligent enough to *comprehend* why we are here."

"Escort them from the building," she said to the guards. To those on the front desk, she said, "Remember these two. If they enter the lobby again, phone New Orleans P.D. They may be violent."

We gave no resistance while flanked by our escorts out the doors and down the front steps.

"Violent?" we said in unison.

"She's shown the first cracks in her façade," he said. "She couldn't hold her poker-face, and what you just witnessed was an unintentional tilt."

"I now understand." We crossed the strip of one-way road and walked the riverfront away from where we had parked. I assumed he knew where he was going. "After all her best laid plans, we fled from our office in the middle of the night, and she believed we could be manipulated. Our showing up today, inside her "castle," flipped the chessboard. She was not prepared for a confrontation on your terms."

"Not this soon," he said.

Lush, perfectly manicured greens and a ten-foot modern sculpture carried the interior theme with us to the open air. More symbols of company status. I was reminded of J.C. Landon wrinkling his bespoke Briani suit. As this was not a through street, traffic was sparse. We passed the turn for the underground garage and continued to the adjoining building where he stopped in front of a sign for "Le Petit Plat."

"So, you have a plan, Admiral?" I said.

He brought out his burner phone and retrieved messages. We crossed to the café.

Not your average company lunchroom on the inside, it more resembled a place to feed the French President. Late afternoon, we took the only available table. Most customers wore tailored suits and ate with folders or briefcases on the table between their *petit plats*. Others dined with company guests pretending nonchalance.

"Excuse me, sir." The man seated at the next table bent to retrieve something from the floor. "I believe you dropped this." He handed my boss a card, but his blue eyes took in the room.

"Ms. Korikova, I don't believe you've met Mr. Brown," he said under his breath. "He works for Patty Gunston."

Mr. Brown nodded for me, then returned to his sandwich. The waiter materialized, and we ordered tea and finger food, and he whirled away.

"She apologizes she could not be here in person." Brown touched his earpiece as if he had someone else on the line. "They wouldn't approve of her involvement."

Mr. Vagelle turned the card over and slid it across the table. A message had been scrawled on the back:

"Tracker Lic Q2K M8."

"Hers?" I tried not to smile. "She should not advertise. Russian schools teach chess to their young."

"The first word matters. Already taken care of?"

"We are efficient," Mr. Brown said to his earpiece.

"I like this guy," I said. "Very James Bond."

The waiter arrived and Mr. Brown all but flew from his chair. He skated a few dollars across the table.

"The service here is terrible, and the food is worse!" He leaned my way. "I would not bring a beautiful young lady in here for a glass of water on a hot day." His eyes flicked to a light fixture then away. He strutted out the door as I caught the black spot on the light's base, the camera lens.

The waiter nearly dropped his food tray.

"I believe we should find another place to eat, *mon cheri*." Mr. Vagelle noticed something I did not. He laid a five on the table and assisted with my chair, to the waiter's chagrin. "We have a long drive ahead. You should use the powder room. I'll wait for you outside."

As he pushed through the glass doors, I saw the car with "Security" on the fender and a blue light flashing on the dashboard. Before I passed beneath the "les Toilettes" sign, black Security jackets moved in on him.

I could do nothing to help. They apparently had no interest in me.

Ten minutes in a toilet stall is a long time, especially when the nerves are rattled. When no one came for me, I poked my head out, then followed my hunch all the way to the sidewalk. I turned for where I had left my car. Less than thirty feet later, a black Lexus pulled alongside, and I nearly ran off until Mr. Brown lowered the passenger window.

"Don't go back to your car just yet. Climb in."

I climbed in the back. He drove slowly until we cleared the castle.

"Your boss will be okay," he said. "Ms. Gunston has been advised, and she has already phoned his lawyer."

The LBRi logo block hovered in the mirror. The sky had deepened its blue, but my skin prickled as if anticipating a hurricane.

7

Mr. Brown parked near the rail yard, and we waited. I did not ask what for. I only waited for one thing, a call from Mr. Vagelle telling me he needed a ride.

Mr. Brown attempted conversation several times. He glanced at the mirror with concern, but my mind lingered on a narcissistic young woman and my fantasies of ripping the lovely hair from her head.

Mr. Brown opened his door then opened mine as another black Lexus crunched onto the gravel alongside. Patty P.I. wore her sandy ponytail above the collar and her smile beneath broad cheekbones. She waved for me to join her. As I left his car, Mr. Brown offered his hand. I pretended not to see it.

"Thank you for all you have done," I said.

"Anytime." He opened Patty's passenger door. "Something you would like me to do from here, Ms. Gunston?"

"You've done good today," she said. "Go over to Charlie's, have yourself a nice steak on the company. Easy on the drinks. You might get a late call from me if things get heated. *Capisce?*"

"Gotcha, boss. Have a…have a quiet evening, Ms. Korikova. He'll be okay." He closed the door.

"A bit tense back there?" Patty drove us away.

"We have been through worse. It is more—I get frustrated when there is nothing I can do but run. I do not like running, not that kind."

"Sounds like it was his call to make. He knew where he was going, and he wanted you on the outside. Like when he called me a couple nights back and told me to keep my distance on this. We can do nothing if we are all locked up."

"Or like my Papa taught me when quail hunting, when the dogs get too close to the nest, mama bird will fly to lead the threat away from her young. My boss has a bad habit of sacrificing himself."

"I've known him longer than you have, Alya. Not as close-up, obviously, but maybe my distance allows me to appreciate your mama quail's instincts. Now, where would you like to go?"

"Do you know if the police served the warrant for my apartment? I would like to see if they took the few things I might need."

"Open the glove box," she said. I did. "Detective Pedersen picked it up before the inspection. He asked me to return it to you."

I unwrapped the hand towel and cupped my mini-Mossberg—my *bedside security*—in my palm beneath the dashboard, out of view of the passing traffic. I checked the magazine. The steel had a mystical way of smoothing out my nerves. *Security.* I tried not to think on the imperious clack of stiletto heels while I had it in my grip.

"Oh, and please trust me on this. In my long association with your boss, I have never known him to be so...what's the right word, *attached* to anyone else. Don't question his instincts too much where you are concerned."

"My mama bird," I said.

"Sort of."

"I imagine they will have someone watching my apartment." I needed to know if they had missed the important things.

"Not police, but I'd be surprised if your clients didn't have at least one set of eyes on your place. I doubt they'll try anything with two of us if you want to stop to pick up a favorite toothbrush."

I nodded and stuffed the Mossberg in the pocket I had sewn to the inner lining of my satchel.

She soon parked against the curb, amid a tight line of cars, around the corner from my building. I estimated we had an hour of daylight left.

"Did you spot 'em?" she said.

"*Da*. Two chimneys in the front seat smoking themselves to death."

Strolling like we had just come from a long day at the shopping mall, we turned before my building and took the open side stairway to the fourth floor. The only people we passed were a couple of loving young boys, smelling of a day's worth of hashish, trying not to fall over the railing as we walked by. They tittered long after we had turned the corner.

Inside my apartment, a minor train wreck, but nothing unsalvageable. Most drawers had been pulled, cabinets swept, closets emptied to the center of the rooms.

"This happens way too often here."

"Occupational hazard." Patty checked the fridge and asked if she could take a sparkling water.

"Take anything in there that has not yet curdled." I crossed to the bedroom and dragged the overnight bag from beneath the bed. I filled it with underwear, toiletries, and what I considered essentials for not knowing how long I would be away. I checked my desk, checked the bankbooks and credit card taped behind a drawer. "Not quite a professional search," I said, transferring them to my satchel. They had not found my second laptop, hidden above ceiling tiles, so I connected it to the printer app and made two more copies of our contract with LBRi.

I found the pipe wrench beneath the bathroom sink, brought it to the bedroom and turned the bolts holding the long radiator to the wall beneath the window. With a little effort, I pulled the fake radiator front and flipped it on the bed.

"Now that's something you don't see much of in New Orleans." Patty stood in the doorway.

"Radiators?"

"False radiator fronts to hide a Kalashnikov. Jesus, girl!"

"Yeah, well…" I laid the AK on the bed and began to disassemble it. Halfway broken down, Patty stopped me.

"Shhh!"

I listened. Footsteps on the landing. Whispers stopped outside my door. Patty bent and removed a small pistol from her ankle holster. I flew into reassembling the Kalashnikov—something else Russian children learn in classrooms at an early age. The doorknob moved and the lock rattled as I slapped the magazine into place.

The larger man bulled the door open and the two of them lunged into the living room, pistols leading the charge. They froze when Patty pressed her weapon to the first man's ear. Their eyes bulged when they saw me in the bedroom doorway, the AK-47 pressed to my shoulder.

"Who wants to die first?" Patty made Bogart dialogue sound like a party. "Drop the hardware. Now on your knees."

"And nobody pees on my carpet," I said.

She used their belts to secure their wrists behind them. I told her where to find my box of duct tape and she pushed their chins to the floor and strapped ankles to wrists. Dropping the magazines from their twin Glocks into my overnight bag, she pulled the slides and left the rest of the handguns as evidence. She took their wallets and keys.

"You're gonna be very sorry." The large man hissed when she stepped on his kidney.

"Do you know me, *To-nee?*" She read from his open wallet. "Of course, you don't. But guess what, *To-nee*, I have your name and address and the keys to your car and house. Oh, and is this your lovely wife and daughter?"

"If you even—"

"Tony! If I get so much as an anonymous phone call, or a meter maid who tells me you mentioned what happened here today, I will end everything about you." She pressed her pistol to the back of his head, pushing his nose to the floor. She let him hear the slide click back. "Do you believe me, Tony?"

"Yesss."

I disassembled the AK, wrapped the parts in bath towels and packed them with reverence in the overnight bag. When I came out of the bedroom, Patty finished texting.

"Our *friendly* on the force is notified," she said. "They should be here in twenty. We should be gone."

Before I followed her out the door, I leaned close to the smaller of the two intruders.

"I need you to understand. Today is not my *good mood day*, and still you are alive with no new holes. We can remain friends so long as you never trespass here again." I threw in a few lines of Russian and finished with, "…or I will bring the whole Moscow *mafiya* down on your neck." I slammed the door and hoped no one peed on my carpet.

Patty concealed the broken doorjamb as well as possible.

"Um, just because I'm the curious type," she said when we were far enough from my apartment, "do you still know people in the Moscow—?"

"I have not seen Papa since I ran away at fifteen, but these dopes will never know for sure." I let her carry the overnight bag.

"As I've said before, anytime you want to come work for me…Please tell me you've never killed anyone with that *radiator-accessory.*"

"One of many lessons I took away from Moscow, life is better when you are over-prepared. When people see it, you would be surprised how quickly trouble goes away." I shut myself into the security of her Lexus once more. "Do we go back to wait for his release?"

"Back at the apartment, I got a text. Landon's Security had handed him over to NOPD. Some bullshit charges, harassment, threatening company officials. I don't know which precinct yet. And his lawyer can't go to a judge or file for release if they keep transferring him around the city."

"With enough cops in the city willing to accept donations from a company with so many *important* local citizens."

"It's late. I don't know, but he may be in overnight. Where do you want to spend it? I'm on retainer, remember."

I was surprised Patty P.I. knew where to find our safe house. Not that I was jealous, but I never knew it existed until this week. I noticed she kept an eye on the mirror as she drove.

She said she could not stay but went inside with me and checked every room in the estate. "Even the slightest concern, you call me. I will have a car close by."

"My boss does not have many friends, but he chooses them well."

Sounds in the dark.

I struggled into sweatpants, grabbed the mini-Mossberg from the nightstand and checked the clock. *3:12*. I descended the palace staircase, pausing with each step, until a light from the kitchen crossed my path. No voices. I took shallow breaths so I might hear easier.

"I'm in here," Mr. Vagelle said from behind, and I whirled with the pistol up before recognition hit.

"Der'mo!" (Shit!) I lowered the weapon. "I am too young for a heart attack."

"I'm sorry. Didn't mean to wake you."

He sat in the shadows. A small wedge of light bled into the den from the kitchen and sparked off the bottle beside him. I dropped into a facing chair.

"First, tell me you are okay," I said.

"I am okay." A long silence, apparently meant to quiet my nerves. "Would you like to go put a robe on?"

While I wore sweatpants, I realized the rest was only the thin T-shirt I had slept in.

"*Der'mo*, again!" I said. "Is that all you are going to say? I spend all day wondering if they would find you floating in the Delta. You are not being kind to me, Nicolaus."

"I know. Sorry."

"Stop saying you are sorry. Where is your head? You are sitting in the dark, drinking and making plans. For what—? Oh. Y*ou know!* You are intentionally unkind to me tonight. This means I will wake up tomorrow and you will be gone. And maybe I will sit here for a few days, or however long it will take for Patty to come by and tell me where the funeral is."

"You are being melodramatic." He poured more bourbon into an already half-full glass.

Lifting free of the chair, I nearly said more, nearly shouted it, but realized it would only be more *melodrama*. I left him seated in the dark. Hurrying through the kitchen, I grabbed a bottle of wine and a tall glass and continued up the painfully long staircase to my room. Someone else's room. In someone else's house. *Der'mo.*

8

I did not drink. I sat on the edge of the bed in the dark for a long time.

I woke beneath a hillock of pillows and duvet and struggled to free myself until morning light blinded me. Then he was there, in the room, asleep on the chair beside the window. The clock read 6:57 and I studied him for a time as he slept. On the way to the bathroom, I hit him in the face with a pillow.

"What!"

"You are a son of a bitch." I closed the door behind me.

"It's a gift," he mumbled. I turned on the shower.

Tammany Parish, Mandeville, presented a series of inland lakes, country clubs and houses worth considerably more than the dream home where we had spent the past couple nights. Naturally, I was sure the late Martin Boyle came from the same type of royal blood as his business partner, J.C. Landon. Mr. Vagelle drove. Not our habit, but my old Impala was still parked where we left it the day before. Or maybe he thought the Mercedes would add dignity in this neighborhood.

"I don't expect to learn much from her," he said. "If we can get in. It's merely one more box I'd like to check off."

I watched the professionally hewn grounds roll past.

"You are still angry," he said.

"I am still angry." I tried scowling. Instead, I touched the bruised cut above his right eye. "You make friends everywhere you go."

"The official report said I tripped while resisting arrest."

He winced and steered us into the driveway, stopping before the gold-tipped black iron gates. A uniformed guard left his hut and approached with an actor's smile. Mr. Vagelle handed him Landon's business card along with his own identification.

"This is just a courtesy call for Mrs. Boyle. We've been hired to inquire about her son's case."

"Do you have an appointment, Mr. Vagelle? Mrs. Boyle is not seeing visitors presently." He bent to examine me in the passenger seat. Returning to his hut, he picked up the landline. Two more guards met us at the front steps and instructed us where to park.

"Developing a twitch from all this security yet?" I said. And as we neared the front steps, "Try not to trip today."

He leaned into the walking stick, a familiar affectation for putting older women at ease. The door guard ushered us into the foyer. The lady of the manor offered a greeting she had learned in finishing school, but her pale eyes wavered and her breathing appeared rushed. A middle-aged man in a tight tweed sport coat, introduced as Dr. Davies, maintained a discreet distance, but his eyes were as jumpy as hers. He followed as she led us to a parlor. She only needed one sofa table to steady herself en route.

"Our deepest condolences." *Are the sedatives wearing off or just kicking in.*

"You are Russian?" she said. "I don't know as I have much to tell you. I'm…with all the arrangements…But if James—Mr. Landon sent you…"

"I promise not to take too much of your time," Mr. Vagelle said. "My company has been hired to check into the recent tragedy." He nodded, and I passed her a copy of the contract, which she dropped onto the loveseat's embroidered garden.

"Maybe you are from Estonia, or the Czech Republic?" she said. "I had a pen pal as a child, from Estonia."

"Lithuania." I offered my sincere smile. Just the half-lie I give to most who question my accent.

"Do you know anyone in Estonia?" As if everyone in the Eastern Bloc knew each other.

I apologized.

"Mrs. Boyle, we are sorry for your loss," Mr. Vagelle said. "I thought perhaps you'd be able to tell us something about your son. Maybe conversations you'd had. Anything those not quite as close to him might have missed."

"I'm sure I cannot…Lithuania?" she said.

"We understand this has been extremely stressful on you. With what I can gather, there is much too much gossip about poor Jefferson."

"Jefferson," she said. Dr. Davies searched for an escape.

"And this is what I would like to avoid. Maybe just a bit of background. Maybe you can tell us how he liked his first year at college. Any concerns. Things like that."

"We…had not been close these past…You know, teenagers."

"Were there other students, maybe teachers, he was fond of?"

"As I said…"

"We recently spoke with one of his professors. A Marie Honoré?"

The name cleared her eyes like a face slap.

"You dare! Get out!" She pushed up from the loveseat, slipped once and regained her footing. "Where did you hear this? My Jefferson and *that!* You—*That bitch!*" Any finishing school vaporized as she fell against the arm of a chair. Mr. Vagelle and I started for the door.

I apologized again.

"You need to go." Dr. Davies, pretending he was in control, had already wedged his tight tweed sport coat between us. He grappled with the floundering woman.

Two estate guards, Mr. Landon, and his bodyguard met us in the parking lot on the way to our car. The bodyguard filled his suit as one might expect from a professional wrestler. Caucasian, his shaved, tattooed head resembled Melville's famous shipboard cannibal. Landon held out a hand to heel the creature.

"You've been told you have no more interest here." Blood strained at his collar. "The court has issued restraining orders. You are now trespassing, harassing a sick and grieving mother, and I am considering a signal for my friends to hasten your next hospital stay."

"Your attorney needs to step up her tactical skills." Mr. Vagelle took his weight off the stick. "I have been told about my *interests*, but not by the oaf who commissioned me. I have not yet been issued a severance letter, nor the court's restraining order. Legally, *harassment* would require more than a single visit, permitted by estate security, and entrance permitted by the *sick and grieving woman* in question. As soon as she displayed discomfort, we volunteered to leave, with our apologies. If you, the oaf in question, are informing me today, at twelve forty-five pm, that I am relieved of the case, I'll consider this your termination of our contract." He took a single step toward the Mercedes and the guards jockeyed to block us.

"All it would take to terminate more than the contract is a single word." The meat of Landon's face twitched. His thick fists unclenched, then balled into tighter fists. The beast behind him psyched himself up for a loosening leash.

"Your tough boys going to terminate me too?" I said. His head tipped to mock me until I motioned to the front gate. "How about them?"

Detective Pedersen, with two uniformed officers, watched from outside the property. He ordered the gate guard to open the driveway, then approached on foot.

"Trust me, officer," Landon called, "you do not want to get involved."

"It appears I'm already involved," Pedersen said. "Just waiting on an explanation of what I am involved with."

"I can have the governor on the phone in twenty minutes. You will be relieved of duty by the end of the day."

"This is my scared look." Pedersen presented his badge an arm's length from the seething millionaire.

"Detective Pedersen, you are already looking at charges of colluding with a principal suspect in a murder investigation."

"Principal suspect?" I said.

"Mr. Vagelle, Ms. Korikova, you may leave." Pedersen said. "But I will expect written statements on my desk within twenty-four hours. Meanwhile, I will be taking statements from Mr. Landon and everyone else on the property, including those inside the house."

My boss acknowledged, and we quietly boarded the Mercedes.

"That would be your cue to phone your lawyer, or the governor, Mr. Landon," Pedersen said. "Perhaps Ms. Boyle will permit us to wait inside."

We left the gate and pulled onto the main road.

"Principal suspect?" I said again.

"That could only have come from our friend, Dupré. Who is Landon not connected to?"

"Or—Oh, by the way," I said, "I got a text from your neighbor today. Dr. Maiwand. Seems your pals on the Department got their warrant. Hemmings has been pacing and shouting at bystanders since yesterday."

"His charm is in his predictability."

"I need to take a little road trip," he said. "I can drop you off at your car if you like, but after last night's conversation…"

"You need to say something, so I do not think you have run off to your own funeral without me."

"More or less."

"Would you like my company on the drive, boss?"

"That would be my preference."

"Maybe we can stop off at a florist. I will buy you a wreath."

Turning west, we followed the signs to Baton Rouge. Throughout the afternoon, his eyes returned more and more to his rearview mirror. I asked, but he only grunted and shrugged it off, so I adjusted my side mirror.

"I also got an email from our favorite P.I.," I said. "She forwarded a copy of the warrant as well as notes to the court. How does she get some of this stuff? The initial evidence against you involves," I cleared my throat, "a prior relationship with your long-legged *lawyer friend,* sworn to in writing and notarized. Photos are mentioned."

"Did she say we had sex? I might've remembered that."

"Funny. Also," I read another text, "statements by LBRi lawyers on your questionable business practices for every year since the death of Lt. Murphy. Insinuations that Murphy had been investigating you just prior to his death, signed off on by our favorite police chief. That guy has been grinding his cheroot since you first walked onto his crime scene."

"This is a classy group. They'll find nothing, but it helped get them their warrant. Fire off a quick text for me. Ask Patty if she can find a little background on Ms. Boyle's doctor friend, Davies. See if he's a company doctor, or just her primary drug supplier and handler."

Patty buzzed back within minutes.

"She's on it," I said. "With a none-too-subtle warning for me."

"Such as?"

"Telling me to check my inbox. She forwarded an FBI memo on the *Bratva-style* murder of Punter Boyle. They make passing comment about my family history and the tactics of the Russian *mafiya*. Only the FBI would know my real name. I have not used it since crossing the Atlantic nine years ago."

"Alya, please remind me to do something to Landon I will regret."

An hour later, we exited the freeway, detoured through the old town of French Settlement. After a few more detours, due to the flooding of Bayou tributaries caused by a recent storm, we eventually arrived at the remains of a century-old church with new construction underway on the same plot of land.

"When I see scenes like this, it saddens me," I said. "I think about people choosing to stay in a place that is destined to repeat tragedy."

"Many feel the choice is beyond them. Family. Community. Parish. Land that has been in the families since the beginnings of the country. The ghosts of twenty generations. And most couldn't afford to start life anew, even if their heart was in it."

Satchel over my shoulder, I waited at the edge of broken pavement while he approached the crane operator. The workman dismounted and led us to a mobile shack set off the berm.

A loud engine prompted a glance over my shoulder. I only glimpsed the rear fender turning the intersection we had just passed, but I could not help wondering how many dirt-and-pea green vans lurked hereabouts.

"Mr. Vagelle?" I said.

"I saw him," he said.

"Come," said a voice from inside the shack.

The dark, compact, rough man in the orange vest and hardhat nearly leapt from his desk to greet us. His hardhat clattered to the tin desktop.

"Nicolaus!" He grabbed the extended hand with both of his. "You have stayed away too long. You are well?"

"I am, Emile." He then introduced me to, "…my good friend Buzz, Emile, Cook. A man who once saved my life."

"Oh, I believe you remember that the wrong-way round!" Buzz laughed. *I do not shake hands*, and Buzz understood as if by instinct.

"He told me a bit of what you are doing here," I said. "If you come all the way from New Iberia to help rebuild the old church, that is impressive."

"Shush. It's nothing. I have family in French Settlement going back a long way."

"Alya, Buzz is the closest I have met to full-blooded Chitimacha. He once held position in tribal government." He touched a hand to his friend's shoulder, a gesture I had not seen from him before. "Yes, I have been away too long. Today, I don't want to keep you from your work, but I need to consult with you on a serious problem."

"Regarding the tribe," he said.

"As much as I know about your people, I still need a bit of professional help separating fact from fiction. I'd like you to watch something Alya found."

Buzz insisted I take his chair behind the desk. I removed the small laptop from my satchel, and he leaned closer to watch. On screen, the raven Marie Honoré prowled an auditorium stage:

"…so, early Twentieth Century, members of mixed ancestry, like my forefathers, were expelled from the tribe."

"They called it Blood Quantum," Buzz said. "What began as a U.S. government test for legitimacy, for determining Native benefits and such, was later adopted by the tribes to test applicants for membership. We have, over time, amended this to a percentage of ancestral blood, or proof of direct lineage."

"Louisiana has one of the largest indigenous populations in the East. Tribal councils here carry political weight and, of course, they grow in stature as new revenues come in. Who here does not enjoy a night out at the casino? You can put your hands down. It was a rhetorical question."

"They also purchase land to be held in trust for the reservation," Buzz said. "And while the state does have a large indigenous community, the Chitimacha tribe is not the most heavily populated."

"As reservation growth is steady but slow, some tribal leaders think more of the short-term profits. While many of you may joke about the price of swampland, deals are being cut. Huge corporations dealing in transportation and agriculture make generous offers, acquiring cheap land to connect rail hubs to farms and ports, crisscrossing many native communities. They guarantee the destruction of wetlands, some family holdings over a century old, as well as historical sites."

Buzz's weather-cut expression changed to one of uncertainty, then to things darker.

"Many outcasts, like myself, love our heritage but are held out of tribal council decisions because we are not red enough—back to that bloodlines thing. Some of us wage personal legal battles to contest this pre-World War One edict, hoping to restore our lawful Chitimacha heritage."

"You know this woman, this Honoré?" Buzz locked his eyes, no longer pleasant, on the monitor. "Ours is still a relatively small group. If she had applied for membership, I would most likely recognize the name."

"A lawyer," Mr. Vagelle said. "She lectures at the university. As you can see, she preaches love of heritage, but I know her to work for the very company intent on acquiring tribal lands for development. She has an obvious animus for the tribe."

"Not all the old laws are bad laws. Without this, there would be many looking to cash-in on the modest government benefits for our people. But I cannot understand her painting our tribal laws as—what, racism? *Not* red *enough!* If she has Chitimacha in her ancestry, it is not much, I think."

"One more question, my friend. As you are in the trades, would you know anything about a proposed big-money transportation project cutting through reservation land?"

"Our lands are small enough. I don't know of a single leader who would vote to pass such a deal. You are investigating her claims? The council has lawyers too."

"Let us try to handle this, Buzz." Mr. Vagelle took his hand again. "But I will call to keep you apprised. I promise."

"Please come to the house, Nicolaus, when we both have more time. Judith will make a wonderful dinner for you and your friend." He smiled broadly for me. "If you work with this man, I will pray for you."

9

On the drive back, Mr. Vagelle decided on his own detour not too far out of our way. The dead, 19th century, sugar plantation. He parked in front of the equally dead manor house.

"You felt compelled to see it again?" I considered the emptiness of the scene now that the authorities had lost interest. "Not a wise investment, if that is your thought."

He left the car, then on second thought, reached back in for his stick. I followed him.

We both froze to the sounds echoing from within the walls. My hand dropped into my satchel for a touch of comfort. Moments later a six-point, whitetail buck, obviously alerted by the sound of the Mercedes, crossed the threshold from the shadowed interior to the top step. I felt his eyes on me for a heartbeat. My scalp prickled. He walked without fear down the steps, crossed the matted grass where so many cars had parked on our last visit, and he continued into the trees.

"He is giving us permission to enter," Mr. Vagelle whispered. The prickling continued to my tailbone, until I decided his words must have come from his bookshelves.

The interior, also eerily unfamiliar in its crypt-like silence, had been professionally cleaned but for the broken, pink-stained floors, and an overlooked trace of arterial spray on the peeling wallpaper. Disturbed by our entrance, twin crows took flight for another room in the house.

Mr. Vagelle led wide of the kill spot, examining the floor in front of his shoes. He tightened his circle before reaching the point of Punter Boyle's execution. Kneeling to inspect the trauma to the floorboards, he ran a finger where one spike had splintered the fragile wood and opened a larger hole. He swiveled to other gouges and scrutinized them more closely.

"The cutter, no ordinary saw. Possibly an oscillating bone saw, battery operated, of course. Expensive."

"That was the coroner's initial guess on the sternum. Did a surgeon do this?"

"A surgeon would not have slipped so far off target as to make these cuts here. Unless…" He paused, and I gave him space. He rose, and I followed through to the back of the house and across other rooms trying to read his mind.

"Would you like to check the upstairs?" I said once we had reached the foyer again.

"Footprints in the dust, the staircase hadn't been cleaned, let's assume the authorities covered it. Besides, we're losing daylight."

"Boss?" I heard tires crunching up the gravel path.

He moved decisively to the window but stood back from the light. "I have a fun job for you."

"About time."

"Leave the satchel for me."

"Um…"

"Take your handgun, worst-case scenario, but you won't need it. I've seen you run enough to know you can outrun these clowns."

"It already sounds fun."

"Before the van stops, get down the front steps and break to the right. They'll see you, but you should be to the corner of the house before they can climb out. They will be confused."

"Today, I will be the Mama bird." I winked.

"Once you see they are chasing, just sprint off and circle the house. My car will be running before you get there and jump in. A piece of cake."

"What about—?"

"They're almost here. Go!"

I went.

There was a time I lived for the exhilaration, and he knew it. My adrenalin caught up with me, our enemies did not. I heard yelling, but never looked back. I sped round the corner and was to the back of the house before they cleared the first turn. As Mr. Vagelle said, he had the Mercedes running by the time I got there.

I looked back as we sped away. The thugs bellowed when they saw all four tires of their dirt-and-pea green van had been slashed.

I glanced at the fancy walking stick lying across the dashboard. I had named it "fancy" because of the unusually intricate head, worn steel with a minor hook vaguely resembling a wolf's head. There were some who thought it an affectation, or a touch of overly theatrical posturing—he seldom limped or used it as support—but I had learned the history of his fancy stick. Though Nicolaus Vagelle had no aversion to guns, he stopped carrying when he turned in his badge. The cane, with its steel tip and spring-loaded blade, a nearly invisible trigger-lock beneath the wolf's jaw, became a fascination for me the first time I had seen it deployed.

"Your friend?" I said to the stick. "Thank you for trusting me."

"I didn't care to provoke a firefight with one pistol between us. And I'm ashamed to admit, you're a faster runner than me."

Back on Highway 10, pointed towards home, my adrenalin still hummed.

"We both knew they would follow us once we left Emile. So, you did not simply stop for another inspection of the crime scene. You set them up."

"I wasn't sure," he said. "And I wasn't sure I could lose them. Better here than have them follow us back to the safe house."

When we caught first glimpse of the city lights, my phone vibrated. "It is Pedersen." Any earlier thrill dissolved like a puff of steam.

"What?" Mr. Vagelle said.

"They are responding to a fire at Bobby J.'s."

He kicked the accelerator.

Parking the Mercedes on a side street to avoid heavy F.D. traffic, we walked quickly and came out on the facing corner as an ambulance yowled away from the lamppost. The faded yellow sign was gone, as was the window. Fire teams soaked what remained of Bobby J's Black and Blues Club. Beyond the police cordon, crowds thickened. I spotted Detective Pedersen and pointed.

"Tell me Bobby is okay," Mr. Vagelle said.

"Apart from minor burns to his hands," Pedersen said. "The cook couldn't get out of his kitchen in back. He was dead when we got here. Another friend was just taken away in an ambulance. The cocktail came through the big window. Fortunately, if there is a fortunately, it happened before the evening crowd."

"Where is Bobby now?" I said.

Pedersen gestured to a fire engine and the giant resting on the back bumper while an EMT dressed his hands.

"He refused to go to the hospital. At least for now."

I nearly ran to the big man. He saw me coming and hid his face, and I threw my arms around him forgetting my haphephobia.

"It's all gone," Bobby whispered into my shoulder.

"Not all," Mr. Vagelle said from behind.

My stomach shivered and I stepped away and hugged myself, focusing on my mantra: *I do not shake hands.*

"My ol' Jamaican," Bobby said. "Son of a bull-headed—thought he could put the fire out. He's hurt bad." He stared at his bandaged hands. "I got him out though."

"You saw no one out front?" Pedersen said. When Bobby did not respond, the detective walked off to question other possible witnesses.

"You didn't say no," Mr. Vagelle said.

"Do you know a man, white man, thick, shaved head, too many tattoos?" Silence. Then Bobby said, "You didn't say no."

"I don't have a name yet. Your apartment upstairs here, you need another place to stay."

"I have friends."

"Many friends. If you need anything and you don't call me, I'll be offended."

Bobby gripped his knees, wincing with the pain, and watched the ruins smolder.

We crossed the tediously narrow bridge back across Lake Pontchartrain to the regal safe house. "You are okay?" Mr. Vagelle said.

"I am okay." I turned away to the blue expanse.

"You lost your head for a moment back there."

"I will go back to counseling once this is over, thank you." I swiped at something in the corner of my eye. "Will this be over? I do not know how to fight *corporations.*"

"They are hurting my friends. There is not enough wealth in the world to protect them from me."

I was more than a bit surprised to see my Impala parked at the curb. Patty P.I. climbed out as we pulled into the driveway.

"As long as you put my ignition back together," I said.

"Oh, that's hot-wiring old school. We are full-service P.I.s and come with a complete line of locksmithing tools."

"Can you repair an apartment door?"

She accompanied me to the front of the house while Mr. Vagelle parked the Mercedes in the garage. We all converged in the sitting room and the man poured drinks.

"Is Bobby gonna be okay?" Patty said. "I wonder if he's still sitting out there."

"He'll be okay," Mr. Vagelle said. "He promised to go over to East Jefferson E.R. to check on the Jamaican later."

"Why do this to Bobby? I do not understand this way of thinking," I said.

"Because you are not a psychopath," Patty said.

"We would not stand down after she ordered us to," Mr. Vagelle said. "I made her appear weak in front of her boss. Now she's showing us the consequences. Choosing the club was her reminding me I had friends to hurt, and she knows where they are." He glanced at Patty. "I—Alya?"

"I know. You told her," I said.

"I should have mentioned long ago," he said. "I didn't want you to be uncomfortable around her. When you first went to work for me—"

"I gave you permission to share with a few. I remember."

"We agreed it was necessary, and you let me send you to my doctor friend."

"Yes, the shrink." I gauged Patty's reaction.

"You were young. We had to get you to the point where you could be close to people, and you know I shared with Dr. Maiwand, downstairs in our building. Detective Petersen knows, and so does Patty, that's all. I felt it important for the work. And for your growth."

"He knows I can keep a secret," Patty gestured to the fancy sitting room, the *safe house*. "It's not like I couldn't have figured it out after being around you for an hour. To be frank, when he told me about taking on an *assistant,* I did a bit of investigating on my own. It's what I do. I thought it curious I could find so little background, and after seeing you, more curious why I could find no boyfriend, or girlfriend, in your past."

"I think we need to stop discussing this," I said.

"Sorry. It was something, a phobia, I had never heard of. Once I learned—Okay. I got it."

"And we will never talk about this again."

"I swear."

Mr. Vagelle changed the subject expertly, as he did most things. "Patty, see if you can get me a name on Landon's bodyguard. Looks like a shaved animal with scalp tattoos. And have you found anything on Ms. Boyle's doctor?"

"I put a man on it this afternoon. So far, we got William Davies. Yes, he's had a long association with Landon's company and the Boyle family. Graduated UCLA, where he did his residency. Started in orthopedics, dropped out, then reappeared with a plastic surgery practice. Boob jobs in Beverly Hills. Suddenly, the guy disappears from California medicine and, just as suddenly, twelve years ago, opens a chiropractic clinic, then a family practice here in New Orleans."

"You sure he didn't get his diploma from the Department of Corrections? The man changes professions like a parolee."

"He got a bad reputation when caught dealing prescriptions as if handing out Chiclets. That's when he shopped his services around and found some cushy clients like you-know-who."

"You got all that since noon?" I said.

"We are efficient." She winked.

Mr. Vagelle dropped beneath the surface of his thoughts.

Patty stayed and talked about the case, thankfully avoiding my "irrational fear," as the shrink called it. We exhausted ourselves, or the drink did, and she eventually called for a Lyft.

Mr. Vagelle retired. I showered, threw on the robe, and took several minutes in the bedroom chair with the laptop while my hair dried. I needed answers to a few of my own questions. I flinched at movement from the hall.

"Sorry." He turned away. "Your door was open. I thought you were up."

"Not a problem." I dropped my feet from the chair and covered my knees with the robe. "Come in. Old habits, leaving the bedroom door open."

He took two steps into the room.

"I had to check a few ideas," I said. "I was going to ask you before I did anything but I remembered, a few years ago, Bobby invited us to a private party. Mr. Hancock was there, and a Mr. Bonama…"

"I know who you mean."

"And…well, I was thinking, yes, insurance will rebuild, and Bobby can get the money to maybe open another club, but I know how in love he was with the memories hanging on those walls. I was going to ask you if I could write a couple letters, maybe persuade his musician friends to ask their friends and— What?" I saw an odd look there.

"Nothing. I think it's a terrific idea." He propped his shoulder to the doorframe. "Actually, I stopped by to talk about tomorrow, and I have an important job for you. First, I'll be heading out early. I need to get back to Buzz. He's not answering my texts and I didn't want to call this late on a hunch. I led those two thugs right to his jobsite, and after today—"

"But you want me to stay here."

"I just got off the phone with Pedersen. He's putting two men on my building to keep an eye on Dr. Maiwand and Hemmings. He said he'd put in a call to Chief Deputy Dupré. Get a warning out to the reservation. Your job, while I'm away, I need you close to Bobby. Not because I think he's in any further danger after today, but you are a comfort to have around. He likes you and trusts you. Keep him away from his club. Tell him I ordered you to drive him around, talk to friends, whatever. Refuse to take no for an answer."

"I can do that." I wanted to say more. I knew he was thinking about the men in the dirt-and-pea green van. He was wishing he did more than flatten their tires.

He started out of the room but stopped.

"Something else?" I said.

"It really is an amazing idea…for Bobby's place. And amazing still, because of all you are dealing with, if I haven't said it lately, I—Taking you in was one of my better ideas."

I laughed. "Of course, you would turn a kind phrase into a compliment for yourself."

He was gone from the doorway when I heard him whisper, "Because I am a son of a bitch." I imagined him smiling.

10

I did not sleep well. Not that I expected to. I woke when I heard the garage door at four o'clock. I would never get back to sleep, so I prepared for my day.

The call came from Detective Pedersen before sunup. He said he was trying to contact Mr. Vagelle but had only reached his voicemail.

Taking you in was one of my better ideas. I had laughed, but at the timing, not the words.

I was sixteen when I fled the horror of my life, my family, Moscow, and he found me at nineteen. I was homeless here, living at the marina, surviving. *He took me in.* Into his life. I knew the difficulty for him, but it remained unspoken. We dealt with *my issues* together. His shrink friend…then, out of the blue, he told me I needed my independence. I needed to work on things like my English, my social skills, and more, so he paid for my university tuition. But I was not so *unschooled* by life. I had guessed at deeper reasons, partly due to his old-world code of ethics, the shield of a white knight, who may not have been so white, but who hated himself for his grays. So, a decision had been made, maybe the day he took me in, that the line in the sand he would never cross must be drawn around me. And by observing the "proper" knight, I grew more aware of that line widening with each passing year. The closer we got, the further he pushed, until he finally pushed me out. But that was then.

I returned after a couple years and asked for my old job back. He said, "No, a new job, my assistant in training," and I knew he had grown in the two years we spent apart.

Now, at twenty-five, while I occasionally called him "boss" out of habit, I felt more of a partner than an employee. We argued, as always, we could both be pig-headed at times, but our arguments never lasted. I have never disobeyed a serious request from him until this day. Well, almost never.

Pedersen told me about the second fire.

He had gotten the news from his call with Dupré, the arson of an old church under construction near French Settlement. One lone fatality, Emile Cook. Buzz. I could not think about Bobby today. Sunrise caught me speeding up the Interstate to my friend.

I pulled onto the gravel across from the pile of wet, blackened timber and ash. With the fire out, the official trucks and cars returned to their caves, a few townsfolk lingered near their pickups. A solemn, solitary man in an orange vest and hardhat pushed a rake through the debris. I approached and he pointed to a man in a gray raincoat kicking the mud off his boots beside a muddier truck.

I introduced myself, gave my sympathies, and said my boss was a good friend of Emile Cook.

"Your boss's name?"

"Nicolaus Vagelle."

Buzz had mentioned the name in the past.

"If it him—least he said it was—you miss him by a couple hour. He talk some with de Fire Chief and de coroner here."

"I need to find him. He was coming here to meet Emile."

"Not sure what to tell you, ma'am. He left in a hurry, him. I did overhear somet'ing he said to de coroner about a crime scene. I t'ought him talking 'bout dis one here."

I thanked him in two languages and sprinted to my car.

I fought to keep my thoughts away from the nightmares and focused on the road.

Pulling onto the winding pathway, I slowed through the canopy of mythological trees. I caught my first glimpse of the dead mansion through their branches. I then saw his Mercedes sideways in the road, hot red tail lamps blurred by morning mist. It had crushed the side of the pea-green van.

I nearly jumped out and ran on but remembered losing my head with Bobby. I grabbed the bag from the back seat, and in less than two minutes held the assembled Kalashnikov on my lap. It would have been one minute, but my hands were shaking.

I did not run. I walked to the wreck, straining for the slightest sound under the noise of the Mercedes engine. The driver's door hung open, the front seat empty, the windshield spiderwebbed with bullet holes, duplicated by the rear window.

The van appeared empty. I rounded to the point of impact where a broken man hung pinned between bumper and side panel. I yanked the handle on the van's rear door, leveling my AK. The space was empty but for a filth-crusted sleeping bag and a broken cardboard toolbox.

Twenty-five meters from the manor house, I sighted the other body. From the throat, a dark stream had spilled down the concrete steps. Sitting on the threshold, forearms resting on his knees, Mr. Vagelle held his bloodied sword cane with both hands.

"Tell me you are unhurt," I yelled ahead.

"I am unhurt."

Legs quaking, I climbed the steps until I stood over him. After a moment, my knees threatened to drop me, so I sat.

A long while later, he said, "Where the hell did you get that thing?"

"I am sorry about your friend."

"Uh-huh."

"Did you call the police?" I watched for the young buck to emerge from the trees, although I knew he would not.

"I don't have the patience to deal with Dupré," he said. "I still have too much to do before they lock me up."

"I checked the tracker Mr. Brown stuck on your girlfriend's car. Yesterday, I asked Patty to forward any schedule updates at the university, in case you ever wanted to catch a lecture." I cleared the AK's forward round as we walked to my car. He stopped at the rear of the van, and I watched him drag the box of tools across the door's mud-thickened sill plate.

"You keep two steps ahead of me for too long, I'll get self-conscious." He lifted a battery-powered bone saw, well-used.

"Maybe you will let me run the business while you are behind bars."

We stopped for a long lunch where neither of us could eat. My phone hummed. I scanned the text then handed him the phone. "Patty."

"Well…" he read, "some physical altercation at a company Christmas party. Old Martin and J.C. in a shoving match, something about Mrs. Boyle. Two years later, partner number-one kicks the bucket. Partner number-two finds himself inches away from full ownership. I assume Martin's wife really doesn't care to inherit all the hard work that goes with running a multi-national corporation."

"Or she imagines she will remarry and keep it in the family anyway."

"That'll never happen, but she can be bought off. However, there's the kid to consider. A nice percentage of Mom's slice had gone into a Trust for Punter, and Punter was entering university on a business education ticket. The more he learned, the harder it would have been for *friend* Landon to guide him."

"And in through the emotional mist tiptoes the beautiful, young, Cajun attorney."

"Coincidentally lecturing at Punter's university after Daddy dies."

"You don't like to believe in coincidence. Landon pushed that button."

We eventually made Baton Rouge, and by late afternoon, I pulled onto the university campus. Three black, late model Expeditions idled conspicuously blocking the parking lot entrance.

"Suggestions?" I said.

"They aren't police and they're not here for tea and a tongue-wag. Their guns may not be bigger than yours but there will be more of them. Their car engines…well…"

"I began driving for my Papa at fourteen." I slammed the gears into reverse, tapped the brakes, spun the wheel, slam-shifted into drive, and accelerated. One-way traffic ran onto the curb to avoid us, and in the mirror the SUVs jockeyed clumsily for position. "Expect the unexpected, *comrades.*"

Cutting the corner of the Faculty Building, my tires chewed up a portion of their manicured lawn. I quickly changed direction three times along the narrow streets of campus housing. Wandering students scattered. A final fast U-turn and I wedged the car snug to the curb in the only available parking space. I cut the motor and listened to her tick.

"Not sure I expected that either." Mr. Vagelle checked his seat belt. "You drove for Hollywood too?"

"Just Papa. He enjoyed running from *militsiya*—police." We watched three black Expeditions roar past the intersection. They split at the next circle, heading to three compass points.

"Give them time to reach the freeway."

"Poor Punter must have been head-over-heels in a flash," I said. "Before he could catch his bearings, he was attending lectures, taking field trips with his pretty professor, changing his major, falling in love with a serpent."

I parked on the far side of campus, street parking rather than the designated lot near the lecture halls. The extra walk would help steady me.

11

"Landon's an Old-World dragon," Mr. Vagelle said. "And dragons jealously hoard their acquisitions. He would've made sure the kid received nothing from the company. Of course, now…"

Lecture Hall 2. Like an image cut from my computer screen, the woman in black faced her slide show and failed to see us enter. We took seats in the back row.

"…forced out of the tribe, lost bloodlines," she said. "We were not *Red enough*. But I still contest this out-of-date edict, hoping to restore our lawful Chitimacha heritage."

She collected her presentation materials with the help of an over-eager student as others, mostly male, flowed uphill to the exits. Finally, with the theater nearly empty, she noticed us. She checked both wings of the stage, confusion blossoming.

"Marie Honoré." Mr. Vagelle spoke loud enough to span the distance. "If you are looking for escape, we are in no position to chase you."

"I am legally bound not to reveal anything company related," she said. "Especially here. Especially to *you*."

"You sincerely believe your company is, at this moment, respecting its legal obligations to you?"

"I have no idea what you mean. Go away."

"Do you prefer shouting the entire conversation for university consumption?"

The lawyer reassessed her position, then descended from the stage as an Adagio in search of musical accompaniment. An elegant metaphor for her pallbearer façade. Or perhaps giving herself time to invent an opening argument. Halfway up the aisle, she halted in profile as if, even in stiletto heels, she might sprint off at the sound of a starter's pistol.

"Apparently—" Mr. Vagelle stepped once along the row of seats but stopped abruptly as the Ms. Honoré checked her exits. "Apparently, you and I had been conspiring for months prior to Punter's murder. Simple enough to *find* additional evidence, company resources what they are. Perhaps eager detectives will locate indigent plantation workers ready to swear they witnessed me nailing Punter's hands to the floor? Where will they find his heart, I wonder?"

"You came all this way to perform a Perry Mason routine? I wish I had you in front of a courtroom."

"As Sophocles warned, Marie, hubris begets the fall."

"Of course." Black satin tresses fell forward to frame the raven's leer in a practiced look. "I knew all about your ancestors before we'd even met, *Nicolaus*—What is your last name these days?"

"Immaterial, *your Honor*. However, I am impressed with how quickly you picked up Landon's mentoring, even his handicaps. After witnessing the ham-handed way he dealt with a *troublesome consultant,* I concluded only Martin Boyle could have had the original brainstorm for the company's expansion."

"You're about to get to the part about me benefitting by listening to this?"

Her first guard dog materialized beneath the stage lights. He dropped his sport coat, apparently to grant us the privilege of his muscle-flexing. He descended from the stage with considerably less grace than the spike-heeled attorney.

"So," Mr. Vagelle ignored him, "you, in all your so-called *indigenous pride,* found yourself in a quandary. Do you make yourself a rising star within the corporation while simultaneously stomping your stiletto heel onto the neck of the Tribal Council? The council that had rejected you since birth? Still just a petulant child."

The corners of her smile wilted.

A metallic clunk, then another, resonated throughout the auditorium as switches dropped and the overhead lights extinguished by rows. The door at the top of the stairs opened. One hundred and forty kilograms of silhouette blocked the evening light from without before ducking beneath the doorframe. Distant light from the stage glinted off the steel in his hand and defined the tattoos as dead black worms across his glistening skull.

Mr. Vagelle rose and signaled me to retreat along our row of seats. I took three steps then pushed my hand into my satchel, disobeying him again. Twice in twenty-four hours, another milestone.

"Damned if I will," I whispered.

Marie Honoré retreated behind the shorter bodyguard, her features disappearing into a mask of shadows. To our other side, Wormhead lifted the steel, took a single step toward my employer, and I put a bullet into his beefy thigh. He did not fall, but his .45 did. Knees locked, and he grabbed the wound. The smaller man-shield in front of Marie decided no move was his best move.

"So, *Baba Yaga*," I said, "when exactly did you tell Landon you had Punter killed? It must have been after he hired us to find the boy."

"When young Jefferson disappeared," Mr. Vagelle said, "he involved us 'little-fish' to avoid any LBRi scrutiny regarding the Boyles, and his less-than-ethical backstage games. Then, once you'd realized we were not so easily *handled*, you needed to involve company resources to deal with us. He must have been a tad upset with you, no?"

"Wrong! You know nothing." She checked the exits. "I could never kill Punter. I—I came to the company through Martin. Through him, I met his son."

"But Daddy also had more than a business interest in you."

"Sure. Why not? Look at me! And one day, Punter walked in on us. Martin tried to make excuses. Then the stress, estrangement with his son and wife—his heart was too old for our relationship."

"*Relationship*," I nearly sang it. "Martin's climax being a massive hemorrhage. You must be good."

"Or you fed him a little something to help it along at Landon's direction," Mr. Vagelle said. "To eliminate *chance* from the equation. Of course, you do know a doctor."

"When I learned of company strategies, what they intended with native lands—" she said. "I would never hurt—"

"I apologize," Mr. Vagelle said. "Before I interrupted, you were about to tell me you loved Punter. That you could never hurt *him.*"

"Wordplay, *Nicolaus.* Weak."

"Enough, *Marie.* Your imagination must be exhausted. While I am more than impressed with your sexual athleticism, you mix far too much fiction with reality and, frankly, I'm bored."

"You talk a lot for a bored man."

"I suggest that Punter's ritual death had been planned for some time, then staged, and you, the psychopath, were there for the execution. Only you could have lured the hot-blooded nineteen-year-old out to the middle of a dead plantation, get him to strip and neatly fold his clothes in a corner."

I lifted the bone saw from my heavy satchel. "A gift from the orthopedist, I presume?"

"Your goons would have tattooed his tongue at your direction. '*No Red*' could only have sprung from your warped views on tribal injustice. They wouldn't have cared about leaving their footprints, but you would have seen your own stiletto heels in the blood and decided to remove any trace of yourself at the scene."

"So, the ammonia and mop," I said. "By the way, we found several dainty heel marks in the dirt where you had parked."

"I will prove that toy in your hand belongs to you, *bitch.* You won't last long, I think." But her eyes betrayed her.

"More hubris." I lowered the saw back into my satchel and substituted it for my cell phone. "Dr. Davies would understand that these *toys* come with traceable serial numbers. I looked it up. When did you first discover the doctor's side-business, trafficking in human organs?" It was a reach of speculation, but her non-reaction said everything. "Were you able to catch all that, Lieutenant Pedersen?"

"We got it, Alya," the speakerphone said. "Operators got a ping minutes after you turned on your phone. We're about thirty minutes out. Tell Vagelle Chief Deputy Dupré is with me, and I believe he's getting depressed."

"Our legal team…" Ms. Honoré began, but failed to close.

"I believe once they are presented with your audio testimony," I said, "while J.C. may be lacking in the creativity department, he would not be in the position he is in—as my *Papa* used to say—without always having a back-up plan, or three."

"My advice, Marie Honoré?" Mr. Vagelle proceeded me up the ramp toward the exit. "You heard the police are on their way. I suggest you wait for them. I don't know your employer well, but I know he is not slow with these sorts of decisions." He paused, turned. "Oh, and to your strategy, throwing your birthright before a jury in order to gain sympathy? All your years of fighting for tribal acceptance, your *respect* for The People seemed obvious to me the moment I saw your gift to Punter. The Chitimacha skull used as a paperweight."

12

"So," I set the heavy Thomson Reuters book aside, "state law demands that archeologists, when discovering human remains, immediately stop the dig and notify the tribe."

After taking our statements, Detective Pedersen had confided that many of our suppositions proved correct, verified in part by a nervous company lawyer, Tyler Coombes.

Marie Honoré had slept with both partners for advancement until Landon recognized her skills and the opportunity, and then devised the means of canceling Boyle's percentage. After that, they found it easy to sexually direct Punter, until—no one knows how—the boy began questioning his father's death. Our femme fatale decided that a second murder would be as easy for her as the first, so she eliminated the growing problem.

That was before Landon hired the consultant, *an outsider to keep the Boyle problem away from company investors. And when we proved too difficult for her, she returned to Landon, for both their sakes. That was when Landon agreed that the consultant would become the goat.*

"That *organ harvesting* was an impressive gambit." Mr. Vagelle paused with the bottle in his hand. "You surprised even me."

"I did not know if it was true. I remembered you asking the coroner about evidence of a *receptacle* to transport the heart. Why else take care with the handling? When I was a girl, I learned about kidney stealing from a friend of Papa."

"Your childhood pains me. I wouldn't have thought to use that tactic on Ms. Honoré. She might have had more knowledge of the practice."

"I do not understand."

"The heart is one of the most difficult organs to transplant and, even on ice, the heart loses viability the fastest. After four hours, without other precautions, cell functions begin to fail. The recipient's survival odds drop accordingly. Still, it was an excellent guess. I imagine Dr. Davies never explained, or was afraid to say no to her demands."

'But once again, I have found a topic you know too much about."

The glass rose to his lips.

Heavy footsteps on the landing, and a hard knock prompted Mr. Vagelle to wave me back. He yanked open the door. The giant hunched with his considerable weight on the doorframe.

"Bobby!" I said. "Are you okay?"

"Come in. Let me get you a drink," Mr. Vagelle said.

"Can't stay." He appeared shaken. "There ain't many knows where I'm stayin'. That's why I come to you."

"Tell me."

"I got a package. With a note inside. All it said was, 'I just heard—More to come—H.' So, I unwrapped it. It was an old horn and a signed LP, signed by his friend, Byrd." He wiped a sleeve across his forehead. "'Twas your doin', wasn't it?"

"Not me, my friend," Mr. Vagelle said.

Bobby shifted his gaze. I could not hold my poker face.

"Ain't no one done something like that for me before. Damn. I gotta go—" and he thundered back down the stairs.

"Boss?" I said. "Is there a chance we can get into trouble again soon? I would like to take another vacation to your friend's pretty house on the lake."

Since our conversation with *Ms. Honoré*, charges had been dropped on Mr. Vagelle. LBRi had suspended negotiations and the pursuit of Louisiana property acquisitions bordering tribal lands. Mr. Landon had taken his family on an impromptu sabbatical to his home on the coast of Kilmore Quay, Ireland.

"As a matter of fact," Mr. Vagelle said, "I've already arranged it with my friend. I would like you to take three weeks, go stay in the house by the lake. Anything you need to do here, you can do there."

"Okay. I know you too well, Nicolaus. Tell me this has nothing to do with Dr. Maiwand visiting his sick aunt, and your landlord's threats of taking a vacation."

"Alya."

"You do not want me here alone while you are out of town."

"Not until I know it's safe. I don't want you going back to your apartment either. Can you do that for me? Patty is still on retainer and she has agreed to check in."

"It is about Emile," I said under my breath.

Monday evening I was still working on case notes when Detective Pedersen stopped in, a Delta Tribune under his arm. He could not fail to notice the suitcases in the bedroom doorway. Mr. Vagelle poured him a tumbler of his favorite bourbon.

"Going somewhere nice, I hope," Pedersen said. "Let's pretend you know nothing about a page-two article in the Weekend Edition." Pedersen laid the newspaper on the coffee table and turned the cover page like he had unearthed the Dead Sea Scrolls.

THE BODY OF AN ANGEL FOUND

IN THE BELLY OF A CHITIMACHA BURIAL MOUND.

"Do you go anywhere without a newspaper?" I said.

"She had apparently suffered from a broken ankle and a broken neck when her stiletto heel stuck in the soft clay of the steps leading into the excavation. "

"Death by fashion statement? That's the first I've heard of it." Mr. Vagelle placed a second tumbler on the desk where I sat, and poured one for himself. I slid the Aer Lingus plane tickets under the desk blotter as he raised his drink to the policeman.

"Do you think we will ever find poor Punter's heart?" I said.

They both put their drinks down.

Ten

A Hazardous

Touch

Trinadsat

Thirteen. My most memorable birthday. Not my best or happiest birthday, but the one I remembered most.

We heard breaking glass. Misha looked at me. I looked at him. Few things intrigued a child like the sound of breaking glass. A violent sound. A sound guaranteed to bring every child everywhere to a fast halt, maybe a held breath, or a dozen heartbeats added to the minute as a young imagination pinballed through a maze of questions. Like the snap of a finger behind the ear, the sound immediately replaced simple playtime with an adrenal shot of curiosity. A sound of possible danger.

Someone, somewhere close, doing something they should not, and proclaiming it with a loud defiance. Enticing.

"Alya…?" Misha said. Maybe I smiled.

We first turned our faces to our back door, thinking some adult would fling the door open to investigate the sound. Maybe order us to "Stay here!" and "Mind your business!" Simultaneously, we decided not to wait. As most children learned early, it was always easier to ask forgiveness than permission, so we launched ourselves down the alley.

Misha Fedorov was a year older, but better fed. I always slowed for him in a race, my best friend. That worked for the best this day, because slowing allowed for us to see the baddies before they saw us. Two boys, older than either of us, hunted the alley ground debris. *For what?* Lean, hungry-eyed, with t-shirts and trousers in unidentifiable colors, they must have spent the night in a coal yard. The taller of the two found a thing of interest. He straightened his back and tested its weight. His perfect throwing stone. He stroked it with both hands. Squinting with malevolence, he turned and let fly.

The gray walls fronting the alley would be an apartment building one day. Today, needing paint and upper windows past the mid-point, it stretched bleak and empty toward a joyless, morning gray, cloud canopy. The lower cut squares had been recently fitted with aluminum and glass. The glass still wore its sticky tags fresh from the factory. The flying stone shattered one of these, the sound echoing throughout the concrete canyon, and the tall boy celebrated with a fist in the air.

The other boy discovered me and he crouched with a stone in each hand, like a brass monkey at the Moscow Zoo, still and expressionless. The tall boy turned to his accomplice. Then he spotted me as well.

"What do you want?" tall boy said.

"Let's go, Alya," Misha said from behind.

"I can throw higher," I said to tall boy.

"Alya," Misha said.

Tall boy grinned and came toward me. He held his hand out, offering his second stone. His friend came to life by inches. This one did not grin, but his head cocked as if thinking. He advanced as well.

"Hey!" Two large men in hard hats and tool belts jogged from the corner of the unfinished building, their sightlines fastened to the boys. I joined Misha in retreat and the boys spun and fled in the opposite direction. Tall boy looked over his shoulder at me before I turned a corner and chased Misha back home.

We sat in Misha's kitchen. Mrs. Fedorov reminded me it was my birthday when she set a small cake with pink icing on the table in front of us. It made me cry. Misha cut a slice and pushed the plate my way. His whole family was good people. When I had been left alone in the past, sometimes for days, or even weeks, they never let me go hungry. Their kitchen, like this morning, always smelled of wonderful things in the oven.

"How is your *mamochka*, dear?" Mrs. Fedorov said. "Did you vist her yesterday?" She brought plastic cups of milk.

"Papa made me work yesterday." I ate and talked. "He says I am grown enough. He takes me to his work, and we are in a big empty warehouse, and he teaches me to drive. I am not too good yet. I need to be taller, I think."

"Yes, but what about your mama?" she said. "What did the doctor say?"

"Papa will not talk about it. He says I should not either." I focused on my fork with pink icing.

"Eat your cake, dear." She busied herself with more kitchenwork. Cabinets opened and closed while Misha talked and my thoughts circled about my Mama.

"I should go home." I finished my milk and pushed up from the chair. "Thank you very much for the birthday cake." Misha asked if I could stay, and I said, "I should see if Papa is awake."

"He sleeps so late?" Mrs. Fedorov said. "Wait." She opened cabinets, removed paper and a cloth sack with handles for groceries. She wrapped a box of store-bought chocolates I had noticed on the counter when I came in. She lowered it without ceremony into the sack and passed it to me.

"Listen, child," she said. "Today you go to your mama in the hospital. She needs to see her *little sunshine*. But before you see her, you see her doctor. Only hers. You know his name?" I nodded. "You give him the chocolates. It is only for him. You say it is from Mrs. Elin, your mama."

I must have appeared confused.

"This is the way of things," she said. "When we go to a doctor, we bring a small gift. A token, something. This tells the doctor to take special care of our family. He will pay more attention when he has so many patients to treat."

I held the sack open, staring in, unable to speak.

She asked if I needed money for a bus, and my trance broke.

"Oh, no, thank you. It is not far." My child-mind was embarrassed to accept more of her gifts. "I will go as soon as I change my clothes. Thank you very much, Mrs. Fedorov."

My stop home was brief. I worried Papa would see the gift and take it for himself, so I stowed it behind the door in the entryway. I should not have bothered. This time of morning, Papa would continue to sleep. I hurried into a clean dress. Misha was waiting for me by the entrance as I came out.

"I asked if I could go with you," he said. "It is not such a short walk and your arms might get tired carrying your gift."

"And such a heavy box of candies? Well, okay, as long as you don't ask to stop and eat it." I poked his soft belly and he laughed.

We would not take the alley route.

Our building stood as one of a curved string of identical buildings. *Khrushchyovka*—low-cost, five-story buildings, named for the leader who commissioned them. Many such buildings in Moscow had become overcrowded. Some apartments housed more then one family, or generations of a family, in a single one-or-two-bedroom flat. We were lucky. Whatever my Papa did for a living, we always had our apartment to ourselves. It was a long walk just to get past our neighborhood, and a much longer walk to the hospital.

I smirked, glad for Misha's company.

The last in our line of buildings, fourth from the beginning of our hike, had been vacant and crumbling and windowless since I could remember. It would be many more years before they demolished it. We had been warned many times against playing inside. A dark carnival of homeless, alcohol and drug-fueled, survived there only short-term. They could be seen huddling in the recesses throughout our long Moscow winters. As winter was yet two months away, the end of our block was a nest of grubs enjoying what life remained to them in the final days of sunlight. By habit, I took Misha's hand and crossed the street to avoid them.

Heads turned. Two teenagers pressed to the side of the building sharing the butt of a cigarette. They recognized us from the alley this morning.

"Don't run," Misha whispered. "Walk a bit faster."

The short one stuck the butt tight in his teeth and grinned. Of course, they came our way. I clutched the box of candies to my chest and we ran. Other grubs soon lost interest, but not those two. They were a wildfire rekindled from early morning, and they took joy from our fear.

Down the street, across the intersection, we ran between moving cars, but still they came closer. I yelled at Misha to split away, knowing they would come for me first, and I might run faster without him. He refused. I turned between buildings. He followed. They followed.

We turned into a parking garage where I thought people might be coming and going, but it proved dark and empty except for three derelict cars stripped and powdered with concrete dust. I beat my palm on the elevator button, but the elevator was out of service.

Our wolves slowed to a walk. We were cornered.

Misha pulled me away, and we ran up the ramp to the second level. As dark as the first—darker, no windows. We ran and turned and held our backs to a shell of a VW van that had been gutted by fire in a previous decade.

"Ooh, nice of you to bring me a present," tall boy said.

I hugged the present with both hands. They came close.

"It is for her mama in the hospital," Misha said. "Leave her alone."

"Aw, mama's in hospital," short boy said. "I'm going to cry." He reached for Mama's chocolates and Misha pushed his arm down. Short boy punched Misha and, when he fell, kicked him on the ground.

"Stop it!" I hit short boy in the ear and tall boy pushed me hard against the van, and I fell to my knees. "Stop!"

"My *mamochka* is dead a long time," tall boy said. "Maybe I need present to take to her grave, if I knew where she was." They both laughed. They both kicked Misha and he cried and curled on the hard ground.

"Stop!" I struggled to my feet, but tall boy pushed me back down and I dropped Mama's chocolates. Then short boy was sitting on my chest and I could not move my arms, and tall boy was tearing my clothes. I looked for Mama's chocolates, but I saw Misha on the ground crying, watching me through his fingers. I fought hard. I was not strong enough. I was only thirteen.

After that, I could not move.

I lay on the cold floor smelling of concrete dust. The boys were gone, and the walls grew darker with night coming. I shivered in my pain. Misha had fled the garage. I wondered if the boys would come back and hurt me again. I heard noises, then knew they were only birds returning home to their quiet corners.

Time moved by inches, if at all. I could not guess how slow. Then Misha returned, followed by a man. Misha talked fast and cried some. The man wore a uniform, electric worker maybe. He was strong and said some things. He wrapped my waist with his jacket, then he lifted me in his arms. I tried to stop shaking, but could not, and lost sight through my tears.

I remember Misha in the back of the man's van, with me lying amongst boxes and tools and spools of cables as the van bounced over pitted streets. Misha tried to touch me, but I pulled away. I could not be touched.

The man carried me through the hospital doors and gave me to nurses and said he could not stay. I recall saying part of a thank you—but could not finish. I still shook. Nurses wrapped me in a hospital shirt and the man took his jacket and, with sad eyes, he said goodbye. I lay on a paper sheet, behind a circle of hanging curtain, with voices somewhere else and the sounds of shoes crossing tile. I thought I heard Misha's voice. He yelled at someone.

I lay there alone, for eternity.

When a doctor came, his face was empty. A nurse came with him. She had a tired brow. The doctor attended me, asked many questions I had no answers for, and some I did not understand. He looked in my eyes with a penlight, my ears, he checked my fingertips. He disinfected my scrapes, examined other wounds. He told the nurse to swab other, more private areas, and apply medications. As I lay on my back, I stared at the blinding circles of light above until the light burned. I cried a little and trembled with every touch.

"Did your father do this?" the doctor said. I shook my head. "Would you tell me if he did?" He must have read my look of hate, because he turned quickly away. Papa was not always a nice man or a gentle man, and sometimes I hated him, but he would never imagine something like this. "Was it another family member? Someone you know?"

Why would this doctor say these things?

"We need to ask," the nurse said, then the doctor sent her to bring medicines for me to take home. The doctor left my little curtained room, and the nurse returned with a warm blanket. "We are very crowded, but the doctor said you can rest here for a time. We will need your family contact information. Can we call someone to come pick you up?"

I thought about it and shook my head.

"Her mama is in the hospital somewhere." Misha opened the curtain, surprising the nurse. Tears had left streaks in the dirt of his face before drying. He said he had called home, and his papa was on his way to get us. The nurse brought him a chair so he could wait with me. He tried to touch my hand, but I could not let him. I ached with shame that his papa should see me, and his family would know everything that happened. I held my ribs to keep from shaking and I rocked myself as a mama might, saying silently, *It will be okay. It will be okay.*

When Misha's papa and mama and older sister, Nadja, came, I managed to sit up with some pain. Then I stood leaning on the bed. Nadja had brought a long coat and she quickly helped me to cover my torn dress and bare legs. She rolled cuffs on the sleeves.

"I wish I knew to bring you trousers," she said. I thanked her.

"Do you need to rest more, *little sunshine?*" Mrs. Fedorov said. "We don't need to leave right away. We can sit with you."

"Mama, I lost the candies," Misha said.

"No worries, little Misha."

"I need to see my Mama," I said. I would never again feel like *little sunshine.* This was how *thirteen* felt.

"I brought them here," Misha said and his tears returned. "I found the candies and brought them with, and I was sitting in the hallway for a long time. A doctor saw me and he said I could not bring outside food in here, and he took the candies away."

"Candies are not important," Mr. Fedorov said. "We are here for your friend."

Mrs. Fedorov left the room and when she returned, she had the room number for my Mama.

It was a long walk, for how I felt, and Misha pointed to a doctor standing in a doorway talking to a nurse, and sharing a box of chocolates.

"Mama! That's—"

"It is not important, Misha," Mr. Fedorov said.

After an elevator ride and another hallway, they all waited in the corridor as I went into the narrow room with many beds. I found Mama's bed. She was sleeping. I had seen her when she first arrived and they put the cast on her leg, and the bruises on her face were new, and the IV had been connected to her arm. Today, except for the plaster cast—

"She is improving." A male nurse appeared beside me. He spoke softly. "She should be going home soon."

I nodded. Mama heard and opened her eyes. She rubbed her face with an arm and frowned.

"It is late for visiting." Her eyes moved over my dress through the opening of the coat. "What is this?"

"I'm sorry, Mama. I was—"

"This is how you come here. Your nice dress—You ruined your nice dress. And you come here—you embarrass me to all the world. What do people think of you? That I would raise my child to..."

I ran from the room and ran down the corridor to the elevator. I ran through the lobby, and I forgot everyone and everything except my Mama's anger. Nadja caught me in the parking lot and threw her arms around me. I sobbed into her sweater.

As we parked at the curb, I thanked each of the Fedorovs. Mr. Fedorov asked if I wished for him to take me in to my Papa. Explain things. I was too ashamed, and feared what condition my Papa was in and how he would react. If I was lucky, he would not be home. But then, luck had abandoned me for so long.

As I climbed the steps to our door, I was already inventing stories, excuses, just in case. I closed the door behind me and Papa watched from his chair at the kitchen table. Three of his friends occupied the remaining chairs, but I could only see the accumulation of beer cans and empty Vodka bottles, and the familiar sheen to Papa's eyes.

I tried to speak, but stopped as an invisible cable hoisted him from his chair. My knees turned to ice beneath his stare. He pushed the chair aside and it fell. He dragged his belt from its loops and doubled it over in his fist. One of his friends called his name, and I found my legs in time to flee to my room. I slammed my door a moment before he punched it back open.

It was my thirteenth birthday.

One week later, Mama came home. That night, with a crutch under her arm, she came into my room. She set a glass of warm milk on the nightstand, then she sat on the edge of my bed and apologized.

"Alya, I was shocked is all. It took me by surprise. When you ran out of the hospital, Mrs. Fedorov came in and explained. She was very angry with me, but I was still sedated and did not quite understand. Then I laid there, night after night, and I thought of what you had been put through. My poor child."

"It is okay, Mama."

"No, it is not okay. You suffered as a young girl should never suffer, and I could not even put my arms around you. And you were coming to see me."

"Mama."

"I am ashamed. And your Papa…"

"I know," I said.

Several days later, Misha and his mama reported my attackers to the police. They filed papers. Police said they would investigate, but everyone had waited too long and there was no evidence to arrest my attackers. The same day, Papa was arrested for assaulting a doctor in the hospital parking lot. He and a friend kicked the doctor nearly to death after Misha told him the nametag on the man who took away the candies. The candies for Mama's doctor. Papa was lucky the doctor survived, otherwise he would never get out of prison.

One month later, a tall teenage boy was found in a parking garage beaten to death by a length of steel pipe.

Due to the severity and planning of the murder, Misha went to juvenile prison. His mama told me not to visit. His entire family stopped talking to us. Nadja would pass on the street and turn her face away.

On my fifteenth birthday I visited my best friend for the last time.

As I waited in the Visitation Room, alone but for the single guard on the door, I thought of how different the smells were from the Fedorov's kitchen, and a new sadness bathed me in its fog. The walls here were painted the color of dirty snow, the furniture stark, utilitarian, and beaten by time. Ancient floor tiles glistened like they had been greased. A potted plant set on a side table, likely to comfort visitors.

Misha entered, led in by a thick woman, not in uniform. I assumed she was a guard as well. She directed him to a hard-back chair across the table from my own.

I did not recognize him at first. He seemed taller, thinner beneath his forest-green shirt buttoned to the neck, and he reminded me of the boy he had been convicted of killing. His head had been shaved. The angular bones of his face had shed the softness of youth. His eyes dark and deepset, his right ear had a knot in it that would never straighten. The fingers of his left hand and knuckles were taped. And I saw wispy ink lines protruding above his collar. He looked at me once, then away.

"Why?" the word caught in my throat. We sat in funereal silence, me staring at him and him looking at his hands. "They kept me away. I could not be at your trial. They refused to let me speak. They kept me from visiting you. It is so unfair."

"Unfair." He said it softly, to himself.

"I had to sneak here. I saved money. Found a man to make a fake ID, and I lied about my age to get in here to see you."

"It was a mistake," he said and shifted in his chair. "You should ask for your money back and do not come again."

"But...I did not want this for you. I would have done anything to keep you out of here. If I only knew how."

"What's done cannot be undone."

"But you had done nothing wrong," I said. "Nothing."

"And you and me are the only ones who know that. A few others might suspect. Our mamas, my sister..." He glanced at my eyes for the last time. "But you and me are the only ones who know." He stood. "Go home."

"No!" I said. "I will not accept this. Never."

"Go home. It is my gift to you. A thirteenth birthday gift."

The female guard took him out the way they had come in. I tried to stand, but could not. Not yet. I held my fists tight between my knees to keep from quaking. I knew if I let go, I would shatter like a window pane beneath a flying stone.

The following year, I ran away from the memories, and Russia, swearing to never return. Of course, no one can flee their memories. Sometimes the nightmares change. Sometimes they are of Misha, and I wake to my tears. Sometimes they are of a hopeless garage and my back against the cool cement floor. But most of the time, they are the horrified face of the tall boy, glaring up at me as I beat him with the steel pipe again and again, never stopping, again and again, until I could no longer stand, and the steel pipe fell from my weak fingers, and my knees could no longer support my weight.

ELEVEN

HADES' KISS

The Sirens

Witnessing the violent rape of their beautiful companion, Persephone, they turned their backs and walked away, and Hades carried the innocent one with him into the Underworld. The Sirens soon ventured to the Land of Apollo where they found themselves confronted by Persephone's mother, the goddess Demeter, and for the unforgivable sin of abandoning their friend, they were transformed into winged creatures at the hands of the goddess, and cursed to be the bane of Man. (Author unknown.)

"Insensate, the cold heart craves neither warmth nor touch. It knows little of human sensibilities other than that which is visible, a smile, or audible, a scream.

"It can only understand the external signposts of emotion. It beats to a rhythm of pitiless curiosity, or it beats in frustration and anger for that which it can never, in reality, understand. Naturally, this person will never admit to a lack of understanding, because a narcissist refuses to recognize failure in himself."

I had found the lectures online, videos posted by a name I did not know, but I recognized the speaker as my employer, Nicolaus Vagelle. His level, confident, *instructor's voice* had taken up residence in my head these past eight years. A welcome tenant. A welcome voice.

"The cold heart *is, of course, my personal, unscientific, catch-all for first-year studies. I can assume most here know that particular organ is not the culprit. To continue...Failure, minimal self-awareness, and cover-up...*

"Frustration will bury itself deep to maintain this paragon's lies. But please remember, while a narcissist is not always a psychopath, a psychopath is always a narcissist. He is the child who zips a puppy into a suitcase simply to hear the frantic claws. He is the adult who finds fulfillment in your tears."

Possibly late-twenties, but the same slender frame, with the barest hint of premature white dusting his crewcut, this younger version of Vagelle stood geometrically corralled by a large crescent-moon of university audience.

"Never look to a narcissist for sympathy. Sympathy requires a degree of empathy, an emotion that will always be out of reach. It is this inability to feel another's pain that ultimately leads to the destructive behavior."

Typed beneath the video: *"Psych-101: Cop turned Psychologist - Teresi, Lecture Series II."* Use of the word "Cop" in the title suggested the amateur video-maker might have been a student. I had come under the influence of Mr. Vagelle at a time in life when I desperately needed guidance—and other things. I had immediately understood who he was. The person he kept hidden from all but a few. *Teresi.* Though he never said, I often wondered if he suspected I had searched out his previous life. His abandoned name. Understanding him had been an obsession, once upon a time. Maybe it still was. Look at me now; of course it was.

My attention jolted away from the screen with the click of the doorknob. Mr. Teresi—Vagelle—hesitated on the landing, noting my immediate shutdown of the website. Crossing the threshold, he turned to the coat tree, pulled free from his shimmering rain slicker, and never mentioned it.

"Dobroye vecher (Good evening)," I said to his back.

Taking up the newspaper and the day's mail from the dining table, he continued to his rooms.

"You've put in a long day, Ms. Korikova. You may go home." Without a backward glance, he closed his door. I heard water run into the sink then, moments later, the rustle of papers and the drop of his shoes.

It had been this way for two weeks. There had been no serious discussion, no unkind words between us preceding the temperature change. One day it was just there like an opaque curtain. A barrier fallen without preamble.

I unplugged and lowered the laptop into my satchel. I held my fingers to the desktop, steadying, thinking I should say something at his closed door. It was a distant, familiar, teetering moment of uncertainty and confusion that would pass in silence. After pushing into my own raincoat, I slung the satchel, stepped into my less-than-fashionable plastic overshoes, took up my umbrella, and closed the apartment at my back. I hurried down the three flights of stairs and out to the street before I could change my mind.

Many times in this life, I had foreseen, feared, the discussion. The "talk" that would begin with intentions of "clearing the air," but would lead like a loosening leash to the inevitable *throwing-off the soft ties of friendship*. I feared this today, with this man, more than I feared his silence. I could not begin this talk. It would have to come from him.

I found myself running to my car, splashing along the sidewalk for two blocks. I stopped only to catch my umbrella before the Gulf squall yanked it free of my fist. I held with both hands, cowering beneath the fragile shelter. Fat pellets drummed the canvas above and exploded in the surrounding water at my feet with expanding, hypnotic, ringlets I used to distract my blacker thoughts.

His level, confident, *instructor's voice*—his *influence*—had become an addiction. A necessity. I needed to understand him.

Déjà vu. How many times have we been here?

Maybe *he* feared letting go. Feared for my sake. For what might become of me. After all, it was his sympathy that began this relationship all those years ago…

I had not yet turned twenty. I was alone in a new country, grabbing shelter where I could find it, until he took me in. He taught me many things, and he asked for nothing in return. Ten years my senior, I knew from the start he did not *need* companionship. He had been alone too long—and I had been an accident in his life, had I not?

The Fates, according to his Greek philosophers, *never bestow a gift without extracting an ounce of pain in return.*

My trance broke when a pedestrian bumped my elbow. A clumsy moment inserted itself, watching the awkward longcoat, much too-long for the wearer, as she blurred beyond the beaded curtain to vanish amid the flow of bodies, all jostling to be out of the rain.

Shutting myself into my old Impala, I clutched the satchel to my breast.

When did I become so emotional? Little things, a side-glance, a gruff word or two, or no response at all, might feel like...

I watched the rain break and cascade against the windshield and listened to the assault on my tin roof. When it became too much for my nerves, I turned the key and tried to adjust my attention to the traffic.

I have become a child, dependent on Papa's approval. Again. "Well, my soul rebels against manipulation, Mr. Vagelle, Terisi, whoever you are today. I refuse to break. Even for you."

"Hey, lady! You gonna live in that parking spot?" was followed by the blare of horns.

"Empathēs emotional, according to the Greeks, meant passion, literally," he said from my laptop on the kitchen counter, while I fumbled with the corkscrew, bumped the wine glass, and barely heard it shatter in the sink. *"Of course, the English, ever concerned with cutting the throat of subtlety, had abridged that to em-pathy.*

"Aristotle established pathos as a means of persuasion. He understood our responses to art and storytelling, and the author's ability to touch that humanity inside us. The feelings we—most of us—bring to the theater before the curtain rises."

Persuasion. Over the years, I had heard much of this wisdom first-hand, but in pieces. He taught what he believed I needed to know at the time, as if for a child entering into a new life in his dark world. For my survival's sake, I supposed.

On this topic, though he never said, I assumed he was lecturing me on the woman he had most recently helped send to her state-sponsored lethal injection. He seldom said her name.

"And the difference between psychopath and sociopath? A sociopath is made over time, usually by traumatic input or repeated exposure to violence. But a psychopath, she is born with that dead conscience. As I say, her caring-switch is turned off since birth.

"Observe, and be mindful of the little things. She can display the most complex of human emotions because she has made a lifelong study of mimicry. But through all of her masks, from sadness to joy, you catch a psychopath when she thinks you are not looking. When she thinks you have not seen her step around the injured child to get to the front of the ice cream line."

Three days later, I still avoided his office, and he had not called.

"I'm sorry. Sorry to hear you're leaving." Patty cleared the open folder from her desk, signaling that I had her attention. Isolated strands of silver caught the window light as a ribbon of sandy hair escaped her short ponytail. She swept it behind an ear. "I won't ask if this is a rash decision. We've known each other too long, and I can only assume you've wrestled with this for some time." Her gaze returned to the cup of cocoa in her hands often enough for me to gauge her discomfort with the conversation. "Any idea where you're thinking of moving? I remember you once mentioned California."

"That was the dream of a child who heard the fairy tales too often," I said. "I am thinking of a place with lakes and streams. Someplace pretty, maybe Wyoming."

"Maybe save up to buy a horse?"

Patricia Gunston, whom I had nicknamed Patty P.I., ran the Gunston Detective Agency since her brother—co-owner— ended up in Dixon Correctional for fraud. Hers was a boutique private investigations firm in a well-maintained five-story, outside the Central Business District by about a foot and a half. One might view the river, given tall enough heels and the right window in Patty's corner office. "You can name your new business *Giddy-Yup Private Eye.*"

"Sounds perfect for TV. But the more I think about it, I do believe I would like to see snow again."

Though we had not been close for long, she had come into my life via the work and her long association with Mr. Vagelle. Sympathetic in the past, we had grown closer over time, maybe as we each needed to hear a woman's voice on occasion.

She once confided, *"Eight employees, all men, all believing themselves alphas, gets on a woman's nerves beyond the first eight-hour shift."* It had forced her to maintain a macho façade of her own, for the sake of leadership.

"Well, you know I'll miss you. Can't close the blinds and prop my bunny slippers on the edge of my desk with all these balls clacking around here. As I've said before, if you ever need a job…"

"This city—well, since I got off the boat, I see everything here through his eyes. I would never be able to forget…" Imagining this statuesque woman in bunny slippers might have drawn a smile from me three weeks ago.

"Believe it or not, I understand." She swivelled her chair to catch the sunlight. "Of course, I can't understand all of it. I've known him many years. Going back to before he took off the badge. He's always had this hero-complex, as far as I know, but he was different in those days. I hate to say naïve, because he was never that, but he occasionally smiled back then. Almost personable, apart from spending too much time inside his own head."

"Do you know what it was? What changed him? All my years working with him, breathing the same air…sometimes I think he is happy then, from nowhere, he gets smothered by this black blanket. Like he cannot even see me. Like—Like something has died there and he wants it left buried."

"I've seen it in him. In the past."

"I cannot stay with this man."

"It hurts, sure." Again, she gave the cocoa too much attention.

"Sorry to lay all my problems on you. You have been my good friend."

"And it hurts me to hear your troubles, and to know I can't say anything."

"But you know what made him like this. You said, before his badge came off—"

"Forgive me." She set the cup on the desk blotter as punctuation. "I value his friendship too, dear. If, after all your years together, he has decided to keep some secrets, I can't betray that."

Her landline jangled like the 1960s. She answered quickly, then held a hand over the receiver. "Can you take a call? It's Detective Pedersen."

I hesitated then accepted. "Yes, Lieutenant, this is Alya."

He apologized. He sounded uncertain. He wondered if I was okay. He could not reach Mr. Vagelle. He had left messages. He needed to see him, about a friend. Could he make an appointment?

"You need to go back. Talk to him." Patty read my face. "Even if it's to let Pedersen in for his conversation. Even if it's for you to say goodbye. I know you feel you owe him as much."

2

The rain had stopped, but lightning continued to shoot the night sky revealing more clouds to the east. I parked within sight of the apartment windows, not wanting to appear the schemer should he look out. Leaving my rain gear and satchel in the car, I dropped my keys into a jacket pocket, stalling for time. The ground floor window blinds moved as I took the front steps, and upon entering, the landlord popped his head from his portal.

"Good evening, Ms. Korikova."

I smiled and nodded, wishing to avoid a lengthy conversation, and hurried to the third-floor. I have difficulty saying good evening when it is not. Hesitation on the landing, I almost used my key, but after being away for so long, I knocked instead. The door opened almost immediately.

Mr. Vagelle stood dressed as the day I had walked out, gray button-down shirt and khaki slacks, a bit more wrinkled than was his custom. He was not surprised. He would have heard my shoes on the stairs, however, he appeared off-balance.

"May I come in?" I said, and he backed into the room.

"You're here late."

"I have come for a few of my things."

"More than that, I think."

"Do not analyze me now, Mr. Vagelle."

"I'm not analyzing you. Analyzing the time of evening, your composure and brisk entry without returning Mr. Hemmings's greeting, which is unlike you. You did not leave much behind when you left. Your purpose here has a schedule, and I can guess, someone is meeting you. Here? I believe that is him buzzing now. Nicely timed."

"Stop," I said, and touched the outside buzzer on the wall panel. "You cannot help yourself, can you?"

"You brought Pedersen from the sounds of him. He's been calling here for a day and a half, so I assume he called you and asked for an appointment. You could have picked a better time of day. Like during business hours."

"Shut up!" I whispered. He stepped back in shock. I turned to see Frank Pedersen at the open door mirroring that shock, and I felt instant humiliation.

"Um, sorry," Pedersen said. "I didn't know—I mean, I wish I could have come at a better time. I have little choice." Two hesitant steps into the room, and I backed away to give him space.

"You're here to ask a favor, Lieutenant. Some desperation you are in the middle of." Mr. Vagelle walked toward the fireplace, conspicuously placing other furniture between them. He seldom moved without purpose in front of others. He seldom spoke more words than necessary, which indicated to me, despite his outward composure, something had affected a change. "You cannot share this with your friends in the

Department, because someone in the Department may be implicated. If you come for my help, it means the one you implicate probably outranks you." He took the newspaper from the arm of his wingback chair and tossed it onto the coffee table.

A SECOND SIREN FOUND

The headline fell with the fluttering of page one.

"We are friends, right? Almost?" Pedersen continued into the room. "I don't know who to implicate. I can't work this like a case, not without being found out and driven off the job myself."

"I cannot help your friend," Mr. Vagelle said. "The other cop who was *driven off the job*. That would be Ms. Grant, I presume. And that case is three-years dead."

"I've asked her to meet us here tonight."

"Then you will call and ask her to meet you someplace else." His silent accusations pierced me.

I responded in kind, my own expression meant to shame the man, my mentor, my friend, for his unthinkable selfishness. My only thought at that moment was, *I cannot remain here. He is lost to me.*

Pedersen, usually perceptive, crossed to the dining table, pulled a chair and slammed its legs to the hardwood floor, shattering the stalemate. He sat as if his action had its desired effect.

"Over four years ago," he began his story unasked for, "a large party over in Bywater. A young woman was sedated, thrown onto a table and savagely raped while party-goers watched. Some cheered."

I immediately recalled reading about the case, at my employer's direction. "An exercise in lost causes," he had called it. I did not know why.

"A Sheriff's Department officer reported being on freeway detail nearby, assisting a traffic stop when the call came in. He was first on the scene. By the time he arrived, the party had broken up, the building vacated, including the tenants and the woman who had been assaulted."

"These days, police response time can be up to two hours."As was his habit, Mr. Vagelle turned away, posing like he still had an interest in the old landscape hanging above his fireplace. "I assume you're retelling the story for Ms. Korikova's sake."

"The victim subsequently disappeared and became a Missing-Person's case for eight months. A week before she was found, a motorist reported seeing a naked woman fitting her description seated in the middle of LA-1, Lafourche Parish, some ways south of Thibodaux. He never thought to stop and assist, and police there could not confirm his story."

"The woman eventually turned up in Lafayette Cemetery," Mr. Vagelle said to the painting. "She spent the following year in and out of hospitals."

"Her day in court, in her hysteria, she pointed the finger at a number of those from the party. She said they had cheered her rapist while the music played."

"I cannot help."

"She identified several of the onlookers as members of the band, including the four singers. During the trial, a clever-as-spit newspaper man came up with the line: *The Sirens take the stand today. Will they sing or fly?'* Unsurprisingly, the victim lost the case, thanks to her doctors, but the name *Sirens* followed the four singers until they eventually disbanded for parts unknown."

"It's an open police case again, thanks to the two recent murders."

"And the Department has assigned two old alcoholics willing to drag out the investigation until retirement." Pedersen pushed up from the chair with a squawking of chair legs. He turned for the open door. "Thanks, pal."

He nearly bumped into a woman on her way in. Short, maybe five-five without her two-inch heels. Attractive, milk chocolate complexion, built sturdy beneath a longcoat that might have been a thrift-store purchase hanging to her knees. She clutched a well-worn, brown leather book to her hip. Her gaze presided over a managed intensity.

"I'm sorry, Ms. Grant." Mr. Vagelle did not approach.

"Come, Diana." Pedersen touched her arm. "We've wasted our time here. It was a longshot I had to take."

"I know who you are too, Mr. Vagelle." She held her ground. "I seen you plenty, you in your special reserved corner booth, back before Bobby J's club burnt down. He always had good to say about you. But that was then, wasn't it?"

"Now you need help," Mr. Vagelle said. "Not police help. It was too long ago, and you testified at trial against a fellow officer."

"Discharged under suspicion! I left the force before the trial because I was the whistleblower. And contrary to what the lawbook says, whistleblowers in blue have no future there. I was ostracized."

"Harassed, yes. As I'm sure you expected."

"I was told no other *fellow officer* would ride with me. I left when Atius, Lt. Russo, pulled me into his office one day to say he heard a rumor that some future radio call would result in me *accidentally* caught in the line-of-fire. He pulled me from street duty and made me a telephone operator." She tossed her worn leather-bound book atop The Delta Tribune headline.

"She's been a caregiver for Posey Cobb since her ordeal," Pedersen said. Posey was the rape victim from his story.

"She's stuck in a wheelchair ever since." Diana Grant stared at her book. "She still talks to herself. Barely coherent. Early on, before the trial, she had moments of clarity. She talked about her months in captivity, so much so that I began taking notes. 'Course my journals were inadmissable at trial. Afterwards, her health rotted away. I still make notes of our conversations when she's not around, but…"

Mr. Vagelle took up the book and held it out to her. When she did not take it, he dropped it back onto the newspaper.

"I am not a criminal investigator." His eyes offered her nothing. "The Yellow Pages is packed with them. There are nearly three hundred and fifty law enforcement agencies in this state, eighteen thousand officers, and most of them do not like me when I get involved. Pardon me, but I need everyone to leave now. I'm sorry for your friend."

I could no longer look at him. I walked Ms. Grant down the stairs. At the street door, I glanced back to see Pedersen captured in the angle of light thrown through the apartment door onto the landing. Perhaps he was still searching for words.

3

Through the night and into the morning, my thoughts remained locked on those last moments in his room. Our quartet in vignette, like the final act of a play. A tragedy. I dislike tragedies. I have lived through too many of them. I pushed through the wreckage of that moment in search of forward thinking. "Finding purpose," was how *the shrink* analyzed my impulses, once upon a time. My own personal escape route from the shadows.

Thoughts of that scene, *our quartet,* took me to thoughts of the four singers, The Sirens, and the newspaper headline.

Mid-morning streets still glistening from the night rains, I parked between cars a half-block from the Athen's Grocery, three blocks from Mr. Vagelle's building. I knew his refrigerator was near empty. When I caught his lean shape hunched inside the dark windbreaker, the one I had bought for him that Christmas, my heart wished to run to him. *Never again!* I hated him. No. Wrong. A child's reaction. I hated that thing in his past that had forged this person, the person I seldom saw, but would now see forever haunting the shadows between dreams.

When he turned into the Athens, I started the Impala and sped along sloppy streets to his building.

I jumped out, ran the stairs to the third-floor. The newspaper lay on the coffee table beside the worn leather book. Not beneath the book where he had dropped it. I knew him too well. He could not walk past that journal without reading it. I wrapped the book in the newspaper, not caring should he know I was there, and I hurried back to the car. And I hurried the car back to my own building.

...a boy I will not name was walking his dog. The dog broke from him and he chased it through the bars of Lafayette Cemetery between the stones and monuments. The dog was only following its nose. He followed it to the stench that was Posey as she lay unable to move from a pool of rainwater between crypts. The boy saw her there bone-white and naked. He laid his shirt over her and he pulled his dog away and ran into the traffic of the boulevard where he forced cars to stop.

He cried and waved his hands at the cemetery and many thought it was a child's prank. But the boy fought to keep his dog from running back there. Eventually a city worker left his truck and followed the boy back to the pitiful madwoman lapping up rainwater like just another dog.

I read all this from newspaper and police reports.

Once she'd been cleaned a nurse at the hospital recognized her from her pictures on TV and social media shortly after her abduction. An officer saw the name on a police blotter and notified me. She knew I was Posey Cobb's close friend.

Of course Posey fears talking about any of this. Her nightmares are fueled by it. I try not to push. I experience her pain with just a few words and my first duty to my friend is to keep her from pain. She lives with the trauma every day. It tears at my heart.

I set the book aside, then moved it out of reach so I would not be tempted to take it with me to bed. Turning on the laptop, I attempted to reread my old case notes, a private folder I had saved in a hidden compartment beneath other Applications, but I could not get far. Those first pages of Diana Grant's journal brought back all my old fears—my childhood—like a thing I had once drowned bobbing back to the surface. Hugging my afghan, I shivered against long-frozen memories.

Old nerves were laid bare.

Moscow and my thirteenth birthday. The horrors. The assault. The murder.

The reasons Nicolaus Vagelle convinced me to talk with his "shrink" friend, so I might be normal enough to live among people, close to people. The shrink taught me the importance of self-analysis as well, and to whisper the mantra when these fears fought to take control again. *"I do not shake hands,"* reminds me to keep my distance, and brings me back down when I forget that first rule. He gave it the official name, *my haphephobia.*

I had almost come to accept all those future relationships I would never have. Physical relationships. These days, I rarely concerned myself with them—until someone came too close and the tremors returned, and the old razor dragged itself across my spine.

"I will not feel sorry for myself!" I needed a new mantra.

...but how can I let something like this happen to my dear gentle Posey my friend and let that evil get away without punishment? Months since she's been back home away from the doctors and hospitals. I fear she will never recover enough to let me help her.

Invisible handcuffs still hold her to the wheelchair. Doctors say it's less physical than mental though she has been immobile for so long I wonder if she has strength in her limbs to lift herself. No desire to improve they say. I say she has given up on God and the world. Maybe I stay close because I'm afraid what she will do to herself if left to herself. That evil bastard has burned away any sunlight from a woman who was all brightness all joy.

Evenings I read her to sleep. Shared interests from our school days. And I read books we used to enjoy together back then. She trusts me I think. I have made myself her constant companion since she has been home. I cannot abandon her to her shadows. She leaves her chair only when I help bathe her or dress her or put her to bed at night. I know somewhere beneath the surface she is thankful.

Alone in my room sometimes I cry. Then I wonder if all my tears are for her. If not maybe I also cry for myself for my chains keeping me here. Then I feel ashamed and the tears stop.

"You know I like to be upfront. Maybe too much upfront sometimes, but I believe in honesty. At least between friends." Patty P.I. had asked me to lunch on the company dime. "I know this is not the first time you've recognized the man has his demons."

"Of course not. And there were many times we avoided each other because of them."

"We've talked about your own personal demons—I know I promised never to mention it again. But you must've understood, deep, on some gut level, for two people as strong as you both are, you must've realized a kinship in the pain, at least. Maybe not in its origins."

"I get what you are trying to do. *Spasiba.*"

A wraith reflected on my silverware. Just the waiter bearing plates. Patty's Po' Boy sandwich and my plate of *pain perdu,* which I shared with her. The conversation halted long enough to think.

"I know it's a lot of bread for a gal watching her waistline," she said, as the waiter continued to the next table. Then she returned to the topic. "I'm trying to be a friend, you know."

"Yes, I know. And you are."

"He didn't need to confide in me about *your* demon, all those years back. I had guessed it. I'd been watching you since you came on the scene. Watching how he acted around you— Please tell me if you'd rather not talk about it."

I shrugged.

"I may not have known the clinical name for it, but I knew someone long ago, a young girl, but her phobia was much more acute. You seem to manage yours. Actually, it's amazing that you can work at a job like this."

"Okay. Feeling uncomfortable again." I fussed with the napkin, though my fingers were clean. I appreciated her intentions. My needing to hear—

"Just saying, I might not have recognized it in you, had I not known that girl."

"It embarrasses me, as you can imagine. Especially now. This old case has dropped a lighted match into our box of fuses. It has changed him."

"As I can see the case is affecting you. For wildly different reasons, I know."

I watched the silverware for more shadows.

"This Posey Cobb case." She studied me over the rim of her beer glass. "Pedersen is finding reasons to stop by my office for these past weeks. Veiled allusions to a former police Sergeant on the case."

"Mr. Vagelle always said you were sharp as a scalpel."

She coughed beer into her napkin, then hid the smirk.

"Tell me I should not be concerned," I said. "With all of your professional curiosity about what might trigger both of our reactions to the Cobb case, are you planning on a dig into my childhood to find the source of my *psychological issues?*"

"I would never add to a friend's pain that way."

"Thank you. And I promise not to post photos of you in bunny slippers around your office." We finished the topic and our lunch.

"Alya," she said before we left the table, "I won't tell you to stop reading that journal. You wouldn't listen to me if I did. But I ask you to stay away from Vagelle for awhile. I suspect he may be entering into Joseph Conrad territory."

I remembered Conrad from a class at university. It held some difficult lessons.

Of course she can't leave the apartment. At times I find myself hurrying home worrying about her day. If there was ever a fire would she be able to call out to let the firemen know she was there? She has escaped one form of captivity and built another cage of her own.

As I helped her into the bath tonight she watched my eyes. I felt her sympathy for me. For me! To change the subject I finally asked about the two round nickle-sized scars. One on each breast.

She splashed water on her face. Held her hands there.

"I smell meat burning." She grabbed her breasts. "It hurts."

"What hurts dear?"

"It hurts. He hurts. He said 'So you will always remember. So no other man could ever want you.' Coals were red and he fanned them. He pushed the tip into the coals—his pistol barrel—black steel—until the black steel turned red." I hugged her hard. "When he pulled the barrel from the ashes he pressed the burning steel against my—'They will always see this. My brand. My kiss. And they will always know I was here first.'"

She said nothing else for days. Sometimes I believe she wants to talk. I will not press her. She talks in pieces but not in response to me. Maybe she's talking to ghosts. Maybe she's talking to the person she used to be or to the evil hand that branded her. Hard to understand. Broken words. Fearful. Sometimes furious. Or frighteningly sad.

Today she talked of blue angels. Rescuing angels. Large strong carrying her away from the noise. Then an angel carried her into that darker place and his kind words became hateful words that burned. He was not an angel then but the opposite. A beast. He locked her in a cold hard damp place where her forever-night began.

4

Big Bobby J. carried two aluminum folding chairs across the street and opened each on the cracked sidewalk facing Booker St., and his club on the other side. The remains of his club. Bobby J's Black & Blues Club. The façade looked better at night, even with plywood covering the large window and entry. Security lights threw cold white across the charred bricks, like too much makeup on an elderly courtesan.

"So good to see you again, *Dimples.*" His smile came alive in that ebon face.

"John Lee Hooker." I flashed my dimples.

"Ha! Got it in one. You been studyin' the classics. So, what you got there, gal?"

I held out the brown paper bag pinched around the neck of the bottle.

"Now, you know I don't drink alcohol, Ms. K."

"I know, Bobby. That is why I brought the other bag with the two sparking waters." I sat holding the waters between my knees, while he opened the first bag.

"What's this? You brought your own White Zin? You're supposed to wait 'til I reopen my bar. I serve the drinks 'round here."

"This is for you to hang onto." I nodded across the street. "Once they finish all the reconstruction, as I am not a fan of champagne, you are going to use my White Zin to break across the corner of your new building and christen her."

His laughter echoed between buildings, the first time I had heard it in nearly a year. "You are one creative lady."

We sat in the space between minutes gazing at Bobby's past and future.

"She does not look too bad from here," I said. "I miss her. I cannot imagine how you feel."

"She's comin' along. Nearly a year of wrastlin' them danged insurance gators. And puttin' the boot to the contractors to push their reports through the city development offices, showin' 'em we're still structurally sound, our construction is finally movin' forward. Near got that outside fixed-up, brickwork and all. Next we go to work on makin' the insides whole again. I promise to crack this here bottle of yours within six months, if I gotta take my own hammer to them carpenters to speed 'em along."

"You might go through a lot of carpenters."

"Yep. That I might." Another silence. "Sure could use a bit of music on this here corner." He stared at the bottle in his hands. "I still can't believe all you've done."

"Shush. You have thanked us enough."

"I could never thank you enough." He looked away as headlights turned to avoid the detour cones. "After that explosion and the fire, Cookie dyin back in the kitchen, Ol' Jamaican in the hospital, I figured I'd lost about everything in my life. I built this place up from nothin'."

"I know, Bobby."

"Then, right after, findin' out you done what you done…makin' them phone calls. And Kingfish and all them passin' the word, sendin' all them artifacts. Treasures to decorate these walls like before—musical instruments, signed posters, record jackets—Shit! Pardon me. They're still comin' in."

"You keep on, you will have me tearing up again." I passed him a water bottle and cracked the cap on one for myself. "We both felt guilty. That firebomb was meant for us, and here you are the one still suffering."

"Don't you start on that again." His brow lowered. "'Twas evil came through my window that day. Meant for you or the jukebox, don't matter. Nobody to blame but the evil that threw the fire. Nothing changes 'twixt you and me and Mr. V. Anyways, we'll be up and runnin' in no time. What!" *He had caught my long blink.* "Did I say something? Mr. V?"

"I know. I am sorry, big man. Things are not good between us. I…may be leaving soon. I was holding off saying anything."

"Aw! Don't say it, Ms. K." Monstrous hands strangled the paper bag around the bottle's neck. "That's kinda like Tammi Terrell leavin' Marvin Gaye."

I was unfamiliar with them, but understood his meaning.

"We just—Let me ask you, Bobby. Do you know anything about these *Sirens* I keep reading about? I do not know if this is what tears him down now. It seems to have hit the headlines about the same time as—"

"Nothing of the N'Orleans music scene happens I don't know about. They had themselves a trial—I take it you know about all that. Well, afterwards the newspapers, with the help of some on the police force, they painted that quartet as victims of a madwoman. You know the one that disappeared after she— then after they found her, she was ravin', and she raved some about the Sirens, how they kept singing right while she was bein'—you know."

"I know."

"So the group eventually split up, with all the outside pressures and accusations. A couple of 'em vanished to parts unknown. One came into my joint looking for work. I took pity on her, thought I'd give her a chance. A one-night-a-week gig with the band 'til I could see how she stacked up."

"She did not work out?"

"The band and her couldn't get along, so I had to let her go. Heard she picked up a few small gigs around town. Then her body was found a few months later." He seemed unable to look at me. "Somebody messed her up real bad."

"And the other one?"

"If you seen the papers, you know she disappeared after a night at a club out near University Park. They found her just a few weeks ago, messed up same as that first Siren. He's some bat-shit crazy to do something like—Sorry again, Ms. K."

"No worries, Bobby. I was here when the *madwoman* went to trial. I know what came after, and about the mutilations."

"I'll never understand a *twist* like that."

"Good thing most of us cannot."

She doesn't know how long she was locked in that dank cement box smelling of mold and urine and shit. Air came in from somewhere and she found two small holes had been drilled in the cement to one side.

Much of her time in that box was spent with her nose or mouth pressed to one of the holes. She stopped sceaming into the holes when she tasted her own blood on her lips and she understood there would be no rescue.

From other things she said I figured it was nearly a month before the monster opened the door for more than just tossing in scraps of someone's dinner—no plate. She only began eating when she thought she'd starve to death otherwise. She understood at times it must have been scraps from a dog's meal as her tongue found coarse animal hairs in her teeth. Then it was a poorly butchered animal un-cooked with thin strips of hide intact. She almost grew used to her stomach rebelling on her.

After that first month he opened the door for her. Animal and barn smells not quite as bad as her box.

He ordered her out. Barely able to stand she clung to the walls. But he screamed in her ear that she should touch nothing until he allowed it. He allowed her to hug the corner in a stall beside a metal sink. Then a painful light struck her and she realized again she was naked. The pipes rattled. A spigot turned and she got hit by a blast of freezing water from a hose. Something hit her foot. A bar of soap. She scrubbed as he ordered. He ordered her to turn and grab the shivering waterpipe above the sink and other hands plastic gloved hands washed her back and raped her again.

He returned her to her box. And this became a ritual—twice a day or once a week. Sometimes she went undisturbed for a few days. One time he was gone so long she believed he would leave her alone to die in her filth— but he always came back. For eight months.

She never said how she escaped that demon. I believe she never will. Not fully.

I could only suffer bits of the Diana's journal at one sitting, and never before bed, but I could not stop reading. The compulsion made me sick and furious at the same time. And something I needed to reach an end to. Survival. I understood that animal drive.

My own psyche needed protection from those pages, so I created mental diversions to avoid my own past, to avoid my thirteenth birthday, my attacker, the birth of my haphephobia. Each time I read, the memory was ripped raw again by Diana sharing Posey Cobb's horrors. My own *demon*, as Patty P.I. called it, clawed at the edges of sleep.

I needed air to clear my thoughts, or so I imagined. I needed rest too, but I set the journal aside late, after eleven, and I knew I would not find Morpheus by staring at the ceiling.

I almost took the trolley over to the Bourbon Street distraction, until I realized, with all the hoops my brain was leaping through, being confined in a tight rolling box with partygoers would have me waking up on *the shrink's* doorstep before dawn. I took my car and avoided the Bourbon crowds. I surprised myself by *accidentally* cruising the Lakeshore Parkway near the West End Park and Marina.

Ten years ago, *he* had found me there. He was just starting his private consulting business; a client had hired him to find an expensive lost dog abandoned on a party yacht during a hurricane—then he found a nineteen-year-old runaway from Moscow living beneath a shipwreck (a yachtwreck). That first day wandered into the next, and my un-official "adoption," as he used to call it. I did not like the word.

I slowed as I spotted it, the old burger shack where we had found the lost dog. It had been rebuilt, probably more than once in the ten years since our first meeting, as had the entire marina. The shack had doubled in size, and that just made it a larger shack. No wrecks here now, the waterfront had evolved into a wealthy sportsman's breeding ground with shops and restaurants all shiny and new-ish. This was not the first time I had been here since meeting my rescuer.

I pulled into the yacht lot, parked and stretched my legs.

Still active near midnight, boat lights and zydeco competed for attention. Cars still coming and going, a dog-walker looking for any thin strip of grass, perhaps a drug deal or two in progress. A few night-fishermen cast their long rods from atop the seawall. I wondered if any kept an eye out for wandering gators. Couples strolled, but not many. Even in the best New Orleans neighborhoods, predators, four-legged or two, roamed freely after dark. I did not care. I enjoyed the memories of the docks, the sounds of low surf lapping at the pier, the slap and clang of boat rigging, all music foreign to the inner city.

Rounding the burger shack, returning to the car, I spotted a tall silhouette on the dock, hands in his pockets, a pose I recognized. He was some distance away, likely not the man I was thinking of, yet the memories stung. I shrugged at the coincidence and continued on my way.

Lakeshore Drive with the windows down. Scattered thoughts and memories. Driving not-quite-aimlessly in retrospect, I inhaled the bitter breeze from Lake Pontchartrain. When I passed the signs to University of New Orleans, I decided

I should circle for home. I turned before reaching the Lakefront Airport. Not completing the circle, I drove due south without stopping until I had entered the Bywater District.

I pulled to the curb across the street from an address I recognized from the newspapers. A five-story apartment block. An ancient cotton mill reformed in this upwardly mobile, *artistic* community, bought and renovated into a solid-looking accumulation of high-priced, new-age apartments. This was *the crime scene.* The first one. The scene of the party and Posey's ugly rape and abduction. I supposed I had driven here intentionally, though I could not say why.

Still without purpose, I fished into the satchel behind my seat and came up with my snubnose. I tucked it behind my waistband and snapped my windbreaker to cover it. Old habit, renewed by recent upsets.

A young man had stepped outside for a smoke. He flipped the butt to spark against the bricks, and I caught the door before it closed and locked behind him. As he thumbed for the elevator, I hurried up the well-lit stairs as if I belonged there. I waved to him when he craned back to check my rear pockets.

I paused outside the door to the fourth floor apartment, *the party apartment*, but it was late, no light from under the door. I had seen none from the street. Muffled, late-night TV voices from within. The papers had said the previous renter had long since moved away, so this one was most likely innocent. *Of that crime, at least.*

The hall terminated with a door, a pushbar, and a sign that read, "No Exit," which I translated as *roof access.* I pushed, expecting a door alarm, but got none. Taking the short stairwell to the roof, I braved the outside.

The stars welcomed me after so many rainy nights. The half moon bounced sparks off Ol' Miss three blocks away. Night music, this night, was comprised of boulevard noise backed by river traffic, punctuated by the clang of a distant railroad crossing. I navigated to the river-side of the expansive roof. Someone else had ignored the No Exit sign and left a lawn chair, waterlogged marijuana butts, and beer cans. I still could not understand what had drawn me here. After four years, there would be no evidence. Maybe I just wanted to see…

…what Posey had seen that night. The night her tortures began. The night of pain and humiliation. Up here, the assault took place. There had been any number of chairs and tables, legions of Christmas lights strung, a party tent canopy in the midst of it all, and to one side, a bandstand large enough for a band backing a quartet. *The Sirens.*

The hour had advanced into pre-dawn. Posey stood alone at the wall, wine glass in hand, enjoying the view of a sparkling river until a charismatic someone approached and dropped a few lines on her. She was shy, young, naïve, but the songs and drink had relaxed her and she laughed at his lines. She saw the friends she had come with dancing, slow dancing, and she wondered if this casual meeting would lead to something more. It did.

When he leaned in and bit her neck, she was not ready for it. She flinched and pushed gently away, still smiling. As she readied her excuses, he slapped her. Hard. The shock of pain sent sparks to her vision. Immediate tears. She did not hear the glass shatter.

The music carried on. He wrapped her in a powerful hug and apologized loud enough to be heard by others over the Sirens' song. She weakened, dizzy. He stroked her hair, apologized more. She heard laughter somewhere. Felt his breath on her neck, a quickened breathing. He said, "Here. You need to sit down," and he danced her backwards, still in his bear hug. Under the canopy now, she stumbled into a chair, and he said, "A bit too much wine. Sorry." More laughter. He laughed. And the laughter fueled his aggression. Her thighs hit the long table and she fell back. This time she heard as more glasses broke on the concrete. He pressed her shoulders down and she saw his face, blurred by the flood of her tears. He grinned.

And *they* all laughed. Someone clapped and others joined in.

She said, *No,* but it was barely a word, just a sound choking on the back of her tongue. His arm stiffened, pressing her painfully to the tabletop. Posey froze with the shock of it. Disbelieving. Could they not see her tears? She groped for the edges of the tablecloth. His free hand groped and tore her dress and her—

—then the pain.

She looked past him. She scanned the faces. Smiling faces. Laughing. Clapping. She saw the band and The Sirens singing, still singing.

I wept for her. *I wept for my own demons.* The stars had winked out. The night sounds strangled away. There was no sparkling Ol' Miss. I was Posey, and I was thirteen-year-old Alya, in pain— then even the pain turned numb—

I heard the roof door open, and a man stepped through. "Everything okay up here? Miss?"

"No." I pushed past him and down the stairs. I hit another door. Then another.

5

Her father has taken her mother back home to California. Seeing their daughter like this for so long with no improvement has destroyed Mom—both of them really—but Dad has decided to shield his wife from more negative reports. He visits occasionally but on his own. Never with her. He sends money. He thanks me regularly for all I do for his daughter. He pays for groceries and medicines. For the nurse while I am at work. But I don't know how much longer I'll have a job.

We've gone through three nurses so far. Yesterday Posey spun hard from mute and docile to self-destructive fury. I was at a traffic accident in the Garden District when I got a call and had to run home. I met the emergency crew going in. Posey had broken into my room and found my personal items. The nurse discovered her in the tub where she had broken apart a safety razor and sliced both inner thighs. Our bathroom looked like a crime scene. I guess it was.

Again my friend has been placed in psychiatric hospital.

At times, she sings to herself. It's nonsense but I know the lyrics by now.

Hard white light streaking through the blinds, falling across my pillow, I gave up trying to sleep. The shower did not lighten my mood. I dressed, took up my satchel, but immediately returned it to the sofa. I feared the outside today. That light.

In the kitchen, with a plate on the counter beside the egg carton and a pan on the burner, I watched the burner turn orange. The butter began to melt. So did my knees. My head hit the tiles, as did the eggs. Painful tremors tightened my limbs, and I struggled to push my back up against the cabinets to sit, but my limbs refused the orders from my brain. My next instinct was to look for flames. Something fallen onto the burner, but that, at least, had spared me. Reaching up, my hand steadied enough to twist off the burner. With my equilibrium in question, I crawled, elbows and knees, to the bedroom. I did not make it to the bed.

At some point consciousness returned. I could not call nine-eleven with thoughts of EMS handling me, lifting me onto a gurney, into an ambulance, a hospital, nurses and doctors, *my demons circling,* all touching me.

Who else to call? Not Nicolaus! No!

Early-afternoon, I found my phone and called Patty.

Onward to the kitchen sink. I ran cold water into a rag and held that to my face.

The pounding startled me. Patty called my name so soon I wondered if she had been parked across the street all night. I held the wall as I shuffled, hoping my balance would not betray me again. As she entered, I backed away to the couch.

"I am sorry." I dropped onto the cushions. "I had to call someone. I think I panicked."

"Don't apologize. You wouldn't have called for something trivial. You need water?" She brought water, and I tried not to shiver it out of the glass. She returned to the kitchen and I heard her cleaning the mess I had left around the stove. "So, can you tell me about it? First tell me you're okay. If you wanted a medic, you'd have called them, right?"

"I will be okay. Please, you do not have to deal with that mess."

"Shush, girl. Dropped eggs only worsen when you leave them to set."

I held the cool waterglass to my forehead and waited until she finished and returned to the facing chair. She eventually broke the silence.

"I've never seen you like this. And we've known each other how long?"

"I have never seen me like this. Not this bad. Not since I was a teenager."

"Of course, it's all about the case. Posey."

"It is the journal, Diana Grant's." I pointed to the book on the end table. "I know *he* read it. I need to as well. I hate my own weakness."

"You just need to find a way to somehow separate your own horrors from Ms. Cobb's. I know it's important to you, but please don't destroy yourself with it. You're already suffering through a traumatic breakup."

"It is not a breakup."

"Of course it is. You, him. You may both believe that it's like a father-daughter thing, and it may be, but it's as close as you've ever been to a real relationship. It's an attachment of the mind and heart. And you know I'm right, so don't argue with me."

I fought back my response. I finished the water.

"Okay. I'll drop it," she said.

"Last night, I found myself in Bywater. At the apartment. On the roof. I felt myself living the experience. Her experience." Her look said this was not news to her. "When I got home, I kept reading, and—I did not understand how deep my obsession with this was. This morning taught me."

"Still, you will not quit."

"I will not."

"Even with this new *understanding.*"

I shook my head.

The room fell silent as I lay back on the throw pillow. At some point, my eyes snapped open and I realized she had covered me with the afghan. My eyes closed again.

When they opened, the outside light had become the color of soft fire reflecting across a still lake. Patty P.I. sat there yet, reading the journal.

Four months she's been in the hospital. I visit daily. She's mostly quiet they tell me. I have regular conversations with her doctors. They put on a good act of caring. It's their job. But I can sense it is somewhat scripted. Too routine for them. Dr. Washburn—who I call Washrag behind his back— today he gave me the speech about the over-stretched nursing staff and lack of hospital beds. Then I pass all those empty rooms as I walk the halls.

Washrag has apparently gotten to the point of trying to convince the rest of the staff and me that Posey is no longer a threat to herself. He asked me to talk with her family and convince them that in his EXPERT opinion "Dad" should seriously think about relocating his daughter away from this city. (The farther the better.) Like in a longterm care facility in San

Fransisco to be near the family. I called Dad this evening. I thanked him for the month's check then relayed the doctor's suggestions.

Dad got quiet. Said it was something to think about. Then I heard the change in tone as he grew angry. "I'll have a conversation with this doctor tomorrow. After all the money I've given that hospital—! I can't have— What about when some doctor here decides to release her? Is her mother going to find her lying in the garden some night? I've just gotten Barbara used to the idea that her daughter was safe in the hands of professional clinicians! I'll call him tomorrow!"

Posey is back home with me today. I've taken my two week vacation to help her settle back in. I'll use my time to interview nurses.

"Wouldn't you rather take the night off?" Patty had insisted on driving. "Settle your mind some? Just leave that damned book alone for twenty-four hours."

"I am more afraid of losing momentum. If I drown myself in my own night terrors, I may never pick this one back up. I need to pick this back up. I will regret it if I do not."

"I suppose I get it. So now that you are *lead investigator*, do you know your next step? Which case are you investigating?"

"In other words, what would my boss do? My former boss."

"Let's simplify things in our minds, and stop complicating what is already over-complicated."

"You are right, of course."

"Pedersen brought the case to your door. Start thinking about that one, the cold case. The one that gives you all the trouble."

"Do we suppose the other two singers are still alive?"

"No way to know until we trip over them. Sorry, not literally."

"So, maybe all I can do is to keep digging around Posey Cobb and Diana Grant. Get to the beginning, the rape, the kidnapping."

"Are you ready to face the victim? Can you?"

"As my *Papochka* would say, *When you have no choice, attack what you fear.*"

Canal Street to City Park Avenue, past Masonic Cemetery, Saint Patrick Cemetery, passing Greenwood Cemetery, to Rosedale, just shy of Holt Cemetery. The symbolism was not lost on me. Parking proved difficult after rush hour—at any time in this neighborhood—and we needed to circle the block twice to get near Grant's address in a long, low block of apartments close to the Community College.

"Wait." Patty held up a hand to keep me in my seat. She watched her mirror. I checked mine, and saw the dark sedan creep round the corner, the same turn we had made, to stop beneath a broken street light. Three seconds hesitation was all, but it felt unnatural until it started forward again. Then I spotted the roof rack of lights. My unease continued as the patrol car crawled too slow along-side our fender, and almost stopped again next to my passenger-side window. Two uniformed officers in the front seat, both heads turned comically to study us as they passed. I smiled in sarcasm, and they continued on.

"Almost as if they aren't used to seeing couples this time of night parking this close to the college." Patty adjusted her ankle holster and smoothed her pantleg back into place.

Once they turned out of sight, I followed Patty's lead and opened my door. I checked my watch as she locked her Lexus with a beep.

"I wonder if we are being rude this time of night," I said.

"I like rude," Patty said. "You learn a lot by being rude."

Next to the door, the buzzer list told us Grant lived on the ground floor.

"Yeah?" a tinny voice called from the speakerbox.

"Diana, it is Alya. We met a few nights back at Mr. Vagelle's office. I am here with a friend."

The gate buzzed and an inside door crept open. Television sounds carried from behind her as she peeked out suspiciously before inviting us in. She wore fawn sweats, top and bottom, and red UGG slippers with stitched cat faces. I introduced Patty Gunston, and they shook hands while I kept mine in my windbreaker pockets. She asked if Mr. Vagelle had changed his mind about the case. I apologized, saying I wanted to look into things to see if I could help.

"We were hoping to ask a few questions regarding, well, you know," Patty said to break the following silence.

"I have not yet read the entire journal," I said, "but I am familiar. I studied the original case and trial notes back when all this first happened. Is Posey up?"

"She's resting. I don't know that she could handle all this, especially with someone she doesn't know." She led us to the kitchen table and offered chairs. I recognized the bulge of a pistol at her back. The room smelled of hospital disinfectant. Much better than the alternative, as I had experienced with some invalids. Sparsely decorated with what might have been garage-sale furniture, she had taste without much money. Not many *tchotchkes*. A few wall posters, landscapes and animals, all framed behind plastic rather than glass, and two full bookcases. She noticed me looking. "I've started our own little collection. Reading to her before bed gives Posey a place to take her mind."

"I read that in your journal. It reminded me of my youth. Whenever I hit a rough patch, Storyland saved me." I noted a platoon of medicine bottles flanked atop the refrigerator out of reach of the patient in her wheelchair.

"I apologize if I came on a bit rough the other night with your boss." She offered tea and we both declined.

"No apology neccessary. I know how long you have dealt with this. The frustrations from your job, with the courts, with doctors—I respect your strength."

"Well, you know *the job* is no longer an issue."

"Yes. I am sorry about that."

"It ended long ago." She rose, crossed to the kitchen, and poured water from the kettle to a mug. She reused a tea bag. "You sure you won't have something to drink? We have bottled water."

"Do you think she can hear us from her room?" Patty said.

"I keep the TV on. She'll be okay." She retook her seat, perhaps analyzing us.

"Would you care to fill us in on how the job-thing ended up where it did?" Patty kept her eyes off Diana, perhaps hoping her question felt more casual and less like a cross-examination. "I have experience with a number of officers from your precinct. Mostly good, some not so much."

"By the end, I didn't see much of the good."

"I read about your Lieutenant Russo," I said. "Seems he went from fairly supportive to antagonistic in the space of a few months. Could you get no help from the police union?"

"Politics." She turned the mug as if warming her hands. The apartment was plenty warm. "If this happened today, things might be different. Probably not. Too many on the department pissed off after my testimony—me and Posey. After the trial…you don't want to hear all this."

We urged gently.

"Yeah, not long after I took Posey in, Russo called me into his office, relegated me to desk duty. Maybe it was my fault. My priorities had changed. My responsibility, she needed attention. But Atius said everyone in the squad had noticed. Then came the rumors about my 'relationship' getting in the way of my work ethic. Rumors that I had *other reasons* for taking her in, hinting that I was *just another bull dyke on the force.*"

I joined Patty in looking at the walls.

"A few of them knew for a fact where my interests lie. Posey and me are friends since high school, but in a bullpen, once the rumors start, I could have fucked every he-man in the lower Ward and it wouldn't change their tune."

"Lord knows, I'd be pissed," Patty said. "I'd have taken a baseball bat to them."

"Atius more than hinted that a few of my *friends* in the squad were afraid to ride with me. I didn't have 'my head in the game,' and I put them in some sort of danger just by being near me. *Bullshit!* I may have gotten called away for personal emergencies, but everyone there knew I never slacked on the job." Diana glared at me defiantly. She eased with the passing minute. "Nevermind. It's in my rearview. I'll never be over it, sure, but I'm better now that I'm away from them all."

"I wonder if your Lieutenant would speak with me," I said, then heat returned to her eyes.

"Don't bother. The prick's a full-tilt control freak. He'll pretend he's your best friend for a whole minute, but he'll never answer your questions, and likely try to bring charges on you for questioning his authority. The man's a bundle of live rounds hoping for a hammer."

"About Ms. Cobb?" Patty shifted uncomfortably.

"Posey is more relaxed since she's been back with me."

Unlike yourself, I thought.

"These days we work hard on her control issues. *She* works hard. I believe she fears being locked in a psych ward again. But tonight, after dinner, she was cool. She said, 'Thank you, Diana, for everything.' She's started calling me *Big Sis* again. Said I was family."

"Sounds like she is aware of how much you do for her," I said.

"Wasn't always this way. Back before the trial—But yeah, it touches me still. I've never had much family myself. I guess she hasn't had much lately either, 'cept for me."

Early sunset after the time change and I've been getting off swing-shift well after dark. I went to the market after work. I had a funny feeling all week a feeling like something was about to happen or like someone was watching me. As I left my car at the curb a car I had seen in my mirror more then once pulled in a couple spaces behind me. I walked into the store looking back and the driver had not left his car. I scolded myself thinking it the result of being on edge all week. I shook it off. I wasn't in the store fifteen minutes when I got a frantic call from Posey.

"Where are you? I thought you'd be home by now. You're on your way?" She hung up. I hurried my shopping and she called again whispering, "Someone's here. They're jiggling the doorknob." I heard breaking glass in the background. She screamed.

I dropped my groceries at the register and ran. I halted at the curb. Two of my tires had been slashed. I called 911 and sent them to the apartment then I called a friend in the department for a ride. Det. Pedersen. I said it was an emergency. We got home before the first patrol.

The living room window was broken. The doorframe was splintered. I threw my shoulder against the door and charged in Glock in hand. I ran through the apartment yelling for Posey and found her curled on the kitchen floor with a steak knife in both hands sobbing hysterically.

Pedersen swept the rest of the apartment with the first patrol on the scene. He said they checked every nook and cupboard every closet and under beds but found no one. They found the brick that had been thrown through the window nothing more. Pedersen stayed with us after the patrolmen took statements then went about their night shift. He even waited for the emergency handyman to come and screw a sheet of plywood over the window until I could get window repair out to fix things.

The landlord showed up with the same expression he must keep on reserve for his special visits here looking like he's carrying a throat-full of bile. Before leaving he said "Nothing but trouble since you two moved in. A man gets tired of this shit. Never rent to a cop is my new motto."

6

When I mentioned the incident, Diana forgot her tea. Involuntary lip movement, turmoil behind her brow, she pushed back from the table but did not stand.

"That was during the trial, but I never found out who." She recovered quickly. "It had to be more than one, I figured, slashing my tires and breaking in here at the same time. That ain't no accident. I have my suspects. It's a long list including everyone I worked with trying to intimidate me from taking the stand. Or letting me know that we would never be safe."

"Did they do anything to Posey?" I said.

"Physically? No, I don't think so. She never said. When I reached her, she had that big knife, but she never said."

"I assume, to get Posey free of her wheelchair, you have worked with therapists."

"A physical therapist friend comes in twice a week to work with her. Mostly to prevent atrophy and keep up circulation. She—" Diana broke off, and we all turned to see Posey wheel herself to the end of the hallway. Diana rushed to her side and whispered something. Posey shook her head violently, hitting Diana's arm hard enough that I hoped she would not injure herself.

Patty and I stood from the table.

"Posey, we are not here to upset you," I said. "We want to help." She had already whirled the chair away to disappear beneath hallway shadows. Diana chased after her. We heard raised voices, Posey's being difficult to decipher.

"We won't get much more here tonight," Patty said.

I scribbled my phone number on a notecard and dropped it beside the teacup.

"Ready to call it a night yet?" Patty said as we left the building. It was 11:15.

"I keep beating my brain against two questions." I glanced back at the click of a door lock. "The first being the same question Mr. Vagelle posed back during the original investigation. Is the party rapist the abductor?"

"Others have asked that."

"Predator number-one seemed to be an offender of opportunity." Night sounds came thin and distant, routine boulevard sounds, as I instictively listened for footsteps. "Near the end of the party, with many others fueled by alcohol, coke, whatever, once he realized nobody would stop him—some even encouraged him—he let his blood take over his animal-brain."

"The alternative, he went to the party searching for a victim and, when he recognized weakness, her demeanor decided it for him."

"In which case, this was not his first foray. He had the science down. Not the *public* part of the rape, of course. A repeat of that would make headlines."

"See if you can get Pedersen on the horn while I drive."

As we boarded the Lexus, a nearby car engine turned over. Patty caught my body language.

"As long as it took us to walk to the Lex, no one opened another car door," she said. "He's been sitting here for a bit."

"On the phone with Dial-a-Date?"

"Let's see if he follows." She pulled away from the curb, made the first right, then the next. That was when our shadow broke away. Had he recognized the maneuver? "It's a busy city. Maybe I'm getting paranoid. So, what was your second question?"

"The obvious one. Who is killing the Sirens now?" I checked my side mirror, paranoia being catchy.

"Who hates them enough to start hunting 'em all these years later? Could it be the rapist eliminating witnesses, beginning with the band?"

"If so, he has a lot of killing ahead of him. If not, someone has a nasty grudge against music."

"And with the mutilations, the way they were found, he's a raving psycho with more than a few loose lug nuts."

"Possibly the work of more than one person?" The thought invaded from nowhere. "Tarred and feathered. Mobs did that over a century ago."

"This ain't a political statement," she said.

"*Nyet.* Mr. Vagelle always says, do not force conclusions." I lost focus over the blur of sidewalk traffic and my ideas running amok.

"Well, it's an angle I hadn't heard yet. If it was a gang, they would have left footprints, something. Let's rein in the imagination a bit until we have more facts."

Det. Pedersen was on duty, so we drove to him near the Rampart St. offices. Not his Division, but he was there on other duties.

He waited for us in a back booth at St. Anthony's All-Nite Coffee & Go. I wondered if I should genuflect as the bells jingled with the closing of the door. Patty motioned to the young waitress for coffees before we sat.

I posed my first question to the detective about the wolfpack murder idea. It caught him by surprise. After a breath, he shook his head.

"No way. The crime scene was too clean. What brought that on?"

"The feathers and mutilations," I said. "Were both singers disposed of in the same way?"

"The second Siren was dealt with much the same. The mutilations were a bit different, though we kept some details from the press. So has Vagelle—?"

"No," I said. "I read some of Diana's journal. I—needed to look into it. How were the mutilations different? I have been taught that details matter in profiling."

"Oh, you're a profiler now?" He stirred his coffee like he just remembered his usual dump of sugar. His eyes kept flitting to the window.

"You know I am not going to spill anything to the press."

"I think your involvement is a very bad idea. *We* are dealing with these murders. The Department is. And this guy's as sadistic as I've come across. You get too close—even with your investigator bodyguard here—" He glanced at Patty. "Alya, I would hate for you to come under this psycho's knife. The thought chills me."

The waitress had frozen her feet to the checkerboard tiles. The tray in her hands clattered a bit.

"Sorry," Patty said, as she took the hand-off of coffee cups. The young lady whirled away. "We've just come from Diana's," she said to Pedersen. "Alya's looking to fill in some blanks to the story, mostly about the old case, the cold case nobody seems concerned with."

"I brought Diana to Vagelle," he said, "because *I* am still concerned. She'd been a friend on the force for a long time, back in the day."

"But you are concerned as a friend," I said. "We know the Department will not let you investigate Posey's horrors. I promise I have no intention of getting close to the monster. I only need to understand."

"You'll never understand him. No sane person would. Forget it." He splashed a spoonful of coffee and ignored it.

"I know my boss told you about my *issues*. I am sure you suspect where something like that originates. Lieutenant, Frank, I believe I need this. For myself."

He stared into his cup. I stared at him. Patty had been watching the street. Now she stood, took her coffee, and walked outside. I thought she might make a call, but she just stood watching traffic. She shrugged, indicating a deep breath.

"You know this is gruesome on steroids," Pedersen said. "This goes nowhere beyond this table, got it? That first Siren was grabbed after hours, after a weekend working a club. Only she wasn't singing, as the papers said. She was dancing."

"A stripper?"

"That's why the papers were speculating ahead of the cops on this. We couldn't pin the murder on her *Siren* singing career. That had dried up a year prior."

"Reporters began guessing because of the tar and feathers," I said.

"And she danced with a feather boa, so we couldn't ignore that as a sick connection either."

"Until this second siren a few weeks ago."

"Yeah."

Patty stepped twice away from the curb as a patrol car slowed. *Cruising for hookers?*

"But—" Pedersen hid his face from the street. "This new one got grabbed in broad daylight, from what we figure. Only the mutilation was different. Sure, she'd been tarred and feathered like the first Siren, the lips removed...but he—Jesus, I can't."

"Frank, you do not know how much I have seen in my life. In Russia."

"Alya...okay. The meat of her legs...removed from the knees down—okay? I'll never forget those pictures. Never. It still sickens me to even talk about this." His nervous eyes bounced around the diner.

I drank my cooling coffee, then came up for air and said, "That took a lot of work. Not at the scene, probably not. He is a planner. He would plan not to get caught, so he dumped the body far from his butcher's table after he had finished."

"I wish I hadn't told you. Damn-it! Please don't hunt down the crime scene photos."

"I believe I can see it well enough in my head. All those feathers, no lips, and—I guess a bird's legs look meatless. Was it an expert surgery?"

He excused himself and disappeared into the men's room, leaving me to tear at a paper napkin. Something about the mutilations. Hard to think on it for long. But too specific in the message the killer was trying to drop. How insane was he?

When I looked to Patty, she was lowering her phone into a pocket, turning for the door. She noticed me and replaced her worry with a flawed smile.

"No." Pedersen returned, obviously weary of my questions. "No medical man's work. More like a hunting knife and an experienced hunter. Can we stop this now?"

Patty rejoined the table.

"Problem?" Pedersen said and she shook her head.

"Where was the second one found?" I said.

"Near the river. The New Orleans Center for Creative Arts."

"You must be kidding. If he believes this is an artistic statement of some kind, carving up birds, he's a loon without a motive. You may never find him until he drives up your precinct steps and plants his last one."

"It's not an artistic statement." Patty leaned back into her cushions. "The Creative Arts Center is in Bywater."

An emotional set-back. Naturally. Posey has withdrawn from me. All previous attempts at conversation have been flat-lined by some shithead. Shitheads. Make that plural. Terrorizing my friend and simultaneously flattening my tires are related. There are at least two working together. I brought this to the attention of the investigator.

All he had to say was "It might not be the best career move to level blame against your entire department without evidence. We got no prints off the brick. No terrorist entered your home. The tires—you live in a neighborhood where even teenage girls carry a knife. There's really not much we can do. You weren't at the apartment. Are you sure your roommate didn't go outside and throw the brick through your window maybe looking for a bit of sympathy from you?"

"She can't even lift herself from the bed to the wheelchair you ass!" which got me a Letter of Reprimand and a good chewing from Russo. Others in the squad whisper while looking in my direction. Uneasy smiles. This ain't just my persecution complex.

"Will I see you tomorrow?" I said as we angled to the curb in front of my building.

"It is tomorrow," Patty said.

"Earlier, you asked me to give the book a rest for twenty-four hours, and frankly, I can't jump back into reading it this close to bedtime." I dragged the journal from the satchel between my feet. "You can finish reading, so long as you promise to return it soon."

"I promise." Something in her demeanor had shifted. She glanced to both mirrors.

"*Spasiba.* Thanks for the rescue today."

Stiff back, sore feet, the satchel felt like a bag of cinder blocks over my shoulder as I climbed the stairs to the fourth floor. It would be straight to bed for the ailing princess. I couldn't risk cracking my head on the kitchen tiles twice in one day. I only paused to turn the deadbolt behind me and flip the light on. As I did, something threw my senses into hyper-alert, and my hand plunged into the satchel for the snubnose.

Nothing out of place. No sounds but the muffled street traffic. A scent maybe, hardly there, but my living room had something new in the air. I lowered the satchel where I stood and lifted the pistol with both hands. A first step, a second, another wall switch and I could see into the kitchenette. I yanked open the hall closet and nearly shot my raincoat.

Into the bedroom, the closet here was empty of humans, but my dresser—the dresser drawer was not open, neither was it fully shut. I always shut my drawers out of a lifetime's habit. Tugging the handle, the folded nightshirt mocked me with two wrinkles that were not there this morning. My spine turned wintery when I noticed someone else had made my bed.

I raced to the nightstand and pulled the top drawer. My bedside security, the mini-Mossberg—*Gone.* I crossed to the wall radiator beneath the window, the false radiator front. But the bolts had not been turned. The Kalashnikov was safe.

He came from behind, the bathroom. I should have—

The tall man in the ski mask bulled into me before I turned my gunhand. The snubnose flew away. I fell back with an electric pain in my wrist, hoping it was just a sprain, and rolled across the bed toward the corner with my handgun.

He hit the light switch on his way out the door. Then the other room lights snapped out, one at a time. I caught movement from the living room, but he wore black against the night, and I was still feeling for my gun. If he had my mini-Mossberg—but if he realized he would be backlit by the street lights, and I was invisible to him—

I located the snubnose. Then my front door clapped, and hard soles smacked the landing in retreat.

I waited, listening for his return. And when I decided he would not, I inched my way to the living room, slapping each light switch along the way. With every light in the apartment aglow, I retrieved my phone, slid my back down the wall behind the kitchen counter, and I speed-dialed Patty.

"This afternoon, while I slept, did you go into my bedroom for anything?"

"No! I'm on my way back." No hesitation.

Thirty minutes later she sat across from me with a worried Pedersen at my side, rubbing his knees, watching while I filled in the blanks on his stolen firearms report. I said nothing. My fear morphed into anger. My sanctuary had been invaded, not for the first time.

"You recognized nothing about him?" Pedersen said.

"We've been followed," Patty said.

"Why didn't you say something earlier?"

"Don't scold me, copper!" she said with a twitch.

"You do recall my saying how dangerous this case is? I don't think some punk off the street broke in here, without damaging the lock, just to see if you owned a gun."

"Never trust in coincidence." Patty handed me the worn leather journal. "But good timing on letting me borrow your book."

"Diana's diary," Pedersen said. "Have you been in contact with your—with Vagelle? If you see him, tell him someone has him under surveillance."

"Who? Police?" I said.

"An unidentified male reported seeing a person, Vagelle's description, coming out of the *party building* in Bywater. This means someone may be watching you too."

"Stating the obvious," Patty said, and the detective bit his lip checking his comeback. She was nursing a distraction, betrayed by an uncommon abrasiveness to her friends.

But we were all distracted now, no? I stared at the journal in my hands.

"Could this be what he was looking for?" I said. "What else? He went through my dresser, my nightstand. He remade my bed—what else would I have hidden there?"

"Who else even knows Diana's journal exists, let alone in your possession? I've said nothing," Patty said. She examined Pedersen like he knew something, but he pretended not to notice. "But that makes your timing even better, giving it to me in the car minutes before you walked in here."

"Coincidence?" *Pedersen's sarcasm.*

"Someone is desperate." I tried squeezing information out of the leather book binding. "Something, I believe…" A flash of recall. "That sound of hard-soled shoes…reminded me…nothing but dark clothes, but I believe I caught a shine to his leather shoes. Black shoes."

Pedersen's phone interrupted with the intro to a Dean Martin song. He hopped to his feet, his look cutting away from me. "Gotta run! Drop that paperwork off tomorrow."

"Was it something—?"

A single glance told me more.

"What!" I said, halting him at the door.

"Siren number three."

"I need to know—"

"No!" Anger transformed him. "You can't come with. Don't even ask it." He slammed his way out, then yelled from the corridor, "Drop it!"

7

Patty chased after me. She would never let me go alone, and she insisted on driving.

"I am sorry." I refused to collapse. "He is long gone. We have no idea where he went." Post-attack nerves, threadbare and eroding stamina, I tried not to let her see me shake.

Patty turned on the radio, not Lexus factory equipment, and tapped a button for "Alt." A police dispatcher's voice and conflicting static rasped from the speakers. She tapped twice more to change frequencies.

"My brain must be shut down." I massaged my aching wrist. "Naturally, a top P.I. firm would have access to the police band."

"Before we go anywhere, you need to tell me what you expect once you get there. Do you think they'll let you anywhere near the crime scene?"

"I was not thinking."

"No. You weren't. You've been running on emotional steam for days. You're exhausted, and I see it. This is how experienced cops die. You're smarter than this."

"I need to know things. That is—all."

"You don't need to know everything as it happens. Start thinking. No investigator learns anything by shutting down common sense. Sorry if you don't want to hear this."

The voices on the radio called out police codes, responders' status, requested assistance, EMS, and locations.

"Bayou L'Ourse," Patty said. "Again."

"Again?"

"Grab a pen from the glovebox. Write down that address." She pushed on the gas.

"Typing into my phone as you speak."

"Remember where Posey was reportedly seen by a passing motorist? LA-1 south of Thibodaux. L'Ourse isn't close, but it's almost a straight cut through Thibodaux to get there. Wetlands and crawfish farms and skeeter hatcheries out that way. Not much else."

"I trust you are thinking better than me right now."

"So, you'll listen to me?"

"Yes."

"Then let's see how close we can get to the scene."

"Was that not my idea?"

Buzzing of tires over a lightless runway, infinite, with few other cars to interrupt the void. She seemed to read my mind.

"If you want to recline, take a short snooze. It's a bit more than an hour's drive. If I hit a deer, it'll be considerably longer."

"Thanks. I imagine, at this speed, a small razorback might bring the same results. Use to be I could sleep anywhere, but not at ninety-miles-an-hour when your highbeams only shine three hundred feet." I reclined the seat anyway. This far from the city, the Milky Way looked like ten-thousand shotguns had sprayed the black-velvet.

"I've got good night vision," she mumbled.

"You put up with me, Patty. Especially lately."

She failed to answer right away. "Years past, your Vagelle asked me to look after you when things got dicey."

"You are no longer on retainer."

"I'm on retainer so often with him, maybe you've gotten to be a habit with me." Twenty miles later, she said, "You asleep? I do think of us as friends, Alya. And as friends, I need to confess something right now."

"Uh-oh."

"This week, he knows what you are doing. His information doesn't come from me. I don't report to him, but I am on retainer. He told me not to say anything about it, but it feels *not right* keeping it a secret."

"I should be angry."

"But you're not. Because you know I'd be here regardless." *Was she looking for my reaction?*

"Yeah. And maybe because it is nice to know he still cares if I live or—"

"You need to stop this shit, right now. This pity-party crap. You know he would never stop worrying about you. He asked me to keep an eye on you because he doesn't want you wandering all over the *Big Easy* investigating sadists on your own. You need to screw your head on, girl, starting now. Try to understand, he may be struggling with more than you think you know."

"It's this old case he's struggling with."

"Indirectly."

"Well, that tells me nothing more than I already knew."

She upped the volume on the police scanner as conversations became heated between departments—the locals versus the staties, and all ancillary responders with surrounding confusion.

"Still awake?" she said.

"You can stop asking that."

"We're approaching the Assumption Parish line. I expect a flashing police presence on the crime road. They won't let us take it though. Not tonight."

"I assume you have another plan after driving all this way?" I raised my seatback.

"Morgan City is the biggest town this edge of the swamp. The sun'll be up in a couple hours, so I suggest a decent chain hotel. I haven't slept in a day and a half, and as much as I like my Lex, at this age, I'd rather stretch out on a mattress."

"Find a twenty-four hour pharmacy first. I need a toothbrush. My mouth feels like the bottom of a catbox."

If it was large enough to earn the "City" tag, I would not have guessed it. Stamped onto the only dry peninsula between the Atchafalaya River, Lake Palourde, and surrounded by too many other bodies of water not worth mentioning, Morgan City seemed like the first place to avoid in any storm.

"Hard to believe there are so many old buildings left standing," Patty said. "Every ten years a hurricane sweeps through. And on off years, if there's a tornado that touches down anywhere in the state, guess who takes the worst of it?"

It had gone through a number of names over the years, she explained. Originally coined "Tiger Island" by early surveyors who had spotted a certain species of wild cat hereabouts. The Union Army had built a fort here, once upon a war, and it became a military supply depot, and easy pickings for the Confederates. Now it appeared easy pickings for no one.

"Sorry, no-vacancy." The Clarion night manager played his sympathetic face.

Patty leaned her back to the counter and rolled her eyes. She straightened with the vibration from her phone, checked the screen, and took it outside.

"A shrimpers convention, no doubt?" I said to the clerk.

He suggested a Triple Cypress B&B near the lakeside docks. He called ahead and booked us a room with two queens. He told me how he and the missus sometimes drove over for their great Sunday morning brunch. Eyes roaming my shirt front, he may have wished for a longer conversation, but he broke off saying, "You gals look about done-in after your long drive."

I paused with my hand on the door bar. Through the glass I watched Patty in angry conversation with her phone, then I eased the door forward to hear.

"You anticipated this would happen. You planned all around it, and me, and you told me not to interfere, so long as— So what do I tell her now—?"

Deliberately kicking the door for noise, I acted like I had not heard her. She acted as well.

"Brown, from the agency," she said. "He's been trying to get contact information from the scene. Naturally everything is in lockdown, silent-running from the press."

Triple Cypress B&B. From the driveway it resembled a large barn recently painted barn-red, of course, and sporting a long white balcony. Fortunately, the interior favored a real house, and I was happy to open my eyes after six hours and not find hay raked over the floors. We booked a second night, not knowing we would never make it back.

Patty sat in the morning light on the balcony with a styrofoam cup of coffee she had brewed in the room. Diana's journal lay closed on the table, hugging her cell phone.

"I didn't want to wake you," she said, "so, I'll take my shower while you coffee-up."

"Did you finish the book?" I was already pouring.

"Not all. The more I read, the more disturbing it gets."

I feel myself breaking breaking apart by bits. Not just from Posey's condition. No. Work is becoming unbearable. The back-biting and open sarcasm now over little things. Verbal attacks—no longer whispers—these cops used to be my friends. Now even Captain Singer calls me into his office once a week to berate me over the most recent rumors in the squad as if they are my fault. Someone in the squad is reporting to him about my every move.

Is it Russo? Who else has that regular access to the Captain? Officer Dillon had flirted with me for years. We were buddies. Sgt. Glover and me made out on night patrol. Now they've also joined in the sniping. They all want me out. It's the upcoming trial. I know it.

Posey had been back two years when she started talking about "that night." She's remembering more. She told me about others at the party. The drugs. The faces she'd seen laughing during her assault. Even the band members. And she knew the face of her rapist. She had seen him once before. She didn't know his name but she remembered his face. She was getting pieces of herself back and she could finally keep from breaking down long enough to make sense.

I talked with her father and he decided to hire lawyers. Upon examination most turned down the case. No suspect identified. No concrete evidence from the initial crime. Private detectives even questioned Posey's psychiatrists and nursing staff. The court ordered more doctors for her evaluation.

Police investigators interviewed me repeatedly. Lawyers determined that with my alleged mistreatment by my squad and because I had been Posey's sole caregiver for nearly three years and had daily access to her recovery I might very well come under investigation for planting the "alleged facts" in Posey's mind.

They insist the prosecution will tear Posey apart under cross-examination but her father's money convinces his laywers to fight on. They agreed they could at least bring charges against those we knew were present during the crime. The tenant who threw the party and band members and many of the attendees were all blameworthy. They aided the felon with their silence if nothing else.

But they all refused to indentify him.

I assume they are afraid of him. And we all know in this new world of "American jurisprudence" no DNA means no rape conviction.

The case had been building for a full year.

Then it finally happened. I was suspended from the force six weeks prior to the trial date. Investigators brought charges against me. All bogus of course. But it was all designed to discredit me before trial. Like each of them knew what would come out with public accusations.

———

All for nothing.

No evidence merely unproven allegations. Our lawyers brought experts and party witnesses and even the singers to the stand. When defense attorneys attacked me with Police Department discrediting I'm afraid I broke down and cried on the stand. And they claimed that was more evidence of my attempting to blacken the NOPD for personal reasons.

Then they destroyed Posey.

She began to talk but the defense bombarded her with false assertions and inuendo she had no defense for. The jury and the press could see her tremors. She could no longer speak and she rattled nonsense through her tears. Tears ran into her mouth as she stood and screamed. And she ripped at her blouse tore it open to show the courtroom the devil's kisses scarred onto her breasts. The judge could not muzzle her cries and bailiffs rushed the stand. Posey fixed on a face in the room and pointed past the defense attorney to the first row of the audience. A full flank of my former friends. She screamed at where she pointed. She pointed at Officer Jacob Dillon *seated beside Lt. Russo.*

8

Too late for breakfast at the B&B, she found me on the broad lawn poised between two of the Triple Cypress trees, with the satchel over my shoulder, gazing across reflections on Lake Palourde. I was ready to go somewhere. I did not know where— my newly acquired bad habit—but I had to start. Patty came up from behind.

"Day two, there will still be a heavy police presence all day, but we can try for it tonight. Did you read the entire thing?"

I nodded.

"Leaves more questions than I had yesterday," she said. "I talked with my investigators to dig into a few of those questions. There are a number of places I'd like to check while we're out here. First, I need a John Wayne breakfast." In response to my expression she said, "A dozen eggs, lookin' at me."

"I know you're kidding."

"Almost."

I had to say, Main Street, Morgan City, looked better in the daylight than I expected. Someone had found money from somewhere in the budget to have a revitalization of the downtown and the *historic* district. Referring to their surroundings as "The Gateway to the Gulf," local politicians learned to view the city with something resembling pride, because that's how they stayed in office. We stopped in a small Cajun grille that advertised Breakfast All Day. Then, at Patty's suggestion, we reversed course back to Assumption Parish and Bayou L'Ourse.

She stopped in front of the first, "no-name" real estate office in the heart of old L'Ourse. One secretary and one salesperson named Dot. A not-unattractive woman nearing sixty, Dot wore cake makeup that drew too much attention to the landscape of her complexion. She overcompensated with a perm she refused to relinquish since Buddy Holly took the wrong flight. Introducing ourselves as "cousins" looking to escape the frenetic world of Bourbon Street, which she easily understood, we inquired about properties in her jurisdiction.

"We are thinking of something bucolic, maybe a small farm. I think I might like to raise ducks and chickens. Cousin Pat just wants a small garden to call her own."

"You're not from hereabouts." Not suspicious, just matter-of-fact.

"I am Lithuanian until recently." My favorite small fib. "I reunited here with my cousin Pat."

We sat in Dot's company longer than we wished, mainly because she thirsted for conversation with anyone other than her secretary. I tried to keep the fibs to a minimum.

As we were about to say our goodbyes, Dot decided to drop a bit of gossip. "Speaking of farms..." then against any good realtors' sale-logic, she brought up the recent crime scene.

Patty asked her where we could stop to research Parish records, so we might get more backstory on the history of the town.

"Y'all might check with Charles over to the Library. He'd be able to steer y'all right."

We found the Bayou L'Ourse Branch Library. Charles, the Librarian, a stoop-shouldered, shave-headed man at least twenty years older than Dot, straightened his back and his vest. As we approached, his false teeth threw sparks like he could not decide if he should date Patty or me first.

After a minute of flirting, Patty moved briskly onto the topic of public records, questioning if we should make the thirty-mile drive to the parish seat of Napoleonville, and visit their courthouse there.

"Oh no, dear! Unless you've other business way up that-a-way, y'all can access any public records right here on our computer. Here, let me help y'all out." It did not take long for Charles to unstick his trousers from his swivel chair and work his way round the counter and across the short hall to the "public computer." He brought up the Assumption Documents & Information page, and the parish land records. "If y'all know what you're looking for, darlin', I'm happy to do the searchin' for ya."

Patty begged for his chair. As he started away in disappointment, she called to him mentioning the previous day's gossip. The farm.

His excitement at continuing our conversation dropped more county history than we could have ever gotten from a thirty minute drive. We got confirmation on the address of the crime, the size of the property, "considerable for not being a sugar plantation," and the name of the family last to own that property—*Waites, Ed and Martha.*

"But they ain't been around for years. Just packed up their young Timmy after the death of their other boy, and left for parts unknown. Didn't even stop in town to say they was leavin'. Now, all of a sudden, it's the crime of the cent'ry up there. How anybody found the dead woman in all that seclusion, we'll likely never know. Guess the town won't stop jabberin' about this one 'til The Coming." *Especially not if old Charles can keep the jabberin' on life-support.*

From there, research on the property and family smoothed itself out. In 1980, Ed bought the farm from the other family inheritors. Martha gave birth twice. Timothy in 1984, and Chadwick in 1986. By age ten, Chadwick had been in and out of hospitals four times (doctor's reports sealed, of course). By his twelfth year, he had died in an apparent hit-and-run accident on Raceland Expressway. As newspapers reported, his remains had been found alongside the road by a trucker who recognized the signs—buzzards fighting off a murder of crows over a striped nightshirt. From then on, as Dot had said, while the farm remained in Ed Waites's name, the family had recorded no further transactions in the parish records.

Patty called her office and asked them to expedite a search on any remaining family members. We also searched, as we could, with the information we had, but we knew a dead end when we came to it.

"Y'all come again, you care to learn more on our little village here," Charles said. "She's an interesting history, I guar-on-tee." We both flashed him with our flirtiest smiles on the way out. It would give him a bit more to gossip about.

A few more stops, but the rumors there added nothing to our collection, so we departed L'Ourse, caught the expressway, and drove past the Waites farm road. The accumulation of police cruisers bottling the entrance prompted circling back to Morgan City for dinner. Not hungry, just stalling for time.

As our dinners arrived on the arm of a well-rounded waitress, Patty received an email from her office. She studied it for too long, until her eyes closed. She slid the cell phone across the table. The single-line explanation across the top of side-by-side photos said simply, "Notice something?" The first was a faded, beach bikini photo of a younger, laughing, well-proportioned Posey. The second, a cold hospital image dated approximately one year ago, showed Posey, gaunt, expressionless, naked from the waist up, with crude horizontal scars where her breasts used to be.

"His kisses are gone." I said to myself. We could only pick at our food after that.

Midnight, the dark access road tempted us. We could see standing spotlights from the crime scene slicing between heavy oaks and cypress. One kilometer in, a single Sheriff's pickup had parked sideways, blocking the trail from nosey visitors like us. Patty killed her headlights and added to the blockade. We would have no difficulty hiking, as long as we avoided stepping on anything long and leathery with eighty pointy teeth and a bite force of three-hundred pounds per square inch.

Patty grabbed a powerful flashlight and a short .12 guage from her trunk. Of course, I never went anywhere without my S&W snubnose, an absolutely useless defense against even a moderate-sized gator.

Patty clicked off the flashlight as we neared the edge of the treeline where banks of spotlights illuminated the property. Squadrons of airborne insects believed them to be enemies. We scrutinized the front of the farmhouse and barn and the two sheds, one wooden, the other aluminum. An aluminum shed meant the family still had hopes of making their working farm work, up until they deserted it.

The grumble and clang of a generator feeding the lights destroyed any rural calm.

A few steps into the clearing, I tapped Patty's gun arm and pointed first toward the front porch, then the barn. A patrolman sprawled on the porch steps. He would have died first. His head rested in a black pool too far from his shoulders. The second uniformed officer sat upright, his back against the barn door. He had kept his head but, I assumed, not his heartbeat.

I grabbed my cell phone, but bad luck persisted. "No service."

"Go back to the squad car," Patty whispered. "Call it in."

"Only if you go with. We do not split up here."

"We don't know when this happened. The killer—"

"—may still be here. Exactly." I tried to look everywhere at once. "If he is still here, he may have heard us park. Or he may have seen our flashlight through the trees. So, where do we start?"

"The barn," she said. "That officer might still have a pulse."

We circled the yard, wide of the house, both knowing if the killer had a rifle we would make easier targets inside all the lights. Lights aimed at the house windows might give us a chance.

Before we reached the barn, too many bullet holes and too much blood thrown at the barn door convinced us patrolman number-two was also dead.

"We need to both get back to the radio car," I whispered.

Almost on cue, a hard sound met with a barn wall within and we both jumped. More commotion, banging, a shout, a rifle shot.

Patty lunged first, then me on her tail, and we sprinted round the structure, looking for a rear entrance. We stopped shy of the opening. Suddenly, Patty bounded past, looking into the dark mouth, and landing at the far edge of the doorframe. Her look of horror scalded me.

"Man down!" She yelled and broke forward, spun the corner, and sprinted inside before I could raise my hand.

A rifle exploded and Patty flew back out the door.

I screamed her name. I dropped to my knees, shielded by the doorframe for a moment, while working up the courage to dive and drag my friend from in front of the gaping black hole. I never got the chance. Tackled from behind, I rolled with my attacker, me to my knees atop a large man in uniform. I saw into the barn's shadows. Nicolaus Vagelle lay prone, ten-feet out of reach. My vision sank beneath waves of grief, until a burst of pain found the back of my skull, and the world winked away as quickly as it hit. As quickly as the lights of my eyes switched off.

For how long?

From an ash. From a spark. A searing heat. Abstract in definition, blind and building to a cruel burn. Pain returned by inches, as with consciousness, then it spread and grew like a brushfire.

I rolled onto my side in order to vomit, but it never came, and I could roll no further. My knees were bent indefinitely. I could see nothing, though I knew my eyes had opened. My face rested on damp, ragged concrete, as did the rest of me. That was when I realized I was naked. The horrific odors of my box mingled with my new reality, and my all-encompassing phobia multiplied within me like clutches of snake eggs chipping open, releasing their young. I screamed.

Whatever logic remained, flashed to the journal, Diana's notes. I knew she had written, and I had read, the terrifying end of my own life. This was *Posey's box*. And I sweat from the cold and the shaking. I could not halt the screams or the tears. I chanted my mantra aloud, "I do not shake hands!" despite the impotence and absurdity of those words.

I will not break! I refuse! You cannot take me! Papa—take me! Kill me! Where is my madness? Please! And I screamed in my mind for each broken moment of my life. And I screamed aloud until the cords in my throat stretched raw.

I lost consciousness and woke, and repeated that several times until my waking nightmare caught up to my dreamstate. Then I could feel no difference between them.

9

How long?

How long had Posey been boxed here? I could feel no passage of the hours or days. The thought tormented me until I heard movement other than my own. A stuttering movement. A ragged breathing. The moan of a haunted thing. It stopped. A growling, a grinding of stone, concrete moving on concrete above me—the lid of my tomb.

A rush of clean air hit me first, as scant light bled from the opening triangle. Temporary blindness, as the world outside refused to reveal its substance to me.

I knew what came next, as Diana's journal had foretold, and I readied myself for a physical assault that common sense told me I could only fail. My limbs, my spine would refuse to respond to my will. I would remain powerless and susceptible. The tectonic plates above growled further and the lid fell outside the tomb with the weight of a house, then *he* bent over me looming, still mostly a shadow.

He examined me like a biology experiment. The expressionless shape of him said nothing to me. I saw only the faint glimmer of a badge. Then, as sight adjusted, I recognized a face I had seen before. A photo I remembered from a newspaper long ago. A policeman in a courtroom...

His name was Jacob Dillon. When he caught my reaction, everything smiled but his mouth, and he reached for me.

An explosion shook me, and it sounded like death. Not mine. Jacob Dillon fell forward into my box, onto me. My mind flailed furiously, but my arms and legs lay dead.

Then another man was there, pulling Dillon off. He reached into my tomb. He grabbed me, lifted me with difficulty into the air. He clutched me tight in one arm, and encircled me with heavy cloth—a jacket—and he fell backwards with me to the muddy earth. Nicolaus Vagelle said my name. His one arm never loosened on me.

My eyes closed.

I woke to clean smells. Hospital pillows. Detective Pedersen looking down at me. When next I awakened, Pedersen slept in a chair by the window.

"Please!" I tried to say, but the sound must have been enough to awaken him. He lurched to his feet, hurried to my rolling bed-table, and held the cup of water for me. I pulled hard on the straw until he forced it away.

"Take a breath," he said. Then he yelled, "Nurse!" Then, "Shush, don't drink too fast." Then he let me drink more.

"Nicolaus?" I struggled to say.

"He is in post-op, but he'll be okay. We are in one of N'Orleans' best hospitals. He took a bullet low along his side. Broke a rib. Fortunately, it missed anything vital."

"I thought…did he not take me out of that box? He was shot after he killed that bastard?" I coughed and took more water.

"Before. I'll tell you more later, after you've relaxed some."

"No!" I fought my sheets until painfully reminded by the IV needle. "Patty! Did you see—?"

"We have her. She was not as lucky as your boss. She is in ICU."

"No."

Twenty-four hours of emotional agony. Exhausted, I could not sleep. I could not fully wake. When my eyes closed for even a moment, I materialized in that cement box again with all the gut-twisting odors, with the baby snakes coursing under my skin. Nurses spoke comforting words—*I had not been sexually violated.* Nicolaus had reached me in time. Pedersen touched my hand until I drew away in response.

Outside, the sun rose like it always did.

"He will be in later," Pedersen said. "He argued until the surgeons gave up. Your doctor wants you another twenty-four for observation. Can I get you anything?"

I shook my head.

"They tell me Patty is still in Critical Care, but she seems to be improving."

I hid my face.

"I can come back," he said.

"No." I pleaded. "I need to know things. I know so little of what happened. I need to know. Please tell."

A young nurse entered and busied herself around the room. Changed my water, checked my respiration and heart monitor, checked the saline IV.

"Vagelle had been watching the farm on and off," Pedersen said. "We'd left two officers on duty securing the property— You already know about them. The killer took down the first of 'em quietly enough, then used his rifle on the second. Chasing him to the barn, he finished him there. Your boss heard the shots and charged, but he had to chase Dillon into a dark space where he took the bullet. You and Patty arrived at the wrong time and rushed the wrong doorway as well."

"The right...time." My throat felt like I had been swallowing wood chips. I drank. "Mr. Vagelle would be dead if we had not interrupted."

"Yes. Right." He watched the young nurse wiping down the bathroom sink. "Miss, how about you run and fetch Ms. Korikova some breakfast?"

"It should be along soon." She checked her watch.

"How about now?" His demeanor chased her from the room. "You were taken quickly. Vagelle, they presumed dead. Then they took you to a garage, nearly a mile from the house, the back of the property."

"Posey's box," I murmered.

"We suspect, yes." He rose from the chair and crossed the room to the door where he checked the corridor. "That's when Vagelle came to. He found Patty's ankle holster."

"She had carried a shotgun."

"That was gone, but he took her pistol and carried her back to the patrol car blocking the driveway. There, he notified the Sheriffs. With the first-aid kit from the car, he was able to slow his own bleeding, then he went searching for you—yes, all with a broken rib." Pedersen paused, possibly contemplating the effort.

"Tell."

"He couldn't wait for the cavalry, of course. Three hours later he heard Dillon returning through the trees, and he stalked the killer, hoping he would lead back to you."

The young nurse returned with a breakfast tray. I thanked her, but could not eat yet. I lowered the angle of my bed and pulled the pillow over my face.

"But he is going to be okay," I said into the pillow.

My brain began functioning, fitfully, naggingly. Something not right about the story. There was more than *shots fired.* There was a physical attack, a slamming of bodies against barn walls, ending with a rifle blast. And Pedersen had said, *"They."*

I did not notice when the nurse left the room. I felt a hand on my arm and jerked the pillow away out of reflex.

Nicolaus. I grabbed for his wrist and pulled him down to me, and I held him while I shivered and wept.

"I need to—" He pushed away.

"Oh." I gasped. "I am sorry."

His left arm strapped to his chest, Pedersen helped him to the chair. "Don't apologize." Mr. Vagelle slumped like a dropped scarecrow laboring for a heartbeat.

"Should I call for a nurse?" Pedersen said.

"No. I need to catch my breath, is all."

The nurse appeared anyway, the young one. She only said, "You should try to eat, Ms. Korikova." Mr. Vagelle asked Pedersen to check on Patty, and the detective left the room. A few minutes later, he sent the nurse away.

I raised the angle of my bed again and we stared at each other for a length of time. I probably expected tender words.

"I'm sure he told you what happened," he said, and I nodded. "And about Patty. I wish I had done more. You will be…?"

"I will recover," I said.

"That night—" His eye shifted to the door. "Patty said something to the EMT when he loaded her into the ambulance, but he couldn't understand everything she was saying. She kept asking for her phone. Did she mention it to you? About evidence? She said she had gotten evidence from someone at her office, but we don't know who. And her phone has gone missing. We'll ask her about that when she comes out of Critical Care."

Why is this phone his first priority? He is a machine without sympathy. Without lateral thinking.

The hospital room dropped into silence, lifeless. I sipped my orange juice until Pedersen returned.

"You were right," Pedersen said. "She's been lurking around doorways here like she's got no other duties. So I follow her. She goes into a room at the end of the hall, and comes out. I hang around for a bit and a uniformed cop comes out and goes the other way."

"And?"

"Curious, I checked out the room. Nothing. Two empty beds." Pedersen remained beside the doorframe monitoring hallway traffic.

"Tell me, please," I said.

"I'm sorry," Mr. Vagelle said. "We weren't lying to you. We manufactured a bit of a story knowing we had others within earshot. Like our young nurse friend."

"I noticed," I said. "Always too present. So I was right, Dillon had not acted alone."

"Dillon was a stooge." Anger colored his cheeks and he held his side, fighting for breath. "The mind...of a high school rapist."

"He supplied the coke for the party," Pedersen said. "He attacked Posey on the rooftop, but *the farm* came after."

"The farm," Mr. Vagelle said, "the captivity and torture came from the mind of a planner, a feral thing who had been raised for violence without the capacity for remorse."

"He grew up on that farm," I said.

"He built the cages. There were others. Then he recognized a kindred soul in Dillon. Ruthless without direction, hoping for opportunity, but intellectually weak enough to be manipulated."

"So, you must know who this other person is?" I said. "This bastard with the cement box? The warped mind who tore apart and destroyed Posey Cobb?"

"We aren't a hundred percent on that." Pedersen said. "The family disappeared after the death of their second child. We now suspect our psychopath, little Timmy, had somehow lured his brother out to that freeway in the middle of the night, and either pushed him in front of a car, or he drove the father's truck himself. Raised around farm equipment, by the age of fourteen he would have some experience behind the wheel. Either way, his folks disappeared. He grew up and changed his name."

"And most likely joined the police department because he craved authority and violence." Mr. Vagelle studied my reactions.

"If you knew all this, if Patty's office had come up with any evidence, you would have a name. You would go after him."

"All that about Patty and her phone, that was for our nurse friend."

"We believe she has already spread the lies." Pedersen kept returning to check the corridor. He appeared rattled. A strong man that I knew well, he failed to disguise his agitation. "We don't have a name, but the monster will need to silence Patty before she can tell us what she learned about him."

"Don't worry about Patty," Mr. Vagelle said. "She is safe."

"Yes. She was hurt at the farm, but she is in recovery. We moved her to another ward under a different name, as your boss suggested. We put a policewoman in her listed room, her bed, and men we can trust are watching that room."

"I do not—" My head hurt. Almost too much for me to struggle with. "This cannot be all of it. Whoever this animal is, this *monster cop,* what about—He could not be behind the new murders. It does not make sense. What reason could he have for murdering the Sirens? The butchering. The horrific way their bodies were discovered. If he was the cunning manipulator just eliminating witnesses, all of a sudden after all these years, why attract so much media attention with the new crimes? And he would have eliminated his stooge first, Dillon. Would he not?"

"You ask all the right questions," Mr. Vagelle said. "I think you will recover fine."

10

"I refuse to stay another night. I am not injured. If they say no, I will check myself out."

Ten p.m., I still awaited word from the physician on-call about my release. Thoughtlessly, temper escalating, I stripped from the hospital gown and dressed in front of the open closet. Mr. Vagelle closed the hall door with his back to me, preserving whatever modesty might remain had I been thinking about my actions. Fortunately, he was the only other person in the room.

"You know I hate to be touched," I said. "I have been touched enough."

He did not reply.

Detective Pedersen had run down to the Emergency Room earlier with a call of a gunshot victim admitted after a botched liquor store hold-up. Our rat, the young nurse, never reappeared. Mr. Vagelle had changed into his street clothes that afternoon and returned, his arm still strapped to his chest beneath his loose-hanging shirt. He said he knew I would check out one way or the other, and he wanted to be ready for it. He had waited with me since five o'clock.

"You call the shots," he said. "Do we at least wait for Pedersen? I'm afraid I don't make much of a bodyguard tonight."

"Says the man who rescues damsels one-handed." I did not smile, but he almost did.

Shouts from a distant corridor, followed by Gunshots.

Nicolaus pushed me to the floor behind the bed and rushed to the closet. He grabbed my satchel and slid it across the polished floor.

"I replaced your handgun," he said.

More shouting. A scream. Shoes slapping tiles. Another pistol barked and echoed.

An alarm horn wailed, and I found my mini-Mossberg in the bag. I checked the load. "My bed-side security. The gun that was stolen."

"I took it off Dillon's body," he said. "I suspect when you chased him from your apartment, he raced straight to the farm." He drew my snubnose pistol from beneath his loose shirt—he had prepared for this moment. He touched the light switch, then knelt in the far corner giving us two angles on the door. We waited in darkness listening to the commotion wane.

"We must have been right on his tail, Patty and me. But we stopped for the night because of the large police presence at Waites's theme park." I flinched at a hammering on the door.

"You okay in there?" Pedersen shouted. The door opened slowly on our dark room. He found the light switch, and we rose to our feet. "Good thing I called out first."

"What news?" Mr. Vagelle said.

"As you might have guessed, this did not go as planned.

"How many injured?"

"Our policewoman in the bed, she got a shot off. Another guard was taken down in the hall. The killer left a blood trail, but he made it outside. Officers are in pursuit."

"Come. We're getting you out of here." Mr. Vagelle nudged me with his bound shoulder, and I let Pedersen take my arm for a bit.

A fleet of patrol cars flooded the parking lot with spotlights, headlights, and flashing strobes in an inescapable brilliance, yet the killer managed to escape somehow. Pedersen held up his badge to stop a slow-moving black-and-white. He began ordering the driver to take us home, when a voice called from an accumulation of uniforms near the parking lot exit. We jogged toward the congregation, following the blood spots between parked cars, until we reached the crowd.

"Lieutenant," a patrolman recognized him. "We got something you need to see."

The blood trail led to a bloodier mess on the asphalt, and another mess not far from that. Tire treads had dragged the blood from the first mess.

"Looks like," Pedersen traded glances with my boss, "maybe our perp fell and got hit by a car. The car dragged him then stopped here."

"Whoever was driving threw him in the car and drove off with him." Mr. Vagelle walked in a circle, searching evidence. "Two sets of shoes in the blood. Small-ish. Women's sneakers maybe."

"Over here!" called from a melee of patrolmen at the end of the driveway. One of them gagged, then cursed.

We reached the curb and the messy pool of blood there. One officer knelt for a closer look. Two small, bloodied eggs lay in the gutter. Eggs with visible veins, torn fiber, iris and pupils, had been removed in seconds without surgical skill, and disposed of without ceremony.

Lt. Atius Russo never reported for duty and was never found. Neither was the fourth singer—the last Siren.

Six members of the NOPD faced criminal conspiracy charges but, "for the sake of the department," the mayor convinced the governor of the state to intercede and all charges were dropped. The six officers faced Indefinite Leave.

Lieutenant Francis Pedersen received a Letter of Reprimand for his part in bringing "unwarranted accusations against fellow officers." Mr. Vagelle and I both testified to Internal Investigations in a special "closed-door" conduct hearing. Upon signing legal non-disclosure agreements, the reprimand magically reversed itself to a commendation.

The morning after the hospital attack, at Mr. Vagelle's suggestion, a search began for Posey Cobb and Diana Grant. The wheelchair had been left behind in their apartment.

Investigators found the Sirens' butcher slab in the Waites's barn, along with evidence of recently massacred chickens, and more evidence of visits by the former sergeant, Ms. Grant. Cadaver dogs found, and investigators dug up, the badly decomposed bodies of Ed and Martha Waites in another area of the barn. Mr. Vagelle guessed that Timmy, aka Atius Russo, may have avoided the old barn for that reason, and probably restricted his activities there between the house and his distant torture shed. Russo never suspected his own stalker, Diana, had worked there for nearly a year.

Posey's father attempted to hire Mr. Vagelle to find his daughter. His attempts failed.

Patricia Gunston recovered from her wounds and returned to her office at Gunston Investigations, minus a lung, but gaining—in her perception—the honor of a new war wound. She actually framed the surgeon's report and hung it beside her diplomas. Her investigators had been caught reading it, which she privately enjoyed.

After my ordeal at the farm, Nicolaus set me up with his "shrink" friend, and even attended my first two sessions to help me deal with my haphephobia. He demanded I let him spend a week on my couch. He stayed up each night until I had fallen asleep, and he was up before me every morning. He made terrible scrambled eggs until I showed him how a Russian woman cooks breakfast.

Vagelle

"Closure." If a man may be permitted to hate a word, allow me this one.

It is a false word. A weak word. A lie. A fantasy made up by kind-spirited, but simple-minded, authority figures to salve the psychological and emotional wounds of the damaged ones. Parents use it. Teachers. Psychiatrists. Television personalities who need to project their own damage onto pretend guests and dewey-eyed audience members. The gullible.

Closure, in its literal form, refers to the shutting of a door. Bringing to an end. Permanently shuttering windows. Ending a business. Closing a street and rerouting traffic in more viable directions. These definitions were never intended for the human psyche. The tortures of the mind are never fully shuttered. Or healed. Every personal story continues, pain continues, despite restitution, despite judgement or recompense. Traumas of the mind never lose their scars. All scars risk reopening. All it takes is one more sharp edge.

Detective Pedersen asked to meet. Alone. Away from the usual haunts. He picked a place he knew I was familiar with—though not regularly. Not inside the old rot-walled tavern, but nearby, past the Morgan Street Dry Docks, a hundred yards up the jogging path, across the river from the French Quarter—*Algiers Point*. Silhouetted by park lamps, he was a familiar shape in his dark windbreaker, seated on a bench, staring at the high-rise lights glistening off the dark Mississippi current. I watched him before approaching, though I knew he would come alone. He was among the few I trusted.

"So soon?" I said, taking the other end of the bench. I held my arm to my weakened side as I adjusted my position.

"No complications, right?" he said. "Still on the mend?"

Alya

His fourth night on my couch, I lay staring at the city lights dancing across my ceiling. At two a.m., hearing movement, I got up, pulled into my robe and watched him from my doorway. The living room lights were dark. He sat in my armchair, concentrating on the glass in his hand. The bottle of Widow Jane

Bourbon I had bought for him that afternoon remained unopened on the table beside him.

"Not thirsty?" I said.

"No taste for crutches lately." He set the tumbler beside the bottle.

Vagelle

"I'll be okay."

"For now," Pedersen said.

He removed a long manila envelope from beneath his jacket, set it on the slats between us, and slid it slowly my way. He held it in place as he spoke.

"Don't take it yet. I need to talk."

"I understood its importance with your choice of meeting place. You usually hate all my cloak-and-dagger. Tell me. I see it in your face. What horror show is this?"

"I wished someone had prepared me, is all." Cadets from the academy left the walkway when they noticed us in their path. He watched an affectionate young couple strolling with a tight hold on each other like they were afraid of losing something precious. "Before I opened this report—know how much I hate this. I really hate this. When I read the folder, I could not move from my desk for twenty minutes."

"But you need me to know this." I allowed him his lead-in time, patiently.

"It's forensics. From the farm."

"If you tell me Alya will be involved in another—"

"No. Not that. Believe me. If it was, I'd have buried it, no matter the cost. It's—This is about you." He released the envelope. I pulled the folder from within.

Alya

"Might it be your comfort level here? It keeps you from relaxing?" I entered and took the corner of the couch across from him. I could feel his disturbance, though he fought to hide it from me. "I believe I'll be okay without you sitting guard every night. I promise. Would you be more at ease back at your place?"

Outside neon slanted through the blinds to fall across the table, the bottle, and the empty tumbler. It lacked importance for him.

"I'm told you're moving away from New Orleans," he said.

"Do you think Russo is dead?" I said.

Vagelle

The top sheet, paper clipped to the sleeve, was a copy of the DNA report I had previously seen. Confirmation that the extracted eyes found in the hospital parking lot belonged to the missing Atius Russo. Pedersen was gazing across the river. I turned the cover—many pages—an exhaustive examination of the earlier crime scene. The Waites family farm. Another envelope contained a thick sheaf of photos: some black-and-white, some night photos under stark investigator's lights, more photos under daylight, full-scene, close-up, micro close-up. Photos inside the farmhouse, the tiny garage with the open cement coffin—Alya's horror—and many more photos inside the main barn. The *archeological* dig. The family bones, Ed and Martha Waites.

Pedersen was taking a stroll by the water.

I scanned like a machine through the rest of the forms. Medical Examiner reports. Lab results. More. The final sheet was hand-written with a shaky pen. I recognized Pedersen's scrawl:

"I know you never miss much. But I need to clarify this for myself. We know the stories. The farm closed down. The Waites family moved away after the death of their youngest son, Chadwick. But we now know they never moved, don't we? Timmy stayed, raised himself until he relocated to the Big Easy with a new name, Atius Russo, and a job with the department."

Alya

"Is he? Dead?"

"The lab confirmed those were his eyes," Mr. Vagelle said. "But I think, maybe not. I think he may have found another box somewhere."

"And Diana," I said, "with Posey, had killed the Sirens? Mutilated them, tarred and feathered them?"

"In her tortured mind, Diana believed aiding Posey in her revenge might help her heal."

"But she originally came to you for help."

"She knew she could not find the last two Sirens on her own. She caught number three when I got too close and the singer spooked and ran." His voice felt leaden.

"She monitored the police networks," I said, "and when Dillon died at the farm with no sign of Russo, she was also a smart enough cop to know *Hades* would show up at the hospital?"

"You mean Atius."

"It is your Greek drama, is it not?"

…and for the crime of abandoning their friend, they were transformed into winged creatures at the hands of the goddess, and cursed to be the bane of Man.

Vagelle

"Now, with all this," Pedersen wrote, "with so much more DNA evidence, we finally understand Atius was not alone for most of his young life. The Waiteses had a third child. And that little girl grew up close to where you found your friend, inside another cement box. She had been raised by the psychopath until he grew tired of the chore and moved away. I don't know why he would leave her alive after all those years of torture. But, as I'm sure you understand far better than me, by adulthood, she was equally mad."

I found myself standing. I had dropped the papers on the bench. A hand touched my shoulder. I slapped it away out of reflex. He understood.

Of course, her DNA signature had been in the records for many years, immediately identified with her dead parents and her now-sightless brother. Records only available *after I had her destroyed.* The Waites's youngest child made it out alive and found her way to the big city. She grew to be quite the hunter, once she had educated herself, blended into society, and began a career as a popular newspaper columnist with a new pen-name. The last line Pedersen had written on his note. *Laine Baker.*

"Closure is but a fantasy. The bleeding never really ends until the heart beats, then stills for the final time."

Alya

"Diana was fond of the classics." He sniffed and touched the day's worth of stubble along his jaw. A self-conscious move.

"You had seen her bookshelves, too?"

"She'd read them to the invalid Posey in order to distract her from the horrors she could not live with. She built this allegory, this citadel, for her friend."

"I found a note today," I said.

"The one pushed under my door."

"No envelope, I read it. It was short. It just said—"

"'Her soul is quieting. In gratitude, number four is forgiven.'"

"The handwriting matched Diana's journal," I said. "You made a bargain."

For once he looked into me, steady, and held without wavering.

"You told her where he would be. The hospital. You gave him to Diana and Posey."

His eyes held. As did mine.

"Would you like me away from here?" I steadied my breathing.

"No one could blame you. What you've been through—what I put you through. I knew it would compel you to chase this case. Posey's nightmare. Your war with your own demons would never let you simply walk away."

"That is not an answer."

"Then, when you came back for the book, I feared it would destroy you, too. I had to keep you away."

"Would you like me to leave?"

"That can only be your decision to make."

"*You.* Would *you* like me to go?"

"When I took you in, you were a little lost girl…"

"I was nineteen. I am no longer nineteen."

"Your entire adult life has been spent under my—"

"I am twenty-eight, Nicolaus. You are not my father. I understood we always had *the rules* between us. We lived too close, worked close, and you needed to maintain a visible distance. *Propriety, you called it.* For those looking in from outside, you said. Or was it for your own antiquated morality? You are the elder—but for God's sake, is it finally okay to call you by your first name? Patty P.I., even Detective Pedersen, jokes about it."

The words exhausted me.

"No, Alya. I don't want you to go."

"Why not?"

"Do I need to say it?" He watched the glistening of the empty tumbler.

"Finally, you son of a bitch!" I rose and crossed the narrow space to stand over him. "You pig-headed bastard, you will never do this to me again!" I lowered to my knees and buried my face in his chest, and his one good arm held me tight.

END

Please turn the page for an exciting sneak preview of

G.J. Bingham's

next Nicolaus Vagelle & Alya Korikova Thriller.

Hades' Heart

Part I

A Storm's Embrace

The Shooter

...had been to this open field in the past. Had walked the previous crime scene here at its edge. The crime now forgotten by all save those touched by the blood of it. A property now owned by no one.

The expanse of the former sugar plantation bore no remaining evidence of the ancient cane, only the abrupt absence of towering trees beyond its forest brink to indicate the original owner's saws and plows and intentions for planting. Near the edge of that crumbling antebellum estate, the demarcation between oak giants and vacant expanse, there formed a hillock of blown gray lumber. Ancient boards one might assume to be the remains of a workman's barn flattened by hurricanes, or the artillary of an advancing army from another century.

The shooter would not expose herself to the openness of the fields, but beginning at the woodpile, she paced away along the treeline a precise one-hundred meters, where she looked back, dropped the knapsack, unslung the rifle, and lowered to one knee. A soft spring breeze pushed the tall grass from the southeast and she laid the rifle across the pack and tied back her shoulder-length blond hair with a black scrunchie.

When the time comes, remember your coloring.

Her light canvas jacket was enough for the climate. She considered removing it, but counter-argued that conditions might prove different on the given day. The memory of *Papa* whispered in her ear:

"No one ever dies from too much preparation."

"Hush," she whispered to the breeze.

The shooter found a granola bar in the pocket of the backpack to settle her stomach, and followed it with water she had purchased at the Gas 'N Go before leaving the city limits. She sat on the soft grass behind the knapsack, laid the Kalashnikov across her thighs, then located the thirty-round magazine and checked the load.

"Step by step," Papa whispered in her ear. *"If routine is important, never vary routine."*

She smirked, dropped the rifle's safety lever, pulled the charging handle and released. She slapped the magazine into place. As she steadied her breathing, she studied the distant woodpile and found the nearly vertical plank, marked upon her arrival, standing amidst its fallen comrades. Unzipping the pouch at her belt, she extracted the hand-size beanbag, the small minocular, and the AKFST—front sight adjustment tool—

"the most important element to this exercize, child."

Squeezing the beanbag to limber her fingers, she thought out her process—it had been many years and she doubted her muscle memory, until she chased that doubt away. Today was not about her. Today was about her weapon, the old AK, and she was here to eliminate concerns for its accuracy.

Eyes on the upright plank, three-quarters the width of a human torso, and a football field away, she set the beanbag crosswise atop the knapsack, then moved herself into the prone position. With the lower handguard nestled center on the beanbag cushion, confidence returning by the moment, one more pull on the charging handle chambered the first round. She noted again the easy push of the tall grasses left-to-right and tested the weight of the rifle stock for familiarity. The sights were old-school, "iron sights," the kind she had grown up with. The rear sight stood at "P," effective up to 350 meters.

"Nudge that up to 300," Papa would say. *"It's all the same. Now take three breaths, long and slow, out through the mouth."*

Her pulse felt fine, steady. She snugged the butt of the AK tight to her shoulder, not too tight to jitter the hands, and she focused on the rear-sight first. She traveled through the front sight to the distant gray plank. She brought the front sight back into focus and the rest of the world blurred as she released the third breath, held it, while tightening on the trigger.

"Do not anticipate," Papa said. *"Let the bang surprise you..."*

It did.

"…every time."

Lifting the minocular to her eye she could see the plank had moved but had not fallen. All that mattered was she could see the splintered hole where the bullet struck, bottom-right. With the AKFST, she adjusted the front post to the right, she used a pencil to mark the post for reference, then, because her shot hit low, she turned the top screw clockwise. The following five rounds placed within thirteen centimeters of each other.

"Hush, Papa," she whispered to the breeze.

To Be Cont'd.

ABOUT THE AUTHOR

G. J. BINGHAM is an award-winning writer and artist, with more than forty years in publishing. Born in Chicago, he served four years as a Law Enforcement Specialist in the USAF. From there, he began his career in the Arts. Comic books and graphic novels, to short fiction, multi-media, theme park attractions, film, television, and now novels. Winner of The Jack Kirby Comics Industry Award, "Best Graphic Album 1984," for his translation of the epic poem, Beowulf. Co-winner of the Golden Apple Award, nominated for the Harvey Award and Will Eisner Comic Industry Award, "Best Graphic Novel 1987," for "Batman: Son of the Demon." He then moved his talents to Hollywood, where he contributed to film for over thirty years, and won the 1998-1999 Primetime Emmy Award for "Background Designer." His Western Art has won awards and hung in some of the most prestigious galleries in the country.

You can visit his website at GJBingham.com